Mars Armor Forged

MARS ARMOR FORGED

Ben Parris

Blueberry Lane Books

New York

2011

Blueberry Lane Books
New York

ISBN 978-0-9830064-4-2

BlueberryLaneBooks.com

For Lila Wortzman
Resting in Peace
And forever in my heart

"And never did the Cyclops' hammer fall on

Mars's armor, forged for proof eterne..."

—from Shakespeare's *Hamlet, Prince of Denmark*

CHAPTER 1
Life Changes

2034: WASHINGTON, D.C.

SHELLY KASTIN FOUND Harris Culpepper, her HR Director at Treasury, resting his bones behind her desk when she arrived at work. Her antique aircraft models had been nudged about, hinting that he'd been waiting impatiently. She noted with a sigh that the man was not shamed into rising when she entered the office. Starting the day with bad news usually meant it would be an all-bad-news day.

Taking off her coat, she said, "Harris, what is this?"

"Shut the door."

She did. "Trouble?"

"You're losing one of your guys. Louis Coburn."

Shelly did not complete Culpepper's power game by taking the seat across from her own desk. "What do you mean, losing him? He's one of my best trainees."

"He's going into the Black Box."

"Stolen by the Agency?"

"Them or one of the other three-letter outfits." He rubbed his short white hair into disarray, and spread his hands wide. "It's by his own choice."

"No, you must be mistaken. If Coburn was waiting to go into the agency, what was he doing training under me? The Treasury Department was his turnaround plan when the Olympics thing didn't pan out."

Culpepper adjusted the base of a stubby World War II bomber, pushing the model even further out of place. "You know how it works, Shelly. Coburn applied to them first and this is when they came through. He's gone, couldn't even tell you about it."

"How is a covert agency going to handle his famous face?"

"The story out there is that he's going to try for an Olympic comeback. That's his cover. Don't crap all over it by saying anything else."

"Why did you even tell me this much?"

"So you can do the paperwork. Enjoy your New Year's present."

"That's your cue to get the hell out of my office."

"Rising. Rising slowly. I'm an old man."

"You're only sixty. Get moving."

Kastin felt sick. She shut the door after him and set her laptop on the desk. She'd had high hopes for Lou Coburn and harbored no doubts that the Agency made their final decision on him only after they saw how well he was doing at Treasury. Add to that the incentive of picking up an agent with free investigative training, and she knew she'd been raided.

Since the Treasury department still used landlines, she was about to tell her assistant to divert her calls when her cell rang.

"Hi, Myra." She would always pick up for her best friend, Myra Finney.

"You have to talk to this kid, Shel."

"What now?"

"Your goddaughter tells me she's moving to Mars."

"That's crazy."

"She's right here," Myra said. "Tell her she's crazy."

"Thanks for bringing out the big guns, Mom." Whenever Terri spoke to her mother or about her, she sounded younger than her fifteen years. "Aunt Shelly, Mom is just having a panic attack."

"Then so am I. Terri, why would you be moving to Mars?" She worried about Terri. Last week it was Sri Lanka.

"It's years from now, Aunt Shel, and I'm not moving there. The Winter Olympics are going to be held at Olympia colony, and the United States team will probably participate."

"That's impossible."

"Why?"

"Well first of all, you would never hear about a thing like that before I did. And it would be the most off-the-wall thing the International Olympic Committee has ever done. That's a brand new colony up there."

"Coach Eilbock has a friend on the IOC. He thinks it's his business to know."

"Terri, even if that were true, it's too dangerous to go."

"Aunt Shel, the IOC knows what they're doing. We're not living in cave man days. Besides, if I'm chosen for the Olympic team, I'll have a responsibility to go."

"That's okay, sweetie. I'm going to stop worrying. You're not going because there's no way any Olympics is going to be held there any time in the near future. Now if you don't have any other harebrained ideas, I have the largest agency in the country to run."

"Thank you, Aunt Shelley. I'm sorry mom bothered you."

Kasten put the phone away and sighed. Coburn. And now this.

The treasury director chalked it up to New Year's madness as she rubbed Culpepper's paw prints off the bubble windshield of her Bell helicopter. Her troubles eased as she reoriented the compact Curtiss Helldiver, and cleared space in front of the twin engine Yacovlev "Crib." Just when she thought she had everything restored, Harris Culpepper popped back into her office without knocking, his hair more mixed up than ever. He said, "Shelly, it looks like you're going to Mars."

"What?" She thought she was hearing things.

"Funny thing. I just found out that the Winter Olympics is going to be held there."

* * *

D.C. was having one of its stifling August days, with the mercury pushing 110 degrees. The tourists were either wandering the chilled labyrinth of the Smithsonian Institution or hiding under shade trees, hungrily eyeing the Reflecting Pool, wishing they could jump in.

Deep in the bowels of the public buildings, where rooms were two-tone olive drab and battleship gray, a small anonymous arm of the government was quietly justifying its existence, seldom if ever imagined by overheated tourists.

The air conditioning strained to keep the temperature around 80 while the guys from the Department drummed fingers in front of them, waiting for the boss and the new kid to show up. Five men and two women, none under thirty-five, so comfortable with one another around the big table that they weren't particular as to who they sat next to, a different mix each day. It was young outsiders entering their group that they didn't trust, one of whom was on his way.

Castleton spoke first, in low uncertain tones. "So who have you got coming in, Pat? Anyone we could stand?" Chicago born Pat Destry was a good detail researcher, a trusted twenty-year man. Due to his penchant for diligent background checks he always got assigned to make the personnel recommendations for the small, select group, lifting fingerprints, and interviewing neighbors, friends, and coworkers to get his facts. While most people would think of his job as too intrusive, twenty years made it routine.

"Yeah, I got Lou 'The Cobra' Coburn, out of Burlington."

"Lou The Cobra? Sounds like a mobster. They're not gonna shelter him here like some kind of witness protection thing, I hope."

"Nah, you got it wrong. He's a sportsman, fresh out of college. They call him Coburn The Cobra because of his speed and quick reflexes on the snow." Destry used his hands to demonstrate something that looked to Frank Castleton more like surfing than anything else.

"You're talking water, right?" said Castleton. "Because if he's a reptile—"

"No, snow, the white stuff," replied Destry.

"Don't tell me he's one of those lunatics with the wooden sticks on their feet?" someone else chimed in.

"Bingo, a skier, supposed to be one of the best in the world. He may be even more nuts than Telino here."

"But he is one of us, right?" Castleton persisted.

"He is or soon will be. He's not actually coming straight from Vermont. They had him down in Atlanta for training."

"Oh crap, you plucked him right off The Farm," Telino yelped.

"Is he any good?" asked Castleton, raising a hand in hopes of keeping the others in abeyance.

"He's a kid. How could he be good?" Telino pronounced emphatically. "He won't even have enough clearance to get my coffee. Am I right, Justine? Am I right, my cream and sugar? Of course I'm right."

Justine Rosario, who was the newest member of the group with only three years in residence, kept quiet although she figured the invitation to butt in was Telino's way of saying she was an old hand by comparison to Coburn, and it made her smile.

"Am I right, Dale?" said Telino still looking for approval from anyone who would listen.

Destry said, "Look guys, he's an investigator they stole from the Treasury Department, and in Georgia he blew everyone away. So that's the end of the story." He was done justifying it.

"Sure," said Jonssen, "that's in training. Wait 'till he finds out he's got a desk job. That oughtta cool his hot blood."

"The brass must think you're a Portobello, Jonssen," said Destry, who was getting annoyed now by everyone questioning his choice after saddling him with the thankless job of picking someone. Everyone today had something to add, every one of them a wise guy comment.

"Why do you say that?"

"Because they shut you in the dark and feed you shit."

"What kind of shit?" Johnssen obliged further.

"Haven't you heard?" asked Destry with palms turned upward as Coburn appeared in the doorway behind him, lean and alert, the boss with him. Everyone else stopped to inspect their fingernails. "This Olympics assignment ain't gonna be no desk job. Not for this kid anyway. He's going undercover in a hot spot. The way I hear it, he's lucky if he don't get himself offed the first day out."

Castleton cleared his throat in warning, and Destry turned to look at the puzzled Coburn and their frowning boss, then gave him a shrug with hands thrown high. "Kid, you had to find out sooner or later."

CHAPTER 2
Conception Of Martian Olympics

OUTSIDE MARS COLONY; EQUIVALENT EARTH
YEAR 2033

"THIS JOLLY JAUNT outside makes me a tad nervous."

"Shut up, Devon. Cease and desist. Isn't that what you lawyers say? In a few hours I can make testing choices that the robots roaming these hills would take years to make. Do you understand? Maybe even decades. But I can't do any of it if you won't pipe down."

Devon March replied to that heartfelt request with simmering silence. He was the restless one at the steering wheel, and his boss, Governor Peter Arazine, Ph.D., was the busy geologist who shut him up. And now the filthy bugger sat there grinning to himself. Oh, the privileges of being in charge, of being the bloody governor of bloody Mars. Devon bet that Arazine had dragged him out to the wilderness just to dazzle him. In the five years since man took up permanent and continuous residence on Mars, the populace built homes and factories and science stations downwards and upwards and into orbit and yet could never build enough to make him feel secure. At this point, survival was only possible in one established location known as the town of Olympia, which was quite far away thanks to the mutt who brought him out here.

Devon March locked the guide wheel into a straight line and frowned into his rear view mirror, watching the settlement fold into the lonely horizon that sucked everything familiar to him inside of it. The turn they had made after Vinton's Gap and the bulk of Olympus Mons itself left no evidence of his precious city of Olympia. For all he knew, his wife had vanished into the ravenous sands. It was easy out here to let your imagination run. Wife, friends, home, career, any anchor he ever had: *Whoosh, swept away.* He fixed his gaze on craggy Vinton's Gap to see if it too would vanish and deprive him of the last friendly landmark. Peter Arazine was the only one who would hire on a lawyer and then mistake him for a chauffeur. The governor had said, "Pioneers wear a full set of hats. You're banking your hefty rate one way or the other." And that much was true.

Before March's eyes, a new wind sculpted the clay of Mars and reshaped its surface with a heavier hand than the planet had seen for eons. The enhanced atmosphere grew infinitesimally denser by the day, worried along by the Mother of Invention, which was Necessity, and the Grandmother of Invention, which was Greed. The goal was a thin skin of breathable air eked around the globe, closing a period of millennia in which Mars had laid naked to space, safe from man's groping reach.

March had few qualms about how he feathered his nest. Up until now he had placed great faith in the Grandmother of Invention to speed his fortunes along. But at this juncture he wondered how they could make something of this grudging land. Odd blocks of cold lava were flung like ball-and-jack tokens across the flat plains of fine, sandy dirt. Larger rocks and boulders that once jostled for position among the smaller pieces now sat frozen where time had halted them. He saw gentle puffs of air clear old silt off some of the scattered rocks and spill a fresh layer over others. Most of the hard fragments were peppered with holes of all sizes left by the popping of molten bubbles in antiquity. As the wind gathered confidence, a fluid carpet of particles crept over the broken stones like high tide spreading across a thirsty shore. Orange-red soil plugged the dark recesses in its wake, and lent its own rusty color to everything it met.

In fact, red and orange alternated everywhere he looked. A cold, rusty orb oxidizing like there was no tomorrow, as it had done the whole time Earth civilization was surviving with the fittest, despoiling one planet while peering anxiously over its shoulder towards another. Woe to the man who clocked in too late for one and too early for the other.

March slipped his cramped right foot off the accelerator and let the left foot cross over. At the same time he worked the kink out of his neck, leaning back as he did so. The sky had faded so pale it was almost white. The slight tint it mustered could have been blue or gray. On Earth, white sky usually meant total cloud cover. Here, the engineers were probably centuries from being able to produce that quantity of clouds. The day must have had nothing to color it with the orange dust lurking elsewhere, and no moisture at all. Most other days, the Martian sky was some shade of pastel pink, relieved by nothing but anemic rags of vapor.

Mars was still very nearly as they found it. Empty of water, empty of air, empty of people. An undeveloped back lot of solar real estate. Under this pale sky, his sky, he would raise his prospects and call back the children he'd sent to live with his brother. He admitted to himself that he was not a genuine pioneer, one who would break his back for future generations. He would do whatever it took to prosper quickly.

"Look where you're going," said Arazine. "We're almost at the transition." Jovis Tholis, or Old Number Fourteen as Arazine referred to it, bit off a chunk of the sky where it swelled the land ahead. A healthy size by Earth standards, the mountain had long attracted the attention even of Twentieth Century mapmakers. But Olympus Mons, miles behind in the opposite direction, reared up larger than any known object of man or nature, reaching endlessly for the limits of the atmosphere like a thing possessed. That was a darker red, the color of anger. One delicate ribbon of road stretched out across the barren plain between the two mountains, insinuating a fine crack through its middle.

This was the Devil's Golfcourse, that desolate place the Oxford-educated lawyer had heard talked of in the bitterest tones, so named for its Death Valley counterpart on Earth.

The smooth man-made road terminated abruptly, and their transport, a new creature on the landscape, scrambled onto the lumpy ground, jolting its two passengers until it learned to make corrections. The Spider had four articulated legs on either side, each ending in a wheel. The legs undulated at their joints to gulp the shocks while holding the compartment secure and level. Some of its wheels spun against soft patches even while the others negotiated hard terrain. The individual wheels had their own eyesight as well as their own motors and computer chips, adjusting speed of rotation for a uniform ride. Clever little thing.

"We don't have much time," Devon put in.

"That's why we're hurrying."

Although he obeyed Arazine's instructions to head for Jovis Tholis, March was appalled at the distance they were going and the chances they were taking. The travelers had penetrated nearly two hundred sixty miles east by northeast into the Tharsis Region where they first began to mount the Tharsis Bulge. On the pavement, they had been clocking eighty miles per hour. Now they lagged to sixty, but on the field of rocks it seemed like they were going a breakneck, irresponsible speed with the bug legs flipping like the fingers of a doped up typist. They had run out of paved road because it was further than anyone regularly traveled, and the dust storms were getting more frequent and worse each day. A few years of weather data had not prepared them for the sum of Mars' dangerous eccentricities, especially when you added the unknown element of mankind and his tampering. The new reality was: Dust can be lethal. Arazine tried to shrug it off, but March was the more practical of the two. He had been brought up on the unpredictable English rain, and had seen what the unpredictable Martian wind could do.

On top of the list, no one knew they were out there. "The governor and his counselor don't owe any explanations," Arazine had said before they left. Filthy bugger.

"Are we nearly wrapped up, then?" March asked his boss.

"You'll know when we're done," said Arazine slyly as he cataloged one of his samples, "and I promise it will be well worth our trouble, old chap."

Peter Arazine, who was sixth generation American from New York, or *N'Yawk* as he called it, did not use expressions like "old chap" unless he was trying to needle March about his English accent, reminding him that it remained long after he thought he got rid of it. March heard his London dialect sneaking out of his own mouth and it troubled him. Worse, Devon March still referred to people from The States as "yanks," lunch was "dinner," and cookies for desert were still "biscuits."

March was British born but he was no Anglophile. His pseudo-secret ambition was to morph into something more Americanized, an idea which he stuck to even on the Red Planet. Not that he wanted Arazine's outlandish New Yorker accent to rub off on him. Of course, if Arazine continued to do his Brit imitation, there was little chance of that happening.

"Maybe all this is worth your trouble, Peter, but I'm slightly tense."

"You mean to say that you're a wreck. You'll have to credit me to know what I'm doing."

"Based on what exactly?" Arazine the man was an enigma to him. As the Chief Scientist on Mars and the former manager of two giant national laboratories, he was the natural choice for colonial governor, technically the only authority on the planet. The position took little of his time with Olympia policy dictated by officials on Earth, and the title seemed to have been imposed on him without his asking. Most of his staff took him to be industrious and modest.

Devon March, as Olympia's Corporation Counsel, had a little more insight. Like Thomas Edison, Arazine was an avid patent filer, stayed off the Nobel Prize track, and concentrated on developing applications, staking his claims and marketing holy hell out of them.

"So what are you attempting today?" said March.

"You may as well get it into your skull that everything I do goes to keep us in the Fourth Orbit." The Fourth Orbit was how first generation Martians sometimes referred to life on their planet. The fledgling colony was only authorized to operate for one more fiscal year, and if their mandate was unfunded they could be swept back to where each of them came from. That's if they were lucky and the relief ship arrived.

"There aren't any congressmen in the Fourth Orbit," March said petulantly. "You should be on Skype pestering them."

"I'll do better than that. I'll shake them out of their trees."

"How about getting the colonists something to eat?"

They were both startled to see the front right leg of their vehicle retract over their heads before sinking, and three more trail in a rippling cascade, much higher than the legs ever went before. Behind them was a massive boulder, deftly and automatically avoided by the Spider with little more teeth rattling than a city pothole produced, but considerably more consternation from the humans in the Spider's gut.

Arazine looked at March accusingly. "You were lucky that time. Watch the steering now," he cautioned. "If we hit anything too big, the Spider's going to rear up like a wild horse."

March did as he was told, unlocked the steering and took it back into his own control, steady ahead for now.

* * *

Arazine switched from referencing the topographic map to consulting the tectonic. He followed structural trends, such as fault lines, and axes of synclines and anticlines. Although it was a flatter, more forbidding picture to anyone looking over his shoulder, he read it without difficulty. The tiny red dot crawling past these features on the screen represented the Spider, the only thing on the Devil's Golfcourse that moved.

While Arazine tracked their progress on the maps, he also kept his professional eye trained on certain boulders. He wasn't interested in the more common, vesicular rocks familiar to him by their diminutive size, blocky shape, and dark color. He already catalogued those as cooled chunks of basalt lava, which if you saw one, you basically saw them all. No, he wanted to see what else the old eruptions kicked up from the subsurface. That would tell him what hid down there and what the history was.

An update flashed, advising Arazine that a mob had broken into the recycling farm and devoured all the fish. Three technicians hurt. He slapped it off before Devon could see it.

"You'll pardon the question," said March as he checked the elapsed time of their current mission, "but what could be so important this far away from the settlement?"

"It's the geothermal work of the consultant from our sister planet."

"Havislaw Valdeen? The chap they sent away for income tax evasion?"

"His tax problem is an old story. Do you want to learn something or don't you?"

"You mentioned some pretty odd theories to me. Something about a trigger that can open trapped energy. Can't say it made any sense to me."

"If you wanted to understand Valdeen Catalytic Factor you should have studied science instead of law."

"But the man's papers on that subject are unpublished." March pushed the Spider to its top speed. "That's not a good thing in scientific circles. I know that much."

"I don't care whether his papers appeared in some pretentious journal," said Arazine. "I've seen the runs on his Catalytic Factor and my experts have duplicated enough of his results. I'm convinced that Valdeen's techniques will boost my geothermal output exponentially."

"You haven't stolen any of his documents have you? I need to prepare a defense for you if you have."

"You barristers always have your excuses for wheedling out information, don't you?"

March closed his eyes and spoke slowly. "How did you get them?"

"He sent the lot of them to me from prison."

"Does he know that you've shown his work to other people?"

"No, he's very high strung about who sees it." As Governor of Mars Arazine thought himself beyond Valdeen's reach.

" I don't suppose your plan accounts for what would happen if he found it."

"I won't be the one to tell him. And if you do, I'll make sure whatever happens to me, happens to you first."

"Fine then, no one tells him. Let's assume his methods work perfectly. Why do we need the temperamental professor here in person? "

"The short answer is, Valdeen's a materials scientist. I certainly don't know how to melt rock."

"So there's something in science you still haven't grasped."

"Piss off, Devon. If I don't understand fully why and how it works, I'm going to have one hell of a time developing its applications."

"That's another thing that bothers me. What makes you think that one of its applications includes dunking it into a volcano? If it's as good as he claims, all we need to do is hook it into a power plant."

"Stop the car, Devon. Stop the car," he said.

"All right. All right. What now?" March cut the power while Arazine popped out, nearly sailing in the one-third G force. Arazine hopped unsteadily to a boulder, and marked its precise location with his remote unit. He photographed the boulder in its original position, lifted the edge to peruse the soil underneath, and suddenly mashed it down on a streak plate to check the color it bled. Then he slipped his geological hammer out of its sheath, and lopped off the end as easily as a shepherd relieves an animal of its fleece. Lastly, he brought out a small chisel, split off a delicate wedge to include the untarnished inner face, and hurried back.

Arazine eagerly examined the cross section revealed on the inside walls of his sample. "Looks like I made a good choice with this one. These amygdales at the top tell a good story." Amygdales, as he had told March on the way out, were vesicles, or remnants of gas bubbles, that later became filled with minerals such as calcite or quartz. These minerals were probably deposited by passing ground water long after the rocks were formed. He may have been holding a sample of one of the oldest rocks in the field. Arazine was so excited he would have gladly explained the concepts to Devon again, and was getting ready to do just that.

Apparently sensing a long-winded lecture in the offing, March said, "Don't give me amygdales, Peter. You haven't answered my question. Can't we just stick Valdeen Factor in a power generator and have all the juice we desire?"

"For now, yes. We can try it." His head wrinkled with irritation. "But it's not gasoline we're talking about. When my plan kicks in, we'll be tapping elemental energy on a grand scale--heat from the core of a planet. Much further down than the twelve kilometers that we're capable of digging with current technology. Vast amounts of energy, practically for nothing, for anyone with the stones to go after it."

"With a volcano involved, the effort sounds a trifle dangerous."

"Did they call you a boring twit in England? Because that's what you are."

Instead of answering, March flicked the wheel so that the Spider rattled them both.

"Let me amend that to a touchy twit," said Arazine. "Well, it's more than a trifle dangerous. It's extremely dangerous. If it weren't so volatile, someone would probably be tinkering with one of Earth's volcanoes right now, and then they wouldn't need us."

Arazine took an even smaller slice of his rock sample and snapped it into the testing chamber of his remote lab unit. A red light winked on, and he punched the button for the standard test series. The light switched to green as it checked color, luster, hardness, composition, internal structure and impurities. The mini lab confirmed his amygdales and also found tiny xenoliths, chunks of even older rock that were caught up in the liquid flow when his rock was still a puddle of lava. "I'm willing to take the chance here on Mars where I can get the work done without major interference from regulators."

"We're still subject to Earth's rules you know."

"Yes, the lawyer in you reminds me of rules every day, but those restrictions are not enforceable at this distance."

"How does this help my cause?"

Arazine laid aside his field lab. "You're always whining at me, 'Why are they pulling the plug on us?' The consortium is tired of waiting to see the benefits and finding themselves S.O.L."

"And getting us lost in Tharsis today is going to change all that?"

"Let me put it this way. If my plan works, we'll guarantee an autonomous Mars. That's what you want, isn't it?"

* * *

One way or another, Mars was going to be the new suburbia and Devon burned to get there first. In any case, March never acknowledged his motivations, his lust for personal authority, so he couldn't admit to sharing anything in common with Arazine. But did Arazine know what he was doing? March liked to think of himself as a limited anarchist, always waiting for the shakeup that would thrust him to the top, and never wanting the chaos to last beyond that. That meant he had to be sure of the risks. "What makes you think you can control a volcano?"

Arazine snickered. "You think they're uncontrollable? That's what they said about nuclear power. 'How can you control something that started out as a bomb?' they said. The nukers made a few good power plants, suffered the occasional near meltdown in silence, and christened their movement a success."

"I wasn't one of its cheer leaders."

"Here we have non-depleting alternative energy, and a head start because much of the same technology of building a nuclear facility applies to our project as well."

"How?"

"We start with a small volcano for testing purposes and wrap a factory around it, including cooling facilities. We toss in some containment walls and redundant systems, things we've learned to do already. Meting out the energy is as basic a concept as the stepdown transformer on low power appliances. Even a lay person like yourself can see that geothermal is less dangerous than nuclear, removing the radioactivity threat."

"Are you forgetting we're destitute? Not to mention that your plan depends on getting Havislaw Valdeen over here."

"I'm willing to wait four years, maybe five before we can even start tapping anything out of the volcano. But I'll get my cash and I'll get my scientist."

"Valdeen's a long way away," March reminded him.

"Yes, but his vulnerable nephew, Nils Barkley, is right here in the Fourth Orbit," Arazine said. It sounded as if he was planning some kind of extortion.

March shifted around trying get his circulation back, thinking that perhaps Peter Arazine was better acquainted with the Grandmother of Invention than he was. On the heads-up display, the weather gauges twitched and spasmed. Nothing recorded, no warning came. Either the reading was false or it couldn't be measured. March wasn't sure about the wisdom of the direction they were headed. In his rear view, Olympus Mons loomed behind them undiminished, basking in its anger.

CHAPTER 3
Jovis Tholis

WITH ARAZINE ENGROSSED in a spot analysis of his latest sample as the Spider sat at rest once more, March took it upon himself to venture out of the safety of the vehicle and grab a black chunk of basalt to admire. He found the volcanic rock a bit smaller than an English football and considerably less smooth. Attempting to turn it and instead coaxing it eight inches in the air with the slightest nudge, the surprised March snatched it back. Thinking it to be the consistency of a giant biscuit, he tried to squeeze the lava product to bits with both gloved hands, and couldn't. Frustrated that it didn't give, he made to punch it and then recoiled when he remembered that he was in an airtight suit that he couldn't afford to puncture.

Their precious suits made these little field trips possible, and maybe even pleasurable if Arazine wasn't around, covering every inch of skin in luxurious flexibility without the hindering bulk of their predecessor models, which March recalled all too well. Now each man wore a layer of long underwear that held the tubes for food, water, and excretion. Over that a rubberized frogman skin suit to equalize air pressure, followed by a tarp quality plastic backed with aluminum to hold pockets and screen harmful rays. The last layer was a hard harness to mesh the suit with the polarized helmet and brace the air tanks and instruments. This arrangement was known as a Hybrid, the compromise between the old "hard suit" and the ideal soft suit that developers hoped would follow in the future. The insulation of the Hybrid shut out the ultraviolet radiation and freezing cold, and kept in the warm, dense air, making the life and death difference that he took for granted. March had no intention of being the first to test the suit's limits.

Getting the scientist's attention with an excited shout, he said, "These stones are lighter than they look, but they aren't soft at all. I thought they were supposed to be spongy."

"Spongy doesn't mean soft," said Arazine in blithe distraction, "it means porous. If something is soft to begin with, then being porous will make it more resilient. That's where you got confused. Toss that out. We don't need it cluttering up the Spider."

Feeling a vague resentment that he was being treated as something less than an adult, March complied by pitching his rock back into the field of stones, and watching it kick up a cloud in the distance before he got their transportation moving again.

"Can we really rely on this fellow?" complained March as he verified that their course was as direct as possible.

"Which fellow is that, old fellow?"

"This Valdeen, after he's been in jail?"

"Let's don't quibble about that, as you English would say. You or I could just as easily be in prison in three year's time, and on much more serious charges." The transplanted New Yorker smiled as he worked.

The hair on March's neck prickled when Arazine used a word or phrase that he thought was what the English would say. He didn't want to be reminded of it, much less hear it from a yank who was baiting him. In a rare burst of candor, his psychologist once told him that there was an element of self-loathing in his aversion to all things English.

However Arazine phrased it, the young legal advisor couldn't argue with the sentiment that he and his governor were tramping on treasonous ground. Their seminal government seemed to be taking on problems like water bubbling through the boards of a leaky rowboat. "I still don't trust him, and I don't for one minute believe that tax evasion was Valdeen's only crime. Look what happened to his last partner."

"As my mother would say, you don't have to marry him, so you can stop carping."

March cast a worried eye on the rear view mirror again. Try as he might he couldn't locate Vinton's Gap. Ahead the land was rising. "Peter, I know that you're busy, but shouldn't we be turning tail for the colony right about now? We're practically brushing against Jovis Fourteen, and that's far from home, such as it is."

"All of Mars is our home now, Devon. The reason we're getting so close to Fourteen is because we're going for a visit."

"Visit?" Devon felt a chill at the suggestion. "I thought you were just collecting rocks and using Fourteen as a steering point. I mean, I knew you'd go there eventually, but I didn't expect you'd drag me along. What are we going to see over there that you can't see anywhere on the way?"

"We'll be exploring the volcano itself."

"You mean to say Jovis Tholis is a volcano?" March instinctively slowed their vehicle as they neared the rocky ramp that encircled Jovis' base. He fought an urge to wrestle the Spider around and whip it like a mule until it reached Olympia. Although he had almost gotten used to the deceptively gentle flanks of Olympus Mons, he felt uncomfortable with anything that had once spit live lava. "If Location Fourteen is actually a volcano, why isn't it called Jovis Mons or something like that, the way the other old puffers were named?"

"*Mons* is how astronomers decided to refer to the Tharsis shield volcanoes with their relatively gradual slopes. The term 'Tholis' describes a steep-sided structure like our Jovis here. But rest assured, Volcano Fourteen, as it was once called, is definitely a volcano."

"A very frigid one, I should hope."

Arazine bent his head down and scraped at the boulder chip he was working on. "Don't be so sure. According to Roman mythology, Vulcano was where Vulcan, the god of fire, kept his forge. The Romans knew the hottest place in the world when they saw it."

March glanced at Arazine to see if he was having him on. "Hot? That's a load of twaddle when you consider the dead volcanoes we have here. I mean, they're all extinct aren't they? They haven't gone off in millions of years, have they?"

"Volcanoes don't rest easily. Extinct was how they described Krakatoa before it wiped out thirty six thousand people."

March looked at Arazine more curiously than before and shuddered.

Their Spider stalked up the side of the mountain, with knee joints bobbing high above the fragile compartment. Servos whined laboriously at the combined effort of raising the Spider's loaded weight in unequal increments while keeping the inhabitants aligned with the horizontal as humans preferred to be. Step, correct, step, and correct. Finally it compromised and tilted them slightly to follow the cant of the surface. The wheels were now retracted and the legs tread on the more secure multi-pads. Even so, according the to the dashboard, the localized chips measured the slippage and found the levels only marginally acceptable.

When men and machine were more than halfway up, the Spider began to scramble and hunt to find secure footing. Unlike the procedure on level ground, it avoided stepping on protruding rocks or anything that might tend to fall away. Inside, they began to feel the turbulence. March clutched the safety handles with white knuckles. After faltering twice in a row and adjusting its center of balance, the Spider planted its pads firmly and refused to go any further.

"EXIT," it warned loudly. "Fail-safe triggered."

"What is that?" March blurted.

"Mechanical wisdom," said Arazine.

"Can't you get the damn thing moving?"

"I suggest *you* get moving."

"EXIT NOW," the Spider demanded.

"I don't care for the way this thing is acting," March complained as he experimentally shifted his weight.

Arazine swung his legs over the outside of the vehicle and gestured rudely for March to follow. "You're scared to death is more like it."

"With good reason. Tell me the truth. Why do they call it this contraption the Spider X-2?"

"It's like any other equipment. X stands for experimental."

"That's what I thought. What happened to the X-1?"

"Never mind. At the speed we're doing things, everything is a crap shoot."

They hauled out the equipment they needed and left the itchy rover where it had stopped. As soon as they stepped clear, March saw their only transportation skittering rapidly back down the embankment, disappearing in a haze of orange dust. "The bloody thing is out of control."

"It's doing what it's supposed to," said Arazine. "Waiting for us in a safer place."

"I wish I could join it."

March and Arazine struggled along on foot, resorting to hooks and ropes when necessary. Even with light gravity to assist, March had no picnic hauling the weight of his Hybrid and pack. Every so often his feet slipped, and his fingers barely held. The Chief Executive forged ahead scarcely looking back at his companion except to tell him to "haul ass." If this were Earth, March's lack of climbing experience might have been fatal.

Arazine, on the other hand, climbed with the experience of many geological expeditions. He stopped to scoop rhyolite and andesite samples on his way, keying into them with some chatter about how Fourteen must be the parent of these specimens. The lighter basalt could have been spit onto this surface from another volcano, he said, whereas rhyolite and andesite, by their nature, didn't go far. The delay gave March a chance to catch his breath.

Guided by the sure-footed scientist, they eventually hauled ass right up to the volcano's lip, and pressed tentative feet on its broad shelf. From the edge, the surface fell away almost straight down, far beyond what a person could survive if they toppled even at low gravity. Below them, the caldera floor was carved naturally into stair-step terraces much the way Japanese farms were contour cut into the less-ancient mountains of Honshu.

"Here we are, Devon, the grand old mouth of grand old Number Fourteen. The sight is sobering even for me."

"Why do you call it Fourteen instead of Jovis Tholis?"

"I've gone back to the generic names for now because us Martians are going to re-christen everything eventually. There's no point in accepting the labels the astronomers tried to shove at us. I'm not using kilometers either. Speaking of which, do you have any useful suggestions for Fourteen's new name?"

March looked all around him. "How about Mount Too Bloody Big?"

"You think it's vast? You could drop Fourteen into the crater on top of Olympus Mons and still have room for the town of Olympia itself. Maybe you live too close to Olympus to have noticed."

"Be that as it may, I think I can just see the sun reaching the lowest level of the basin in one corner about a kilometer below us." As an afterthought he added, "It certainly looks safely dried up with all those cracks."

Arazine said, "That's not the true floor. What you're seeing is the surface that was formed when the central plug subsided over and over again after eruptions. That step in the center is the remains of the lava from the last explosion that cooled and hardened in the caldera. When your eyes adjust, you'll notice that there is one particularly large crack that continues deeper. It's too dark to see where that leads."

"So I wouldn't actually see the lava broiling in there even if the volcano were capable of producing some."

"No, you wouldn't see it. But you'd better hope this thing has got some fire left in it somewhere. If it's entirely extinct, we'll be out of business. Come, Devon, I'll let you do the unscientific part."

Arazine selected a dark rock at his feet, one of the stragglers that never made it down slope. In size and shape it resembled a cinder block, toasted dark as Cajun chicken. "Here's one of your spongy basalts. You're so proud of that pitching arm, why don't you heave it down there, but get it into the deeper opening. Don't let it hit anything else."

When March looked skeptical he added, "Give it a few tries if you have to."

"It won't take a few tries."

March held the basalt like an American football and gave it a strong throw toward the center of the enormous caldera. He couldn't believe how long it flew and how slowly it arced, turned, and was pulled under before it passed from sight. Though it seemed to go into the crack, the block appeared so small by then that they couldn't tell for sure. March thought he would have noticed if it went skipping away.

After a while, March bumped his audio feed and cocked his head as a dog would to better hear the echo when it came back up. He imagined the rock falling unhindered inside the empty expanse. Falling and falling.

They waited and listened to silence until the lack of reply after so long went beyond his imagination. He looked at Arazine. "Are there really such things as bottomless pits?"

The scientist smiled. "It may be four miles to the bottom. Sound moves much more slowly in the Martian atmosphere and dissipates over distance, so you would never hear the echo. So far so good. Now I'll need your assistance again," he said as he unzipped his pack. "We need to do some probing to see if the central conduit has a reasonably unimpeded path to the magma at the bottom."

Arazine disemboweled his secret packages and the two of them constructed sonar devices in thoughtful silence, broken only by quiet and clipped instructions from Arazine. With all the odd pieces assembled, they set up the pulses that would range invisibly into the cone and the crust below it, and return to build overlapping slices into a single image.

Sweeping around the rim for a final inspection, Arazine stopped, nodded to himself, and jogged the system into action. It immediately began to gush silent data which he compressed like autumn leaves in a barrel. The viewer allowed March to see what Arazine was creating, three-dimensional pictures drawn from reflected sound. He found that the bowels of the behemoth were a complicated affair a long way into it, not at all like the straight shaft of a well. Branches piled upon branches, twined like the layered nest of a cormorant.

Arazine remarked vaguely that they needed to trace the most likely path directly, giving March no time to digest the remark or prepare mentally for what he was about to do.

"Keep your eyes in the viewer," Arazine ordered as he pulled the strap tight through the buckles around the young attorney's helmet.

The image in March's visor changed subtly when digitized and he felt as if he were walking toward the inside edge of the caldera against his will. He tried to stop but his legs would not respond. "What the hell? Don't tell me we've gone Virtual!"

"I already haven't told you."

The approach to hell seemed a safe path around the rocky lip. Yet the sensations were as realistic as the images. Abruptly they leaped across the volcano's ample gullet, arching like launched projectiles toward the very same crack that swallowed the basalt. Inside, the darkness was lit with the eerie colors the computer imagined for the interior walls of the volcano.

For March it was an extreme roller coaster with no car to ride, desperately grabbing handfuls of thin air while his partner's laugh echoed on the near wall. Trying to close his eyes was futile. The virtual image had tapped into his brain, leaving him no escape. They followed the turns that Arazine willed, swept flat sills at high speed, and through switchback dikes that terminated in dead end blisters, whipping back out of them just as quickly before screaming toward the next one. In the last phase, they were sucked into the cavernous branching conduits in a breathless vertical plunge, the path of the rock that March threw, the place he dreaded, an unending fall. Against the wind, he pulled into a fetal position and tried to endure, endlessly swearing to himself that none of it was real.

March was shaking when they jumped into darkness. He didn't know if the ordeal was over or if his brain finally shut down the horror. But the visual had been so convincing that his pounding blood was threatening to overwhelm his eardrums when normal daylight returned, bringing his breath back to him in ragged gasps.

"You're now a junior member of the U.S. Geological Survey Team," Arazine pronounced with glee. "Best ride in town."

"You bloody bastard," March croaked back after he tore the harness loose.

Arazine smirked as he crunched the fresh data. "I hope you're not mad. It won't kill you. I just gave you the same thing today's kids pay for." He watched the progress line fill while March worked at unclenching his hands.

When Arazine saw his probe results, his chest swelled. "I'll need more information, of course, but the depth access is incredible. It's looking like this will work. Unlimited energy. And think of this: Nearly all the gas that escapes from volcanoes is water in the form of steam. Do you know the value of water on this planet, Mr. March?"

March eased slowly to the ground to steady himself and reached a hand down to make sure he arrived. Something in his inner ear was making the yawning caldera seem to drift around him and he didn't want to end up with a hole underfoot where solid ground should be. "I'm still concerned about a few small details," he said to Arazine with an unrepentant, sarcastic tone.

"Such as?"

"Such as, we don't own this planet yet, Peter. Where are Earth's authorities going to be while you're putting this shebang together?"

"Any authorities visiting Olympia are going to be removed from the equation one way or another. The people behind the scenes who really hold power will be on the side of profits, our side."

The attorney had no question on that point. He must have decided not to learn more about what his client meant by "removed."

The two men made their way back down, Arazine with confidence, March still shaky until they reached the Spider. Instead of running away, it waited with tense excitement like some strange arachnid puppy that saw good times ahead. They stowed their packs inside and tumbled in after. March was grateful he didn't have to waste a second turning any ignition key to get it going. He took off in high gear to put some distance between themselves and the dangerous volcano.

Flying over the fields of scattered rock known to geologists as the bedding plane, he had many reasons to hurry. Not least of all, the nutrient rations he sipped through the straw in his Hybrid had run dry. As March grew hungrier, the rocks on the way appeared to him like large heads of lettuce, rounded out by the shadows each one cast. My first mirage on the way to a breakdown, he told himself.

As they headed west by southwest, March could see the sky giving way to darkness in the South some 200 miles away. Not the darkening of a beautiful sunset, but a shadowed mass with sharp boundaries much as a tornado looks invading a cloudless Kansas plain. He felt a shiver wash over him. It could be, he thought, that the virtual trip is taking its toll and I'm seeing my second mirage.

He had no such luck. The Spider provided a weather report on a heads-up display, splashed on the windshield to get his attention. Instruments showed the disturbance bringing havoc to a "sea" called Mare Sirenum, with barometric pressure falling in a region to the North of it, a place called Memnonia. Storms like this one moved to any adjacent area in which barometric pressure fell, and would continue moving along the line of falling pressure, which was now represented on the map by an arrow pointed North. Memnonia was the last region that bordered on Tharsis, the area that included both the town of Olympia and their present location. That meant that the pressure arrow now pointed to them like an accusation.

"See what you've done?" said March. "We're going to get our skins flayed off by that playful little wind back there."

"Most dust storms are nothing."

"This one is something. It's one of the strong ones we've been getting. Instead of being encircling the globe, it's concentrated."

"I've noticed it." March thought he heard false confidence injected into Arazine's voice. "I have it worked out," Arazine continued, "and we can make it. I have complete faith in your driving ability, Devon."

March checked to make sure there was nothing blocking the accelerator from hitting the floor. He pressed down until there was nowhere left to push. Although the storm had a longer distance to travel than March and Arazine did, it had the advantage of moving much faster. Both men understood that if the Spider had to stop at all, as it might in the case of faulty equipment, they would become two Martian notables that would not be seen in Olympia again. So March had no intention of stopping. The most troubling thing for him was being forced to move partially toward the disturbance, pushing slightly south as the storm tracked north. March locked the Spider into top speed and kept it in the best route possible, worried about the volcano at his back, imagining it smoldering maliciously, adding its own billows to the gloom.

"I've been doing some thinking, Peter. I'll do anything else that you ask of me, but where are we supposed to stand while this Volcano Fourteen is erupting into clean and profitable energy just a few hundred miles east of us?"

"You've misunderstood me completely. I have no intention of setting off a valuable volcano and making it untouchable. All I want to do is tap into the heat that's way at the bottom. When people use geothermal energy in places like Reykjavik, they don't have to explode something to do it. They have access to some heat source, which is what I'm trying to do. We could never drill a shaft to the depth of Volcano Fourteen's conduit. That's why we need to utilize the ready-made shaft that's there. At the bottom of it, we'll find enough heat to spin a turbine until the end of the next century. We may use anything from Valdeen Factor to old-fashioned dynamite to start it churning, but that's all. We're talking tiny amounts. There is no major activity left inside this planet to trigger a devastating eruption."

At least you hope so, March added silently.

And the storm that was following the pressure arrow advanced into Memnonia like a moving trap.

CHAPTER 4
Brush With The Beast

THE DEVIL'S GOLFCOURSE behind them, home loomed like a beacon to soothe March's palpitating heart.

With death's wall in Tharsis now, it was a false relief. The Spider crawled a jagged line as turbulence rocked the small craft beyond its capacity to correct. A heavier gust made it slip into the unpaved shoulder, lurch drunkenly from the sudden tilt, and pivot in an effort to move ahead. March fought through a 360-degree turn while its legs did a mad dance. Finally they resumed forward progress.

Until now, Arazine sat through the long drive home telling March he was confident the timing was on their side, however narrow that side may have been. Here, a grain of doubt must have crept into him. He tucked his head down.

The port loomed at teasing distance. Everyone else on Mars no doubt had their surface projects abandoned and the access doors sealed for the past half hour. Lights dimmed throughout Olympia as the air jets of the perimeter went into overdrive, drawing down the onrushing air and throwing it back at itself to stave off the frenzied charge. The system wasn't designed for a challenge of the magnitude they had seen recently. At a certain point Olympia's precautions would be overwhelmed by concentrated wind. Nothing that wasn't tied down would be left. Stragglers in bad storms had to use the sand lock to join the city if they wanted to enter in one piece, and if things got bad enough, even that entrance could shut down with no override possible.

Arazine called three times to link them to Gatekeeper's software, having been too far at first, and getting it wrong the second time because of an unsteady reach that refused to land on the proper keys. Grabbing one shaky hand with the other was no help at all. He punched in again, saying, "Gatekeeper should never ever deny the governor access. I'll have the damn thing ripped out if it does."

March stared with rounded eyes at the port growing too quickly in front of them, still a wall and not yet a door. Refusing to slow down as they closed in, he would rather have slammed into the solid concrete than give himself to the rending dust. Caught in a sudden updraft, the Spider's legs had to dangle at full extension to reach the ground. When only three legs touched, guidance was temporarily ceded to the wind.

Arazine wrapped his fingers under the edge of the board for support, pressing the buttons with an awkward thumb. "Yes," he said, "got a connection." His final summons made the doors budge like fingers casually unclasping, slow and unmindful of the explorer's plight. As if at a signal, both men threw their weight at the Spider's inside wall in the direction of the entrance, and March, at least, imagined that they jolted ahead. The Spider scurried in, scraping its edges against the metal fingertips with a burst of wind clamoring all around.

Only when he saw that the Spider would fit through the partially opened doors, only when he heard the scraping protest subside, did March cut his throttle and apply the brakes, pressing with hysterical euphoria, adrenalin surging in his right thigh. Compressed air and airborne particles forced their way from behind like a collective lynch mob, adding to the inertia and buffeting the Spider so violently that it hit the far wall with a crack that rocked them inside the compartment. The rest of the momentum sent them in a rotation along the wall, petering out only when they had made a complete circuit. Stunned and dizzy, March made no attempt to keep the craft from spinning.

Then they were still and seemed unable to move, talk or think.

The ache from his bruises brought March out of it.

"Shit," he said when he noticed that he had bit his tongue. He sucked at the salty wound and managed a weak smile as the metal fingers fully sealed again and the chamber regulated pressure. Arazine looked slightly concerned when the wall's stress sensors called for and ran a self-diagnostic before they could be admitted through the inner door.

Arazine said, "Without a clean bill of health from the stress monitor we won't be allowed to go anywhere."

March was so happy to be sheltered that he didn't recognize the potential problem or notice the time lag. Helplessly giddy, he spent the time collecting himself, ready to deny any difficulties, ready to seem perfectly normal. And why not? he asked himself, their ordeal on Olympia's doorstep was nothing compared to what could have happened if the doors hadn't opened.

While they watched, a minor repair to the air lock wall was automatically effected with a light spray of concrete. When all of the sensors reported no significant damage, another set of fingers separated, revealing the brighter lights of the inner corridor. Gatekeeper apologized for the delay. The Spider checked its own integrity before it dug its wheels out from the accumulated sand and strutted drunkenly to the hallway. March squirmed because the suit couldn't process his volume of sweat, and some of it burned his eyes.

As they rode the Spider back to its port, seven knee joints aligned, one leg dragging, March heard the little thunderclap that kicked the ubiquitous sand outside. But not for long, he thought, converting his fear to more controllable anger. Anyone who doesn't like sand up their ass had better of stayed on Earth.

* * *

Now that the danger was over, and the hallway ride relatively smooth, March said, "That was a bit of a close one. Do you still believe we can trifle with volcanoes on Mars?"

Arazine said, "More than ever. Actually, I feel slightly euphoric. You saw the fury of this planet in that storm. Imagine the possibilities of tapping into forces like that."

"You're crazy. You may need a billion dollars or more. You'll spend a pleasant few dollars just in the repair of this toy of yours."

Arazine grabbed his partner by the shoulders. "Tell me, Devon, what is it that brings people, resources and economic prosperity to a city faster than any other single event?"

"Is that a rhetorical question?" March thought it rude to have any questions put to him that weren't rhetorical, particularly in the wake of a crisis.

"Not exactly. I'm asking you to think now. What hauls a city out of obscurity?"

"I can call several things to mind. There's the discovery of precious materials, a lot of pioneer cities founded that way. Supposing Olympia's nitrites weren't so hard to ship back, we'd be loopy with cash. If the Atacama ever runs out we can name our own price." March was referring to the desert that spanned parts of Peru and Chile, the Earth's chief source of essential nitrites in one densely packed region. The vicinity of Olympus Mons in which Olympia was built was blessed in the same way. The governor himself regularly sold a small amount smuggled onto Earth-bound ships through a tolerated gray market.

"Massive shortages on Earth can't be counted on. What else occurs to you?"

"There's the instance where a major business or industry is relocating. Usually the big boys like to start their own town from scratch. But there are no advantages to starting a boomtown here. The proverbial railway isn't exactly coming through any time soon."

"Maybe it is. Keep ruminating. I can smell the wood burning."

"You're very smug, aren't you? I can figure this thing out if you can."

"Go ahead then."

"Well, there's the occasional Big Science project like the one that created Olympia itself. Unfortunately for us, that sort of thing always falls flat when people tire of seeing how their money is wasted. Just look what happened with the massive particle accelerator in Waxahatchie, Texas. It was twenty years before your government stepped foot in that bear trap again. I give up."

"Try the next Olympic Games."

"Sporting events in Olympia? It's preposterous."

They had already docked the Spider and emerged. Arazine popped off his helmet and stepped out of his suit while March struggled to do the same. Within the boundaries of Olympia there was no need for supplemental oxygen tanks so they were unmasked as well. The governor made a face at the way they both smelled but he was determined to finish his explanation. "In our warm season, it's just right in this part of Mars for a winter competition."

"You mean skiing and things like that?"

"Why not? I've always said that the tourism industry is the key to our survival. That's what we've been developing here in case you haven't noticed."

"Our little ski lodge and facilities in Olympia? The Olympics is more than tourism. Don't let the town's name go to your head. It's fanciful and nothing else. We haven't the capabilities."

"We've had the snow making equipment operating for years now, a forty million gallon capacity reservoir just waiting for the money to fill it. Some people have given their lives mapping out the trails, and building the facilities and lodgings. Holding an Olympics is the next logical step."

"For a giant maybe. There are resorts on Earth in operation for fifty years that haven't hosted an Olympics. Who would take a decision to put one here?"

"It pays to have allies. I have a certain friend from the Chinese embassy stationed in Belgium. That's where they're making those decisions now."

"In a Chinese embassy?"

"No, the Olympic Committee sits in Belgium."

"So what has your friend got to do with it?"

"Those choices are strategically made. And he has a certain amount of influence."

March still didn't have Arazine pegged. He wasn't entirely a Thomas Edison. If he had Olympic ambitions designed to attract large-scale funding, he was a lot like P. T. Barnum as well. Ventriloquism and hypnotism should be added to his act. "Friends or not, Peter, Mars is the last place anyone would put The Olympic Games."

"I'm confident that's just what they'll do. It's a matter of pushing the right buttons. In China, they refer to it as *guanxi*. That means 'connections.' Without us, the Chinese have no foothold on Mars. They began an excellent space program at the turn of the century, but us Americans got scared and moved three times as fast. So they've been shut out of Mars so far. With us as partners, I can offer China a sizable acreage if they provide the right kind of help. They have an interest in seeing us take charge. They're never going to have a second chance."

"So long as you don't give away too much. There's going to be a lot more people than your Chinese friend involved at the end of the day. And they're all going to want a piece of it. Before supporting you, I'll need time to think."

Arazine sized up the gangly March with his longish hair and his thirty-year-old baby face. "Sometimes I think you were never cut out to be a radical, Devon. Your problem is that you never learned to think big."

* * *

Arazine and March used the rear entrance of Town Hall, past the workers and the police line barriers, their shoes clumping on the temporary wooden bridge that spanned the foundation trench. The other side of the building was completely inaccessible under even heavier construction, as was the governor's office at the moment. Pedestrians and construction workers watched their leader's progress with varying degrees of interest. Arazine waved to everyone and to no one in particular, a habit he was getting used to since he came into public service.

They proceeded down the hall and squeezed into the Office of the Corporation Counsel, crowded as it was with the governor's furniture commandeering space. Arazine let March sit at his own desk while he took a guest chair after the door was tightly shut and locked. He looked pleased.

"The construction is going well," said Arazine conversationally.

"You went and contacted them, didn't you?" pleaded March. He re-stacked file folders until he could see the other man. "You've spoken with your Chinese Embassy friends."

"Of course I did. Let me tell you, it wasn't easy."

"You haven't been playing fair with me. I didn't pass on this decision. What wasn't easy? They didn't agree then, did they? I knew they wouldn't have it."

"No, not that. I meant the connection was awful. You know how these ultra-distance calls are. The delay in the signal was maddening. Every time I would say something, it would be met with silence like he was mulling it over or making me wait. Only he hadn't heard anything yet. It seems a much longer delay when you're talking about something important. Then when I finally heard his words, I answered immediately, and he had to wait. It was like playing chess by snail mail."

"Were you able to convince him?"

"Easily. Like I told you, it's what he wanted and what he was waiting for. Before I came along, he just didn't know how to get it. Now he'll scramble to do whatever's required to make it happen."

"It's all very well and good to make plans among yourselves, but I still don't believe this is going any further. I mean, the Olympic Committee has to make a sensible judgment, don't they? Your man won't be able to push it through over common sense."

Arazine reddened. "From what I've seen, the process is political, not sensible. If the IOC could decide to put the Olympics in Nazi Germany in 1936 when they had five years of shocking news to change their minds, or in Munich in 1972 where people were lined up and shot by Carlos The Jackal, or even in hospital-poor Moscow in 1980, where an injured athlete shared an infirmary bed with cockroaches, they can certainly decide to put it on high tech Mars in the twenty-first century."

Arazine so worked himself up as he spoke, that with his last line he pounded the table for emphasis. The over-stacked files tipped over onto the floor.

CHAPTER 5
The IOC

THE SCHELDE RIVER flowed unceasingly through the greater part of Belgium before reaching the streets of Antwerp, washing along on its way to the North Sea, the English Channel and the vast ocean beyond, as most of Antwerp's inhabitants filled the dark with their dreams. Abdul Harouk slept abreast the banks of the Schelde in one of the most graceful old Belgian homes amidst a rare tract of green, his bedroom three levels high overlooking one of the finest river views at the bend where the torrent flows east to west.

Less than five hours after Peter Arazine cast his line to Earth, Harouk was roused at two in the morning by his new servant and informed curtly that there was some kind of policeman downstairs.

The girl was gone. Empty bottles were scattered with unidentified trash and clothing. The pulse was pounding in his head. No time to dress, he wiped the drool across his knuckles and hurried.

Stumbling from room to room, he flipped on lights as he went, a little too late each time, crashed with his feet, barked his shins with a yelp, and shuffled finally into his study where he appeared ridiculously clad in a red silk bathrobe and unmatched blue and green slippers. From beneath his crusted lids he saw his visitor reposed like a

Bedouin chief, with overcoat closeted, contented smile, and cigarette glowing in a notch of the ashtray, as if Harouk's home were the intruder's private tent.

Chul Huk Chang was the man's cursed name. On the floor stood four sturdy chairs marking the corners of a square, each focused on the center of the ornate rug Harouk had imported to remind him of home. The same rug that was beneath Chang's camel-filthy feet. Not that this communist oriental knew what a camel was save for the level of grime that he shared with it. The rug wasn't there to please anyone but Harouk, and this wasn't the room in which he received visitors. Yet Chul Huk Chang, who was not exactly a policeman these days, occupied the chair at the far right extreme and his body language spoke of supreme confidence and damning evidence. How did he know about the girl? Harouk wondered. Why would he care?

Harouk took a short, dreadful step inside the room looking for hazards, still adjusting to the light, still thinking too slowly. *Has the butcher come for me tonight?* Did the girl mean something to him? I have to focus. Visits from Chang were rare and always uninvited. He came for blood or he came for money. Which would it be now? In the years Harouk was in personal contact with him, it had been money-related so far. Was there reason for things to be different this evening?

The Chang he knew most recently was a top ranking member of the Chinese Communist Party with diplomatic status, confidant to the Premier and the Chairman, a career manipulator, probably a spy, anything but the diplomat he claimed to be.

Harouk was privy to only a few of the murderous highlights of Chang's earlier vocation. As a teenage member of the Red Guard in the so-called Cultural Revolution, Chang began his career as a kind of state-sponsored gang member in 1967, terrorizing the countryside, slaughtering household pets as icons of the old ideas, thriving on chaotic destruction. Soon an important commander in the People's Liberation Army, he spent much of the Nineteen Seventies under the Minister of Public Security, expertly torturing political prisoners for the names of their freedom-loving companions.

Then Chang disappeared for a while, presumably sharpening his manipulative skills abroad, surfacing again in China in the late Eighties as a valued member of the Central Committee. There he was one of the radical powers who precipitated the Tiananmen Square Massacre when his ilk feared democracy would take hold. In the Nineteen Nineties his blood stained resume was tucked away in the official files, while Chang himself was rinsed pure by a mandate that he must be popular. His most unwavering belief was that the vision of Mao, The Great Leap Forward, was somehow fulfilled by the birth and life of Chang Chul-huk, as he was originally called. When his view proved unpopular, he kept that message to himself, and so survived wave after wave of purges.

This man was Abdul Harouk's houseguest in the early morning. No matter what he seemed on the outside, Harouk reminded himself, Chang would never be more than a barbarian. The politician had to have more on his mind than Harouk's slattern from last night. Harouk prayed it was Olympic Committee business and nothing else.

As the head of the International Olympic Committee, Harouk had become the target of the powerful. He often fulfilled small favors, petitions from special interests.

Usually it was a matter of how a delegation's demands would be suffered, where they would be placed at events, with kings, queens, and presidents at ringside, and so on. Also he would make clandestine arrangements to smuggle out athletes from war torn countries or cover the less noble political embarrassment of some aristocrat's offspring arrested for vandalism. Praying that by satisfying small favors he could avoid large and perilous ones, he sometimes found himself walking a rope. Money and prestige with their attendant governments and power blocks were at one end, and the IOC Chairman was at the other. Who was he, after all but an appointed fop who had to know his place? With Chul Huk Chang calling for favors, it would be a deadly game of cat and mouse.

He fought the impulse to shake the sleep from his face. Admitting any level of discomfort would please Chang the torturer for too much. He had to show strength, or at least play the polite role. He had nowhere to retreat.

Harouk said, "Forgive my appearance, sir, but why could you possibly want to drag me out of my bed?" Such outbursts counted as bravado. He knew very well that Chang could pry him out any time and have him bounced into the coldest and darkest of jail cells with a nod of his head if he pleased. And undoubtedly, even more. He shivered at the thoughts that nipped the edges of his sleep-clogged brain. *Have I triggered his temper with my impertinent question?* Harouk's hands involuntarily rose to his temples. He practically slapped them down again.

Harouk thought he saw a trace of genuine urgency nestled within Chang's silence. He realized the visit might concern a demand for some radical change. It had been suicidal to shift the headquarters of the IOC out of neutral

Switzerland and into Belgium. Proponents argued that
Belgian soil was also neutral, with Antwerp itself the site of
a glorious Olympic Games in 1920. The truth was that
Antwerp was far more vulnerable to outside manipulation,
especially these days, more than a century later. What some
thought was an experiment in trust was actually Chang's
heavy handed intervention, for Antwerp happened to be
one of Chang's political playgrounds.

The people's representative sat sipping Harouk's tea,
gently tugging at the liquid with his top lip outstretched. He
hadn't bothered getting Harouk's servant in since he
preferred to fix it himself and so do it properly. The gold of
his watch caught the light as he raised the cup again to his
lips. Chang was contemptibly well turned out. He looked
as fresh as if it were 9 a.m. on a Monday rather than two
a.m. on a Saturday. With unparted hair slicked back, he
sported a new manicure and a high gloss on his black shoes.
Not garish patent leather but quality soft leather, machine
buffed to a ceramic glaze. The difference in their states of
dress gave Chang a decided psychological advantage. Or at
least Harouk believed so. It was no coincidence that Chang
rushed Harouk out of bed. Harouk wondered if Chang
dressed this way in the torture chamber, and hoped never to
find out.

The diplomat nodded almost imperceptibly for the
house's owner to sit down. He didn't waste a single motion.
Inside his civilized wrappings he had eyes like a buzzard,
blind to everything but life throbbing away in mortal pain.
He saw people as living dead, allowed to walk around as
long they remained useful to him, then assuming their
rightful place in the ground. Remarkably, damnably, he
hadn't said even a word so far. His buzzard eyes remained

locked onto the IOC's top official, who was not so much sitting as he was assuming the shape of the chair.

"Little man, there's been a change of plans," Chang said, pulling a long draft under his lip immediately after. Chang addressed him in Flemish that was even better than Harouk's given the time he'd spent in Belgium or across the border in the Netherlands. Language was a gift that he had. He used at least seven tongues including the ones from his native region. And didn't have a pleasant word to say in any of them.

Harouk felt his gut laying low, with a bouncing headache glancing off his skull. "We haven't spoken in eight months. What plans could you and I have?"

"You have an announcement to make, Abdul."

"Go on." Harouk wondered if he really said what he heard himself say, since he didn't want to hear more. Chang's dark nature was so carefully shielded that the answer could be anything at all. "What kind of announcement?" he added bravely.

"The next Winter Olympics is going to take place in Olympia. On Mars."

Harouk nearly smirked, a nervous mask of humor. So it was Olympic business that Chang came to speak about after all. Holding Olympics on another planet couldn't happen, though the suggestion was enough to make the Arab more than a little uneasy under the circumstances. He let out a controlled breath, distressed that things would be difficult, relieved that the butcher did not arrive to take him this evening. Then he did something that would haunt him later.

Like a trained idiot in a moment of weakness, Harouk recited what was on his mind. "Olympics on Mars? It would take more than an announcement. Of course I will help as much as I can. Still, I must point out that trying to have the Olympics there so soon is wishful thinking, Mr. Chang. With all due respect, you may not know much about the development of that region. The little town of Olympia is very nearly dead. They'll never be ready for an Olympics by '42. Truthfully, I never even thought of Mars as a possible Olympic site before, but I would say you should shoot for 2046 at best. But of course you know that. When you said the next Olympics, for a moment, I thought that you meant to suggest that there should be an Olympics on Mars in '42. I apologize. It was presumptuous. The late hour must be affecting me." His breath came up short. Having built a box of sand he found himself sinking deeper and deeper. He wanted to sob, wanted to slap himself, wanted to wake up and fight.

Chang let him ramble to a halt before continuing. "I said nothing about '42. I'm talking about 2038, the year of the Twenty Eighth Winter Olympic Games. I made the decision only hours ago and we can't afford to lose a single day of preparation. So you see why we are in such a hurry to complete the formalities."

Any trace of expression evaporated from Harouk's face. He pulled the silk robe tighter around him as if he couldn't afford to reveal anything more. "The 2038 Olympics is not the next one, it's this one. The one that's coming up right now. You don't know what you're asking. The '38 Olympics are supposed to be in Trondheim, Norway. We announced it to the world. The location was selected by my committee well in advance so that we could have seven years of preparation. That's the way it's done because we must have that time."

"You of all people should know better, Abdul. Short term planning can and has been done. The Olympics that happened here in this city were announced in April of 1919 and took place in the Summer of 1920, just eighteen months after the end of World War One, and at the same time the Allies continued to occupy Germany. Need I remind you that Belgium was devastated in that war? They didn't need seven years."

"Things are more complicated today. It's hard enough for a host country to set up on Earth. Forget about Mars. The Oslo government has taken almost a billion dollars worth of loans from the International Monetary Fund and various investors. They've matched it with nearly a billion of their own." Harouk the official sat a little straighter as he talked, engaging Chang with the facts and figures of inarguable truth.

The People's Representative eyed the cigarette he had left burning. "We will pay the Norwegians for their trouble."

"From what source?"

"Let my government worry about the funding. You will do what is necessary."

"I am the Chairman of the IOC. My agreement on this matter is not one of your formalities." Harouk realized he made a mistake as soon as he said it. He watched Chang slowly close and re-open his eyes. Harouk retreated back until the hard chair stopped him, and lowered his head. In the silence, he could hear the Schelde churning outside his window, like himself always struggling to turn the bend from East to West.

Chang filled up the space that Harouk vacated. He wore a pale smile that promised retribution, punishment that would bring him extreme pleasure. "Look at the luxury around you. Wouldn't it be nice if you had some progeny to leave it to?"

"I have a boy and a girl," the IOC Chairman said vacantly.

"No, *I* have the boy and the girl."

Harouk paled. "Mine are with the nanny. They have to be."

"Hmm. Did you miss an appointment some hours ago? Were you not planning to pick up your children, but picked up a slattern instead? Your own decadence betrays you." Chang hid his face behind his cup yet Harouk could see his cheeks rise and spider web lines stretch from the corners of his eyes.

Harouk gasped, the last bit of fight drained out of him. *The monster enjoys himself. So Chang did have a connection to the girl. She was a spy. And now I pay the price.*

At once, Harouk saw things in a different light. He would give his full cooperation but the project would not go on for long. *Be absolutely humble now*, he reminded himself. *Even Chang cannot accomplish Olympics on Mars. The price of defiance had suddenly gotten very high, while the likelihood of fruition seemed very low.*

"I misspoke from my ignorance and meant no offense, sir. Allow me to serve you in any way I can."

"Good, groveling works best. Get to work at once and we'll announce it next year on the anniversary of the Mars exploration project Viking. The Americans lap up anniversaries."

Harouk's eyelids lifted with comprehension. Chang was right: The Americans would pay for anything. And their political force combined with that of China and its allies would be overwhelming. Harouk wasn't foolish enough to ask why a location on Mars was so important to Chang, how he had gotten such an idea, or who he had been in contact with. That knowledge would be more fearful ground than the IOC official ever dare tread.

No wonder Chang hadn't thrown him in prison. It wasn't the Chinese who would meet the repercussions in the gargantuan task of shifting an Olympics to Mars, it was him. Harouk felt the skin of his face tighten from dried sweat. He held on to the hope that Chang could still change his mind. Had to change his mind.

"If you pardon me, sir, my staff is not going to have time to prepare. Not to mention the trouble we'll have with the advertising contracts. The extra facilities and support systems that you will need on Mars, together with the costs of shipping from one planet to another, will far exceed the Norwegian expenses. If you find the project cannot be done you must be prepared to postpone."

Chang finished his tea and clicked it against the plate as he set it down. "Visitors will expect Mars to be Spartan. Scale it down if you run out of cash. Reconvene the committee this morning and get it done." Chang was apparently tired of playing with his food. Tired of dead men speaking so loudly.

"With respect, sir, you have my vote," Harouk said, "but there are eighty-nine independent members of my committee to convince. How will I persuade any of them to vote 'yes'?"

"I didn't leave it up to your limited persuasive abilities. Bring them back in, and you will find that they vote that way now."

CHAPTER 6
Valdeen's Original Sin

2012: SUTTER CREEK, MARYLAND

DOCTOR HAVISLAW VALDEEN nestled the empty tube among the others in the "dirty" rack, ready for sterilization. Penciling the result of his last test of the day, he moaned slightly in anticipation of his eventual triumph. Among fanatics reaching at least as far back as the Nazi era, there had been many who told themselves they did evil things for the sake of science, and some, like Valdeen, who knew they did science for the sake of evil things.

Valdeen broke out his Nikon to take a photo of the room for insurance purposes and almost lost himself in the viewfinder. The morning light gleamed off a forest of laboratory glass. His Sutter Creek facility had the latest in vacuum chambers, scanning and tunneling microscopes, cyclotrons, and anything else a multi-functional, fully equipped lab might need. Beautiful in its deception, Valdeen never even touched most of his machines except when he used one to prop open a door. In fact, he accomplished his miracles with almost nothing.

Only two people knew why. One of them was Valdeen himself. The other was in the way.

Valdeen snapped the shutter.

"Um, what was that?" his partner murmured across the vast gulf of his mind. Although physically present, Doctor

Edward Merris was neither in Hitler's Berlin nor Valdeen's Sutter Creek. He was hunched under a table with pin-fed piles of statistical data, starting his shift early, and working in his peculiar trance. He yanked heavy reams of paper from topless cardboard collection boxes in their homes under several of the printers. As Merris once explained, he learned from painful experience that he must work with the old-style continuous feed paper so that sheet after sheet would stay in sequence. Otherwise he would continue to jettison half his most valuable data before his first home-wrapped sandwich at lunch. He had to buy the ancient equipment at a yard sale.

With a sniff that said *I'm in control,* he traced his way down the columns of words and figures by means of a no-nonsense metal-edged wooden ruler, and endeavored to leave a pencil tick on every line he visited. In time, he flopped the double page over to grow a second pile, and started anew from the heights of the following page.

He seldom remembered to close his mouth while he worked. As a result, the first sound he made usually wasn't a word at all. "Uh, did you say something?" he prompted Valdeen for the second time.

"Nothing you would be interested in." Valdeen stared at his collaborator's back. *What a shit head. Why would I be saying something to you if I didn't have to?*

Merris responded with a noncommittal, "Uh-huh," having obviously forgotten that he had asked Valdeen a question. Valdeen knew his collaborator so well he believed he could read the man's mind. Merris didn't want to seem like he didn't know what was going on. Holding the paper close to his eyes as he worked, his left hand flew up every few seconds to resettle the heavy glasses on his sweaty nose.

Copious fingerprints clouded a different spot each time until the lenses were coated with the frosty haze of oblivion.

Merris said, "Did you make a lot of progress, last night?"

"I ordered five new machines," said Valdeen.

"Don't we have enough by now?"

"Merris, you're a clown."

Merris laughed. His own quirks amused him, so he took no offense if Valdeen noticed it too. The fact that Valdeen partnered with him was proof of respect, not malice.

"What about your stats from last night?"

"I did the usual," Valdeen replied automatically as he cleaned up his work area, sorting out hazardous and nonhazardous materials. The hazardous refuse went into red bags marked for proper disposal. He had no desire to draw unwanted attention to their operations by inviting a fine for some stupid mistake.

"You didn't document it very well, Havislaw." Merris' paper mountain caught in the middle, forming a sort of pup tent between the two piles. The shadow nagged at him, so Merris took a whack at it with the back of his hand while he was in the middle of the next page.

Doctor Valdeen winced at the use of his proper name, and the implied reprimand that went with it, but it was a waste of time to correct Edward Merris, especially at this stage, so tantalizingly near to the end of their collaboration. In Valdeen's estimation, Merris was halfway to idiot savant, limits Valdeen understood all too well, and dealt with accordingly. "Would you care to back that up?"

"Some of the things you wrote here don't make sense at all. Like this one." Without even glancing up, Merris chalked up two pencil marks for the item in question. "You see what I mean?" His rounded shoulders did not shift even a fraction. He didn't seem to realize that Valdeen couldn't see the paper through his head.

Valdeen stood still. If he were to answer, "Yes, I see what you mean," without being able to see the page in question, his partner would have no trouble believing him. Ed Merris was like a keyboard full of ice cream. Some of the essentials had short-circuited. True, he had made his contribution here in the laboratory these last three years. Even Valdeen had to admit that much. It took an unorthodox scientist to unlock the secrets of chemical bonding, and Merris certainly fit that description. But those trials and errors were yesterday as far as Valdeen was concerned, and Merris was mostly a bother at this juncture.

"It will all come clear to you later, Merris. We're closer to cold fusion than you think."

"Uh, we are close," said Dr. Merris, while he resumed his line-by-line inspection with the vagabond pencil ticks, "but I'd love to see some of our early results replicated by other labs. That would show us that our results are valid."

Ending his inspection of yesterday's data, Merris dipped into a barrel of rubber gloves, and tugged a pair up to his wrists until his fingers were encased in tooth-decay yellow. He selected a clean jar from the shelf together with a simple screw clamp to hold it in place against the upright. His first attempt captured his thumb inside the clamp with the jar. He smiled, close mouthed, at his own talent for being distracted, and where it got him sometimes. This time he concentrated. The second attempt held the mount firmly on the jar without getting any of his fingers involved. From the shelf he picked up a beaker of foamy liquid which he poured just up to the white tape mark on the outside of the glass. The jar filled quickly but he caught it just in time. Amazing. Anything that didn't involve his intellect, such as a physical act, he usually treated as an autonomic function. Since filling a lab receptacle was more complicated than breathing, one successful maneuver was an uncommonly good accomplishment for him, a private thrill.

Valdeen bored his eyes into Merris' broad back. "Replicated in other labs? Have you been sniffing formaldehyde? That would be showing our rivals what we did and teaching them how we did it. Listen carefully, Merris. This is the Holy Grail of Chemistry that we're working on, not one of your school projects. I do not want the Valdeen-Merris-Catalytic-Factor-Holy-Fucking-Grail-of-Chemistry reproduced in other laboratories. Am I getting through to you?" Valdeen zeroed in as he spoke, folding his huge frame down until they were eye-to-eye so that Merris could catch the breath and spittle of his words.

Edward Merris, who had his school projects far behind him, smiled slightly even while the muscles at the corner of his mouth puckered and fought against it. *Havislaw disagrees with me and he's probably trying to make me laugh,* Merris decided. He had met people like Havislaw in the past, even while attending MIT, the Massachusetts Institute of Technology, fifteen years earlier. At least Merris *thought* he met other people like Havislaw. He never understood schoolmates well enough to recognize the distinctions between one person or another.

As his Aunt Carol often complained, he never understood most people in his life. Social intercourse seemed to have so little to do with his work, unworthy of diverting his energy. If his project partners and coworkers didn't press him, they never found out if he had parents and siblings, if he came from anywhere or if he liked anything. It didn't even matter to him that he ascended to valedictorian in his class at school. The concept simply amused him momentarily before he got back to work.

He was, however, forced to talk to people when they became as misguided as Havislaw Valdeen. This time he said: "What do you think? That they're going to steal our research? They can't steal it. We've already gotten a chain reaction on one level or another with the substances we've been using. If we make a full report in the right places, everyone will know that we got there first, we'll be documented in print. What am I telling you for? It's not as if you haven't published something before."

Valdeen again invaded Merris' line of sight, his stare cold and vengeful, out of proportion with the offense. Without being able to recount the reasons, he felt slightly threatened at Merris' suggestion that they break their vow of secrecy. Havislaw Valdeen was not someone who could stand to be threatened.

CHAPTER 7
Games Of The Chairmen

2034: NEW YORK, NEW YORK

"YOUR FULL ATTENTION is requested, Mr. Valdeen," said Chang with the thin, unpleasant smile reminiscent of a torturer about to apply his craft. Valdeen sighted down the long barrel of his nose at the much smaller man, and said nothing.

Chang's painting gallery in the Soho section of Manhattan was closed to the public in the morning, two discreet guards posted outside. Havislaw Valdeen saw the wisdom of their meeting in the United States. It was less suspicious for someone with official diplomatic status like Chang to hop from nation to nation than it was for a former convict to head for a communist country.

Valdeen grunted in reply. He could not abide a patient thought or gesture for Chul Huk Chang as they waltzed awkwardly through the halls of the converted warehouse, both of them acting as if the other were the reluctant virgin. Valdeen made sure he came off as ruffled, unkempt, large and brooding. He didn't care to be summoned like dog to master, essentially an echo of what Arazine was already doing to him by forcing him to go to Mars. *Whatever Chang wants to happen, must not happen. So what is it that he wants?*

Chang was small, thin, immaculate, and calculating, like the paintings he fashioned for his gallery. He gave little away. According to Valdeen's information, Chang had no love for Caucasians in general. He thought of colleagues as tools that had to be forged, and believed some nonsense that art should lead off all discussions.

In a disgusting display of pride, Chang swept a thin hand toward the section of his own paintings paired off in comparison to the masters that hung next to them. If Valdeen turned his head to look at the art works, it was only by reflex. Although he knew and enjoyed Chinese art, he looked away with as much contempt as he could muster.

Naturally all of Chang's masters were Chinese, and all imbued their subjects with several traditional elements. Spiny leaves made way for bare trunks that led down to knotty roots, bent trees grappled with ornate pagodas, inky dabs of vegetation dappled the foreground, water flowed endlessly over multi-faceted rocks, and hills layered back until they dissolved into distant mist. The heavy inks were dominated by verdant lines, supplemented by subtle blue, red, and shades of tan.

Chang's works were just carbon images of the originals at their sides as far as Valdeen could tell. He didn't examine anything closely as someone might do if they were interested, or wished to seem interested out of politeness. All he would recall later were rectangles that were either very tall or very wide.

Chang administered lectures on technique to his unwilling student as they walked. "Nothing is the same as Western art," he admonished Valdeen as if he'd doubted it, "not the brushes, not the paint, and not the technique, except what was stolen from the Eastern masters. And not properly stolen, mind you, but ineptly copied and then co-opted to another context. The Chinese honor and learn from the masters by attempting to reproduce them as closely as possible while injecting their own life forces onto the paper. Westerners merely scavenge."

The diplomatic poseur also took the opportunity to brag about the extensiveness of his flower and rock collections which he had personally arranged to match sections from the paintings. He droned about how each diorama echoed the harmony of nature until Valdeen considered spitting on the next one.

Chang responded to Valdeen's disgust with only a minute crease in his brow. He said, "Chinese art differs in ways the Western mind finds difficult to understand, the concepts alien. Each stroke represents thousands of years of tradition and accepted technique. Western painters follow no basic techniques and ape their masters only to exploit them."

"I see now that Eastern art and Western art have something in common," said Valdeen. "All of it is a waste of time since the invention of the camera. So-called creative types dab at canvas to avoid the real world."

Chang colored slightly, yet held his composure.

Valdeen stopped short of cursing Chang's masters and their ancestors, but added, "Why did you bring me here if the place is bugged and instead of real business we have to talk about your scraps of old paper?"

Chang said, "Incarceration has given you a different perspective, Havi."

"May your horizons be broadened the same way." Valdeen looked down at Chang with unvarying intensity, as if each of his words had equal and immediate importance. He knew that the effect disturbed Chang's need for cleanliness and order. Valdeen had just eaten a pizza with generous amounts of pepperoni, garlic and onion so that he could offend with bad breath as well as bad manners. The more crude and physically ponderous Valdeen could be, the more he could control the agenda.

"There is no problem—no bug—Dr. Valdeen. We can speak freely." The Chinese communist appeared momentarily impressed by the effort Valdeen was making to disrupt him. Of course crudeness had its place in the power plays of Chinese history too.

Valdeen recalled the Tai Chi master crap in Chang's file. The little propaganda maven believed himself to be as hard and enduring as the rock plateaus captured on his walls. He had been known to say that as long as he could feel the ground below him, he could draw upon its energy. Garbage. The elderly Chang did not look to Valdeen like someone who could defend himself. *Let him understand that I can snap him in half.*

Chang stuck with his maddening, deliberate pattern nonetheless. Their walk led them in a circuit through the gallery so that they had almost arrived again at the starting point. Chang took ten more perfect steps before uttering his next words. "Do you know Governor Peter Arazine, Mr. Valdeen?"

There. At last he had said it. Valdeen suspected that if he hadn't been such unpleasant company Chang would likely have begun showing his collection of entrails. "I know Arazine," said Valdeen. "If you're asking for my evaluation, he's in over his head."

"Has he contacted you in a scientific capacity?" Chang asked.

"I wouldn't exactly call it that."

"What was his request then?"

"He hopes to steal my work and make himself rich."

Chang cleared his throat. "I am sure that is not what he said."

"Not in so many words."

"But you are confident his motives are decadent?"

"Peter Arazine only knows how to be obvious."

"Has he made you any promises?"

"He likes to offer percentages of something he doesn't have. Like a planet. He's also willing to do certain favors for my nephew, who lives on Mars. The implication is that if I don't join him on Mars, he's going to give my nephew a hard time."

"Does that concern you?"

"My nephew can handle himself."

As they returned to the main building, the scientist lagged but soon grew tired of irritating Chang, and followed him inside. Finding the television switched on and broadcasting an unscheduled press conference, the rationale behind Chang's timing with the gallery walk became clear. On the large screen, Abdul Harouk, who looked as if he hadn't slept or shaved in days, was making the official announcement of his committee's new decision on the location of the Olympic Games. The crowd, bristling with questions, could hardly be contained. Harouk's shoulders jumped at every movement as though he feared an assassin among the questioners.

Turning away from the broadcast, Chang said, "If you please, Dr. Valdeen, when you reach Mars, there's something I want you to do for me."

CHAPTER 8
Quid Nunc

2012: SUTTER CREEK, MARYLAND

DR. VALDEEN, THE chemistry miracle maker in his early forties had the dimensions of a stone monument with an especially wide upper level. He used his booming voice like a cannon on the heights. At an unremarkable five feet eleven inches, people his own height always swore he was gigantic. Intimidation was an end in itself for him, casting around, knocking people over, focusing his intense gaze from behind the large muzzle of a nose that filled his face. Starting out mild, he could build to a crescendo, unabashedly working up a contrived rage to master any situation at hand. He could even redden his cheeks at will for hot, unpredictable flashes of temper. Most people would do almost anything to avoid provoking him because it was never clear what would set him off. His wife, who had seen the act more often than most, knew better but apparently chose not to be comforted. He'd heard he tell her friends that knowledge made life all the more frightening.

These last couple of years Valdeen didn't get easy intimidation practice because he was not at home with his wife. He worked long hours with Edward Merris who rarely took cues from facial expressions or tones of voice.

This MIT moron is somehow disconnected from normal reactions, Valdeen concluded. He should sense danger. Anyone who was paying attention would be cringing by now. A calf in a slaughterhouse would understand better.

Valdeen took a deep breath and did his best in a volume too high by half. "Don't be an ass, Merris. We can't show our results until we get a very substantial chain reaction."

As Merris tightened the jar mount to make sure it wouldn't slip, he said, "I think my Aunt Carol would like you. Well, not actually like you, but she would find you very interesting."

"I don't care about your Aunt Carol or any of your slack-jawed hayseed relatives. The public may know too much about our research already, thanks to that idiot we order materials from."

"What? You're talking about Norrick?" Merris swiveled around a bit, letting the wooden ruler slip away, forgetting about his check marks.

That got his attention. Phil Norrick was their agent for dealing with several equipment and supply houses. Merris was often kept busy unwrapping items and returning the ones that didn't work. Whether their project had use for them or not, he tested equipment, filled out warranty cards, and lodged the appropriate complaints with Norrick. Then Norrick, who was completely taken in by the flurry of unnecessary activity, would make apologetic noises and promise to do better next time.

The Sutter Creek Laboratory also engaged a private disposal service who could report carrying empty boxes away for the items Valdeen and Merris kept, if anyone were to inquire. It was all part of an elaborate subterfuge in case rival scientists paid off their supplier to find out what the laboratory was up to. Merris often complained about the time it drained from their real work.

"You said Norrick would never figure us out because we keep ordering things we don't need, to camouflage the things we do need. It didn't even matter if he had a big mouth, you said. That's the only reason I agreed to buying all this junk." Both of Merris' hands flapped up briefly, butterfly-style in his rotten-tooth gloves before coming to rest.

"*You* didn't buy it," Dr. Valdeen reminded him. "Research grants bought it." How does a man like this function? Valdeen wondered. He acts like he shelled out for the extra equipment himself.

"You know what I mean."

Valdeen walked away, knowing the conversation was done. Like a family pet, Merris would forget about the unpleasantness in a moment and go back to his food bowl.

The senior scientist removed his sweaty lab coat, rolled it in a ball, and pushed it in the laundry bin. The rubber gloves went into the wastebasket nearest to the gyrotron. He took the goggles from around his neck and slipped them onto a brace for the thermal cycler, putting it in service as a hanger. His work was just about finished for the day. Of course, he still had one very important thing to do.

* * *

For once Edward Merris was glad his research partner left the room. The distractions were getting too much.

Valdeen called from the other room, "Merris, don't forget to put on fresh gloves. We don't want contaminants."

"I don't need to change gloves. I just put these on. It's my first experiment of the day." Irritation was plain in his voice, but his chubby neck and short patience with human interaction kept his head from turning very far. He wasn't happy unless he was totally absorbed in his work so he was anxious to get back to it.

"Is it your first?" Valdeen called out from nearby the other side of the door. "Yes, that's right," he answered himself. "Because of our staggered shifts. Well, if you have everything in place, try adding some potassium nitrate to the mixture." After hearing no sound from Merris he added, "You do know what potassium is, don't you?"

"You're very funny, Havislaw." Merris turned to scrutinize the charts posted on the wall. He read through them twice. "Wait a minute, Havislaw, that's not on our testing schedule. I couldn't possibly... Where did you go?"

"Use what I left for you there." Valdeen pitched his voice to carry from the adjoining room. "I've run some figures. Potassium will save us a lot of time."

"Save time?"

"Yes."

"You think so?"

"I know so."

"I could try it."

"You'll do it!" the cannon boomed.

"All right, all right, I'll do it." Merris' voice trailed off into a mumble, thinking, *Valdeen's specialty is materials science, so he knows.* Merris would add the potassium experiment to the chart later. The chart was there to remind you of what you tried, whether it worked or not. He fantasized about not adding the experiment to the chart at all if nothing happened. *What would Havislaw do then? He'd have a fit, that's what.*

Merris reached for the flask without looking and almost knocked it off the table before getting hold of it. Seeing that nothing was lost, he felt another small thrill of triumph. "Is this the preparation over here?" He spoke loudly into the jar, causing his nasal voice to echo, and his breath to fog the sides.

"Yes, yes, yes." Valdeen forced his muzzle into the room for just a moment before retreating again. "Don't spill any. I've measured it out for you in exactly the right amount."

"I'm not going to spill it. Please, what do you think I am, some kind of klutz?" Shaking his head, Merris added the remainder of the potassium from the jar. It rested on the film at the surface in a powdery lump with little particles flaking into the liquid below. He sloshed the jar around a bit, impatient to make it dissolve. The clump yielded and mixed well. Satisfied, he breached the isolation seal to add the mixed portion slowly into his electrolytic cell. Carefully, he re-sealed the experiment and noted the conditions at that moment.

Then he waited, looking for a spike in the temperature reading on the thermistor. If cold fusion were taking place, they would get more energy out than went in, energy that had been stored in the chemical bonds. Things got very quiet in the laboratory. *We'll save time, Havislaw tells me. So let's see it. Show me how we save time.*

The MIT valedictorian settled his glasses back up on his nose in his usual sloppy gesture, keeping one eye on the electrical resistance heater calibrating the experiment. The frame didn't arrive at the top of his sweaty nose, so he pushed the glasses again. He watched closely, holding his face close in front of the basin, waiting, his hands soaked and itchy inside their rubber sheaths. Check the clock. Check the thermistor and back to the experiment. Oh yes, something there, churning. His eyes widened, and he clutched at his note pad without taking his eyes off the cell. He scrawled something quickly and tore off the sheet, balling it into his hand in an unconscious spasm.

"Valdeen, I GOT IT." Even as he called out, he realized that the amount of potassium nitrate he used was a very bad idea.

The explosion separated his head from his shoulders. Merris' blood spattered every part of the room, every piece of elaborate machinery and glassware Phil Norrick ever carted in.

* * *

Valdeen uncovered his ears and came back with his hands in his pockets, unwilling to touch anything because he had scrubbed clean for the day. Also, the investigating officers would need the scene in pristine condition and the senior scientist was nothing if not cooperative.

Dr. Merris lay on the floor dead, one hand still gripping the jar, the other closed. Most of the missing head was nearby with its mouth still open. Valdeen could almost hear him say, "Uh."

"Good work, Merris. But I got it yesterday," the miracle maker remarked to his partner. "Only with much less potassium. You'd be surprised by how little it takes to set off the Valdeen Catalytic Factor."

Havislaw Valdeen walked over to gaze out the window and into the deep woods beyond, thinking how much it resembled the Black Forest in Germany and wondering what it would feel like to be the richest man on Earth, plundering the world's cheapest new energy source, and savaging everyone within his reach.

"Oh, by the way, Merris," he told to the remains, "the world is going to be a very different place from now on. You wouldn't have liked it anyway."

CHAPTER 9
Torrent

2034: NEW YORK, NEW YORK

CHANG SURPRISED HIMSELF by breathing a sigh of relief when the crude soulless one was gone. He braced himself in the doorway and drew strength from it. Above his head, at the entrance to the painting gallery, in a space four feet high, was simply the character *tao*, formed of two chinese pictographs, *ch'o* and *shou*, out of a dynamic collection of brush strokes. Naturally, Valdeen had been totally oblivious to it. It meant the road, the path, the way, and with its associated ideas, much more. The symbol *ch'o* represented a left-footed first step, and the *shou* represented a head, or thought. The left foot itself was like *Yin*, the Female Principle, the moon, darkness, a force turned inward. When combined with *shou* or *Yang*, the Male Principle, sun and light, it signified total harmony. Side by side, the two pictographs were a single character which meant wholeness from head to foot.

Yin and *yang* could also be two swirling water drops, one white, one black, never separated. Contained within each, a reflection of the other, a black spot within white, a white spot in black. The painting gallery had only the pictograph versions which looked like a thicket of reeds.

Tao gave truth to painting because it was also true for life. It was the Way.

For Chang, the transition to his elder years had not been an easy one. From pampered rogue, to killer, to ideologist, he had made many adjustments. He survived by finding balance so that his conflicting worlds could mesh.

Valdeen offended his whole sense of fitness, a man without taste or proportion. He had an abiding intensity that Chang had shed in youth and judged unnatural in a man of middle age. He made Chang's head hurt. Still, he had to concede that Valdeen had his uses, and Chang was reminded of an old proverb: *One may cut down a great tree with an axe, but furniture is made with a hammer.*

* * *

WASHINGTON, D.C.

The U.S. Senate hearing on the Martian Olympics took a disastrous turn for its chairman when Dr. Sanheiser took issue with his questioner and muttered the words, "Useless dickhead," all too audibly.

This breach of protocol in the Senate chamber opened the door to talking out of turn and escalated to shouting. Someone angrily threw a pile of documents at his subordinate for laughing, and the papers fluttered to the floor. The title of the stack was Mars Colonization--Phase II.

Photographers leapt from their pit and had to be corralled back by security, while cell phone cameras popped up across the room. The Martian Olympics had dominated the imagination of the American people for the past month, and the story was amply fueled by this witness. Television crews rolled live.

Senator Evan Brandenberg slammed his gavel repeatedly as the shouting progressed. The top official let his head sink into his hands for a moment, sweating the heat of the floodlights, hoping to allow the disruption to gradually lose strength and peter out.

His attempt to correct the situation turned out to be a mistake. The image of the chairman with his head bowed made for a good picture in itself. The Senator from Colorado led the committee that would either support Olympics on Mars or shut down that support. He was sorry he had gotten into the middle of this nonsense. As a former astronaut, Brandenberg believed strongly in the space program in principle, meaning that he wanted some kind of new development plan to go forward. When and how such a plan could be implemented to best serve conflicting goals would have been a fair question.

Yet the President had bluntly told him he had the choice of steering this committee toward the administration's position or losing his hard won support from the White House. When Brandenberg balked, the Chief Executive got specific. Did he, Evan Brandenberg, want a military base to close in his state, losing who knew how many jobs? Personally losing who knew how many Colorado votes? No, the President thought not.

Even if Brandenberg could assert his independence regardless of the consequences, he was not sure he knew the right answer. His panel, which was split down the middle, sprung into being when the International Olympic Committee, via Abdul Harouk, made the startling announcement that it would shift the upcoming Olympic

Games from the cradle of skiing's birth in Norway to an unstable colony millions of miles from the surface of Earth. The Norwegian government had somehow gone along with the change, saying that the choice of Norway was not originally unanimous and therefore a mistake. Were they made happy, or was their new position bolstered by threats?

As stated publicly, the IOC intended to either find the money to land the Games on Mars or hold no Olympics at all. Having no Olympics to participate in didn't sit well with Brandenberg's country. Things that didn't sit well didn't reelect well. And the prospect of holding the Games on Mars was creating an optimism that hadn't been seen in the United States since the 1990's. "Imagine twenty-foot high-bar jumps and seventy-foot running jumps!" went the advertising, which neglected to mention that it was a Winter Olympics only, and those particular events were likely to remain summer sports.

In any case, record-breaking sports reigned supreme when generating viewership. At last, outer space had some use! That kind of appeal was undeniable.

As chairman of his committee, Evan Brandenberg sat heavily with the deciding vote. The majority of public pressure was on him to come down on the side of funding the Mars Olympics, and to see to it that his committee cleared the hurdles. Still there was just enough well reasoned and documented opposition to bury him if the plans went sour.

His desk lit with a reporter's question about what the plan would cost. The public, however, did not know the dollar amount involved and that didn't matter one bit. Whereas the abandoned Star Wars defense program was once assessed to be the size of eight Manhattan Projects,

Mars Colonization Phase II, with the Olympics as its first goal, would be something on the order of twelve Manhattan Projects.

Meanwhile, Congress ran a circus. According to the screen in his desk, the press was already calling it Brandenberg's lost concerto. The Post pointed out that it was more like *concerto grosso,* a style where the full orchestra plays contrasting sections while a small group of soloists do the important part. Journalists sensed that the decision-making process was corrupt even if they couldn't prove it. A scandal of major proportions was brewing somewhere down the line.

Having indulged himself in this rare moment of self-pity, Brandenberg was ready to take charge once more. No one in the room had run out of things to say so he banged the gavel hard enough to make the water in the pitchers splash up. "Come to order. Come to order." In the raucous shuffling, an old banister cracked. "Come to order, you brainless asses!"

His chamber went silent. Brandenberg could see surreptitious cigarette smoke twirling in the stillness and rising toward the high ceiling.

He relished the silence for a few more moments, and remained standing when he spoke again. "Dr. Sanheiser, I remind you that you cannot use that language in here. Senator Davis is not an expert, as you are, but he is qualified to question you on any relevant matter. That is the nature of these proceedings. I must warn you that there is a limit to how much of your flamboyance this hearing will allow."

Brandenberg regained his seat, which squeaked as he swiveled to his right. Because his committee table curved outward toward the gallery, he had an unobstructed view of

Senator Tom Davis of Wisconsin three seats down. Black plastic glasses dominated Davis' face, plastic arms straining to reach pink-tipped ears, his hair sweat-soaked from oversized pores. The water in front of him clouded from his dripping, making the pitcher look as if it were filled with antacid, which he probably could have put to good use at the moment.

"Senator Davis, continue."

Davis coughed to cover the awkward scene, shuffled his papers in front of him, tipped his heavy glasses up, and finally resumed. "Dr. Sanheiser, you've been an outspoken supporter of U.S. participation in the Mars projects since long before Mars was selected as the site of the next Olympics. In my opinion, the Mars settlements you urged on us are no more than off-planet pork. If the so-called colonists are not self supporting up there, they ought to be pulled out and all programs shut down. Not expanded, not rewarded, not redeemed. Now you suggest that we pay vastly more than our share for these Olympics. What will the American taxpayer get out of pouring more money down the drain on Mars?"

Sanheiser, pugnacious as ever, placed a long, wordless gulf between them. When he spoke, he made an effort to show that it was to the rest of the panel, and not to Davis; directing his comments to wiser heads. "Gentleman, if we continue our vision and belief in Mars for just five more years, we will begin to develop a second Earth. It will make the California Gold Rush and the Spanish conquest of South America seem trivial."

The murmuring started but Davis' voice cut above it. "We're talking about a ball of rock, a cold ball of rock millions of miles away. Don't romanticize it!" By the end of his sentence, his face flared red with frustration. The chamber erupted with laughter with the press core whooping it up more than anyone. The Senator from Wisconsin was famous for quickly losing control and he had accomplished that twice already in one day. Davis' face flushed deeper in response to the laughter. The writer from *Washpol* was already posting that "the Senator screamed like a baby hyena abandoned in the wilderness."

Brandenberg rescued Davis as best he could by thumping the gavel head into its base. "Dr. Sanheiser, when we come back to you tomorrow, this panel will want to hear you justify your theories with facts."

Sanheiser stiffened, glared, and retreated quietly to the back row. Brandenberg slapped the remains of his gavel onto the table. Sanheiser was actually Brandenberg's star witness, one who was going to help the President's party ram the plans home. But Sanheiser had to be kept in line, and at the same time, it was no use making enemies with Davis.

"Our next participant—" the Chairman began.

"Pardon me, sir." Brandenberg's senior aide showed him the results of an unofficial congressional voting poll. The sentiments of the full congress looked unfavorable for the Mars project, possibly enough to scuttle any positive recommendation that came out of the hearings. If such a vote became official, everything was over. Failure would make Brandenberg a traitor in the President's eyes, just as surely as if he had willfully gone against him. That left Brandenberg with a painful, if necessary, decision, and no time to huddle with a political priest. He had to co-opt his most impressive critic.

"Our next participant in this proceeding will be Shelly Kastin," Brandenberg announced. "She's a former Special Agent with Treasury, and a specialist in science and technology issues." In a government system where the slothful were rewarded with a job for life, she was one of the few whose extra hard work made up the shortfall of the others, and kept the whole machine running. Whatever his differences with her, he counted on the fact that deep down, people like her wanted badly to cooperate with people like him for no other reason than to keep the system functioning.

* * *

Knowledgeable heads turned faster than the simply curious ones when Shelly Kastin stood and made her way to the podium, her eagerness and confidence hushing the crowd.

Pausing at the witness bar, she noticed it was sheathed in pool table green, a good color for gamblers. She moved the microphone down to the height of her mouth, gathered her notes, poured a cup of water for herself, sipped at it quietly. Those who would remain in control took their time when they sat in this hall, and she had no intention of being intimidated or sidetracked from the essential facts she wanted to convey. She knew she had the curse of bustiness to overcome.

When Kastin was settled, Brandenberg said, "Ms. Kastin, do you have an opening statement? If you do, keep it brief."

"Yes, Senator, I do. Are you aware that there were sixty one incidents of terrorism last year in the United States alone?"

"It depends on how you classify acts of terrorism, but I am aware of something in that ballpark," said Brandenberg dryly.

"The public is not aware," she retorted.

"Are we to believe that you are an expert on the subject of terrorism now?" Some of the witnesses laughed uncertainly.

"Terrorists continue to co-opt advanced technology. Wouldn't you say that the two subjects are inseparable?"

"Please get to the point if there is one, Ms. Kastin. You're not here to try this committee's patience with questions."

Kastin cleared her throat. She was aware of the momentum of history and the upstream battle it would be to go against the direction of the Olympic movement but her conscience demanded she air this hidden issue to help the public make an informed decision.

"My point is this: We can't stop terrorism in one of the safest countries on Earth. The incidents increase each year. On Mars, our defenses will be much more vulnerable. Our resources are thin. Out there, all it will take is one madman to destroy everything we're trying to accomplish."

For the first time since the contentious hearings began, Brandenberg pulled a smile. "That won't be a problem now."

"Pardon me sir?"

"I agree with you. I don't operate in ignorance you know. I've been following your investigations and find them credible."

"Does that mean you'll recommend scaling back development of Mars?"

"No."

"Does it mean that the United States will decline involvement in developing a Martian Olympics?"

"Not at all."

"What does it mean?" she said above the rising din.

Brandenberg paused to cover the mic and whisper to his aide before continuing. "It means, Ms. Kastin, if this project goes ahead, I'm recommending to the President that you take charge of enforcement in Olympia. If you are really concerned with the safety of the Olympic Games and the people involved, you will accept."

"Sir?"

"I've sought advice on who should fill the post, your name was submitted, and I'm comfortable with the decision. As Security Chief, you, Shelly Kastin, will be responsible for the success of the entire project. Or its failure."

He glanced up at her stunned face. "That's okay. No need to answer now."

* * *

Shelly Kastin's feet punished the pavement on the way back to her hotel room in the humming center of Washington D.C. under a milky haze of sky. The unseasonably warm air smelled of rain thick in her lungs.

She was furious with the hearing panel, and specifically with Senator Brandenberg. His grandstanding should have come with a display of pyrotechnics. She found it more than a little surprising to be offered a position by someone who apparently didn't like her.

He certainly had no reason to be warm and fuzzy. She was, on balance, against having any further developments on Mars, let alone an Olympics. Let alone being in charge of security for an ill-advised adventure. Or whatever it was that he and his cronies actually had in mind for her.

It irked her, too, that her HR director Harris Culpepper had predicted this offer. So she had done the sensible thing and politely told Brandenberg not to hold his breath. The way plans in Washington usually worked, someone would float a trial balloon and see how badly the idea would get shot down. It perfumed the stench of even the most unsavory intentions. If the proposal didn't draw too much flak, it had a sporting chance the second time around when the concept would seem less shocking by repetition.

Judging by the unlikely amount of time allotted to accomplishing their Olympic pipe dreams, it seemed that the administration was actually aiming at four years down the road. If the plan got squashed, its boosters could claim it would have been great if only their opponents hadn't shot it down. In any case, even long-term projects were funded one year at a time with rules that could change each year, and the entire project could be scrapped regardless of how much had gone into it. When she told Brandenberg all this, he turned it around by saying that her healthy cynicism would make her the perfect administrator.

Brandenberg then extracted a promise from her to at least be present at the hearing when Dr. Sanheiser came back the next day with his charts.

The next day had found Shelly Kastin again in the wood-darkened hearing chamber among the rabble of witnesses, the infectious excitement of the reporters, and the tolerated columns of blue smoke.

All awaited the pugnacious Dr. Milton Sanheiser with his inarguable data, scripted sound bites, and great, unrepentant set of balls. Glaring pointedly at Senator Davis this time, the middle-aged researcher explained that science had already determined that Mars possessed all the basic materials needed for human existence. Maybe more so than what was available on the surface of Earth at this point. Virtually no more raw materials had to be exported to Mars for its development to be a success. The picture he painted showed ultra quick advancement in settling the new planet if they got the economic boost that an Olympics would bring. Otherwise, the colony would have to be dismantled, and the people in Congress who threw money at it in the first place would develop popularity problems. And he never took his eyes off the giant pores of Tom Davis when he said it.

Meanwhile, the fees corporate advertisers were willing to pay broadcasters for a spot on Mars were staggering. Members of the House who wanted the project fully funded in advance floated a much more radical proposal. Their school of thought envisioned industrialists paying the full cost in exchange for land grants, in the way the American railway system had been established. If that weren't enough inducement, investors would also have rights to further exploitation. Those who funded it could then recoup their money by direct receipt of advertiser payments, pay-per-view fees, and tourist money. The final step in the plan had tax dollars going to a United Nations environmental improvement superfund. Kastin didn't care who got reelected and who didn't, but on the whole, it began to sound rosy even to a skeptic.

At the end of the day, she had still rejected the offer. True, she had a strong grasp of the issues, and experience in running a large operation, but a security expert she was not. It would take a lot more than a request from Brandenberg to make her change her mind. Some part of her wondered if he realized that and would do something about it.

She walked the neighborhood of grimy bricks and aggressive beggars, which was not so far from the land of domes and white columns. As a stream of yellow fluid projected from the alley, a soft trilling tickled her leg. Picking up, she said, "Kastin here."

Through a haze of static, the caller identified himself as the President. Cell phone infrastructure could never keep pace with demand. Kastin pumped the volume and pressed the phone to her face.

"Yes, sir?"

"The project," he said, "is going through. You and I have to meet."

* * *

Devon March, sitting proudly in his preferred driver's seat known as the Office of Corporation Counsel, was among the primary recipients of Earth dispatches. Since his boss was out of town so to speak, he ascended to the very first. Reading the display, he licked his lips with growing interest.

"Well, well, well," he said. The big deal had been sewn up, and the United States was going to unwittingly do Governor Arazine's bidding after all. They would provide the major funding for Olympics on Mars. They even had a security chief picked out if she went for the job. Shelly

Kastin. Wasn't she somehow connected to the materials specialist, Valdeen? If not, what made him think of the two of them at the same time? He would have to check up on that. Meanwhile things looked cozy.

Start your own Olympics, pay to open a volcano, juice up its innards to set it cooking under controlled conditions, and you've got yourself a golden fireplace for your kingdom.

How exciting to watch from so near and yet from such a position of relative safety. As the right hand man he could be enthusiastically supportive of the gamble without looking suspicious. As long as Governor Arazine was the chap sticking his neck out. *Go, Arazine, go. If it works, you're a genius. If not, I denounce you for a madman.*

CHAPTER 10
Ambitions

2037: STEAMBOAT SPRINGS, COLORADO

THE SNOW, CALM and majestic under acres of pine. Lou Coburn knew why everyone came to Steamboat Springs for in the winter. Champagne Powder, so dry and light it can't be made into a snowball. But put your skis on it, and you were gliding in heaven. Though Lou was in the freestyle moguls competition to punch his Olympic ticket for a clandestine mission, there was no place he'd rather be than the top of the Voodoo Trail.

Lou checked the mechanisms on his short, flexible, twin-tipped skis, wondering if he'd still have his chops when he landed on Mars for the Games. Olympic trials normally took place about two months prior to Day One. This time the selections had to be made the winter before the planet hop, which was coming up in the launch window of June 2037.

Anticipating his turn, Lou did six reps of an alternating-leg hop to warm up. He loved moguls like an addiction. Colorado could cloud up sometimes, but today blue sky reigned, and the sun stretched to starburst through his polarized lenses as he sized up his task. When the start buzzer sounded, Lou poled up, tucked down and hit the zipper line. The field was littered with bumps between one and two-and-a-half meters high. Half the score in the qualifications was based on ability to carve the most direct route while maintaining upper body composure. He kept his head and chest forward and shoulders level while his legs pumped to soak up the shocks.

A quarter of the score measured the degree of difficulty of the tricks the skier could manage after launching up a sequence of ramps. After 36 meters of left and right banking turns, Lou had his choice of low kicker or high kicker, and he went for the high one, a 4-meter slope that would heft him 16 meters over the snow. Known as "The Cobra" for his sinuous movements and startling speed, he used his air off the first kicker to execute a corkscrew flip with a triple twist. For most people, that was the maximum the hang time allowed. For him it was a warm up.

Landing in the chowder and recovering quickly, he went right back to carving turns, minding his line, watching ahead, and making sure he got to the next kicker at the right speed.

For his second aerial, he again chose the taller offering, and this time pulled out five blazing twists with an Iron Cross. The finish line came screaming up right after the transition. He pulled a fist pumping, side-slipping turn to stop, and his tally posted fairly soon with results that amazed even him. The last quarter of his marks had to do with time on the course. He'd sacrificed some fraction of seconds to the elaborate nature of his tricks, but easily secured his place on the team.

Team Captain Gingold pounded him on the back. "What the hell's wrong with you, crazy man? Whatever it is, I love it."

Lou could feel the wry smile on his cold face. According to the fitness board at Spook Medical, as he called it, something actually was wrong with him, and it wasn't that he wanted to get himself killed. From what they'd told him, he could blame it on what he thought of as his chemical bartender. It seemed that the hormones and neurotransmitters that fed into personality made for a complex and murky sea. They said that the human brain has excitatory and inhibitory neural mechanisms that exist to balance each other at the appropriate times. His was not the average mix. It made him want to do things like extreme sports and espionage just to feel the exhilaration normal people experienced when their football team won a game.

If he understood right, his new employer's concern was that things like low serotonin levels had also been known to lead to criminal behavior. In the end, they'd decided their new agent channeled his thrill seeking into positive areas. Lou left the trial course feeling lucky his chemical cocktail had only left him borderline insane.

His fan club at the bottom included his best friend Yves Loitte, his blonde girlfriend Barbara and Yves' girlfriend Terri. He leaned into congratulatory hugs all around.

Yves gave Lou a friendly shoulder crash. "Where have you been, Cobra?"

Lou squinted in mock confusion. "I thought you knew I went out for a winter skinny dip in the hot springs. Wasn't that your naked ass I slapped?"

Yves laughed. "Can you forgive us, Barbara?"

Terri said, "You'd better be looking for my forgiveness, mister."

Lou said, "So now we all go to Mars, huh?"

"Except for me," said Barbara, giving Lou a punch on the bicep. "My job doesn't give me a year off."

"It's less than that," Lou said defensively. He knew that Barbara would ease up as she always did, but this separation was a huge adjustment for her.

Barbara said to Yves and Terri, "Who's going to take care of this half-domesticated animal?"

Terri said, "My Aunt Shel will look after all of us."

"Well I want souvenirs," Barbara said as if that settled the matter.

Yves said to Lou, "Hey, you want a real edge in the Olympic Games? You have to learn something about Mars. Join me in auditing part of Professor Brisini's geology class before we go."

Going back to school even for one class sounded like the dullest thing Lou could imagine, but it was just what his employers had ordered. Lou said, "Sounds like solid, crazy fun, brother. I might just do that."

* * *

OLYMPIA COLONY, MARS

"What the hell is Brandenberg trying to do to me?" Governor Peter Arazine barked as he shoved away from his desk.

"With Kastin? Nothing at all," replied his council, looking over his superior's shoulder for some information about Brandenberg's Shelly Kastin. Oddly, the screen on his oversized desk said nothing about the so-called Security Chief. His boss just happened to be perusing synthetic fuel reports.   Another ugly story.   It took a great deal of the slowly produced resources to run an Olympics, especially with Martians responsible for fueling trips back to Earth or the orbiting stations.   Arazine wouldn't be Arazine if he couldn't think on at least two tracks at once.

"They don't know a damn thing about our private plans," March reassured him.

"Brandenberg says I will have to answer to Shelly Kastin for the duration.   What is she, some kind of medieval overseer?" Arazine demanded.   "I never even heard of her before."

March could smell the aggrandizement in that last remark but he left it alone.   "It's too soon to say," he comforted.

"A top investigator coming to Olympia to help us run things, that's trouble.   If you can't recognize that, you're a schmuck.   I don't know the British word for it."

"We don't know that she'll accept the extra responsibility.   They're still chatting her up."

"You're too damn naïve, Devon.   I don't know anyone who would turn down an opportunity to take control over this planet."

"You're panicking," said March, afraid that Arazine would retreat from his lucrative plans.

"No, I'm thinking ahead.   Kastin's interference is only a matter of our timing versus hers."

"Our head start has to count for something."

"Not when she has the power to impeach me.   No, we have to implement my second plan early."

"Meaning what?   I didn't know anything about a second plan."

"Meaning we need to start the revolution," said Arazine, trailing almost to a whisper.

"Revolution?" March repeated, even less audibly.

"Today wouldn't be too soon," his superior answered.

"I'm sorry, are you talking about revolutionary politics or revolutionary science?" March asked half seriously. "Let me in on it, won't you?"

"I'm talking about politics for the sake of science," Arazine said, his voice warming. "We'll overthrow ourselves, the government of Olympia."

"What are you talking about? Are you out of your mind?" March was used to guessing games from Arazine but this one he couldn't fathom.

"Not a real one, Devon, just something to cover our tracks. A sloppy, bloodless uprising, kept small. A little mischief where no one gets hurt, more ominous than anything else."

"That's creative."

"It will have to look realistic," Arazine continued, ignoring the sarcasm. "Enough to show that there are malcontents among us, but not enough to alarm authorities on Earth before we take tight control of Mars."

"You mean dictatorial."

"Whatever."

"We would be the instigators?"

"The instigators and the victims both."

"To make sure Kastin can't operate?"

"It can serve many purposes, including keeping her busy. Hopefully, when the problems crop up, Congress will see that Mars ran better under my full authority, and they'll send Kastin packing, leaving me to straighten things out. Martial law works wonders."

"Now you're talking," said March, a slow smile creasing his face. Opportunity in chaos was something he could understand, and a smoke screen like the one Arazine proposed would be easy to pull off. There were lots of people weary and hungry enough to engage in a bit of civil unrest. Let the revolution's converts believe what they wanted about why it was happening, whether it be for money, for power, or for autonomy. The cause would have a surfeit of volunteers.

"Our main problem will be keeping the disturbances from getting out of hand," said March.

"You have to have the stomach for collateral damage. It won't be much."

"Brandenberg's committee gives you no choice, do they?"

"By putting Kastin in here, they really don't."

"What's next?"

"We'll call the movement Red Freedom," said Arazine.

"I like that. It sounds deliciously subversive."

"If anything goes wrong, we'll never be implicated because the uprising will appear to be against the Martian government rather than Earth. Whatever else we do can be masked by the confusion."

And Devon March thought one more step ahead: *Anyone who has slighted us in the past can go to hell in the process.*

* * *

BOLDER, COLORADO

"Who here thinks we are fortunate to be alive in this era?"

Professor Alan Brisini, posturing in front of his desk, bristled with exhilaration as he surveyed his sea of students in the theater-sized classroom for the day's lesson.

Someone in the cheap seats called out, "What era is that?"

Brisini was well aware of how they watched his face, which was basically a quizzical pattern of permanent mirth like a theatrical Greek comedy mask. His facade differed only by his great, bushy eyebrows pasted way up high with a surprising range of independent movement. The students knew that when he hoisted the left one, he was ready to continue.

"As any of you who keep up on current events will know," Brisini said, "the planet Mars has been chosen as the site of the next Olympic Games. I say that this defining moment will one day be recognized as the single greatest event since mankind discovered fire." He paused for the students still entering his room from the back.

Sessions with Brisini filled the house with his main group and kids auditing Geology 101 without credit. When he returned next semester, his exuberance would be simulcast. Hopefully, he would broadcast to two planets, and it wouldn't matter which one he lived on.

That was not the way he pictured his lessons when he first became a teacher. Good teaching was always an individual process; not everyone learned in exactly the same way or at the same pace. The larger the group, the more you were forced to homogenize and leave the less adaptable behind.

Somewhere in the room, a student coughed, and others got caught up in the reflex but all waited patiently. How different people looked when they were turned towards you, listening, he thought, their faces appeared round and open.

"It's the second time man has turned to space," Brisini continued, "and we know it's a serious commitment because we've got an Olympics on Mars.

"Since ancient times, Mars has been affectionately referred to as Earth's sister planet, and thought of as a viable world. We often feared that people more advanced than us lived there. Projecting our own human nature on these conjectured inhabitants, we assumed they would kill us and rape our women if they got the chance. Only later, when robot probes landed on the Red Planet, did people begin to see the Fourth Orbit as too ancient, too depleted to support advanced species, or any species.

"Now we have people living on Mars. That's a long way from its 'canal' days." He reached behind to press his hands on the top of his desk for leverage, and settled himself onto its surface in one fluid hop, leaving both feet dangling. "That's enough chit-chat from me. What more do we know about Mars?"

The professor leaned back and folded his arms, preferring to let everyone tackle a question in tandem until he caught something that interested him. He tried to call on all one hundred twenty kids on his roster to see how they processed information, and reviewed their names aloud with the remarkable accuracy peculiar to the best of the teaching profession.

Open palms rose from every corner of the room, but not from every student. He pointed to a kid on the far left who hadn't raised her hand.

"Me? It's another planet after Earth?" the young woman answered. Lucky thing Joanie had her looks.

Without comment, Brisini then pointed to the one secretly reading the folded newspaper on his lap. Brisini cleared his throat with his other hand until the student took notice that the teacher wasn't talking anymore and people in the vicinity were snickering. He looked up to see that the finger had stopped at him.

"Mars? It's older than the Earth," came the sheepish reply.

The teacher nodded, satisfied that the kid was partially listening at least, and moved on from left to right, to the red-haired girl, Marissa Melendez.

"It has two moons."

"Uh-huh," said Brisini.

His roving pointer next found the lanky athlete, Lou Coburn.

"There's underground water, and I think they have wells."

"Yes, water. Very good." He would get back to how much.

Meanwhile, he picked the anxious one, right next to Coburn, Yves Loitte.

"It's mostly iron."

"Aha. Mostly iron. Interesting answer. Why do you say that, Mr. Loitte?" The professor was always happy when Loitte spoke up. This was one student who wanted to go to Mars more than anything. Like his friend Coburn, Loitte was an excellent athlete, so he had a serious chance of qualifying for the Olympic Team.

Loitte had talked with Brisini about his chances several times after it was announced that Brisini would be going into space as only the second teacher since the Challenger disaster in the last century. The professor was ready to turn in his teaching certificate to go to Mars if he had to. Luckily it never came to that.

Encouraged, Loitte stood up to clarify his answer. "The whole thing, the whole of Mars, is colored red. We can see that all the way from Earth. We know the red is iron, so there has to be more iron there than anything else."

"I see. So if you ate some pie and your teeth were stained blue, we could assume your teeth were composed mostly of... blueberry?" said Brisini, his voice rising to an incredulous tone at the end. The class howled with laughter while the professor boosted one of his thick eyebrows to an impressive elevation. Loitte was surprised at first. Then he looked around, smiled, and took a bow.

Brisini was quick with that sort of analogy. Such was the learning process. He wouldn't put Loitte through it if he didn't think the kid enjoyed it. Plus he knew that the boy's skiing coach would do far worse.

"I'm glad you brought that up though, Mr. Loitte. In fact, that ferrous material you see coloring the planet is less than two micro millimeters thick. It's a thin film coating on a sandy silt silicate. Now say that three times fast." That joke got him various guffaws and giggles. "Now does anyone know the scientific name for that ferrous material?" With his look of irrepressible mirth he added, "Mr. Loitte?"

The class burst out again.

"No, no, I want to hear his answer," said Brisini.

"Ferric oxide?" said Loitte, regaining his seat right after.

"Good, that's right. Ferric *oxide* coated over silicon di*oxide*, mixed in with aluminum *oxide* and so on. Is everyone getting the picture?" He heard murmurs of assent all around. "We know we can live there because oxygen in one form or another is locked into just about every mineral on Mars. So we know that the most abundant element on Mars is what? Say it with me class: OXYGEN. Everything depends on that, and one other thing."

"What's that?" asked Ms. Melendez out of turn.

He squinted peevishly at her before answering. "I'll get to it. I should also say that while chemically, Mars is remarkably similar to Earth, there is one big difference. Even though iron makes it's presence so obvious—as Mr. Loitte pointed out—Mars apparently does not have an iron core like that of the Earth. There is no magnetism to speak of and no Van Allen belt. So it's ferrous material is distributed very differently for some unknown reason. Isn't that *iron-ic*?"

The class gave a collective moan. Brisini laughed now.

"Mars even has the other critical element, water, as Mr. Coburn observed, most of it waiting for us underground. In short, our sister planet has everything humans need to sustain life. Yet the information is rushing at us so quickly from Mars that we still don't know everything we'll find up there. Speaking of which, we have a guest today to tell us more about that."

The class turned to see the ruddy-faced fiftyish scientist with the snow-white hair. He was a rugged man, packed just barely into a neat blue suit. Responding to the attention of the class with a quick, tentative smile, he gave a half-hearted wave to match, then he folded his hands, one over the other, to wait. Most of the students looked a little uncomfortable as they usually did at the possibility of having a stranger take over the class.

"Since you asked, his name is Dr. Logan Avery. And he just may be the world's foremost volcano specialist." Avery shook his head in vigorous disagreement. "No? In any case," Brisini continued with a lopsided smile, "since the Olympic Games will be conducted on Olympus Mons—a point you all forgot to bring up, by the way—I thought it would be appropriate to learn something about volcanoes today. Give a warm welcome, please."

Dr. Avery strode down the aisle to polite applause, and took over the podium. He unfolded a few pages of notes from his pocket and pulled out a pair of black rimmed half-glasses to hold ready. The glasses together with the suit fitting tightly over bulging muscles contributed to make him an oddment.

Brisini stood nervously to one side, worrying about the etiquette quotient of some present, and hoping Avery would get started before their attention flagged.

"Thank you, uh, thank you. As Professor Brisini was telling you, our efforts on Mars are centered on the volcano, Olympus Mons. That particular spot was important to the first settlers on Mars for its climate and resources. It was also excellent for geological research."

"Excuse me," said Melendez, "Geological would be the wrong word. That's an Earth science."

"Wait until someone calls on you," countered Brisini from the sidelines.

"Semantically, you may be correct," said Avery, stroking down his perfectly white hair to calm himself. "I didn't want to confuse everyone by introducing new words right up front. So we'll stick with 'geology' for now."

Brisini nodded his approval that Dr. Avery was taking charge.

"As I was saying," Avery continued, "the International Olympic Committee chose the same site because it had a slope suitable for a ski resort. As you may know, the once-volcanic location originally caused some concern when Olympia was first built. I am here to say that if colonization doesn't work, it won't be because of danger from dormant volcanoes."

Coburn raised his hand as he spoke. "Has anyone tested it?"

Avery said, "We've never been able to bring a volcano into a laboratory, grade school science projects notwithstanding."

The group laughed and Avery said he appreciated how Brisini had warmed them up. He found his place again and went on, "Since we can't duplicate the conditions that prevail miles below a planet's surface, we can only theorize about how materials behave under that kind of pressure. There are three basic types of volcano. Quiet, explosive, and intermediate, named after the rate and manner of lava flows. The other method--"

"What type is Olympus Mons?" asked Coburn.

"It's not a matter of what Olympus Mons *is*. It's a matter of what it *was*. Lava once flowed freely and abundantly throughout the planet. It left the core and the mantle much the way steam escapes pipes and valves. The eventual thickening of Mars' crust from this very activity, millions of years ago, closed those valves like the turn of a spigot. In its time, Olympus Mons was the most active of all volcanoes in terms of sheer volume of matter escaping. And still there were many other mountain vents on Mars that would have made Earth's volcanoes seem like fumaroles. We're familiar with the images of the Martian landscape with its thousands of chunks of rock. These scattered remnants, known as *bombs*, came from the most violent of explosions."

Marissa said, "You call that dormant?" That got a laugh too.

Brisini need not have worried about his guest's popularity, given the topic.

Avery unfolded the special glasses, found a place for them on his face, glanced around for raised hands, and seeing none, continued.

* * *

WASHINGTON, D.C.

"I need your help," he had said in the rich, familiar tones that any American could identify.

There was something magical about a request from the President. The power of the office had its allure, even for sophisticated Shelly Kastin. Enough so to change her mind after Brandenberg's committee evidence softened her up. She comforted herself by realizing that very few people had the experience of working with the President, and no one could predict how they would react to it. The way he could scale himself down from national orator to infectiously enthusiastic friend gave her a sense of shared confidence. She fended him off for two days to clear her head before coming to a final decision. However calculated the efforts to convert her may have been, the reasoning behind her decision, and the outcomes, were her own.

Other people never would have guessed that Shelly Kastin had to think things over. Those around her were used to her conclusions coming spontaneously and mysteriously like a cloudburst in summer, sudden and definite in duration even if the common man wasn't privy to its secrets.

Like anyone, Kastin could harbor misgivings, but she saw the job on Mars as a challenge and a responsibility. Even though she didn't fully admit it to herself, she also thought of the offer as a kind of confirmation of her ability and qualification. She had never gotten that kind of validation from her family or her ex-husband Richard. The President himself said that he needed her and that she would get all the help she asked for. Senator Brandenberg, he explained, would handle that assistance personally.

Today she would go through the preparatory materials and the first briefing in a hurry. The committee told her to leave as soon as she wound up her affairs on Earth; the sooner she reached Mars, the more she would be able to accomplish.

She wasn't kidding herself. It would be damned hard to relocate to a pioneer colony in the midst of holding together humanity's first and foremost Olympic games on the Red Planet. It was already hard. She contacted Richard, and of course he made a fight out of it. He was against her putting the house up for sale after she wrested it from him in the settlement. She shot back that when she took possession of the house she couldn't have foreseen an assignment on another damn planet.

To tell the truth, she was sentimental about the house herself with its flagstone path winding under a canopy of young willows. There were times when the house was all she had while her husband was chasing other women. But it all had to go. If he still wanted it, he could buy it. The blessing was that their marriage was without children. That gave them no extra lives to destroy, and when it came to Mars, fewer people for Shelly Kastin to say goodbye to.

Given how many final arrangements she had to make, she joked that she was beginning to feel like someone who was in ill health and advanced years, as though her life were being wrapped up. And if that weren't enough, Brandenberg suggested that she make out her last will and testament, just in case—something that would have shocked her if she weren't expecting it.

Kastin pulled out the box of materials provided for her journey to Mars, Brandenberg's Care Package, as she thought of it. The first item was a report on the available management resources. She read from the top of a list of people that were supposed to help her when she got there.

Peter Arazine was first, listed oddly enough as an inventor. That was like listing Bill Gates, the founder of Microsoft, as a software engineer. There was no one on Earth who hadn't heard the name Peter Arazine by now. As the first governor of the tiny Mars colony, he was the subject of thousands of articles and recycled five-minute interviews.

Yet the list of real and manufactured facts about him only hinted at what kind of man he was. Around NASA it was said that even people who knew him didn't know if he was a hero or an overzealous imperialist. According to the President, Kastin would be akin to a temporary military governor, which placed her above him. And it meant that he could be very valuable to her if he chose to be. Whatever kind of guy he was, it would be easy for him to resent the arrangement.

Lieutenant Governor Marty Richfield held his position only because the law required a back-up in case the governor could not function. He had been given no role and in government and didn't seem to mind.

Then there was Harris Culpepper, who was going to be Keeper of the Holy Records or something like that. If he was sensitive about being a direct report to her, too bad.

Ellen Saftig, she was fire chief and everything else, just like in small towns everywhere.

Next came Logan Avery. Interesting.

The first three were strangers, the last an acquaintance, some kind of geology specialist. She didn't follow the details at the time he told her, and the report didn't go any further. Whatever he did was all right as long as he was competent at it. He said and did what he had to, and these were the values Kastin admired most. So he would be helpful no matter what.

She would select her own group of people for the most part. Her number one assistant, Zack Younger, had agreed immediately to join her. Every time Kastin got a new job, she stole Zack Younger from the previous job with a better offer. Now she had put him to work right away so he could establish a rapport with Governor Arazine.

The rest of the people on the list, well, they would have to be checked out.

Kastin reached back into the care package and came up with a book. HASKELL'S OFF TO MARS!, it was called, one of those fifty-dollars-a-day tour guides for the hot spots. It featured a crude map of Olympia, a service directory, and suggestions on how much to tip. They suggested visitors bunk with the natives until hotel prices come down. That book was probably a gag. She tossed it off into a scrap bin. The luggage pile just had to get smaller.

The phone rang then as it did almost constantly these last heady days. Somehow she didn't like the sound of this particular ring.

"Yes?"

"It's Zack." That would be her assistant.

"What's wrong?"

"I received a message from Governor Arazine in Olympia colony." His tone raised her hackles.

"Read it to me exactly as it's printed, Zack."

"Yes, chief. 'Journal Entry Cleared for Upper Level Distribution. At seven-oh-six ante meridian today, a tin box loaded with dynamite ignited in Outpost Eight, blowing apart the main storage shed and destroying the drilling equipment. Our thin air spread the debris over a two-mile radius. Fortunately, Outpost Eight was unmanned at the time. We are hoping the non-lethal nature of the attack was intentional. We found a message laser-cut across the site's dedication plate: Courtesy of Red Freedom. You'll be hearing from us again soon.'"

CHAPTER 11
Assignments

AT 7:50 AM, Jim Hrelcik touched down in Beijing as quietly as he had landed in dozens of American cities in a non-election year. The senator had taken a commercial flight to Tokyo, and a private flight for the last leg. Unlike a vacationer with provisions for a long stay, he kept only one small bag outside of the luggage compartment, held close. And unlike a business trip or matters of state, no official stood on the sidelines to meet him at the airport, no photographers to snap a thousand bothersome pictures. No constituents to cater to either.

He shouldered his carry-on luggage and wandered from the thinning crowd. A red and yellow cab he hadn't called pulled up directly in front of him as if waiting to ferry him to his destination. No one else got in. The driver did not step out to help him, nor did he draw a gun or make any threatening gesture. Assessing the battery powered ZAP SUV without a word, Hrelcik got into the back, and it took off in silent haste. As if mystery cars whisked him through the Chinese capital every day. But he didn't have to guess which of the twenty million inhabitants had made the arrangements.

Although he remained wary of his host, Hrelcik still gave himself credit for knowing who had real power and who were mere puppets. Abdul Harouk, the head of the IOC, wasn't the sort of man who went looking for trouble. He wouldn't change the site of the Olympics at the last moment and have the weight of the world fall on him. Not of his own free will.

No, Hrelcik knew what type of man it took to ram through the idea of an Olympics on a distant planet. The same one who worked behind the scenes to bend Hong Kong to the whims of the Premier the moment it was released from Britain's control in 1997. The same man who had the largest role in maneuvering the IOC out of Switzerland and into Belgium. And Hrelcik was certain that Chul Huk Chang was a man with whom he could "do business."

With four decades behind him in public office, Jim Hrelcik was Congress's top international maven. Foreign affairs was a specialty that many of his peers avoided, giving him a power that rivaled even the members of the nearly omnipotent domestic Ways And Means Committee. Now Brandenberg, a leader from the opposition party, had unexpectedly given him oversight of the red planet on a silver platter, the most foreign country of all. Unlike those who looked a gift horse in the mouth, the seasoned pol accepted the proffered horse and led him to the blacksmith for new shoes. Brandenberg obviously had his own reasons for Hrelcik's appointment so Hrelcik owed him exactly nothing.

But maven or not, the congressman was operating outside normal channels when he sought the trail that led the Olympics to Mars. He had no illusions about the legality of what he was doing. The Twenty Eighth Winter Games were an irrefutable fact of life now, and no one, neither Brandenberg nor any of his own supporters, had asked for its origins to be investigated. His job began after the fact and called for him to look over Shelly Kastin's shoulder. Certainly he was not authorized to sniff around Beijing for his answers.

Hrelcik didn't care about trifles. He proposed to share some bits of information with Chang in exchange for some of the American dollars that had misguidedly ended up in China. Nothing important, mind you. A few special updates that Chang wouldn't come by otherwise. Just a little something that he could trade for a comfortable retirement. Knowledge of any improprieties he uncovered in the genesis of these Olympics would be his insurance policy against anyone who begrudged him his rightful share.

The cab went as far as it was allowed and quietly dropped him off near a busy street. There, Hrelcik suffered a brief spell of anxiety. With so many foreign people rushing around him, it was impossible to see where he was. Had he gotten into the wrong cab after all?

No, in a fleeting gap he was relieved to see Chang standing without a visible escort on the other side of the road, hands behind his back, waiting for the river-sized flood of bicycle traffic to ebb. As it petered out, Chang practically swam through and greeted him halfway, a compact man with slicked back hair. Hrelcik was pleased that Chang shared his passion for good grooming. Finding the similarities between himself and his opposite number was what made the congressman so successful in foreign affairs, just as being a Garden of Eden snake was probably what made Chang so successful at spying. In fact, both were inordinately pleased at finding each other, as if they were family members separated by a forgotten war and finally reunited. Though in his eighties, Chang was sufficiently robust to briskly devour several blocks at his side. They entered a nondescript skyscraper and took the elevator to a restricted floor that had been stripped barren.

Hrelcik was struck by the fact that the high party member looked somewhat like Chiang Kai-shek before the moustache. A long face with flat cheeks and tight eyes, his hairline pushed back from the onslaught of a bulging frontal lobe, his chin fixed in place by an invisible strap. A hard face even when the man was obviously happy.

"Mr. Jim Hrelcik. It is so good to see you again," said his host.

To Hrelcik's apparent confusion, Chang added, "We met at the American Embassy? Ten years ago?"

"Oh, of course," he lied. He had no recollection of such a meeting and didn't care if it were true.

"It was wise of you to come here. Please sit."

Out of his element, the large empty room gave Hrelcik a touch of agoraphobia, the fear of open spaces. Surreptitiously, he passed his hand along the underside of the table.

"It is clean," said Chang with a smile. "We allow no place for bugs to hide."

"Your English is perfect," said the visitor, less because he believed it than to distract from any offense he might have given. "I didn't know you were educated in America."

"I wasn't," Chang said unblinkingly. Most people Hrelcik knew might have elaborated at that point but Chang was apparently the type who offered nothing of his past unless he could see an advantage to doing so.

"Very good though," Hrelcik shrugged. He hadn't expected the opening stages of negotiation to be so difficult.

"What do you bring with you?" Chang said. "You promised a little information 'to get started'."

"You promised a little cash," he countered.

"You already have part of it. While you were *en route*, I had it transferred to your special bank account in the Caymans. You may check on that if you find it important."

Hrelcik determined its importance by watching Chang's body language. He noticed the hard features, the way the tiny muscles in his chin pressed his lower lip against the upper while the corners of his eyes pinched together in a wicked gesture, the head slightly tilted back in a challenge. Not the beneficent fatherly face of a Mao. Not what Westerners thought of as the typical Chinese expression at all. Hrelcik was becoming slightly disenchanted by his new friend. "No, I trust you," he said meekly.

"Then we proceed," said Chang.

"All right, here it is. I found out something interesting about the inception of the U.S. Olympic involvement." He held his breath, waiting to see if that was an acceptable subject. He raised the issue to get details he needed confirmed for his insurance policy against prosecution. In effect he was asking for a favor that would put him in Chang's debt.

"I would be interested to hear it," Chang urged.

"It seems," said Hrelcik, "that the United States Government, without the knowledge of Congress, actually began spending money on the Olympic project before the congressional hearings even began."

"Before it was approved?" Chang asked.

"Yes. Certain agencies began taking bids from contractors for specific designs in advance. They actually went forward, made the company selection, and funds were released. Senator Brandenberg was aware of the advance spending and did nothing to stop it. He himself was probably behind the appropriations, but I can't prove that. Unless someone had some further information to add."

"Why blame Mr. Brandenberg? He is the same as the Soviet dog, *Laika*, who suffocated from lack of oxygen a week after they shot him into space. The satellite that bore the dog's corpse continued to operate much longer, as does Brandenburg's committee."

Hrelcik snorted at Chang's refusal to help him pin it on Brandenburg. Instead of commenting on Russian experiments from 1958 or whether his colleague was equivalent to a dog's corpse, the congressman said, "But you already knew everything I just told you, right? Those contracts were with Chinese companies."

"If our other commerce is satisfactory, I may give you the leverage you seek," said Chang with a long, cold look. Then they got down to their real business.

* * *

ALEXANDRIA, VA

Evan Brandenberg, U.S. Senator and nominal former astronaut, tested his stocking feet on the concrete terrace, and lifted a glass to the flight of the Taurus 2, just launched. Inside the walls of that stout cargo giant were the first prefabricated elements for the factories that would build Olympia into a true city, a real colony suitable for the Olympics, suitable for conquest and the pages of history. Maybe he would go there himself someday, and become one of the cynical footnotes.

This evening he celebrated in solitary, pacing the balcony because his was a personal burden. Very few people were in a position to be as duplicitous as he was. He was never a hero or someone who claimed to be. His boots never kissed lunar soil. He wasn't one of the famed twenty-four Americans who journeyed to moon orbit and back between 1969 and 1972. He participated in manned flight aboard the U.S. Space Shuttle Endeavor, teasing at the periphery of Earth after three hundred fifty other people had already flown in space. His was the era of the watered down, post-Challenger space program in the agency politicians no longer trusted. *Go slow, you flying assholes! Try not to blow anyone up!*

Nothing like the heady days of Senator Ty Babcock, one of the first men to touch space when it was a forbidden realm, swept into office by the morbid curiosity called fame, kept in office by a hard head and his natural aptitude for the common touch. And by his fame.

Brandenberg wasn't elected by his limited celebrity, although some of his constituents must have recalled his background and given some him points for it the first time around. After his freshman season in congress, his limited past in space was forgotten and there went his advantage. He adopted a new way of life where as a career lawmaker he purported to serve the public, special within small circles because he counted as one of the few experts on the subject of extraterrestrial progress.

And what else was he becoming in this era of perverted decisions? Politics, much like his previous profession, involved plunging into infinite space, linked to the familiar world by a thread of imperfect communication. But in the halls of Congress the only ground control, the only voice in your head, was your mutated conscience. *Did you know right from wrong when you went in, Evan Brandenberg? And how often did you have to go through wrong to get to right?*

The Senate leader was personally connected to some of the individuals involved in the latest Mars project because he had buried them in the outland. He couldn't see the Taurus 2 in the sky when he looked up from the balcony, but he thought he could see a sparkling orange point of light, no bigger than stars that were light years away, and he pictured the athletes, the soldiers, the private citizens struggling there in the coldest of cold wars.

Shelly Kastin, whom he had somewhat shamed and deceived into going, was the one he worried about most. Brandenberg had gotten to know her better since he gave her the assignment so he looked at her case differently now. He didn't trust or understand his own motivations anymore. Did someone have to have made their whole career in the Department of Defense to be prepared to take charge of security on that hostile red planet? Shelly was so much in demand elsewhere that she wouldn't accept the job if she didn't think she could do it. Politicians took charge of whole countries without being an expert in most of what they did. He posed the question to himself this way: Since no one can really safeguard against a determined terrorist, every thinking person has an equal chance, don't they? Or did I send her there, following my original plan, as much to get her out of the way as anything else?

The man on the terrace in his stocking feet didn't have the answer. All he gathered by his introspection was that his decisions were tainted by the nature of his chosen profession. Some people could accept that. While he tried to decide which kind of person he was, things were beginning to look grim. So he toasted the little orange star, and drank and drank and drank. He chose straight whiskey because to him, the stuff tasted as awful as he felt. At the bottom of the glass, he saw the Mars mission for what it was, a desperate gamble.

The wheels in motion on that planet spun in every direction in a crazy clay clockwork directed by a mad conductor. Brandenberg doubted if there was one person who knew everything that was going on. Not Abdul Harouk, as Chairman of the IOC, not the President of the United States, not ambitious Governor Arazine of Mars, and certainly not himself. With that he called to mind the newspaper evaluations of his performance. Am I at least one of the *concerto grosso* soloists playing a leading part or does each participant just think that they are?

The whiskey burned its way down. He pitied anyone who got in the way.

CHAPTER 12
Man On Mars

MARS EQUIVALENT EARTH YEAR: 2038

THE DISTANT SUN poured watery light on Team Captain Bill Gingold as he led the American skiers in a sloppy counterclockwise jog around the base of Olympus Mons, making the solar system's largest known mountain a giant running track. Having taken the dusty skirt in increasing daily doses, their absent coach had joked they were building to do the whole thousand-plus-mile circumference. Each man secretly thought it possible for the Martian skiers, but not for them. This day's run, possibly their last, followed a melancholy drinking celebration at the end of training.

"Forget the Games and Coach Kashvili. This is an unbelievable high," cooed Mackie vaulting unsteadily for the sky with every other step. His last lurch and kick went nearly as high as Becusi's head.

"Hey, watch it," Becusi yowled.

"Gravity is for suckers," said someone way at the back. That sounded like a maximally sloshed Turpin. "I don't even need any skis to run this hill. Gimme the medal now." He sprang and whooped. Gingold pulled back to keep an eye on him.

"You drank enough to blast up there on piss power," said Mackie.

Stumbling on a small rock, Turpin said, "Why is it that the drunkest people…who always tell me that I'm drunk?"

Mackie laughed. "You got that a little mixed up, sport."

"I wonder what it's like to get balled on Mars?" Becusi yelled at the mountain.

"You haven't yet?" said Jimson. "I've been mounting anything with a hole on this trip."

Gingold said, "Turn around and walk, you sick hump." As captain he was their surrogate leader in the absence of their coach. Now the rattling sounds of congestion filtering out of his faceplate tipped him off that he was developing a nasty cold. First the coach went down with a bug and now him. He prayed it was an Earth germ and not a local one that had waited a billion years to incubate in human flesh.

"Why should I shut up?" Jimson said. Then he yelled in the general direction of City Hall, "It's not my fault the Clayheads forgot the babe station."

"Screw those loser Sculptors, screw them all," Turpin said. The local residents referred to the terraform planners as the Sculptors, and infused them with the kind of reverence usually reserved for the creator of the Universe.

Having paused, Turpin started off in the wrong direction.

Gingold grabbed his shoulders and rotated him to safety. "Just keep going," he advised, fighting a congested cough. His ragged charges actually loved Mars. They didn't love to admit the very real prospect of losing badly.

When Jimson turned around to look at Turpin, he noticed the personally designed suit of a teammate in the distance by the green and silver snaking around his torso. Yves' one and only sponsor had paid for it. "Look at that. It's Yves 'Too-good-for-everybody' Loitte posing on that hill. He thinks he's auditioning for commercials, that dummy."

"That dumb dope," said Mackie. "Drag him down here with the rest of us fallen angels."

"Let him work out," said Ivanovich.

"Why is that, Ivy?" said Mackie.

"The team sucks badly enough as it is."

"That's your opinion, Ivy League. You can't guarantee it sucks badly enough."

"Yves has a chance. Coburn vouches for him," said Gingold holding his cough until the end of the sentence.

"Wisdom from Phlegm-gold and the Cobra," said Jimson, "who also is not among us today. If Coburn was a genius, he'd be on some other team."

"Keep talking, Jimson," said Turpin. "While we're all jacking off, Loitte's gonna walk away with the gold."

Jimson said, "He's from the same planet we are. He's not gonna get gold, silver, bronze, or a tin cup." Turning to the mountain he shouted, "Hey Loitte," while struggling to take off his helmet.

"Stop that," said Gingold. "It's time to go home," by which he meant their lodgings.

"No, I want the showboat to hear me better," Jimson said. Before anyone could take his drunken efforts seriously, he managed to finish twisting the catches, and threw his helmet away. "Hey Loitte, you stupid s—" He wheezed, unable to get a breath, and then collapsed.

Ivy, who had gone after the helmet, struggled to get it back on him. After a reconnect, Jimson took a shuddering breath and then fouled the faceplate with a splash of vomit.

"That's too damned funny," Gingold coughed. "I was hoping this run would sober you-all up. Let's go home."

* * *

Yves Loitte with his worries, didn't care what Turpin and Jimson, or any of his drunken teammates, might think. He shouldn't have been so badly in need of another trial run so late in the game.

Though skiing Olympus Mons was beginning to feel natural to him in fits and starts, he needed the physical adjustment to click. He would welcome it any time now, although it was probably too late. With the games themselves only two days off, his only chance was to ditch the team and its ailing coach, and find his own way.

The late afternoon was clear and the wind tame on the inhabited side of the mountain. The corridor looked like a stolen and transplanted slice of Mars' North or South Poles. Artificial snow made a smooth blanket of the gently sloping cross-country section. It should have taken little or no conscious effort for his athletic frame to cover a distance. On this planet, Yves weighed precisely fifty-eight pounds, which reduced his skis' friction and opened the door to greater speed. Instead, Yves began to learn the hard reality that Mars made skiing a new sport. Control issues—the risk of overpowering the course—exhausted him, and the visual cues continued to throw him off.

As he launched himself across the slope attempting to pretend he was on Earth, he looked too far ahead and suffered a wave of queasiness. The hills, the ridges, and the drop-offs were exaggerated to an incomprehensible scale, the course a minor wrinkle in the vast lava dome of an ancient peak. Not a product of nature as he knew it on Earth. He felt the massive hills roll under him like restless serpents. The great faces of the cliffs retreated from his approach like dreams chased by the waking mind.

The snow itself conspired against him. Even though bare rock sat more than a kilometer distant, reflections from those red surfaces tinted the soft expanse in front of him pink like a candy land mountain. His rebellious mind tried to adjust, said the pink was really white, or told him it was sunset. Yet every time he spotted the rocks, he knew better.

He pushed his poles gently down and back in two strokes to pick up a little speed. With the first push he watched the ground. As his ferrules bit snow on the second pass, his gaze ranged far ahead of him to pick out man-sized artifacts. He could see the domes of town, with buildings rising no higher than one level suburban sprawl. Gray shapes mixed together with the yellow green of fresh trees and shrubs.

The Martian Olympic Park on the edge of the city of Olympia nestled in the shelter of the dormant volcano he skied. According to the official map, the nearly flat outer section from the midpoint elevation to the lava terminus would be used for cross country skiing while the inner segments provided enough variation to utilize them for all the other events. Every terrain existed within the same general area because of the complexity of geological events over eons without significant weathering. Encompassing the Olympic Village, the communication center, and competition arenas, the park was perhaps the greatest technical achievement in the history of man.

Correcting his trajectory slightly, he steered toward base camp. The few others on the course were at various stages of doing the same, headed for the Martian horizon as though they knew where they were going. The planet was one huge unexplored territory. Until now, the space highway that brought people there was not very well traveled. They usually waited for a window of opportunity every twenty-six months when the trip was relatively short and most fuel efficient.

The majority of the spectators, even his own mother, would be home on Earth watching the Olympic events on television, tuning in to the previews right about now. Usually several million people came personally to see the Olympic Games when they were held on Earth. The visitors on Mars at the moment consisted of over one thousand athletes. Then you had the scientists, International Olympic Committee personnel, security, maintenance, a handful of very wealthy spectators and, of course, the Martian settlers who lived there to begin with. Maybe a presence of twenty five hundred souls all told.

Yves' girlfriend Terri, an Inspector Trainee with Earth's Environmental Protection Agency, had explained patiently that the new eco-system was very fragile. Oxygen and nitrogen had been partially restored after a billion years lacking. As parched riverbeds drank fresh water, the revised world got divided up between microorganisms, humans, and their pets. With the exception of these particular life forms, it was all there before, but Yves could not comprehend how people could now frolic where pioneer explorers struggled just a dozen years earlier.

The one thing Yves could easily equate it to was the beauty and the loneliness described in the diaries of the earliest settlers. These were people like Yves who saw the need for new frontiers. Until now, Earth's oceans, pretty much conquered in the late 1990's and the aught years, were the last place left.

When he came sliding out to the end of his run, Yves pulled a deep, greedy breath from his Nitrox tank, the supplemental nitrogen and oxygen cartridge that allowed him to exert himself in the thin air. Yves allowed himself to coast to a long, easy stop as the ground leveled out. He could see several of his competitors skiing off to the sides. No other Americans seemed to be present.

Nils Barkly of the Martian team must have kept out of sight at first because he took Yves by surprise. He approached the Earther from behind, cutting in front to intercept him, and pressing uncomfortably close as he halted. Then he ski-walked in a rotation so that they were face to face, only with Barkly looking down from his greater height. The two competitors originated from the same orbit. The former Swiss national shared Yves' classic skier's physique; lean with bunched muscles that flexed with every movement. Barkly, however, handled the light gravity as though he were born on Mars. Under the helmet the corner of his mouth curled like Mack the Knife. "So it's Yves Loitte from Earth," he said.

Yves couldn't fathom why the European-born Barkly insisted on pronouncing Yves' surname like "Detroit." The real way should have been more like LU-WAH-t, with the "t" barely vocalized, but the whole Loitte family had long since given up insisting. The conversion irked Yves only when someone who must have known better still said it incorrectly.

"I've seen your mug shot," Barkly went on, "I've heard the stories about you. Do you always journey so far in order to lose a tournament?"

Yves' skin crawled. He was painfully aware that nationals from most other countries judged him strictly by his official standing. People like his friend Lou Coburn would have laid odds that Yves was the most promising raw talent amongst the Americans, and that meant exactly nothing. One of the best skiers on Earth, Yves' poverty had hindered him with poor equipment before his first sponsor came along.

The top members of each team were famous in the sports world and Nils Barkly was the easiest to recognize. A deep gash divided his face as it sliced across his forehead, turned downward through the center of his left eye and continued into the middle of his cheek, half an inch wide at some points. The open part was like the raw meat of a cow cleft by the butcher's knife. The old wound could be seen even through the glare shield, marring an otherwise boyish face, strikingly good looking when viewed in right profile. The defect he lived with could make him look sad or vicious, depending on his expression at the moment. When he worked at being sincere, his disfigurement made strangers feel sorry for him.

Like others who had encountered Barkly's aggression for the first time, Yves Loitte wondered whether the Martian skier was in a perpetual state of anger, always anticipating mistreatment because of the way he looked.

Used to being unpopular as an American, Yves was ready to make allowances even after Barkly's first remark.

Not that he planned to back off as though he couldn't take the heat. The mistake would be to treat him differently from other competitors. He gave Barkley's words hang time in the air.

"Are you deaf?" said Barkly, leaning toward him, one hand cupped to the vicinity of his mouth. Perhaps mistaking Yves' reaction for fear, he pulled off his helmet, and tucked it under one arm. The ram's head insignia emblazoned on the top glared threateningly, peering out from a dark crimson circle. He wasn't breathing hard and he didn't appear to need spare oxygen.

Barkley said, "A little advice, Loitte. Here you are practicing on the easiest slope. I don't know how you thought you were doing, but you look like shit. I can help you understand. It comes from living on a soft planet with tiny mountains like lumps of oatmeal. You and the other soft Earthers don't even know why you're here. Best to stand aside and watch how real men ski."

Yves kept his helmet in place. Even if he had the brightest future in the solar system, with his standing in the Olympic Trials, any kind of fight could get him thrown out, and with his whole career ahead of him, he wouldn't fall into that trap. Barkly engaged in the posturing that competitors have used to intimidate each other since the beginning of time.

Yves said, "And how did you get here on the easy slopes?"

"I approached you because I thought you were a woman. I see I was wrong. You are a boy, skiing like someone with a squirrel in the *derrière*." Barkly smiled as Yves' face darkened.

Yves said, "You Martians sit here on your low gravity butts for years, sailing around the planet like there's nothing better to do. Meanwhile you've got the highest mortality rate in skiing. You don't even know how to stay alive. Is that how your parents were killed? Was it carelessness? Incompetence? Was it your fault?"

As Yves' response came spilling out, he realized how terrible as it sounded, how he had gone too far. Backpedaling though would make things worse.

Barkly studied him. "Don't think I hate you just because you're an Earther, and don't share our history. I hate you because you're an Earther *and* an American. No, a French heritage traitor skiing for the Americans."

The Olympia resident was right in one sense. American-born Yves didn't know firsthand about the hardships Martian settlers had endured. He had no responsibility for them and he wasn't going to do battle with history. His training taught him to focus on the present and what he needed to do to win. "That's your problem, Mars man. If you'll excuse me, I'm going to use this time to practice. I'm gonna get real good and make you proud." Yves began to turn away.

Barkly shoved Yves hard enough to knock him on his back in a twisting fall that made the skis pop off his feet. Yves snatched one ski pole into his hands and whipped it across him as a barrier, ready to strike with it if he had to.

Barkly began to frown, and then caught himself, converting it to a smile. He laughed so hard his head recoiled. "You will never medal if you can't stay on your feet." Then he pulled his helmet in place as he turned and lit off into the snow.

"Welcome to Mars," Yves said to himself.

* * *

Nils Barkly rabbited out of there while he could still master his emotions. No less a concern was his special suit that blew oxygen into his face when the helmet came off. The unrecycled air would have run out any second.

The reflexes of Yves Loitte had taken Barkly by surprise when he discarded one pole and used the other as a defensive block. The American could have easily lashed out and damaged his attacker's legs from that position if he was inclined to revenge. A move like that would have put an end to the competition before it began, and more importantly would have shattered the Martian's self image. Such prowess from the foreigner was not what Barkly expected.

His American opponent also surprised him by mentioning the death of his parents in order to gain a psychological advantage. If Barkley were in Yves's position, he would have done the same.

The images from that time were still vivid. The last day his parents lived provided his clearest memories of them. Kit and Inge Barkly were hired for Mars as professional trail planners. They made their living at resorts designing ski paths tailored to beginning, intermediate, and advanced skiers. The job called for determining the length of a particular course, the location of the start and finish, and what kind of challenging twists and turns fit the contours of the slope, the objective being to make a trip both safe and exciting. For Nils there was never a profession more mysterious, more exclusive, or more demanding. You had to be a mountain climber, a skier, a surveyor, and an artist.

There was never any question for him about other choices in life. He would always be a trail planner like his parents.

The Barkleys wanted a job where they could work together as a family and the consortium that brought them to Mars provided that opportunity.

Their only son joined them that day because he was an excellent skier and already an important member of their group. Because of the weight advantage, they were twice as well outfitted as any comparable Earth expedition. They carried ropes, shovels, claws, cleated boots, ski boots, skis, poles, altimeters, cameras, thermometers, nitrox tanks, cartographic recorders, first aid, and more, stowed in weighty backpacks and front packs for balance. Individually, the items were lightweight, collapsible, and combinable. One extra meal filled every sack in case they didn't get back by suppertime.

The family took pictures and surveying measurements and sang while they worked. They encouraged Nils to figure out complicated issues for himself as much as possible. When he faltered, he marveled at their inexhaustible supply of answers.

The routine was to return to the village at the end of each day by skiing along one of the snow paths the planners used for testing purposes, allowing an ample buffer of hours against the approach of sundown. Even though the paths were carefully selected and flattened, regular maintenance was impossible and new snow blew across them daily. All routes were considered rough backcountry, nature driven and unpredictable.

Before setting downhill that day, his father Kit insisted on digging a trench six feet deep, which was the first step in checking the stability of the chute to make sure the snow wouldn't slide out from under them. Though the method was not infallible it gave some assurance. Most people would skip some of the standard procedures, but as a professional and a safety expert, Kit wouldn't have it any other way. So Nils sat patiently charting the type of snow they stood on while Inge measured the temperature differential at various levels in the cross section revealed by their trench. They found a slight difference in the temperature readings, nothing most people would worry about.

To be even more certain, they scored the outline of a pie wedge into the walls of the trench to form a block the size of a boar. Then the family systematically attacked the surface of the block with their shovels. Seeing that it didn't give way, Kit, who was the heaviest of the three, jumped on top to see if any of the icy snow would break away. The other two were poised to grab him if he went flying.

After several hops, the pie wedge did not separate. That was all they could do. The beginning of the path, at least, was safe as per the tests.

The Barklys pushed off, skied without incident, and admired the pale saplings that were taking root, poking green needles through the snow, serving as a special reminder to the thoughtful traveler of how recent was life on the planet. Those would remain stunted for decades, but the artificial trees nearby served a dual purpose, planted for psychological support, and as kilometer markers for reference. If travelers lost track, they could scan the tags.

Down they went in sidewinding rhythm, one family member checking on the other at intervals. Their pace was leisurely, their formation single file and well in sight of each other, with Inge following Nils and Kit following them both, obviously admiring his wife's firm ass and wishing for once that the boy wasn't with them.

Then Nils did something his father had asked him never to do. He glanced behind him to take in the view as he worked left in a transverse. The boy didn't cause the problem, but his move gave him a chance to see the end coming.

Horrified, he watched as a house-sized ice shelf detached from a point above them with a booming crack, a silent fall, and a bouncing crash when it hit the slope. He shouted into the sound of the chain reaction that followed, gesturing madly, fighting for control. He could hear the snow thunder, rattling the slope behind them. Listening, watching the mass grow, and knowing they couldn't outrun it.

The Barklys disengaged their packs and braced for the shock that would slam into them from behind. Kit, who saw Nils' warning movements first, pulled the S.O.S. flare from his belt, triggered it until it was empty, twitching at it twice more to make sure. The flares soared away, struggling to outshine the daylight. Inge glanced back at the wall of death, took a deep breath, and pushed Nils so violently to the side that she fell, face pressed in the snow as the white terror bore down. She recovered a standing position in time to feel the back-spraining impact. The menace built relentlessly, heaving them upwards at first, over three times the height of a man, with still more snow and ice above. Kit and Inge backstroked furiously to try to stay on top of the snow when it came, but they had waited too long. Kit disappeared first and Inge was the second to go under. Nils flailed his arms like the others but only briefly.

The young man who was pushed out of the direct path of the avalanche eventually slipped off a rock face, plummeted fifty meters through the open air, and impacted on a bridge of snow that broke his fall with a jolt before it gave way to a crevasse hidden beneath. He plunged again, his body tracing the opening as it went from three foot wide, to two foot wide, to just less than the width of his rib cage, which flexed, then cracked and fixed him in place when his organs couldn't squeeze any tighter. The external bleeding was stanched by the pressure of the rocks. There he stayed.

The search party immediately found Mr. and Mrs. Barkly with the aid of the flares and their avalanche transceivers which led searchers to an area marked by strewn out back pack provisions from all three of the trail planners. Kit had died of suffocation, and Inge was too badly injured to survive or offer any last words. Their condition was to be expected. The man assigned to gather their possessions was more surprised by what he found. No matter what else they carried, they still proudly made room for their Swiss passports.

Then there was the matter of their kid. The physical evidence that young Nils was originally with his parents wasn't enough to help locate him since his transceiver broadcast no signal at all. As the rescuers would discover later, the device had been crushed in his belt and jammed up into his broken ribs. The ice-penetrating radar units were still in transit from Earth. That left the search for Nils up to guesswork until the shipment arrived.

While the search party feared for Nils' air density even if he were in an air pocket, he had been pushed much further than his parents and was fairly close to the village where the escaping air was denser. Just enough air was available to supplement his nitrox rations for his limited lung space and lack of movement, but he landed where no one was looking. Each and every person in the colony was desperately needed, so the search went on. They wanted, at least, to retrieve the body.

For days, he listened to his name echoing in the distance while he slowly starved on a diet of melted snow and the crumbs of his only meal. With the pressure of the rocks against his chest, he couldn't draw a deep enough breath to answer them. He called out for as long as he could in a near-whisper, using precious gulps from the supplemental nitrox tank to do even that.

At the same time that the weather turned especially harsh, the team got the word that the ice-penetrating radar had never been shipped. Without any hope, they were forced to call off the search earlier than expected. It was this decision that saved the life of Nils Barkly.

On their way back to Olympia, the team ran into a field of man-sized cracks in the ground, covered mostly by snow, but visible enough to experienced eyes to show the danger. The expedition went single file with a meter probe, bound to each other by ropes, lashed to a large supply sled in the middle for anchorage. Those who fell into the cracks were held by the counterweight and got hauled up immediately with only minor injury. Most of them had a turn falling in. It was on one such occasion that a rescue worker spotted the small object that was Nils, illuminated from the light in the worker's helmet, forty five meters below, desperately, automatically sucking the last of the warmer air from his nitrox cartridge to keep his lungs from freezing.

Nils was incoherent when the other settlers pulled him free, during which the treacherous crevasse tore a hideous gash in his face. In his hospital bed he did a vigorous backstroke against an imaginary avalanche. The staff had to tie his arms to keep him from destroying his life support. When he came out of shock, and heard the outcome like a sentence pronounced on him, his parents dead, he made a pact with the mountain that Olympus Mons would never claim another Barkly life. It would be an empty pledge if he ever left the vicinity of the volcano or allowed others to master it better than he did. Within his trauma-soaked mind, this resolution made sense.

He kept his facial scar unaltered as a constant reminder of the price he paid, the dangers he faced, the dangers he would face again.

The transients couldn't know what it had been like in the years before, when Mars was tamed with the blood of its settlers. It hardened Nils Barkly until his cold dark eyes plugged the weaker emotions. Now he lived to wring emotion from others. Especially foreigners.

* * *

Shelly Kastin pressed her right fist to her left palm, eye-to-eye with her goddaughter Terri Finney, both of them ready for a fight. Kastin had scanned enough dossiers to come to a surprising conclusion. Of those currently on Mars, young Terri had the greatest expertise with Karate, a hobby she shared. She found it ironic that this child she helped raise would become her *sensei*-away-from-home. Technically.

As they circled, Shelly said, "This is your chance to get even with me for trying to keep you from coming to Mars."

"Ancient history. Anyway, I came around to your point of view."

"That'll be the day."

They started practice by turning aside direct assaults and ducking under roundhouse kicks, which the security chief did easily.

Shelly said, "Step it up, girl. I'm not going to learn anything if you hold back."

"I think I'm only in the mood to beat up skiers today, Aunt Shel." But as she said it, she tried for a lunging front kick at head height. The jump was the easy part. When Shelly deflected her, Terri ended up in a shaky recovery a few meters away. They had come over in the same launch window, and were in the process of getting used to the transition from shipboard's two-thirds gravity to the red planet's one-third pull.

"Boyfriend trouble?" Shelly asked.

Before Terri could answer, Zack Younger entered the gym and cleared his throat. "Chief, the, uh, man you requested has been located. You told me to inform you immediately. On your orders, we are very discreetly detaining him until you arrive. He won't even know he's being held unless he tries to leave the building."

"I wish I could do that with Yves," Terri said quietly.

The chief reconfirmed the wisdom of picking Zack. He knew when to be discreet. There was no telling what the public might make of it if they knew that their Security Chief and Mars' governor had such a tenuous relationship. She turned to Terri with a closing bow. "Sorry about getting you into the *gi* for nothing. I know you need to train for your skating."

"I needed a break. I'll pick up another partner here."

Shelly said, "I know you'll be fine. Try to take that tour I told you about, and give my regards to your boyfriend. I'd give anything to switch places with you right about now."

* * *

Zack took his chief to Town Hall and steered her to the governor just before he tried to exit. Arazine took a firm step toward her followed by an ungainly half-step backward.

"Governor Arazine," said Kastin, "this face-to-face has been a long time in coming."

"I'm sorry, Madam Security Chief. I have no time for your face now and I'm sure you to tend to have slatters of mate. Matters of slate." His breath stank of alcohol.

"You've stalled this meeting as long as you could. We'll sort it out now whether you're half in the bag or not." Shelly Kastin did not consider herself heavy handed. She didn't breeze into Town Hall and displace anyone physically. Her operations were housed in a special facility at a respectful distance. Since she had arrived and established herself with her small group, Arazine and his staff had given them a wide berth. No advice, and scarcely a word had passed between the two groups. She worried that while the transition and division of power was going smoothly enough in most ways, lack of communication lines would be a critical error in the event of a crisis during the Games.

"Let's get this over with then," growled Arazine, "you're in charge. I accept it. End of story."

"Understand this, governor: I have zero desire to remain on Mars when the Games are over. I did not invent the situation that brought us together, nor will I take advantage of it. For the duration of the Games, I have temporary control in matters of state security only."

"Which is the army way of saying: if it stands still you'll paint it, and if it moves you'll fuck it. You have a death grip one way or another."

"You and I will have as little overlap as possible. I take over all functions only if an emergency arises."

"What you deem an emergency," he said extravagantly.

"Doctor Arazine, it doesn't help if you're going to be cynical."

"If I'm going to be cynical, best I be cynical on Mars." He winked. "There were enough cynics back on Earth, so we shipped us here."

"You've inebriated," she stated simply.

"A lot of people think that until they've had a few themselves and see things my way."

"You can think of me as an adversary if it serves your ego to do so. Just don't for one moment let it interfere with the smooth functioning of the Olympic Games. If you do, I will put you out of the picture for the duration. It can get public, it can get ugly, it can get embarrassing. I'll have no sympathy if you get burned."

"Finally I meet somebody who gives guarantees." Arazine ended the meeting by stumbling away.

Now Kastin understood why she hadn't heard any complaints from the governor so far. Apparently, he reacted to his temporary loss of power by drinking. Her briefing materials had noted a high rate of alcoholism on Mars. It was disappointing to see that the problem began at the top.

She had studied his hands during the exchange. They weren't red, raw, rosy or purple, just even flesh tones like his face. Neither did he radiate alcohol from every pore. So he showed no obvious signs of a problem that went back a long way. He was also fairly well groomed, as much as most men bother to be. All of which seemed to indicate that he wasn't an alcoholic or that he hadn't been an alcoholic for long.

Even though she would have liked more cooperation from the local government, and she now pitied the man in charge, Kastin felt a morbid sense of relief that Arazine had not chosen to pit himself against her, which would have caused a major distraction to add to the trouble that Red Freedom stirred up. All she had to do from here was to put aside any feelings of guilt for whatever she had to do if the man decided that tacit resignation didn't suit him.

CHAPTER 13
Signs Of Trouble

"WARNING. TEMPERATURE IS LOW AND CURRENT AIR DENSITY MAY CAUSE SHORTNESS OF BREATH. PLEASE TAKE APPROPRIATE MEASURES."

"Yes, I heard you, Gatekeeper. And I'm careful by nature. I guess you can't just take my word for it." Terri Finney checked her suit integrity one more time, pressed for the airlock again to show she was ready, and the inner door admitted her without any further complaint.

Check the suit, check the suit, check the suit, they drilled into you. Redundant safety is the key to survival. Like the song says, "underground with the air jets blowing and the nitrox tank flowing, that's where I'll be." I got it already, Terri thought with a smile. They must think us Earth-siders are a dumb bunch.

She stepped through the outer door into the pre-dawn light, walking carefully as night lamps winked off and objects took the color of the new day, which once again was basically red. Her Hybrid felt unexpectedly light and airy. She had a sudden impulse to throw her arms in the air and skip like a little girl skips on Mars, see how high she would fly.

"Hah, that would be some excuse for losing the competition," she mumbled. "Fall down, twist your ankle and ruin everything. No sir, I'm going to behave today. My second childhood waited this long, it could wait a little longer."

The sun broke crimson on the horizon as she arrived at her destination, making it seem that it was sunset even while advancing light affirmed the dawn. Cold air blew through soft shadows cast by the Olympia Tourist Center, already buzzing with human commerce by this time of the morning. Vulgar though it may have been in its conception, the design was actually quite pleasing so far from home. A composite replica of one of the early mountain lodges of America, the main house sported huge wood-synth beams supporting a steep, green-shingled roof. An early soda pop machine in cherry red, circa 1928, waited out front with a pair of old time gas pumps in cherry red to match, their oval globes frosted white. The beams were rough-cut with distress marks, but the wood-synth benches that adorned the porch were smooth and inviting.

Perched in the foothills among the largest pines available, the Tourist Center was just twenty nine hundred feet above theoretical sea level, and tailored to appear as though it were high in the mountains. To complete the illusion, patches of snow adorned the top of every surface, including the paths leading to and from, in a charming mosaic. Who could believe Mars was dangerous when they saw sunrise over the homey Tourist Center? she wondered.

The Canadian figure skater stretched out a finger to plug her fingernail interface into the service billboard for her choices. Payment transferred with a confirming chirp. Gazing again at the Tourist Center and its surroundings, she now gulped air scented by fresh pine, beds of old hay-colored needles, and the occasional whiff of a mountain stream or the musky odor of a deer in mating season. The signal that triggered the scent reserve in her nitrox tank would give her ten minutes of rapture instead of the odorless monotony she was breathing before.

She let her lungs expand to the maximum, hold there, shoot it out quickly, and suck it in even faster. The next time, she did it slowly to savor it as she realized she must. The same combinations would never come again. She recalled Yves' friend, Lou Coburn triumphantly declaring, "Happiness packaged and sold."

Actually, the deal was a hidden bargain. Mars rotated just a smidgeon slower than the Earth, about thirty-seven minutes extra per turn. Instead of scrapping the twenty-four-hour timetable that everyone lived and loved by, the geniuses from Geneva simply told their clocks to go that much slower. Now each person was democratically doled out an extra second-and-a-half for every minute they had before. Therefore ten minutes of Mars time on the scent boxes were about fifteen seconds longer than expected. She wanted to start a book of riddles beginning with, "How do you sell happiness at a discount?"

As she sniffed and entertained herself with time calculations, she wondered how much better the experience would be if Yves were there to join her. Extra thirty seven minutes or no, he lived by the athlete's schedule just like she did, and their pleasure would have to be taken in fleeting moments. Some of her leisure hours would always be spent alone. Terri kept her helmet cam running so she could share her adventures with him later.

She hurried across to the simple kiosk for tickets, and bounded onto the street car-style land rover marked "Big Orange Tours," grabbing the straps to make sure she didn't fly off again. Barely keeping your balance was a common experience and the people already seated observed the etiquette of looking away from the next person's embarrassment.

Terri estimated that there were about twenty-five others aboard. She gazed briefly at each of them with her fondness for studying people, using her first glance to see if she had any friends among them.

New faces for a new planet, unidentifiable with the exception of one. Although she had never seen him before, she had an idea who he was, a college teacher named Brisini, with a first name of Al or Mike. Or Pete, or something else with one syllable. The correct name would come to her if she stopped trying to remember it.

This professor had two lucky graduate students with him, each working on a master's thesis judging by the conversation in progress. They were bouncing advanced concepts off of him rapid fire, and he was looking very sly as he led them to their own answers. Brisini was pale with black eyebrows mounted high on his forehead, matching his thick black hair, with cheeks of tough stubble that looked like they could never be shaved clean. His eyes were cheerfully squeezed by the impish smirk frozen to his face. Once in a while, one eyebrow would inch even higher than the other before settling back in its place. This had to be the professor Yves was always raving about from his school. The one who knew "everything." There could be no other. Riddle number two: *How many teaching Brisini's were selected to go to Mars?*

He seemed totally absorbed with pointing out details to his students. She would introduce herself later provided she could get a word in.

She turned her attention instead to the man in charge of the trip. The Martians she had met so far hadn't been too friendly, but this tour guide, a thin Martian with strong, round cheekbones under an old-time train conductor's hat, at least looked cheerful. A robust showman, the nametag sewn into his headgear identified him as Horace, and he came to life, robot fashion, as soon as his rover was in motion. He swelled his narrow body with a deep breath while the passengers murmured in excitement.

"Big Orange Tours is proud to welcome you to Mars, The Happy Orange Planet," he announced over the public address system. "I'm Horace your guide."

A beautiful, well-dressed passenger shouted, "No!" as though she had strenuous objections to the guidance of Horace. Her toddler had just climbed up a stability pole in the vicinity of the tour guide. He took it with aplomb.

The rover descended from its picturesque locale into the Village itself. "Our main attraction today is the Olympic Village and the town of Olympia, host city to the first Olympic Games to be held away from the planet Earth.

"I'm not playing your games," the beautiful woman said loudly enough for everyone to hear. She could reach the little girl if she wanted to. She chose to sit with her arms folded and do some pouting of her own. Terri didn't care for this type of mother.

Horace colored, but went on, "In addition to Olympia, the only official city on Mars, we have twelve exploration sites expanding our world even as I speak; construction goes fast at one-third gravity. The village and city together describe a ten-kilometer arc within the rim of Mars' best-known landmark, the great Olympus Mons."

"There's nothing so great up there," bellowed Ms. Pouty. "I'm disappointed that you won't compromise." She ignored calls from fellow passengers to shush.

Terri wanted to shout, "Your baby is two! She doesn't know that word." Terri revised her estimation. She detested this type of mother.

The little girl's response was inaudible.

Horace cleared his throat. "Mars is angled the same as Earth, only much more distant from the Sun. That's why you have to wait for Mars' double-length summer to hold a Winter Olympics. It is now twelve degrees Fahrenheit with an expected high of thirty. It's much colder on the slopes, and the temperature everywhere will drop a hundred degrees at dark."

Ms. Pouty shouted, "I don't believe you. I'm not going to listen." Covering her ears, she brayed, " Nyah, nah, nah, nah, nahhh." Then everyone fell silent for a few moments, disbelieving that the juvenile woman could be oblivious to the disruption she caused.

Terri could hear the rover's tractor belt churn through the snow. They passed umber barbs of thistle and octillo touched with faded green, and a sign that reminded them to "PLUG INTO THE SCENT INTERFACE TO GET THE FULL EFFECT." Horace spun the big wheel toward the Village.

Someone said, "Can we throw her off the bus? Or under it?"

Cruel as it was, everyone laughed, including Terri. Ms. Pouty looked perturbed.

Brisini stepped in with the confidence of a great entertainer. He waggled his versatile eyebrows at the two-year-old, told her to be good, and she let him take her down from the pole. He put the girl back in her mother's arms, but not without a warning waggle for mom.

Terri led a collective "thank you," and received a welcome waggle in return. Ms. Pouty didn't say a word.

Terri had a fanciful premonition that the rest of the tour would be more eventful rather than less. When they visited the outdoor gardens with experiments in mosses, liverwort, and lichen she feared that mutant springtails and mites would launch a mini-attack against the meddling humans. When they crossed a deep trench with water flowing under a clear shield, Horace describing the dam, she thought it would surely burst.

But she found it hard to keep her mind on the tour when it became clear that the Olympic Village itself was the only attraction that Big Orange Tours was willing to show. The snow, air, and ozone factories that fascinated her, as well as the outlying areas, were off limits to civilians. There was also high security at the recycling plants, and the greenhouse complex, which you could only glimpse from outside the tinted domes. She had stopped off there the day before and tried to get a close peek through the polarized wall before a caretaker came along to drive her away.

As an Inspector Trainee with the Environmental Protection Agency with so much to learn, she felt more than a little disappointed. In three more months, her badge would take her any place she wanted to go.

As Ms. Pouty and her baby launched into a fierce staring contest, Terri sat back and let herself think about the future. Her new job would be purposeful, preserving human life and the biodiversity that supported it. Others found meaning by becoming doctors in Latvia or fighting for human rights in Tibet. Terri had a calling born out of a need to preserve order in a chaotic world, the entire realm of human existence. There was no point in being a candleholder if the whole column of wax melted on top of you.

So many athletes failed to plan a life after Olympic competition, much less to plan for something important. They forgot that an Olympic athlete's life consisted of two parts: Before and After. The singular focus required to win pretty much dictated that attitude. Everything you experience as an Olympic athlete builds up to a single moment where you do what you're trained for, and then drop into a slot—Gold, Silver, Bronze, or Nothing.

On the way, the only certainty is that practice comes before everything. The phase following competition—what you expect to be the greater part of your life—is shrouded in complete mystery. You don't know your potential for any career outside of sports. Any doubts, any hedging of your bets in the Before phase can undermine the entire effort. So Terri divided her mind into two parts, one bent on physical achievement, one racing toward the future. Now and again her confidence would slip despite the theoretical advantage that came from having a purpose. The truth was that like everyone else she too was rooted in the Before. In two weeks the Games would be over and she would be struggling to fill the void.

For discipline's sake, she had to come back to the skating. Two weeks seemed like a lifetime away, or someone else's life. Skating was here and now. The skating and the anticipation and the expectation. The power and the demand for precision.

Terri had trained with her father through the years, catching his approving smile only from the corner of her eye. He pretended to be stern and unyielding all the time, but they both understood.

This time she faced it on her own. This barrel-chested ox, her inspiration, was coughing up blood when she left home, a smaller version of the man who had reared her. He insisted that she must go ahead without him; he could see her glory on television. But how could she see the look on his face when she won or feel his comforting arms around her if she lost?

Terri Finney, the pride of Thunder Bay, only noticed when she was the pride of her father. A tiny pair of ice skates was the present he gave her at the age of four. She couldn't remember a time when she could walk but not skate. It became a road map to his heart. When she tore her ligaments in practice her father worked a second job to pay for a physical therapist. He learned all he could about the treatments, and helped nurse her back to top form. He promised that she would come out of it better than new, no less. Skating was the thing she must do for herself, he reminded her, the reason she would find the strength.

She brushed her wet cheeks and took a deep breath that lifted her sagging shoulders. In a way, she didn't actually think the old ox could die. He was a war veteran in the most useless of wars, as he always reminded everyone. She preferred to pretend he stayed home out of stubbornness. She urged him to come, told him it wouldn't be the same without him there. And of course her mom had to stay home with him. They had debated the subject for weeks but he made his decision and he had just enough strength to stand by it. Her most enduring fear was that he wouldn't be there when she got back.

Terri never expected fate to put her in this position. She thought she was going to Trondheim, Norway, a place that was actually prepared for an Olympics. No one would believe the new venue could work until they actually pulled off a success. If they did, Mars would make a mint while the athletes got short changed. If it had been any place on Earth her father would have dragged himself out no matter what his condition. "Even Ontario isn't as cold as Mars," he had said. "That's the wrong place for me to die."

Times like this hit her with a cascade of recollections of those who had passed during her lifetime and the regrets she associated with them. The most painful was her great grandfather, who she first remembered meeting when she was seven years to his ninety-seven.

With a sudden irrational insistence that he had one week to live, he had checked out of his nursing home in Toronto, hoping to spend his final hours with his relatives in busy Thunder Bay. So he came to join them, a stranger to her in the small house. Terri at that age was highly suspicious of new relatives turning up, especially one going from non-existent to omnipresent, one so odd, so impossibly old. To think that her mother had a living grandfather with her own grandpa already gone, strained her imagination. To her, family meant someone that you knew all your life. People didn't just appear from nowhere did they? The idea that the little man she met could own that mystical relationship with her mother was the kind of nasty make-believe that put monsters in your closet.

He was thin and strong like a rail stood erect in dark, baggy clothes. She remembered white stubble on soft skin, watery gray eyes, and resilient muscles of knotted iron exposed daily in white tank tops. He was also the shortest adult she had ever seen, the height of a kid. What deception he carried to be so old and young at the same time! No wheelchair, no cane, no shortness of breath like her grandma, his claims of mortality seemed incredible, unworthy. She sensed such a feeling even among the grown-ups. If they didn't believe him, why should she?

Each day he grew more intense, maybe even stronger, and insinuated himself into the family, resuming a role Terri had never witnessed in the first place. But the frightening part was that he began each day before shaving with arms extended asking Terri for a kiss. "Kiss, kiss, kiss, give me a kiss, sweetheart," he said, using the same words every time from deep in his quavering throat. The first two days it sounded like a question, in the middle of the week, a petition, by the end of his stay, a prayer. She would approach, come near, see the wet eyes, smell the foul breath on red lips, hear him plead at her hesitation. She would inch closer through the ninety year gap between them, teeter on the brink of decision, and then run like he was a beast, a pretender for her love already parceled out among the relatives she was born among.

He had no other requests, spoke no other words, had no other chance, understood no other way. A liar, Terri decided. If she had her way she would unmask the imposter and throw him in the street. The strange, invincible little man could not be planning anything good.

Like a light bulb, he glowed more brilliantly than ever just before the end. In little over one week, very much as he said, they put him into the ground to trouble her no more.

He had done no harm, left nothing of himself but a razor and a comb. She tried to remember his name and realized she didn't know it, had rejected it along with its owner. Shocked and empty, she had glimpsed an ancestor like an apparition, a generation offered to her and lost through neglect.

After that she fed herself a steady diet of shame made potent when the tearful years after the event were so much more than the hazy life that preceded it, and the mind of an adult could pass judgment on the child she was. Her rebuke must have killed him, she often thought with the same irrationality that she once ascribed to his decision to come home. She couldn't have been more wrong in her actions or more wicked. The image of him with arms extended, lips red under pale skin perpetually waiting for that kiss, was the one that haunted her still.

Horace interrupted her sad thoughts with a heavy foot on the brake, sending his guests rocking forward against their seat belts. Terri started when she saw barren Mars encircling her instead of bustling Thunder Bay. The tour guide pulled the rover to the side of the road by a display of shovels in the ground and antique exploration equipment. He placed his conductor's hat over his heart and called for, "a moment of silence for the explorers and settlers that gave their lives for this land."

A sign outside urged, "PLUG IN NOW AND GET THE FULL EFFECT. ONLY ONE HUNDRED CREDITS."

Terri stole the time to pray for her father and her great grandfather. Damn the settlers and the separation they brought her.

Despite the fact that she was out in the company of strangers, she drifted off to gentle sleep filled with dreams of abundant fresh air without the aid of a nitrox tank or a filter mask, her father smiling openly.

By the time the tour rumbled back toward the kiosk, Terri's nap was over, her mind clear. Like the sky when dark clouds passed there was nothing left. Ms. Pouty and company were gone, probably having escaped the pitchfork mob at a rest stop.

Terri substituted her shadowy thoughts for ones of her boyfriend, Yves, and the renewal that came with the first twinges of caring, making a place for someone new in your heart.

She saw his pale, wind worn face with the dimples that popped in and out as he spoke. She wondered if she would have a chance to spend some time with the skier if he ever paused in his practice. She had been seeing a lot of him in the past few weeks, as much as their schedules allowed. He was good boyfriend material. He was a little stubborn and single minded, and he didn't know much about ecology. But she could teach him. And if it didn't work out with Yves, there was always good old Horace The Tour Guide.

The passengers heard a squeal followed by the scrape of metal on metal, slivers of machine flesh torn and gnashed with an inhuman scream. Terri's small hairs stood on end, bringing a warm flush against chilled blood. Brisini looked a little green, the motion of his face stilled. His students gasped. The rover lurched to a halt, tripping on its undercarriage just a meter short of its station. The engine whined and sighed, then faded out like it was finished forever.

"Heh, lucky we got back." Their host had already switched off the public address speaker so he had to shout. "I said: Lucky we got back." Horace smiled, a thin cover for his embarrassment. "Nothing to worry about folks. Just a little Martian pixie dust in the gears."

* * *

Red dust formed swirling clouds along the busy dirt path. They must be saving precious concrete pavement for more critical areas, thought Yves as he tested his angry boots on the inadequate surface.

Contrary to everything he had learned about the way he was supposed to behave as an athlete, he was still fuming about his confrontation with Nils Barkly. There was something about his encounter with the Martian that was more threatening than it appeared on the surface. He had seen this complex mixture of emotions in people before but he couldn't put a name to it now, couldn't quite identify Barkly's brand of fear-driven fury, or he didn't want to.

Yves planned to hit the noisy Martian markets for the rest of the day. His coach always said, "Whatever's got you by the throat, walk it off." That simple advice actually worked. Yves became absorbed in the marketplace with the wonder of a foreigner. The Martian village that settlers made their living in babbled along in striking contrast to the Olympic Village. The burlap tents, the volume of bickering and bargaining, the odor of donkeys carting merchandise, and the local residents milling around, made it seem like a trading post from some old movie.

Moving off the main road into the stalls, Yves decided to take a closer look at what the vendors were offering. Stacks of pottery formed a narrow path. There was some fine work here, much of it well painted and glazed. Was

Martian dirt suitable material to make clay pottery? He added it to the list of things to ask Terri.

Turning the corner to the next row, he spotted an oddly familiar sight in these strange surroundings. Lou, "The Cobra," Coburn focused his penetrating stare at the harmless knick-knacks. Cobra poked at the ones he was interested in and brushed aside others, making comments to anyone who would listen. It reminded Yves of the first time he saw him in the college bookshop and discovered he was in several of the same classes with the garrulous oddball.

A lean American skier with all-seeing eyes, Lou was the only real friend Yves had in the Olympic Village. He certainly knew him longer than the other team members even if they hadn't spoken very much for a period of time. They had drifted apart after Lou got a government job that he kept very quiet about. Top secret and all that jazz. In college, no subject had been out of bounds, so when Lou refused to talk, it put a strain on their friendship. That separation could not hold. Their mutual love for sports competition with both of them ending up qualifying for the Olympics, threw them back together and it felt like the old days.

Lou spotted Yves watching him. "Hey, I don't remember blowin' a dog whistle. What are you doin' here?"

"Hey ya lousy bum." They slapped hands right to left, and then reversed. Neither could remember the origin of that ritual, but it was a tradition.

"Hey, hey," said Lou. "What do you think of this one for Bar? You know what she likes." He held up a dark frog-faced figure sitting awkwardly on something Yves couldn't identify.

"I don't know, Cobra. Who could figure out a woman's taste?"

"You must have known something about her when you introduced us."

Yves remembered how he had told each of them that he knew the other for years when he set them up. It had to be done that way. Otherwise Lou and Barbara would never have agreed to meet on a blind date. Well, that wasn't exactly true. Barbara might have. Barbara Barrescuito was a go-along, get-along delicate doe of a girl—the perfect complement to Lou's personality. They called her Barbara Barracuda, one of those opposite labels, just for fun. Yves introduced the two nicknamed friends to each other because he wasn't compatible with her himself.

Yves preferred strong, active women. The more activities she was involved in, the sexier a woman got. Terri was the perfect example. Being on the U.S. team, Yves could get all the groupies he could ask for. Instead, he wanted someone who was unimpressed by his status because she had status of her own.

The Cobra and the Barracuda may have been the first blind date in history that worked out so well but Yves had predicted their union and he was happy to take credit for it. "To tell you the truth, Louis, she just told me she wanted to meet the skinny punk with the crew cut. I told her, 'If you can get him out of my room, he's all yours.'"

Lou shook his head and laughed. "You sonuvabitch. Just tell me what you think of this thing."

"I don't even know what it is."

"So much for the sensitive soul of a skier." He tossed frog face back on the rack. It tipped onto its side. The Martian shopkeeper, who didn't seem to be watching or listening or even awake up until then, ran up flailing his arms. "You pay for broken items," he said. "You're a very bad man."

Lou examined the wronged frog and saw that the thing hadn't even been chipped. Both men ignored the merchant and took his advice to move on.

They stayed on the main road, tracing back the path that Yves had just walked, an uncomfortable quiet settling between them.

Lou was not one that could go long in silence. He said, "Are you out here shopping for Terri?"

"No."

"Shopping for yourself?"

"No."

"So what brings you hence, Yves?"

"Nothing."

"Uh huh. What crawled up your Olympic-sized A-hole and died there?"

"Who says I'm in a bad mood?"

"When you start giving me short answers like 'No,' and 'Nothing,' I know something is awry in Loitteville."

Yves glanced at Lou and pressed his lips together. When he tried to frame an answer nothing came out.

Lou stopped. "I hope I'm not going to have to tie you to one of those horses and drag you through the streets before I find out what's on your mind."

Yves laughed. "It's nothing really. I had a run in with someone from the Martian Team."

"The marzipans, that figures. Nils Barkly, by any chance?"

"How did you know?"

"Everyone knows him. Those are the wages of being famously obnoxious."

"That's a relief. I thought it was just me that rubbed him the wrong way."

"If you think the Martians are antsy, the Norwegian athletes are hopping mad."

"At least their anger is not directed at us. They're fuming at the committee."

"To add insult to injury, the IOC won't let them do their traditional ice sculptures because the water is needed for snow." After a pause Coburn said, "I suppose Barkly said some things that hit home?"

"Close to home," Yves admitted.

"Ah yes. Wasn't it Yves Loitte who said, 'No one can own a mountain. You have to fight for your right to be there.'" Lou used his best stentorian tones.

"I said that before I found out there were mountains the size of countries."

"Yves, what do you say we get some lunch?"

"No thanks, I just want to wander around. I didn't expect to bump into anyone."

"That's too bad. I spotted this really authentic Martian joint with original Martian recipes. Or so they say. New gastrointestinal germs await you."

"Authentic, huh? Okay, why not."

The sign over the genuine Martian eatery declared it "Little Green New York." Their footsteps echoed. Yves looked around at vacant seats and the tacky green figures drawn as cartoons on the wallpaper. "Not a very popular part of New York, is it?"

"It's early," said Lou settling into a booth. "Check your local customs book. 'Marzipans pop on the feedbag approximately eighteen and-a-half minutes late on account of a half day's local time difference'," he said, looking up and tilting his head as if trying to recall the exact details of the fact he just invented. "Yeah, that's it."

"Hmm." Yves picked up the menu. "Look at that." They had the MARS MENU on one side and the more comforting EARTH MENU on the other. The MARS MENU featured such items as Extraterrestrial Delight and Human Stew. The illustrations were frightening.

Yves said, "I'm officially chickening out." He flipped back to EARTH MENU. The New York steak managed to look expensive, using the standard photo of a juicy grill-marked sirloin with garnishes. Like the culinary equivalent of the family picture that comes with a wallet. "And I bet it's an ordinary hamburger," he finished his thought aloud. "I would kill for a pecan pie."

"Hey, what are you two doing over there?" The disheveled waitress carried a cook's spatula and brandished it threateningly. "Oh, look what you made me do," she said when some grease flicked off of it. She wiped both sides on her apron.

Yves frowned accusingly at his wiry friend.

"We came in for lunch," Lou offered.

"Dincha see the sign? 'WAIT TO BE SEATED,' it says. But you didn't wait. You trounced right on in. You Earth people got some manners on you."

"Uh, yeah. It looked empty. Do you want us to get up and come in again?"

They looked at each other and laughed.

"Matter of fact, I do. Them seats are reserved. Over here will do you fine." She showed them to a spot near the kitchen, and she just kept walking.

"Wait a second. Can you take our order?"

"No."

"Why not?"

"It's not my table." She disappeared into the back.

They looked at each other. "Lou, let's get out of here."

"No. It's the same all over. The Martians just have to get used to us. Besides, you know you can't stomach that cafeteria food they serve in the Village."

They ended up staying and waiting over an hour for the food to come. The New York steak turned out to be a bad hamburger as Yves suspected. The meat appeared to have a lizard's footprint on it. The Cobra gave his endorsement with a cheerful thumb's up. "Yessir, that's a lizard's footprint, you lucky devil. Green Gekko, I'd say. Probably strolled over it to get to a juicy cockroach."

"I'm lucky I ran into you today."

"Oh I'd say you are. Hey, speaking of Greenies, what's happening with that girlfriend of yours?"

Yves put down his fork. "Terri?"

"That's right. Terri, who-knows-what-she's-talking-about, Terri. Are you gonna give her a break or what?"

"She told you about our different points of view? It's nothing."

"Why aren't you with her right now?"

"Terri and I are very close. We're just sharing a disagreement at the moment. What are you looking at me like that for Cobra? You agree with her that it's not time to have an Olympics on Mars?"

"Yves, I have to talk to you." Lou pushed his plate aside. "Terri knows what she's talking about."

Something in his tone made Yves looked directly at him. Lou Coburn had suddenly turned very serious. "What are you getting at, Lou?"

He lowered his voice. "Two or three decades ago, no one could find the money to send expeditions to Mars. It couldn't be done cheaply and Congress couldn't see the short-term benefits. Our generation was born with zero expectation of seeing Mars in our lifetimes, let alone living there."

Yves said, "We learned that in class. That was before our scientists sent the automated fuel factory ahead of the manned launches so that outbound ships from Earth weren't saddled with the weight of fuel for the return trip."

"*In situ* propellant production, Brisini called it. Yes, that made manned visits affordable, but we needed much more than that"

"Right," said Yves. "Advancements in physics that changed the whole ball game. Don't ask me to explain it. I never could." He went back to chewing.

"And we implemented it so fast? Yves, American scientists found a way to process vast amounts of oxygen and water that weren't here in a useful form before. We had advances in power generation that were completely unpredicted in that time frame. Before the Olympic decision, scientists claimed we were at least thirty years away from the technology we're using today. Doesn't it strike you as strange that it's only 2038 and we have a city that's ready to host the Olympic Games? I'll tell you what happened. We're talking about doomsday economics. The former Soviet Bloc countries in the Mid-Nineties faced a situation where seventy five percent of their surface water was undrinkable and thirty percent of their food contaminated.

By 1994, Poland was so polluted that they had to train their athletes elsewhere.

"Meanwhile, Russia still had Chernobyl-style plants in operation or scheduled to go back online to shore up their economy. Six of their reactors partially melted. Not vented the way our Three Mile Island did. Nearby, concentrated levels of ultra-toxic Strontium 90 were four hundred times normal. Many other reactors were in populated areas close to Western Europe. Life expectancy for men in the former Republics went down to age fifty-nine. Japan in 2011 had six reactors of their own on an earthquake fault. You know what happened when that earthquake triggered a tsunami. Not to mention everyone's leaking nuke subs that crashed."

"How did the industrialized nations let it happen?"

"In the old Soviet Bloc, their motto was production at all costs, and weapons at all costs. By their definition, neither the Soviet State nor the post-Soviet state could pollute. China's biggest troubles came next when they went for Soviet style manufacturing. By 2000, it was panic time at the Earth Summit. Air, water, soil, forests and wildlife were worse off than before the Montreal Accords."

"Which was what?"

"Forget about that. The whole world was in trouble. Wild pigs in Germany were still radioactive three decades after Chernobyl. When the U.S. had its next nuclear accident, and calculated the tens of trillions to control global warming, a mega-investment in Mars started to make a whole lot of sense."

Yves shook his head in disagreement. "We were destined to head for space."

"That's just my point. Everyone vaguely thought we were destined to go to Mars, but there was never a current value to it. You don't spend hundreds of billions in cash on a vision quest. Only when you stack it up against the fact there was not enough money in the whole world to stop coastal cities like New York from going into the sea does planet hopping begin to look like a bargain. California's Highway 1 already took a nosedive."

"Werner von Braun said we could have gone to Mars on 1959 technology."

"We were technologically ready to fling ourselves across space. It's vastly more difficult to terraform and settle the planet. We relied on a concept known as 'uninvented technology.'"

"Uninvented? That does sound pretty stupid."

"Think about plans like The Human Genome Project and the Strategic Defense Initiative. They were conceived and budgeted under the blind concept that we could arrange anything we wanted because future tech would catch up with us. One had mixed results. The other didn't work at all."

Yves had never seen Lou looking so urgent. He didn't like it. "You and I weren't born at the turn of the century. I have to think it's been sorted out at this point."

"Yves, everyone has some idea of why we came to Mars in the first place. Not everyone knows why an Olympics here is so urgent right now."

"The first colonization movement sort of fizzled, right? It didn't meet expectations. So I guess they're trying to beef it up again."

"It's reasonable for them to try again. The Olympics will force things along much faster. The problem is the price of how they pushed it through and what happens next. It's being run by the Pentagon's Advanced Research

Projects Agency as a matter of national security. That's serious business."

"Is that who you work for?"

"No comment."

"I'm not going to ask where you're getting your information then, but I thought corporate sponsors were running the Olympics."

Lou shook his head sadly. He leaned close and spoke even softer. "They are and they aren't. I've seen the files because I've worked on these projects."

"Wait a second. Are you sure you should be telling me this?"

"So far everything I've given you are things you could have dug up yourself given the time." He stopped to take a drink and casually glance around for the waitress. Her lackadaisical attitude pretty much guaranteed them privacy. "I can tell you that government, private, and university money from every major industrialized nation went pouring into research. The terraform experiments to make Mars habitable took on a war-time urgency. Anyone who got in the way of a Mars project never worked again. We're still in the middle of it right now. Every dollar we have is on Mars."

"That sounds like a good thing. The planet is being developed isn't it?"

"Yves, it's the ultimate risk. Worse than that. These dollars aren't going into fixing the problems on Earth. Mars can't be changed fast enough. And there's not enough time between Creation and Eternity to shuttle everyone and future generations to the new planet. I can picture some elite group leaving the bulk of the population behind on a dying Earth while the fortunate escape to a relative paradise, blowing up the bridge behind them. There are ways to achieve that. Just think about it, Yves."

Yves thought about it. But he thought more about the thrill of the Martian slopes and how they beckoned to him every moment he was away. What could he do about politics except wring his hands? Selfish as it seemed, Yves happened to be one of those people Lou mentioned who never thought he was going to have this opportunity in his lifetime. At least not while he was still young and strong. It just seemed unlikely that the government didn't have a better plan than the one Lou was envisioning. Olympia was the next Plymouth Rock. The first generations would be rich, but there should be plenty left.

"It seems to me that the more people they ship to Mars, the less strained Earth's resources become," Yves reasoned.

"That's true enough if you don't count the fuel and shipbuilding costs. But if you net out the number of births versus the number of deaths on Earth, you find that there are one hundred twenty million more people on Earth each and every year."

"No way to make a dent in that."

"Yes, and that's not even the worst part."

"What is?"

"There are other things going on here. Things that even I don't know about."

CHAPTER 14
Point Of Entry

DR. TRAVIS ZILJIAN, as Valdeen called himself for now, rode the last leg of his journey to Mars on the Akagi Shuttle, comforting himself with the thought that many first-time would-be terrorists were not on anyone's Terrorist Watch List. That included him. He used the added cover of being the replacement for the U.S. ski team's doctor.

The shuttle made a smooth transformation from space vehicle to planet-bound airplane, experiencing no more turbulence than a terrestrial flight. An easy landing was the least they could do for him. He hated any kind of traveling, let alone a trip that took months. It smacked of the incarceration he had suffered in earlier life.

When the shuttle changed functions, it settled into an even path, cruising at a lesser altitude than it would have on Earth since the cushion of air began in a lower place. The visual cues for this difference were hard to decipher since the land had an unfamiliarity and a sameness to it. Because of this, only a few passengers with the most delicate inner ears could guess how close they were to landing. Since there was always a traveler or two whose hobby it was to figure this out, the cabin buzzed with the news of their descent.

Valdeen anxiously peered through wispy cirrus clouds to the rocky orange obstacles below arranged in seemingly impossible variation. Here and there, almost imperceptibly, a patch of doomed green life, browned and withered at the edges, had been planted in open-air experiments. It would be a few minutes before any man-made objects were below them, even more before full-fledged outposts appeared.

Valdeen squirmed toward the dark of the interior cabin, lifting his knees in an arc to wedge his legs the other way. He was among men and women of science for the most part, callow ones at that. Acne was king on their neglected faces. Whelps who were actually comfortable in this flying snuff box. More than comfortable, in fact, they thought they were engaged in some kind of adventure. Some of them were even counting up the colors they saw on the ground the way kids play in the back seat of their parent's car.

Valdeen could recognize their smug, neurotic postures under any circumstances; engineers and botanists, radiologists and mathematicians, zoologists, astrobiologists, and worst of all, the social scientists. How disgusting did the human animal have to get? Except for himself, existing as he did on a different level, it looked like a damned nerd convention.

But they were receptacles of information if nothing else, he reminded himself with a mental sigh. With some effort, he admitted they held more than could be learned from the window. *It's time to be charming. Pull the cheeks, shrink the eyes, drop the mouth slightly, and you've got the classic smile.* Shielded by his new identity as Travis Ziljian and a serviceable expression, he turned to the man seated beside him. "You said your name was Medcamp. What is it that you plan to do here?"

Medcamp was a small man with thick, curly black hair that shined and sat still like laminated black paint. Young as he was, he wore the deep facial lines of a happy puppet carved into his dark complexion. Though his know-it-all grin broadened at the man who was taking an interest, his mouth still looked hinged.

No question seemed too abrupt for Medcamp, as though he had been waiting the entire Akagi leg of the journey for his seat partner to ask him something. "Not planning much, I'm afraid. I'm probably superfluous. You see, I'm a geochemist." The smile necessarily waned a bit as he spoke, but quickly spread across his face again when he finished, hinting that Medcamp fished for a license to say more.

Dopey nerd. "Yes, I know what that is. As a geochemist, you're an expert on what the Earth is made of. Can't you become an expert on what Mars is made of? I'm sure you don't have that much competition yet, a man as smart as yourself."

"This is what my employers are hoping, Dr. Ziljian. But you must understand, Mars presents a whole different set of problems. I'm a geochemical prospector to be exact. Some call me the miner's friend. I specialize in finding the minerals we need to stitch together our modern lives."

The miner's friend helping our modern lives. I hate him already. "They could use that kind of knowledge here," he offered pleasantly. Valdeen rubbed his cheeks to take inventory of his face. He had to insure that the friendly expression hadn't fallen off it. *High cheeks, parted lips, and narrowed eyes. Good.* Smiles that didn't include the eyes looked phony.

"I don't know if that kind of knowledge is accessible here," said Medcamp. "For instance, a basic technique of geochemistry is to take leaf and root samples at various locations to see what they contain. The plants will tend to soak up whatever metals are in the ground. If those metals turn out to be useful ones, we know that we found the place to dig and we build our industries around the spot. If a plant has not absorbed a mineral that interests us, then the mineral is either not present or is not likely to be near enough to the surface to make prospecting practical. So plants represent signposts. Very convenient. But what if each growth pattern is separated by several kilometers as it is here on Mars? Then you may have no plants to look at in your target area. No signposts."

Valdeen found himself genuinely interested in the answer. *The little puppet is telling me something. I hope that shit consuming grin doesn't crack his poor wooden face.* They almost didn't notice the gravity shift until a view of the ground below filled the window. The plane banked into a well-controlled left turn, leaving only the very squeamish alarmed. Valdeen glanced casually, and couldn't help but see the areas where huge cracks carved the desiccated soil into nearly-fossilized blocks. There wasn't any green in sight here, just as Medcamp described it. "I get the point," he conceded. "No plants."

"You, I might add, have a much easier job." Medcamp found room on his face to smile more broadly, showing that he meant no offense.

"How so?"

"I understand that you are a medical doctor for a certain athletic team. I take it you're in your sixties, so you have a great deal of experience in sports injuries. You'll be looking at people just like the ones you've always looked at. Some of them may even be your old patients transplanted here."

Valdeen frowned thoughtfully. This doctor business wasn't a good subject for him to get into since he knew so little, yet he didn't want to seem evasive either. "Actually I don't know what to expect. The differences between the two planets could easily cause—"

"Excuse me, you two." The man in front of them had twisted around in his seat. They both stopped talking to look at him. His blocky face looked familiar like someone Valdeen had seen on the news. It rounded at the edges like well-worn dice framed by silver hair cropped so short that it all stood at attention. He had a small chin that disappeared into his neck and the soft, loose skin around it. Valdeen noticed he wore an expensive suit, freshly cleaned or brand new, with a pointed handkerchief that matched his tie, and concluded that the man was not a scientist.

"Are we bothering you?" said Valdeen with a forced mild manner that belied the sarcasm. He was interrupted at a convenient time but resented the intrusion just the same.

"Not at all. I'm Congressman Jim Hrelcik from the United States." The overly groomed man let that sink in as he searched their faces for any impression he created. Valdeen recognized him, but would not give Hrelcik the satisfaction. He had noticed that the politician made a point of never saying Representative Jim Hrelcik, the customary title being less descriptive to the average man. If Hrelcik could have gotten away with it, he probably would have made "Senator Brandenberg's Congressional Watchdog" part of his name.

Valdeen said, "Yes. And?"

Hrelcik said, "I was wondering if you could tell me about the air on this planet. Where can it be found? Is it still poisonous? Is there enough of it? What have you people done to it?"

"I can answer that," Medcamp grinned, eager to field so many questions. "The first objective on Mars is air density and greenhouse gases so the engineers put mirrors in orbit over the South Pole to heat up and release the carbon dioxide there. Oxygen is something they've been pumping out from a number of stations for five years now. It's a long process to say the least. Meanwhile, there are strong bursts of air around the perimeter of the town that come up in jets. That keeps the air inside from escaping its boundaries before our experimental flora and fauna can get a lung full, so to speak. Whatever leaks fills the planet for our descendents."

"Hold the phone, here. Are you saying we can breathe on the surface, outside of the domes and the buildings?"

"As in stepping outside and taking off your helmet? No, I wouldn't recommend it for more than ten seconds at a time. Assuming you had enough air, and provided you chose a warm day between the hours of twelve and two, your exposed skin would need at least a four hundred strength sun block against the ultraviolet light that reaches us. Even then you're taking a high radiation count. If you came out on the wrong end of the eleven year sunspot cycle, one solar flare could poison you." He laughed briefly at the bitter truth of it.

"Sounds like the open space air is a lotta PR crap."

"It's the least practical part of everything that's being done here, if that's what you mean."

"Has open space breathing ever been achieved?"

"Within the town of Olympia there are permanent settlers who occasionally breathe outdoors if they're not doing anything strenuous. That behavior is not allowed, but they presume to know how to protect themselves. It's the low gravity, and lower demands on the body that makes breathing possible at all. And it takes a long time to adjust to the differences from Earth; the air produced seeps out quickly, so they've made it oxygen rich to compensate."

Valdeen listened quietly while Hrelcik scowled. "How rich in oxygen?" The congressman made his question sound like a challenge.

"Well, on Earth, air is approximately twenty one percent oxygen, and seventy eight percent nitrogen, which is useful as a buffer gas. The air mixture Mars Colony generates is closer to thirty one percent oxygen at this time, with a corresponding decrease in nitrogen. It's thickened out with existing carbon dioxide but still comes out thin. You would probably faint fairly quickly in an unwalled environment."

"Where are the Martians getting all that oxygen? Are they sucking the air out of Earth to stick it on Mars?"

Medcamp chuckled. "Oh no. They don't have to do that. Chiefly, they separate oxygen from domestic carbon dioxide. To supplement that source, forty percent of Mars' crust is composed of trapped oxygen. Even more so on the moons Phobos and Deimos. We need only unlock the element from the minerals it combines with."

"You get air from rocks? That sounds like quite a trick."

Medcamp was delighted. Between Ziljian and Hrelcik, he had found two such inquisitive people on the same flight. "Actually, that is exactly what happens. The process is conceptually simple. You could do it right on your own kitchen table with mercuric oxide. Aided by a Bunsen burner, of course. You heat up and melt out the mercury in one container, liberating pure oxygen, and recapture that oxygen by means of a tube. On Mars, we use a more efficient process because of the scale, but we can repeat that 'trick' with almost any material. It just takes a few trillion specialized bacteria and much bigger containers. And oh yes, someplace to dump the enormous volumes of slag." His short laugh sounded inappropriately mirthful.

Hrelcik said, "If you can't really breathe outdoors, and none of us will live to see a day when you can, why does Governor Arazine bother using up any oxygen outside of the shelter domes? And why the hell would anyone risk his life outside?"

"They are building for the future. The immediate effect is psychological. Makes everyone feel better."

Hrelcik narrowed his eyes and grunted in response. "Like I said before. PR fumes. Better not light a match to it."

"What brings a congressman to Mars, Mr. Hrelcik?" Valdeen's Travis Ziljian voice was guarded. He hadn't yet figured out how this new element would affect his plans, felt certain it wouldn't be in a positive way.

The seat belt sign flashed its compelling signal, leaving the question hanging while the passengers searched for their safety harnesses. Hrelcik found what he wanted, grappled the two ends and forced them to click. Medcamp discovered contentedly that he had never unbuckled the fastening and could leave things as they were.

Valdeen ignored the advisory and held very still waiting for the politician's answer.

"Fact finding," Hrelcik spit out when he had strapped in.

Valdeen snapped, "Well you found some facts now, didn't you?"

* * *

When Terri collected herself, she noticed that the teacher, Brisini, was gone as were his eager grad students and the rest of the passengers on the tour.

"Sorry about that small glitch, miss," Horace said in a polite effort to rouse her. "You were the last one on, I guess it only makes sense that you're the last one off." His red cheeks fairly popped.

"Did I look that bad?"

"Not bad at all, ma'am. I hope you'll still recommend us at Big Orange Tours."

"Could you direct me to the museum?"

"Yes, ma'am, it's that way."

"Thank you."

Following in the direction he was pointing, she could see the tail end of her group entering the museum entrance of the Flying Saucer Dome. So she wasn't so far behind.

The main exhibit just past the reception hall was the instrument capsule from an unmanned Soviet spacecraft that came hurtling down in the crater-pocked region of Phaethontis on December 2, 1971, nearly seventy years ago. It was an odd creature, about the size of the Viking lander, remarkably delicate looking with extensions labeled "multispectral scanner" and "thematic mapper" that would have been exposed to the elements. The high gain antenna was snapped in half, which probably explained why it didn't transmit very much data for the Soviet program in its day.

The little known craft was a lucky find. Lodged at forty-six degrees south latitude, the capsule was often covered by ice from the maximum winter limit of the southern polar cap, and so hidden from the curious. Now the southern cap had largely dissolved.

Here in the museum, its presence had somehow sparked a controversy between some of the visitors and a real live Russian, judging by his accent. Terri wondered at the rotund spectacle with his reckless beard of gray, around whom the lively discussion was raging. He brought to mind an image of a great planet with many small satellites.

Only a few people were actually participating in the cross fire so she quietly asked one of the hangers-on, "Who is that?"

"The astronomer, Andrey Mirovich," the man answered harshly. "If you don't mind, I'm trying to listen."

One of the satellites, a man with sharp, sardonic features under an unconvincing black toupee was saying, "At your age, Mirovich, you spent your formative years under the Soviet Union and its lingering influence. You were young in the old days. So you must still be part communist, right?"

"What is your understanding of communism, Mr. Finch?"

"You're not allowed to make money and you work for the overthrow of capitalist countries. I mean, I don't blame you. You can't help how you were brought up. You're no threat now because you don't have the power to do anything."

Mirovich looked slightly amused. "Without attacking your scholarly definition of communism, I will say that your statement is as accurate as the source from which it comes."

Finch was irritated that Mirovich was trying to confuse him. "Are you saying you're not communist at all?"

"Popular fiction has every Russian citizen spouting off at every opportunity, perfectly versed in Karl Marx. To see that the myth holds weight even now is testimony to how often it was said."

"Can you stay on a subject? What is it your agenda?" Finch persisted.

"Russians want what everyone wants: to seek pleasure and avoid pain. I will not be defined by an accident of geography! I am human, you can get used to it."

"What guarantee do we have that someone like you won't act up over here?"

"Mr. Finch, you are proof of one thing: By repetition, we learn. Whether something is true or not, we learn it." Abruptly he stepped aside and broke through the wall of people with the weight of his body leading the way. Some stared after him with open mouths. The rest looked at each other and smirked.

Terri scrambled to catch up with him, not daring to speak until they were out of earshot of the people left behind. He didn't seem to notice her trotting at his side so she finally piped up. "You put that Finch in his place."

Mirovich was open and generous. "The Finches of the world do not need my help to find their place." He continued to stride away at the same remarkable pace, always energized, wagging a finger to go with his words.

"I'm impressed that you take the time to speak with a critic as unfair as he is."

The Russian laughed from deep in his chest. "Sometimes you speak to one for the benefit of many. When the Soviet Union fell, those who were socialists usually remained socialists. Those who were something else stayed that way too."

Although Mirovich advanced through the corridor at high speed, he didn't appear to be going anywhere in particular, passing obliviously through Zubrin Hall with the great holographic figures of the Martian Underground who made settlement possible. Terri thought he would stop and talk to her. She wasn't used to holding a conversation at this pace. So odd and captivating, nothing was conventional about him. She gathered that the astronomer functioned this way at all times. Not that the old gentleman was competition for Yves. He was, if she were to admit it, not only exceedingly wise but comfortingly fatherly.

* * *

Mirovich, who had an easily aroused sense of excitement about concepts and ideas, had gotten used to people becoming temporarily attached to him. Always ready to step into a fray, he had equally keen instincts about when he thought a conversation was over. "Hello" and "goodbye" were only lately and reluctantly creeping into his heavily accented vocabulary. Typically, he would startle people on the phone by hanging up as soon as matters were fully discussed, not waiting on niceties or ceremony. He didn't take names unless they were given and didn't ask Terri hers.

"I'm Terri Finney," she offered.

"You're an ice skater," he said loudly and with conviction.

"You must be guessing. I'm sure you haven't heard of me."

"You have the legs for it. I'm Andrey Mirovich."

"The astronomer," she said, forcing herself up a decibel to match him more closely.

"I guess I have the legs for it, too," he said with a broad smile that thrust aside the gray beard. Terri noticed that the gray was made up of very definite white and black bristles grown wild.

Laughing, she asked, "Who is Finch anyway?"

"A common spectator. He is wealthy and fat, though not in the way that I am fat. His is the fat of complacency, the poison of his bank account. He is one of the lunatics that wanted to transport the polar ice caps so that they could have iced tea." Mirovich was colorizing one of the radical proposals to deal swiftly with the water shortage.

"Iced tea?" Terri said. "They'd be more likely to get soda pop since the ice caps are mostly made out of frozen carbon dioxide, not water."

Mirovich laughed and nodded vehemently.

Then Terri added, "And, if you use the alternate method of drilling to the water table, you get the bonus of a great deal of heat."

"Very well put. Are you a scientist as well as a skater?" he asked seriously.

"I'm preparing for my job at the Environmental Protection Agency."

"Is this true?" he asked with excitement, pausing in his stride.

"Yes."

"In this area, we could very much use your help."

The last exhibit they passed before the exit door was a miniature scale model of the Akagi Shuttle, which bore the multi-colored Olympic Rings, coming in for a landing at Mercury Interplanetary Airport. Mirovich pictured a miniature terrorist represented inside. There was sure to be one sooner or later. The Olympic Village was painted behind it, rising in the background. They paused to read the inscription below:

> Delphi and Eleusis were only sanctuaries;
> Thermopylae immortalized the names of heroes;
> the Acropolis tells the story of a great city;
> but Olympia symbolizes an entire civilization, superior to cities, military heroes, and the ancient religions.

—BARON PIERRE DE COUBERTIN, *Statesman*

"Hmm," said Mirovich, "another quote rises in my mind: 'The great tragedy of Science is the slaying of a beautiful hypothesis by an ugly fact.' So said Thomas Huxley, Biologist."

* * *

After Mirovich, Finney, and most others vacated the freestanding museum building near closing time, the Flying Saucer Dome erupted. The fireball, exacerbated by the difference in internal and external air pressure, singed buildings one thousand meters distant. Small charges deftly placed were all that was necessary. Three were dead, twenty-eight injured.

* * *

"We have an exceptional situation here," said Guy Moncuso in response to Shelly Kastin's inquiry about the terrorist group Red Freedom. The number and quality of targets had gradually increased since she arrived, from the tiny storage shed at Outpost Eight to three roads leading to the spaceport that had to be quickly repaved with costly concrete after bombs made them impassable. Luckily no vital supplies or services had been cut off yet, which was either a testament to how well they were guarded, or the fact that the saboteurs weren't all that stupid. Or something as yet unexplainable. Studying these questions was Moncuso's full time occupation since he landed on Mars.

The squat sociologist fidgeted in his seat as he tried to explain his take on the day's events. He had the voice of a deep throated goose on its way to becoming a fog horn, belying his serious words. Knowing him as they did, he was immediately convincing both to Kastin and to her sober assistant, Zack Younger, who remained standing.

Governor Arazine, who turned out to be no help at all in preparing security in Olympia for the Games, was not present and not informed of this gathering in advance. Kastin debated whether or not she would later provide him with the minutes of the meeting. If he didn't find out and didn't ask, the answer would be "no."

Guy Moncuso, she noted, was well versed in his specialty, which included military history. "Separatists don't usually arise in such a short period of time," he declared. "Every revolution or attempted coup on Earth had some history behind it or was part of a series of retaliatory moves. Mars was settled recently. I would expect at least one generation to be native to the land before anything of this nature happens, this terrorist activity. So this short time frame for these events is one of the things that surprises me most."

"What can account for that difference?" Kastin wanted to know.

"Looking at it intellectually, I'd say it's a reflection of the runaway technological locomotive we've been riding for the last century and a half. The rate of change since the Industrial Revolution began in 1870 has been exponential. Future shock, which would tend to make people more conservative, has been damped down in recent decades by a society that is constantly speculating about the future as they find their situation rapidly changing. Speculating on the future allows you adjust to it more easily and accept change more readily whether it's for the better or worse. Books, movies, video and VR games normalize changes before they happen. Violence is expected to accompany the changes. On top of that, the distance from Earth to Mars could add substantially to the inhabitant's feelings of alienation. They can rapidly lose their identification with Earth's values."

"You said that the time frame is just one of the things that surprised you. Assuming first that your theory of change is correct, what else needs to be explained?"

"I'm not sure this apparent rebellion of ours can be explained. Not in the socioeconomic terms I'm used to. If I didn't know better, I'd think the entire thing was a fabrication."

"I assure you the movement is real and it is dangerous."

"I know it's real, yet it feels...manipulated."

"Stimulated by outsiders? That could help explain why it's happening so fast."

"Outside agitators and experts at least," he honked solidly.

"Who else is there?"

"I'd hate to be wrong about this, and I'm not sure yet. We have to treat it as real." Moncuso shook his head with confusion. "But to me, the way it's playing out seems contrived, like some kind of game. Are we such geniuses that Red Freedom can't make the slightest dent in our industries or our defense installations?"

"I was thinking the same thing. Maybe they don't want to hurt themselves that much. They would feel the impact of any major actions boomerang back on them."

"A good terrorist would be able to rationalize it, no matter how much damage he caused the people he was supposedly trying to help."

"Let's examine this process step by step," said Kastin. "How many people would you estimate are involved in the Red Freedom organization or share its sentiments?"

"Where there is terrorism involved in a civil insurrection context, it's usually because the malcontents are a small minority."

"Why is that?" asked Kastin.

"When there are a large enough number of people who feel oppressed, they can wage full scale war, a direct confrontation rather than little underground skirmishes."

"You're generalizing. That doesn't help me."

"You're right, of course. In our case here there are very few people altogether. Even if all of them were discontent, they would find it difficult to wage full-scale war against a well-armed opposition such as us. However, the law of averages and the inherent differences between people make it extremely unlikely that nearly everyone is part of a Red Freedom conspiracy. And if the number were more than, say, ten percent, they would act more boldly since they would have enough people or sympathizers to cover each other's actions."

"What's their weakness?"

"Leaders of such groups often overestimate how many sympathizers they actually inspire. Therefore Red Freedom may force a confrontation with us before they are ready."

Zack said, "Great. We don't find out their weakness until they attack."

Kastin said, "Zack is right. Keep working on that. What do you assess as their level of danger to us?"

"I'm guessing somewhere between a minor to intermediate threat. If they go unchecked, they can certainly shut down the Olympic Games."

"Worst case scenario?"

"Your guess is as--"

"Wrong answer, Mr. Moncuso. No matter where it leads, I need you to continue to draw preliminary conclusions from the information you have currently. Then I'll take those opinions for what they are."

"Well, if the terrorists manage to seize power, we will be in the unhappy position of trying to take control away from them. If your security forces are not imprisoned, they will at least become a disadvantaged minority themselves. Because of our isolation, and the delay in getting reinforcements, success for us will become exceedingly difficult."

Kastin shot a glance at Zack who was up on the balls of his feet. At the signal, he ended the meeting immediately, ushering Moncuso out the door so they could get to work on what they'd learned.

The military governor ordinarily wouldn't have called in a military sociologist, but under the circumstances, she found herself listening carefully to this one.

* * *

The Akagi Shuttle's wheels kissed Martian ground like an autumn leaf touches a river, and taxied to a gentle stop at Mercury Interplanetary Airport and Spaceport.

Valdeen tried to ensure he was in last group of arrivals, but the crew pushed him out along with his seat neighbors through the boarding rings that linked the shuttle with the terminal. Everyone bounced with a light step.

Intellectually, Valdeen was not surprised at finding the gravity at thirty-eight percent of what he lived with on Earth. He wasn't entirely unconditioned for it either. They had spent the better part of three months *en route* in a halfway house environment that ranged between Martian conditions and Earth conditions in every possible respect, which meant that they had given up a third of Earth's gravity already. Valdeen understood that his bone marrow would have gone into a kind of hibernation if he didn't give his muscles a workout that would at least mimic normal gravity values on earth. Some of his peers onboard had never exercised that much in their lives. But walking freely in a large open space and even less gravity was something else again. He had the uncanny feeling that he could walk straight off into the air if he wanted to.

The band of newcomers were herded through a detector for weapons of metal or plastic design, then past a pair of military police, one male, one female, ready to frisk them. Most of the passengers were so grateful to be on solid ground that they didn't mind the procedures at all. Medcamp showed his carved grin to everyone around him. Jim Hrelcik pushed ahead of the group like a battle commander leading a charge. Consequently he was the first one stopped, with a firm hand to his chest.

"Pardon me, sir, if you will stand still for a moment?"

"What do you think you're doing searching me? I'm a United States Congressman."

The MP couldn't help but smirk slightly at the reference to a nation on a different planet. He backed off swiftly when he was finished. And only when he was finished. "I'm sorry, sir. I'm following my orders." Hrelcik replied with a long icy stare.

Valdeen took the same treatment quietly, watching them search his person and his bags as easily as if it were someone else being prodded and poked. He had nothing to worry about. *To find a weapon you have to be able to recognize it. They won't.*

He ignored the man he identified as Peter Arazine, who was at the end of the line flashing his white teeth at one passenger after another. The politician's palm locked into theirs to make the desired impression. He had a few glib distracting words for each as they handed their passports and papers over to an assistant. The assistant perused the papers, ran them over a scanner, and machine stamped them.

When it came Valdeen's turn, he met Arazine with the languid motions of an ordinary jet lagged passenger who had no particular familiarity with the famous man, dipping his head perfunctorily and moving on as soon as he was allowed.

Hrelcik had stopped to speak with the governor as the line moved past them so that the arrivals could be helped into protective suits with nitrox tanks attached. Being a politician himself, Hrelcik didn't say anything until his fellow passengers had gone by. Valdeen doubled back to see if there was anything worth overhearing.

"Don't tell me that all of this security is for you, Petey," Hrelcik sneered. "With the size of your population, you're not much more than a glorified mayor. And not even that since Shelly Kastin came along."

"No," said Governor Arazine, ignoring the insult and sharing a nodding grin for anyone who glanced back. The group was being instructed in the use of nitrox for the fourth or fifth time. "The precautions aren't for me," he said through his brilliant teeth. "All of this security is for Mars."

CHAPTER 15
Management Support

ROLLY INGREM SET the plastic snack tray in front of his workstation and eased his natural born bulk gratefully into the large padded chair. Highly conscious of his comforts having been born with a bone structure that called for a great deal of flesh if not fat. The large chair was new, something the specialist had nabbed in his various one-man commando raids on unoccupied executive quarters. The execs got his regular-sized chair in return, and probably wouldn't even notice it for a long time in that maze of vacant rooms. The cool switch was one of dozens of tricks he routinely pulled for fun and profit. What heaven, to be alone in a room with a computer and food and the many free things he liberated.

When he wanted to see what a successful man looked like he gazed into the darkened computer screen and grinned at his silhouette of uncombed hair. Most often it was the only mirror he consulted so he kept it unlit when it was out of use rather than employ screen saver graphics that would deny him a reflection. Ingrem noticed in that image, as everyone else did, that his head was too massive even for his sizeable frame. "My head is so big because it's so full of government bullshit," he liked to say, regardless of whether or not people were around to hear his complaint. Shrugging at the thought, he rubbed his hands together, and gave the screen its life. Rolly Ingrem, Life Giver.

"Oh, I'm sorry," he said, smiling to the empty room. "Does anyone here want some of this tasty sustenance? No? Great. More for me, then."

Management Support Specialist was the best job Rolly Ingrem ever had, and Sub-level Three with all of its empty offices was the most hotshot place to work. Opportunity came when the project designers didn't get as many people over to Mars as they had hoped. Until Management Support was fully staffed, Ingrem had a good deal of discretion about the best way to utilize his hard working hours. In his opinion, frequent breaks were essential. Comfortable with the fact that he was an oversized kid, he realized he needed a lot more recreation time than most people, and also appreciated a quiet area where he could think out loud. They even let him pick his own shift: two p.m. to ten p.m. with a break at five o'clock for lunch. He kept close track of the time so he wasn't cheated.

Refreshments in place, everything looked right to him. Time to get started on the essentials. Of course, the jobs he granted himself weren't the same as what his supervisors thought were important. For one thing, he gave himself the chore of testing his private collection of antique video games to see which were the most enjoyable. Then he could pass them on to his coworkers in return for other small favors. Since some of the people he swapped favors with were managers, Ingrem figured it was all part of management support one way or another. So this was the task he would toil at for the rest of the afternoon. The computer wizard he knew himself to be was grossly talented, so too bad if other things had to wait. Those who disagreed with his sense of entitlement could eat a turd.

Ingrem dialed up "Thunder Gods," a re-creation of the outlawed gasoline-powered racers where the wheels were taller than the bodies of the cars.

Old programs were the best, he thought. And let's face it, the government does not use state of the art computers so you might as well go in for the classics when it comes to software. You can't even get this baby anymore.

He guessed that the manufacturer of the video game didn't want anyone to get too titillated about something you couldn't have, like a gas powered engine or a passenger space too small for the mandatory car pool. Not having the real thing wasn't something he minded. This version of the racing cars was realistic enough for him since players were expected to scientifically design their own cars and modify them based on experience. You were given no data on the success or failure of previously known designs, and you had to manipulate dozens of variables. So winning the race was not just a matter of steering. You were as responsible for the car as the original drivers were, and Thunder Gods determined the results from the choices you made.

Ingrem's fingers nimbly picked the arrangements for the configuration of the Thunder Track itself. He selected one of sixteen options, and previewed the layout. While he watched the graphic display and listened to the trumpet call for the racers to line up, he paused to snap open his drink and get the food sorted on the tray the way he liked it, beverage at the left hand, main course right, desert waiting at the back.

Now he needed the car itself. The four categories were Formula Ones, sports cars, stock cars, and dragsters. Because he was a man of élan, Ingrem went for the Formula One every time. From there he switched into custom mode and began with a few cosmetics. In a few quick strokes, he conjured a blue job with white stripes and a tall air foil wing in the back, something he added for fun, not knowing whether it really helped the speed or not. Satisfied with the look, he gave the chassis a series of horizontal supports, and chose to locate the engine in the rear, a 12-cylinder type with 48 valves. The bigger the better. "V" style rather than flat, chalk another victory for savoir faire over aerodynamics. He sized the wheels right up to the legal limit and made the tires from a composition he previously developed and saved, consisting of synthetic rubber with resistance resins, zinc oxide, and carbon black in a radial pattern--all intuitive choices from a long list the game provided. Finally, he christened the car Number 98 and had it roar up to the starting line.

His creation sat revving up alongside the cars that were selected and designed by the program. As Ingrem understood it, this wait simulated turbo charging, a procedure which injected high-pressure air into the engine before the race to increase performance. More realism for your buck.

The racers were belching out a prodigious amount of illegal black smoke, giving him great vicarious fun as he waited for the checkered flag to drop, when the screen interrupt flashed his homemade distress signal. His motoring pleasure vanished behind it.

"Shit." He had the computer set to alert him when he had already ignored two work orders and just got a third from the same source. It was four fifteen p.m. according to the alert. "Couldn't it wait 'till tomorrow?" he said uselessly.

The work order was from Harris Culpepper, the head of personnel. Apparently, the old man had been pinging since three fifteen. *Harris Culpepper sending three inquiries in one hour? What the hell could be so important coming from him?* Culpepper never struck Ingrem as a guy who cared if the bureaucratic wheels were in motion or not. He was too busy being a senior citizen and playing electronic shuffleboard. Rolly Ingrem stroked his beard as he poked up the specifics. The answer came dancing past his nose.

"Oh crap. Oh stinkin' crap." No wonder. This work order came routed through Culpepper as an intermediary for Security Chief Shelly Kastin.

Shelly Kastin, the *de facto* governor, they called her. With Arazine off on a drinking binge, she had carte blanche to run the whole planet. And you didn't keep her waiting. She was the I'll-rip-you-a-new-asshole type.

Her orders called for printouts of the passports with entry visas from the people who came to Olympia in the past week.

"Passports? Unbelievable." The Chief's request wasn't really time consuming. It simply wasn't worthwhile. It was a stupid way to squander Ingrem's energy since the new arrivals were already checked out before they left Earth. Chief Kastin, of course, wouldn't see it that way so it had to be done.

Meanwhile, there was no sense in wasting his game altogether. Ingrem spared a moment to request the outcome of the race based on his car design, his recorded level of ability, and other conditions imposed on the race in question. It only took four or five seconds to watch the last lap play out in super speed motion made slightly jerky by missing "picture frames."

The contest ended with a blast flash from his own car, which was skewing sideways in front of the others when disaster hit. An explanation hung in the frozen frame: TERMINAL OVERSTEER, NO SURVIVAL. That meant that the back end of his stylish Formula One tried to get ahead of the front end before he totally lost control.

"Killed. I hate that. I gotta go for a front engine or somehow get better traction next time. Yeah, right after the stupid passport thing."

Ingrem cleared out Thunder Gods and put the passports on screen, flipping them by one at a time. Sometimes it was a good idea to figure out why Kastin asked for something so Ingrem wanted to take a quick look at the documents himself before printing them out. After all, he was the one with specialized access to these files and he had to make sure he was digging out the right one. His automatic set up called for a speedy page-through at a rate that was comfortable for him to glance at.

"Yup, yup, and yup." It all looked fine. Nothing special, though. He poised his finger over the print key while the last items flew by.

"Wait, wait. What the hell was that?" The last item, which remained on the screen, listed a passenger named Travis Ziljian from Billings, Montana. The listing had no photograph. It displayed a blatantly empty square in the midst of text where the picture should have been.

"That can't be right." He paged away and then back only to find the same empty spot.

Where did that sucker go? he thought. It had to have a picture when this Ziljian guy landed because they wouldn't have let him debark without it. All the others had photographs right in that spot. Yet Ingrem saw that there was no image in front of him. He couldn't escape that. Could the original scan of the passports fail to electronically translate a photograph, a single photograph and none of the others? Very unlikely, and he would have to get hold of the hard copy passport itself to test that theory, which was not an option.

It was time to get his prodigious brain in gear. He wasn't used to having any serious problem when it came to computers. Something was wrong with the file and he didn't have a lot of leeway to fix it. Chief Kastin was going to be pissed if Rolly Ingrem didn't come up with an uncorrupted passport file. And doubly pissed because she was kept waiting an hour for something that he should have known was incomplete. This was technically part of his job.

First things first. The glitch might be easily fixed. He cleared out the file and called for the passports again. The process seemed to take longer on this shot, with the hard drive growling softly and the activity light flashing like a spinning gem before it spit something out. Good signs. He went straight to the end of the whole batch of records to check that last one. And nothing had changed.

This was bad.

Ingrem tried to modify the contrast in case the picture was present at a very low definition. The maximum contrast just made his eyes hurt. "What's wrong with this thing?"

With a few nibbles on the keys, he tried for enhancement and reconstruction. The program enlightened him with the following message: NO IMAGE PRESENT FOR RECONSTRUCTION OR ENHANCEMENT.

"Damn you." Normally, any room with a computer in it was filled with joy. Any room with several devices was paradise. Just a single one that wouldn't cooperate was hell.

"This just sucks." He was well versed in the procedures on what to do next. The manual dictated that he do a full trace and hunt down whoever had handled the corrupted file since it's creation. One of his coworkers had screwed it up somewhere along the line. Some lame keypunch jock was going to pay for giving him so much grunt work. But finding the culprit could be a ball buster. In the interim the finger of blame would rest unfairly on him.

The Management Support Specialist tilted his large head back in deep thought. If he really had to, he could start that tracing project later, sacrifice a little leisure time to get even. Meanwhile, there could be another way to go...

The phone rang on Line One, the high priority channel. Ingrem didn't need to pick up any receiver since it gave one ring and put the caller through on speaker. Sensors indicated the presence of the person being called so there was no use hooking the line to a voice mail to dodge the caller, and rigging any avoidance mechanism would lead to instant trouble.

Kastin didn't wait for him to say hello. "Ingrem, why can't Culpepper get in touch with you? Understand that you have a job to do or I'll get someone else to do it."

Even though the government never sprung for teleconference video, it still felt like the whip cracker was right there in the room with him when she spoke. Her message was rapid fire and clear, his post was at stake. It was no idle reference; Kastin's threats had a way of coming true, she would move him right out of there and into a real job.

Ingrem made up his mind just then. "There was some trouble Chief, but I've got it now."

"Any problem I should know about?"

He managed to sound just bored enough to be innocent, and just interested enough to be reassuring. "No problem at all. You'll have the whole file in five minutes." She cut off as soon as he said it.

Rolly Ingrem loosened his shirt collar by pulling out his tie. "That's right there's going to be no problem. Why didn't I think of this before?"

He hunted down a game program called "Master Detective." It wasn't on the hard drive so he had to find it on the shelf, and drum his fingers while it loaded in. Soon his hands were flying over the keyboard.

Top quality security measures prevented him from scanning a random photo into the passport file from outside of the system. The options in Master Detective, however, included a feature that allowed you to build or modify composite photos so you could share them with someone playing the game elsewhere. That person was shown a crime in progress and became the game's witness. Another player helped the witnesses create a model of the perpetrator based on their memory of the image on the screen. It was really a rip off of the same sketch program the cops and other authorities used in their routine operations, but it was great. Co-opting it for his purposes would be easy stuff.

Like the pretentious authors of the detective game, Ingrem believed himself a master of digital space. He could drain its secrets and lock others out at will. Smarter users than him believed that even an out-of-date machine like the one Ingrem took for granted had unfathomable idiosyncrasies that demanded respect. But no matter, these things were not at issue.

Ingrem dominated his computer and commanded its allegiance to himself. Suppressing any reverence he might have had as a child, he ascribed awe to the realm of the novice. He thanked the software when it cooperated in getting him out of hairy situations but convinced himself that he was just being gracious in his acknowledgements or indirectly thanking himself for being such a talent. After all, what did a machine do without instructions? Nothing.

When Ingrem saw that he had the right program up on the screen, he enlisted his own custom software to break into the program code that told the game how to function. Jumping the copy guard hurdles as well as any mental athlete, he searched out the sub-routine for building your own photo. When he found the right section, the anti-theft devices made it difficult to see where the necessary instructions began and ended. "You're not fooling me with that," he said.

He solved his problem by lifting the photo manipulation part and several lines of surrounding garbage that he could clean up afterward if necessary. Next, he grafted a copy of the photo sub-routine onto the passport program itself. A few small changes were necessary to fully integrate it, and there it was.

"Problem solved, I bet. Just in time for my five o'clock lunch break, too."

When he recalled the passport program, it now appeared to have the flexibility he needed to make changes. Once there, he combined several pictures from other visitors into a new face for the Travis Ziljian entry with very little discrimination in the parts he chose. He also had the option of building the picture from scratch, but as usual, his way was the quickest way. The last step was to match the skin tone of the various pieces, which he remembered to do. When he was finally done, Ingrem sat back in his sweat and smiled at his creation.

"What a freak." The ersatz Ziljian had a shock of white hair, deep sunken eyes and frail shoulders. It wasn't a pleasant face or one that you would want to study closely. Ingrem could find the right photo some other time if he felt like it. Then again, it was probably not a good idea to touch the file anymore, so maybe he wouldn't. Meanwhile, this picture would do nicely.

"Good. For all I know, that's exactly what the Ziljian dude looks like."

CHAPTER 16
Mirror

DEVON MARCH KEPT to a normal pace, giving the reluctant nod here and there to those who recognized him. Fewer and fewer people appeared, friend or stranger, as he jogged the ramps down to the lesser used levels where the lighting was dimmed to save resources. One foot in front of the other, and that sort of thing. Yes, nice to see you too. Keeping up appearances, as they say, not nervous at all. Three more steps and a turn. He looked and listened to the quiet passage before he continued to the peaceful corridors of Sub-Level Three, the part he thought of as the Red Freedom section, where he was very much in control.

The nosey buggers could mind their own business. No one had a reason to stare curiously after him as they seemed to be doing. As Corporation Counsel, March was perfectly entitled to be on the sub-level. He just didn't want people knowing precisely when. Or showing up uninvited when he went about his special work.

March ran the blind maze from memory in a route that included doubling back to see if anyone followed. He keyed one of several unmarked doors that bore an empty nameplate like the rest, and sealed it up again behind him, feeling safe in the unused chamber. The furniture was free from wear, layered in dust. March unzipped and peeled off his outdoor clothes. He raised his shoulders apprehensively when he heard frantic shuffling coming from behind an inside wall.

Kitty Honera popped out of an inner room to get a look at him. Her eyes were large with surprise and long lashes. Her hair was tamed back except for one uncooperative blonde lock that flopped forward decisively. "Is that you?"

March dumped his outdoor suit into a musty chair, raising dust like the basalt he tossed into the field of stones on his first trip with Arazine. "Yes, it's me. Who else were you expecting, the milkman? Have you got it done?"

"Partly." Her English accent remained much stronger than his even in the space of a single word. Or at least he thought so, and took comfort in it. She had a rough and common accent to begin with. As a result, he didn't trust her and his comfort was in knowing he couldn't trust her instead of wondering if that was so.

"What do you mean by saying, 'partly?' 'Partly' doesn't swab the admiral's poop deck, and we've plenty of poop around here. Ziljian's picture had better be out of that passport file, and the new photo in place."

"It's out and I'm getting to the rest."

"Getting to it? You're getting me agitated. The Akagi already landed at the airport. Ziljian's out strolling around like he hasn't a care. And Compton--"

"Who?"

"That's the cover name of our boss."

"Oh, right."

"Compton headed off Kastin. Went to greet and process the shuttle passengers by himself. He dealt with the passports so far. But those files will be forwarded to Kastin for review this evening." March checked his watch. 4:14 p.m., it read. "Look at the time."

"I know all that."

"So have you got his picture out?"

"I just said I got that part done, but you interrupted my work after that, didn't you?"

"Are you saying you didn't get the new picture inserted? You just left a blank hole in it?"

"I can't very well keep the bleedin' file open while I find out who's mucking about in the other room, can I? I didn't know that was you then."

"Right. Let's get back to it."

They moved hastily into the room with the terminal and Honera plopped down while March stood over her like a condor. He knew nothing useful about this computer system but he was damn well going to stay and keep his nose in it just the same. He had invested too much in this for her to get it all bunged up now.

Honera gave the keyboard a few expert clicks to return to her place, and watched. March smiled, comfortable to be supervising directly.

Her place in the file on view was restored only as a last image with explanatory text appearing below. Honera froze when the wrong words came across the screen. She sat back with her mouth open as though contemplating the unfairness of the world from its inception to this moment. She said, "Only a few seconds ago..."

"What's wrong? What's that?" March said in alarmed reaction to her posture.

"Someone's got hold of the Ziljian file."

"What do you mean, 'someone's got hold of the file'?"

"Take a look for yourself what it says: FILE IN USE."

"The Ziljian file with the passports in it?" He clutched at his hair.

"That's the same bloody file we're talkin' about, Devon."

"Pike, pike, not Devon! When we're working on this project I'm Pike and you're Penny. And the boss is Compton!" He pulled out a caffeine pill and swallowed it hard, without water.

"I don't think I fancy that tone of voice," Honera warned, folding her arms.

"You're not pressing any keys, Penny."

"And I won't be if you keep this up."

"Alright, fine, I'm sorry. I'm very calm now as you can see."

"Come up with some ideas then," she said.

"Alright now, for a start, who could be checking the file? It can't be Kastin yet. She's tied up at an official dinner with Arazine. I just spoke to him. Do you have any way to check who's gob-spit is all over this thing?"

"That bit should be easy for me."

"Good girl. Go to it."

She queried the computer about the user. It returned a string of code. "Yes," she said tersely.

She dipped into the drawer for the orange book with its classified listings, and began to thumb its soft pages.

"Did you actually get hold of the bugger's access code just then?"

"Not his access code. Only his user code. That's available so that you can find out who's using it, but you can't get on the computer and pretend to be that user yourself."

"I don't want to hear the theory. Just tell me who it is."

"I found it. His name is Rolly Ingrem. Kastin must have asked him to fetch a printout or something. He's a Specialist Second Rank in Management Support. That's not terribly important."

"It doesn't matter how important he was before he got his fingers in the pie. Anyone who gets hold of this information the way it is now could be deadly to us. Get the file away from this Rolly person right now. Just kill it if you have to. Just wipe it out. You can do that can't you?"

"No way."

"What do you mean 'no way'? You don't want to do it?"

"I mean I can't, Mr. Pike. It can't be done."

"You mean you don't know how. Can you work on the Ziljian file at the same time as this other guy is working on it? That should do the trick."

She looked at him like he was a dolt. "Nothing goes like that. I can't kill it or steal it away. If people could work on a file at the same time, it would be chaos. I can't do anything while he's got it."

"What can we do then, eh? If he sees the entry corrupted we could be blown. They'll track down whoever did that piece of work and that someone will turn out to be you. And the someone standing next to you will turn out to be me. They won't call us Penny and Pike at that point, they'll call us Jailbird and Life Sentence. You had better think of something fast." He reached for another pill.

"Wait a while," she said, stopping him cold. "There's one thing we can do. Watch this." She tapped the function keys and the passport file appeared with a blue box covering the bottom.

"What's that? It looks like the passport file. I thought you said we can't get to the file."

"We can't. It's a picture of what it looked like a moment ago. By successively updating the queue, we can watch what he's doing. Practically."

"Practically?"

"I mean, we can see the commands he uses just after he's done them."

March leaned forward. "All right now. That's something. At least we can see if our heads are on the chopping block." A bead of sweat ran off his forehead and onto her hand. "What's he up to now?"

She checked. "Damn, he must have noticed the picture missing." Honera pushed her hair back and it flopped forward again.

"How do you know?"

"He's isolated it twice. He must have had a reason."

"What will he do about it?"

She took a deep breath, clicked at the board, and watched the operator's command unfurl. "It's predictable. He's trying to find out if the picture's really there and won't show up on his screen."

"What now?"

She tapped the function keys in the same way as before and let the screen update. The previous command was there in the separate blue box, together with a new one. "Ooo, the guy works oh-so-fast."

"Don't sit there and admire him! What's he doing?"

"He's trying to boost the pixels every which way."

"Damn it, we're blown. He'll see it's no good."

"Wait." She repeated the procedure again and saw something unusual. "Now isn't that funny?"

"What? I don't like funny."

"That's very odd."

"What's odd, damn you? You can tell me, you know."

"He's left the program."

"Grab it!"

"I can't. He's got it locked into some kind of reserved mode."

"What's he doing? Did he give up?"

"I can't see until he comes back. If he comes back." Honera's screen was blank for a minute. She tried to break in while March wondered what he would be instructed to do about Ingrem. Would Valdeen or Arazine be able to do the right thing? Murder was an option. March was angry enough. He wouldn't be able to carry it out personally, but he could get it done.

The program was active again. March was alerted by Honera's excitement. "Something's different," she said. "He has a new set of commands."

"New in what way?"

Honera was busy figuring it out, gently shaking her head. "So that's it. He's imported a sub-routine."

"Why? Haven't we been through enough?"

"I don't know yet. It's nothing I've ever seen." She gave it a few more clicks and watched. Her pressure on the keys sounded to March like rats scuttling through marbles, a reckless sound of entropy heralding nothing but disaster. "I can't believe it," she said.

"Tell me!"

"I think—yes. He's replacing the missing snap with a bogus one just like...what I was about to do."

March gave her a blank stare. "I don't understand."

"I do. This is going to be easier than I thought," crowed Kitty Honera with a smile of relief. "Someone's doing my job for me."

* * *

After Mirovich moved on, and she heard the muffled backfire sound that local police assured her was nothing, Terri saw an interesting couple with a five or six year-old boy. Their golden sashes, proudly worn, identified the family as privileged citizens of Olympia, and suddenly she felt the urge to learn something about the lives of anyone who would travel so far to endure the hardships of the New World.

"What a handsome little boy. Was he born here?" she asked the parents, careful not to ask if the boy was a "Rusty."

"No, he came here with us in the last window, about a month ago."

Terri squatted down to speak to the child himself. "This kind of excitement must be very new to you, isn't it?"

"No," said the boy with certainty. She laughed and glanced up at his parents before trying again.

"I mean, you live on a very strange planet now, don't you?"

"No I don't."

"All that time on a spaceship, and now you breathe nitrox and play in the light gravity, isn't that something?"

"So what?"

"Isn't that odd?" she asked, straightening up.

The mother put a hand on the boy's shoulder, protectively. He shrugged it off. "Gustavo doesn't trust strangers," said the mother.

"I don't trust Third Orbits," Gustavo amended.

The father added quickly, "There's nothing odd about it, Miss—"

"Terri."

"Kids adjust very quickly. They aren't dolts like us, agonizing over everything."

"Look," said the boy, "there's the crazy giant man again."

"May I have your attention, may I have your undivided attention, please." A tight knot of suggestible people gathered around his compelling voice without reserve while some stayed at the fringes out of curiosity. Still others heard enough and stayed well back.

"My name is Travis Ziljian, the American Team doctor. If I could just have a moment of your time, I would like to speak to you about a matter that concerns us all. I was put upon to come to Mars as I'm sure many of you were. As much as we may be making the best of it and even enjoying the novelty for now, I'm sure you'll agree, the journey here was a matter of considerable inconvenience and expense. Those of you who are athletes had no choice and those of you who are spectators know that you paid too much. Am I right?"

There were murmurs of general agreement at the last statement. The new Martian settlers, including Gustavo and his parents, and the rest of the gold sash crowd angrily went on their way. Most of the small cluster stayed to hear more.

"You had to disrupt longstanding plans of going to Trondheim, leave many friends and loved ones at home, invest maybe a year-and-a-half in round trip travel time, and take substantial risks with your personal safety. Depending on the time of year, you could be as much as two hundred million miles from home on a planet experiencing mysterious explosions that the police sweep under the rug. It's shocking when you think about it.

"While we can no longer change the location of the Games, we can do the democratic thing and let our objections be heard and demonstrated so that the future of the Games will have a voice. I propose that we hold a candlelight vigil in the Olympic Stadium. My staff has worked hard to prepare. Listen for the announcement of when the demonstration will take place. I trust that none of you will disappoint us."

The assembly let out a small cheer of affirmation and Ziljian went on to work the next crowd, honing his sales pitch as he went. Mars in the first century, Terri thought, and everyone is holding court. Heretics, prophets, fools and sages alike. At least one of them is making sense.

* * *

"Not so fast, Penny," Devon March warned Kitty Honera. "What's he about? What's Ingrem's game?" His forehead was tighter, his skin a shade darker than usual after the close call they had with Ziljian's missing file photo. They had yet to get a look at the new picture Ingrem had inserted.

"He's a lazy bastard is all. Anyway, it doesn't matter anymore. There's nothing to be done for it," Honera replied quickly. She was still fiercely pecking at the terminal, glancing down at her fingers only when she had to.

"Why is that? What are you doing now?"

"Take a look right there. He's transmitting the passport file to Shelly Kastin right now." She pointed and he gave the screenful of digits a foggy look.

"Transmitting it? Why didn't the imbecile print it out and send it to her like she asked?"

"He's probably doing both."

"How do you know he's linked up to Kastin right now?"

"I've got her user code memorized. I recognized it in part of Ingrem's transmit command when he sent it over. It's all in my head."

"You amaze me sometimes."

"Thank you. Me mum always told me I was pretty smart."

"What's wrong with you, Penny? Don't you understand that we can't just leave things this way?"

"What's the difference? Ingrem did the same thing we were going to do, didn't he?"

"That's just the point. He did it and he knows what he did. He takes that knowledge with him as long as he lives."

"Maybe he's balmy. He doesn't care what he does."

"Maybe he's balmy and maybe he's a blackmailer."

"How would he know who to blackmail?"

"There's Travis Ziljian for starters."

"That's bollucks. How could you blackmail someone for having his passport photo screwed up in the computer and then changing it yourself like Ingrem just did? Who's to say that's Ziljian's fault?"

"Alright then, maybe not Ziljian. But even worse, Ingrem will trace down the person who changed it in the first place. Your size five kangaroos must be all over it."

"That's going to take him time. And my footprints are not all over it, thank you very much. I used someone else's access code and an out-of-use terminal. Never used the same codes or locations twice. Clever, right?"

March jumped up and started circling. "Ingrem ought to know better than to start with us. If blackmail's his game, he'll soon find out who he's dealing with. We're in too deep to let it go. This photo business was supposed to be a minor detail before you went and screwed it up. Now it's blackmail and...and...who knows where the cycle ends?"

Honera said, "I am not going to let you pin it on me. Don't forget who was the one interfering with my work. It would have gone perfectly well if you hadn't come barging in, stopping me in the middle. So anything that follows is your fault. I'll tell it that way to anyone who wants to know."

"No need for that, Penny. Accusations among ourselves aren't going to help anything. I wonder if we should confront the little bugger."

"Oh no. There's no use going to Rolly Ingrem and letting him know who we are and what we worry about." She smiled at March's dumbstruck look. "We don't have to be forced into any suspicious moves. It's his turn now. We'll just have to wait and see."

CHAPTER 17
Newcomers

JIM HRELCIK HADN'T bothered to unpack his meager belongings when he dropped the unusually light luggage off in his room. He was used to not bringing much with him and leaving the bags closed anyway, especially on his jaunts to visit Chang in Beijing. There were trips where he never unpacked. He just bought the things he needed along the way. Of course now he felt a pang of regret. This was Mars after all. *The shopping here could be more difficult than in China.*

He knew he would have to rush to the heliport after a stop at Kastin's office. That visit had turned out very brief. He hadn't seen her since a year earlier when she was getting ready to leave for Mars, and she wasn't happy to see him now, especially when he demanded a guided tour by air. He guessed that she would just as soon get rid of him by granting him anything he wanted, and he was right. She caved in to the surprise inspection.

Hrelcik took the continuous-run bus back to where the shuttle had landed, thinking about the things that Medcamp had told him about the air in Olympia, and checking the integrity of his Hybrid all the while. Once he arrived at Mercury Interplanetary, the attendants informed him the heliport he was looking for wasn't part of the spaceport complex, so he was in the wrong place. The transportation he sought was strictly non-commercial, in other words, military.

Hrelcik commandeered a patrol vehicle to take him the rest of the way. According to Kastin, he was supposed to find a pilot named Grove, who would show him around. Someone pointed to Grove out on the ready pad, the guy with the wide face and thin red hair.

* * *

Hal Grove was talking to one of the young athletes when the crazy old man trotted up and hotfooted like he couldn't wait.

Grove ignored him and said to the athlete. "So you're The Cobra, huh? What's that?"

"A nickname. You can call me Coburn, or Lou if you're more comfortable with that."

"I'm not comfortable with either one."

"Like I was saying, that's an amazing bird you have there."

"We don't call them birds."

"It's a fine piece of machinery then."

Why did he have to be so nosey? Grove wondered. Skiers should stay in the skiing zone or whatever they call it. Claims to know nothing and looks through me like he knows everything. Well I'm not going to tell him anything. He can get his kicks somewhere else.

"So why *do* they call you Cobra?" asked Grove. "What is it, like, no one can trust you? You're a snake? That's a good picture of a snake there on your jacket so I can believe it."

"Excuse me, Mr. Grove," Hrelcik interrupted.

"Excuse *me*, old man," said Grove. "I'm talking to someone."

"You don't seem to be doing anything important so I'd say you're done now."

"Who the hell are you?"

"They told me I could find you here. I'm Congressman Hrelcik." Lou Coburn took that opportunity to slip away quietly. Grove looked after him to make sure he wasn't actually going deeper into the restricted heliport area. When he was sure that Coburn was headed for the bus that led safely back to the non-resident quarters, Grove finally turned back to the new arrival who was already getting red in the face. He couldn't decide which of the two he disliked more, the Cobra or the fossil.

"Did you hear me, mister? I said, I'm Congressman Hrelcik."

"So?"

"Don't be impertinent. I'm here for a tour."

"The tourist center is over that a-way. Congressman."

"I'm here for an aerial tour in one of your choppers."

"It's not a chopper."

"Helicopter, whatever it is."

"This heliplane is not for tours."

"It is now. Get it prepped or anything you have to do."

Grove looked at him closely, up and down. "What are you, the oldest man on the planet? You must be eighty or something."

"Seventy two," Hrelcik corrected testily. "What's your point, son?"

"Nothing. I just didn't know they let someone travel to Mars at that age. It probably isn't safe for you. I'll have to get special clearance for you to fly and that will take some time. You'll probably want to wait back at the hotel, take a nice long nap until I can find out. That's if they let you up there at all."

"I go anywhere I want to go, young man, including up in that chopper of yours. Your name is Grove, isn't it? All I have to do is mention this incident to Chief Kastin and you'll be flying ferry service to the asteroid belt."

"Shelly Kastin sent you here? Why didn't you say so, captain? Let's get a move on."

Hal Grove subsisted in a world of scientists, celebrities and superiors, having to deal with them from his position as low man on the totem pole. If his way of dealing with it was to be an asshole, he felt that was the least he could do. Each day got more ridiculous than the last. He was already upset by the pampered celebrity who got curious about his unusual aircraft with its special booster rockets. What was the snake man going to do, add them to his skis? How does the guy expect to be called Cobra and be taken seriously at the same time?

Now he had a big fat congressman in his passenger seat as he lifted off the pad. And this one had big fat expectations. *Totally unscheduled,* Grove griped silently. *How do they expect me to do my job? This just stinks. I'm gonna stand up for myself someday.*

He wouldn't tell Coburn and he wouldn't tell Hrelcik or probably anyone else, but Grove privately called this particular heliplane the Calgary after his home city in Alberta. When he got into the Calgary he was usually alone and thought of it as his sovereign territory. He'd fly over the pines and the snow and multiply them in his mind until it looked like his familiar retreat. Any place was better than here. He still had his throne at the controls, so maybe he could ignore the old guy and enjoy the view.

Something made Grove glance over at his charge in the seat next to him. The man was unusually quiet. He had to admit that the senior geezer actually looked pretty energetic when they were standing on the ready pad. Now, as they took to the air, he looked queasy, definitely ill in three shades of gray, with his jaw going slack like he was going to keel over. *Great, now they're gonna say I killed him.*

* * *

The brochure from the shuttle kindly described the lobby in base camp as "cost effective" with no frills decorating, and high quality materials. Havislaw Valdeen accepted the decor as Post-Utilitarian, concluding that it was good enough for common areas as long as his own accommodations were better. Even Mars had to be divided between peasants and kings, human nature would support nothing less. He'd confirm that theory soon enough.

Blank-faced, he went through the whole arrival process as quietly as possible. His anonymity didn't last. When the American concierge noticed the badge that identified Travis Ziljian as a Team Doctor for the United States, the staff wouldn't hear of letting him carry his own bags. Even though bellboys were in short supply, one was promptly dispatched for him. Many yessir's later, they had him settled in with a basket of fresh fruit and a recent newspaper from his supposed hometown of Billings, Montana. A recent edition had been satellite faxed and reassembled with its original folds. Much cozier than an electronic edition.

Valdeen didn't hurry the bellboy out or prolong the feting by asking questions. He let it run its course with detached indifference and made sure to give an unmemorable tip at the end. That would give the kid nothing to be curious about and keep him from sniffing around, looking for excuses to get tipped again.

After the bellboy left, Valdeen came alive, stalking around the suite, first checking out his physician's quarters with pride, finding room to spare. He got a good deal taking over the team doctor vacancy left by Dr. Koutsaflakis. And damned nice of him to cooperate by dying.

Valdeen's total space consisted of a large apartment, attached to several areas comprising his waiting room and offices. The examination rooms came complete with the latest Robomed unit, which could be wheeled from one place to another. Wonder of wonders, it was American made. What a beauty, he thought. Dispenses medicine and gives advice without getting suspicious. The manual said it could even do some surgery! Precision down to fractions of a millimeter. That would really come in handy for someone who didn't know what he was doing. How hard could posing as a medical doctor be when you were starting out as a scientist? He tossed the Robomed manual onto his pillow for a little night reading and slipped into a Hybrid.

Governor Arazine's office in Town Hall was his next stop. Valdeen could visualize its location along Olympia's main street, right in the midst of avenues named Goddard, Korolev, Oberth, Tsander, Tsiolkovsky, and von Braun, the rocket scientists.

What he didn't expect was to find Town Hall still under construction, chunks of red soil gashed in one place and heaped up in another, warning flags papering the building itself. It troubled him in no small quantity. How much of the maps he studied for sabotage were proposed blueprints only? He would have to inspect the buildings inside and out to see how much strayed from the plans. Right now he was forced to enter Town Hall from the rear and detoured to the governor's temporary office.

"I wanted to introduce myself," said Valdeen to Arazine when he blew past the admin. He pretended not to notice her open mouth and Arazine waving her off in resignation. She stood by, vigilant.

Valdeen said, "I am the physician for the United States ski team, Dr. Travis Ziljian."

Arazine looked young for a governor, with his original hairline apparently intact, and creases of determination just beginning to take shape on his forehead. The wrinkles around his eyes seemed fresh. He was clearly a bit irritated by the man who dropped by. "Yes, Dr. Ziljian. What brings you to my office in the middle of a working day?"

"I wanted to find the person in charge." Valdeen took a seat across the desk.

"I met everyone at the spaceport."

"That was barely a reception. Less than I deserve."

"I'm busy. Get your ass out of here."

Valdeen rose to stare at the top of the governor's head and then hunkered down to eye level, leaving only six inches between them. "I came to meet the czar of the new world."

"I'm flattered," Arazine said cautiously, "but you must have a better reason than that. We're top heavy with people in charge around here. You don't work for me. Are you unhappy with your accommodations? Is that it? We can make some adjustments if necessary."

"There you go. Don't you find it so much nicer to be friendly? I was actually thinking of settling here on Mars after the games are over. I thought you would be the best person to talk to about that. I just want to make sure that Mars is under a firm hand. I hope to hear that it's controlled by yourself and not by that glorified IRS agent. What was her name? Shelly Kastin."

"I assure you we've got everything under control."

"By what method?"

"Let me put it this way: I've already got everything started in such a way that nothing can hold it back." He looked around, frowned, and finally decided what he was about to say was fairly harmless. He whispered, "Kastin thinks I sit around and drink myself into oblivion."

"I take it you don't?"

Arazine seemed a little disappointed and hurt. "No, I don't."

Valdeen relaxed. "Good. That's comforting to hear. Now tell me—what's going on outside?"

"The construction? We've learned a few things since the original sketches were drawn up. I assure you, it's nothing but improvements."

"Yours?"

"I have the blueprints."

The admin came in to make sure every was all right, and Arazine said, " It was very nice meeting you, Dr. Ziljian. May I call you Travis?"

"Yes, of course, Governor Arazine. I don't usually let people use my first name but you remind me of an old friend of mine who used it quite liberally. I hope we end up just as close."

Valdeen headed out into the corridor and promptly made an appointment with his second contact.

* * *

The pilot said, "I never gave a tour before. What do you expect me to do?... Uh, Congressman?" Grove beefed up the oxygen for his passenger as he waited for some response.

"Talk louder, Mister Grove." Hrelcik swallowed, still trying to get used to the motion of the heliplane. He didn't look well at all.

"I said, where do you want to go?"

"Take me to that outpost that got damaged by the bomb."

"What? The one from two years ago?"

"That's the one."

"There's nothing to see there. They must have gotten it cleaned up by now. What makes you think I know where it is?"

"Are you going to talk back to me or are you going to fly?"

"All right, whatever you say," he mumbled. "I'll get you there, Congressman."

Grove's Calgary leaned over and swung south, across the canals and roadways, past the boundaries of Olympia and into the rarified air where the heliplane's supplemental jets had to kick in to keep them aloft. The extra burst bounced them twenty feet higher before they evened out. By this mode of transport, it didn't take long to cover the distance.

Outpost Eight was indeed cleaned up, and it looked like one of the most important of the exploration posts, if not the most extensive. One impressive geodesic dome held the center like a soccer ball lodged in the sand. Beside it was a tiny airstrip and a number of smaller buildings clustered around in an "L." Several information gathering towers among them had support walls peppered with crescent shaped vents to limit storm damage. Solar arrays of every variety were arranged in two rows, filling in all available space in the paved area.

Abandoned for the duration of the Games, no workers toiled there. Two guards were permanently on patrol because of the original trouble from Red Freedom and the threats that came later. They recognized Grove's signal and allowed the heliplane to land on its special pad. Hrelcik stumbled out, happy to be on solid land again. The marker he sought was only steps away.

The old dedication plate in the ground, ruined by Red Freedom, had been replaced with a larger monument consisting of a brass plate set into an upright stone fixed in place by its own weight. The inscription, like so many things throughout the Olympic Games, was in Latin. It read, "*Non mihi, non tibi, sed nobis*," with it's English equivalent written just below, "Not for me, not for you, but for us."

The congressman was unconvinced about the message. He thought cynically, that the slogan ought to be, "For me and only for me," which he believed was everyone's motto.

Then Hrelcik noticed that the guardhouse door also had an inscription, obviously written by the guards themselves because it was done by hand on the back of a plastic food tray. *Cave canem*, was all it said, with no English equivalent below. Hrelcik recognized it to mean: Beware of the dog. He nodded sagely, those were sentiments he could understand.

"Are we about done?" said Grove, glancing at his watch as though he had another appointment. "Seen enough and ready to go home now? You don't look good."

"I can take it if you can, sonny boy. Take five if you have to. There's at least one more stop we need to make."

They lifted off on jet power bolstered by hubris to head still further South for a visit to the newest of the outposts with its construction in progress. Gaining altitude, Grove set the direction, which required a change in orientation from the way they had faced on the helipad. Those instructions engaged the lateral propeller for rotation.

In the gentle turn, an explosion ripped through the air and the heliplane spun in a corkscrew motion, out of control.

CHAPTER 18
Early Clashes

THIS WAS SUPPOSED to be Yves' first day of quiet contemplation, but things seemed to be getting more eventful rather than less. First there was his less-than-cordial encounter with Barkly, then Coburn weirded out on him with wild ideas about the poorest being abandoned on Earth for a less polluted Mars. Yves was glad the day was over and nothing else could happen.

Stashing away his valuable thermal outfit, Yves switched to indoor casual. Almost as an afterthought, he hit the news update button as he got ready to leave his room. The wall viewer showed a reporter's head the size of an Easter Island monument. "...down the last day before the opening ceremonies, the controversy surrounding this twenty eighth winter Olympic games threatens to overshadow the games themselves. Our experts say it is expected to be the most dangerous since the Munich games of 1972 where eleven athletes were murdered. A group of Martian separatists calling themselves Red Freedom have warned they will stop the proceedings at all costs. This channel recently learned that this is the same group that began sabotaging Martian outposts two years ago. The name of the terrorist group was previously withheld to deny them publicity. Olympians are advised..."

The viewer would shut itself off when it registered that he left the room. The news was troubling but the analysts had pretty much said the same things about terrorists at the last Olympics. If it was as bad as all that, they never would have allowed things to go ahead this year. There was too much at stake for security to be so poor. Anyway he wasn't a soldier or a diplomat. His job was to keep his mind on skiing.

As a rule, he tried not to watch or listen to news because there was sometimes a report that included him. The press liked to refer to Yves as "the underdog of underdogs," and lately, "the dark horse of the underdogs." Not exactly the animal references he preferred.

Letting the door lock behind him, Yves made his way to the lounge, and looked for an unoccupied biofeed pod as soon as he got there. The bios were extremely popular among the athletes as the best way to calm the nerves and re-live past glory. Psychotherapists called it "positive reinforcement." Yves preferred the way Lou put it: *Strapping on the ol' biofeedbag.*

More importantly, he had to unwind before Terri saw him in this condition. The trouble was that a few dates with someone or a few dozen couldn't clear up his innate nervousness about relationships. Although his athlete's build showed through his clothing, trim and healthy, almost speaking for him, he always had more anxiety talking to girls than he did plummeting down a steep chute of ice. His dimples, which showed up just about all the time, made him feel childish. When he put it all together, he couldn't imagine why Terri was interested in him.

The first time he saw her in training camp, his immediate impulse was to say: "You are so amazingly beautiful. I just needed to tell you that." But he managed not to say it. He didn't want her to think something was wrong with him.

When Yves arrived at the athlete's lounge, each bio displayed a pale blue light, warning others not to approach. Yves shrugged. He'd use the time for stretching.

The trickiest muscle of them all and the one most neglected was the adductor, the inner thigh. He stood with his legs a bit more than shoulder width apart, and shifted most of his weight to his right leg, bending it slightly so that his left extended outward to the side. Right away he felt the adductor on his left leg tighten, and held still before it went too far. Shifting his weight to his left leg, he repeated the action in reverse.

He couldn't picture Nils Barkly and the rest of the superhuman Martian Team having to stretch. They probably had the most cooperative hamstrings in the Universe. Many of them were reared in the Alps where skiing was still more highly revered than it was in the less active United States. The magic chain included countries like Italy, France, Austria and Switzerland.

Norway, with its separate set of mountains running throughout, was also a perennial favorite to medal. Basically, people who lived in and around mountains were most attuned to skiing. That was why America's best were usually those from places like Alaska, Colorado, Montana, Washington, and Vermont, and rarely, if ever, came out of Kansas or Florida.

When some of the people from high altitude European backgrounds moved to Mars, skiing remained a national obsession for them. In a recent interview, Yves' teammate,

Marc Turpin, referred to the Martians as "the newest and baddest members of the downhill mafia."

So the individual Martians who would win now were the ones who could best ignore the pressures of high expectations and overconfidence. And America, a country that had its share of skiing breakthroughs in the past, was back to shooting for top five, and certainly not cursed with high expectations.

A biofeed beckoned Yves with its blue light flashing so he hurried over and slipped into the padded seat. Time for a brain massage. The program activated a screen filled with jumping multicolored lines, gnarled and tracked like overworked snow. These colors and patterns represented the athlete's current state of mind. The lines sliced themselves into a rain of confetti, soft, fluttering and accumulating until the ounce scraps covered him in their collective tonnage. He swam up through the debris, determined not to let adversity bury him.

The American team's Underdog of Underdogs had trained a lifetime for his moment, which was not surprising to those who knew that hard work ran in his blood. His father had owned a trawler in the days before Louisiana crayfish turned scarce and their debts piled up. Then Jean Loitte heard about the new granite mine in the East. He packed up his family and fled to Vermont, an area that Jean's French pride found acceptable because it was first claimed by Champlain and settled by France. The move to Vermont was a necessity that the family never thought to question.

Within a few years, the old debts were settled and it seemed like Jean had been a granite miner all his life. That was when Yves had the luxury of turning his attention to the mountains. Part born athlete, part skiing technician, Yves grew into the sport as naturally as the human body follows its DNA blueprint to provide the average person with the number of fingers and toes their ancestor had. The Loitte clan always felt the touch of the land even if they never prospered financially. It stirred Yves' pride on any day he thought about it.

The lines on the screen swirled into a harmonious circular pattern as the Olympian drew into himself and began to focus on where his contentment could be found. Yves' skill in skiing came to him so easily that he always felt chosen for something. As the skier grew up, he claimed one local championship after another. He won a Junior Cup, and too many honors to count before he placed third in the World Cup in his best event. In the year after college, he hit the road, working at resorts, paying his way, hitchhiking from one famous skiing center to the other, right up until the time he had to leave for the Olympics. In doing so, he cut his teeth on every type of mountain on Earth so that he could be ready for anything.

Cooperating with the biofeed, Yves pictured a range called Killington with its six sprawling mountains and seventy miles of soaring trails. He was drawn forward, dreamily floating over the grand expanse. Having summoned this image within a biofeeder many times before, the high white spire of the peak came into focus more quickly each time. Floating as freely as a spirit, he traced Earth's backbone down to the lower elevations, past the frosty Skye Peak, a longer way to round-shouldered Bear Mountain, and finally to the gentler Sunrise Mountain where he found himself standing with his gear on a beginner's trail with crystal clear memory, feeling the way it felt then as though it were happening now. On firm ground, his muscles loosened and his nerves stopped jumping. The familiar sounds came flooding back, the fresh air cool against his cheek.

He was twelve years old on the day of his first race in 2030, gazing at a surface of snow undisturbed by wind, and overtopped by a sky of pure blue. In about ten minutes, Kimbell Welsh would plod in with his father in tow, and challenge Yves to a contest, one that young Loitte would win and win again in years to come.

When Yves reached bare handed into the picture, he could scarcely distinguish his life here as a kid from his distant presence in the biofeed in 2038, which was rapidly being forgotten by some dim version of himself. Crouching down, he scooped cold snow into his hand, watching it turn to clear crystal and water at the edges where it met his skin. He dipped in again and sifted the stuff around in soft, yielding circles while he waited for young Kimbell to make his appearance. With his knowledge of the far future slipping away, followed by his jettisoning of the near future, he began to wonder if Kimbell would show up, and why he thought so before. Winning his first race became a vague, prescient feeling.

In the next minute it didn't matter if the other boy arrived or not. Young Yves smiled as the wet powder clung to his fingers, happy to just be there, happy that his father agreed to go away and pick him up later. He didn't know then but would later learn that the snow on that day was what most skiers considered ideal.

At first, he couldn't interpret the shadow that fell across the biofeed console. It did not signal the approach of Kimball Walsh, but registered in Yves' reality as the sun disappearing behind a passing cloud. Then the cloud was arrested over the sun, fully obscuring it, refusing to pass.

"What fine powers of concentration Earthers have. Always in a daze."

Yves heard Barkly's voice as an alien thing, assaulting his place and time. The words were indistinct as if they wafted down from the cloud itself. Then a rough hand dug into his shoulder. Sunrise Mountain vanished instantly, jarringly. The individual lines on the screen returned, coalescing into a knotted ball of string, expressing his shock at the collision of realities. Yves spun in his seat and forced his eyes to focus on the intruder. "Barkly, you shit."

"Have I interrupted something?"

"You haven't accomplished anything. I was on my way out." The athlete hopped from the machine and tried to straighten up, but found himself reeling.

Barkly clapped a hand behind Yves neck, and wrapped his fingers tight. "Yes, go on. If you hurry, you can catch a flight before you make a jackass of yourself in the morning."

"This is what I should expect from one of Earth's rejects," Yves shot back, all thoughts of diplomacy banished. Everyone else in the room, secure in their biofeed environments, was oblivious to the encounter.

Barkly tried a punch and was surprised to find his blow blocked. The aggressor took a shot from Yves on the side of his head, then came up with a blunt object from behind his back. He caught Yves off guard and landed the object in the middle of Yves' face, slamming him to the ground, ready to strike another blow to make sure his competitor was done.

As he lost consciousness, Yves had just enough time to think: *This is going to make me miss the Games.*

* * *

Devon March entertained his secret guest in a restricted area that he had previously staked out and utilized on other rare occasions--Room SL3-25. Periodically he checked his watch because the timing had to be perfect. Earlier, he had obtained copies of the daily schedules so he could avoid the official meetings that sometimes took place in these fancy conference rooms. Those were the appointments people cleared with the custodial secretary when they did things through proper channels. March suffered the nagging thought that some people, like himself, don't follow protocol. Sure, he could pull rank if anyone showed up. He had the excuse that his own offices were unavailable to him due to construction, but what would they make of the indelicate Valdeen? Would the burly man allow himself to be pushed into a closet, and if not, would anyone sound an alarm?

After Valdeen stampeded in, both March and his guest tried to relax, the lawyer, as usual, having the harder time of it. He brought Valdeen to the conference room both to impress him and to keep him away from the general operations. Wisely, March took inventory of the room, and would do so again at the end of their *tête à tête* so he could leave things as he found them.

Aside from being private, these restricted areas had all the comforts of executive hedonism. Having sweetened the purses of the rich and famous in his profession, March had developed a taste for the good life, absorbed some of their whims, enjoying, not least, the large chairs, overstuffed inside actual leather. His overworked back end longed to linger in each of them in turn, and might have done so if Valdeen hadn't been present. All the chairs but one, that is. During his inventory check, he noticed with some annoyance that one of the chairs, smaller and simpler than the rest, had been substituted in as if someone had made off with the original of the set. Not that he would pursue it. He had enough problems.

March focused instead on the liquor cabinet that made his mouth water, with the other refreshments that he could just see through the wire mesh, right out of reach. Gobbled up and restocked once a week. Pity he couldn't help himself to anything but what he brought along. To him, SL3-25 was more of a picnic spot than anything else, strictly a bring-your-own affair. He didn't refrain from sharing the wealth for want of a key, he simply knew better. And right now he had better stop staring at that cabinet before he got Valdeen craving the forbidden fruits too.

March found Valdeen every bit as imposing as Arazine had described him. His snout alone could set a person on edge.

"Do you want some tea, Dr. Ziljian? I hope you do. It was awkward bringing it in here. I may not do it in future but I suppose it being our first meeting and all that, the added comfort might be a good idea."

"No, I'm fine thank you, Mr. Pike. Have I got that right—Pike? No first name?"

March poured tea for him anyway before he did his own cup, and he noticed Valdeen watching him too closely. "Yes, Pike will do nicely. How was your trip?"

"I hated every moment of it."

"Sorry. It's a pity you couldn't meet with Compton straight off. I've arranged for you to see him casually, later this evening. Out in the open for the first time round. Then other arrangements can be made." Compton was what the revolutionaries were calling Arazine. March hadn't been officially informed of the brief meeting Valdeen already had with the governor. There was no set plan for these details.

"That's an option," said Valdeen.

"An option? I would think you'd want to get started with Compton as soon as you could."

"Why should I? You're the man I want to see."

"Not me. You must have gotten it wrong," said March, immediately suspicious.

"No, you're the one."

"I'm not in charge."

Valdeen latched onto the Earl Gray and gave it a try, savoring a mouthful before he swallowed. "You're not in charge of the planet now maybe. But who knows?"

"What are you about?"

"This Compton of yours, he has very different ideas than you and I."

"Does he? You're both scientists. I'm not one. If anyone has something in common, it's you and he."

"You and I are visionaries. Compton..." He waved his hand at loose air.

"Go on," said March. "What's your theory about him?"

"My theory is that he's a scumbag."

March blew tea out of his nose, mopped it up in embarrassment. He looked down into his cup and then pushed it away.

"Wha...what do you mean by that?"

"Don't think that Compton is on our side. He doesn't have the same goals, and he makes his decisions on the fly."

"So you have been in close touch with him. I knew it. Talk to me."

"Compton is greedy. He ultimately wants to make money. Am I wrong about that?"

"I suppose he does. Who can blame him? You always have a profit motive."

Valdeen said, "You too?"

"It's a normal goal that I share with the rest of humanity."

"I don't think so. You're too smart for that."

"Too smart or not. That's the way it is."

"I'll take your word for it. You know yourself best." Valdeen walked over to the dark wood cabinets and peered through the mesh at the treasures inside. "Do you have something for a weary traveler? Besides the tea?"

"Nothing that we can touch. If the same people schedule a meeting here twice in a row, they could notice something missing. And that will get them checking."

"You're a very careful man. An anal retentive of the first order. Maybe that's a good thing."

"What is it you're after?"

"I'll tell you what I want." He was suddenly intense. "True autonomy for our adopted planet. Mars should never have become a colony run by outsiders. The failures of imperialism time and again should have taught us something. The furthest flung empires have always broken down at some point because the ideology of the mega-state is extinct. No one has the right to rule people's lives from a different orbit in the solar system any more than they do across the cultural boundaries of our first planet. World government never took hold on Earth and inter-world government certainly won't work now." He backed off and softened. "But that's just my opinion."

"Bullshit. You don't live here, you have no stake in it. You talk an impressive line, but you're saying all of that because you think it's my opinion. You know it's my opinion. Arazine's told you everything about me, hasn't he?"

Valdeen raised an eyebrow. "I want it because I know right from wrong. I can make it happen much sooner than later." He noticed March close his mouth tightly and shift his eyes subtly towards him. March could tell that his guest noticed, and looked away.

"What do you think of Compton as a person?" Valdeen asked.

March thought his answer through in earnest, this time stone faced, with half lidded eyes. "I think he's a little too happy, like a hyena." March drank some tea pensively. "I can't stand all that cheering squad rah rah stuff he spouts. I'd like to take a baseball bat, smash him in the head with it, and see if he still keeps on smiling. I bet he would."

Valdeen looked pleased. "Of course. That's exactly his problem. Too rah rah, as you say. Again, would you like to know my opinion on the subject?"

March said nothing, bit his tongue waiting for the answer. He almost forgot that he was timing their visit.

"If I were you, I'd like to see things move along much faster than they are with Compton guiding things. No more five year plans for something that should be happening now."

March thought about having Arazine's smug face out of the picture. With himself most senior, it would move him to the ultimate rank. His mouth went dry. "Can that be done?"

Valdeen nodded slowly. "Anything can be done. You're an interesting man, Pike. I'm glad we had this talk."

March glanced at his watch and regained his feet with a start. When Valdeen was gone, he cleaned up and left the room in pristine condition.

CHAPTER 19
Moves Of The Assassin

A DARK MOTE swam laps in Yves' watery eyes. He woke up on his back. Was it the next room? he wondered. It seemed like only a couple of seconds had passed since he was in the Biofeed Lounge trading blows with Barkly. He didn't remember hitting the floor.

His lip twitched, causing him a sharp pain behind his nose. The glare of white on white throughout the long, narrow room magnified his headache. The sanitized atmosphere told him he was in the Team Doctor's office. Sitting up too quickly, he fell back with a thud. "Ah-ah-ahhh," he said, wishing he could lose consciousness again.

* * *

Valdeen carefully turned out his patient's pockets on the other side of the room. The skier was in no condition to notice. It's a good idea to tiptoe through some identification once in a while, Ziljian decided, if only to see who your friends are. The arrival of Congressman Hrelcik made him wary of the increased scrutiny the Mars mission was getting. Now he worried about undercover agents, for there certainly had to be some on the planet.

Yves Loitte was the name his patient carried on him, which matched up with the name Valdeen was given when the two Good Samaritans dragged the body in. The only other items in the wallet were a picture of a young woman, the room number for someone named Lou Coburn, and a few universal credits.

"Your nose is not broken," said the doctor. "But I've just given you something for the pain. In a moment, you won't feel a thing."

"What time is it? What day is it?"

"You haven't missed anything. You've only been out for an hour."

"My whole head is numb. I think you loaded me up with that pain killer."

The doctor shrugged. "Being a physician is not an exact science. Rather a primitive profession, it seems to me. Anyway, I didn't dose you. I let the Robomed do that. You're not a Luddite are you? A plain old injection is nothing compared to what this little machine can do. Where would I be without you, Robomed?"

"Please phrase your inquiries in medical terms only," the unit replied.

Laughing, he turned to inspect Yves Loitte's wallet more closely, slicing the lining neatly from one end to the other with a scalpel to see if anything was hidden inside. The doctor's large back concealed his movements.

"You know," said Valdeen, "fighting is a very bad idea for you. I've checked your file. You're not exactly a star around here. They don't allow this sort of behavior in second-stringers."

The conspirator chuckled to himself. Skiers were some of the stupidest people he had ever met. And he had met many stupid people in his sixty-six years, many of whom could be blinded by the trappings of respectability.

Yves said, "Are you Dr. Koutsaflakis' assistant?"

"It's Dr. Travis Ziljian. I'm no one's assistant. Your usual Team Doctor couldn't go at the last moment. He had some nasty accident in the office. You're very lucky to have me here as a replacement."

"Koutsaflakis had an accident?"

"He's fine. You'll see more than you want to see of him when you get back."

Yves squinted. "You look familiar."

"You wouldn't know me. I'm from Montana."

"There's some good skiing in Montana. I've been there."

The impostor ducked his face, and tried to appear preoccupied. "I wouldn't know. I don't go near it."

"I saw you somewhere. Are you famous for something?"

Valdeen's shoulders rose apprehensively. Having the wallet in his hands gave him the idea to play a little game of Rob the Rube for a distraction. He turned around and snorted, "I'm probably better known than you'll ever be. You won't have much future if you can't get along with the locals."

"It wasn't my fault Dr. Ziljian. The Martians don't like Third Orbits. You know what's been going on."

"Don't discuss politics with them." Valdeen took out a pad and started keying in. "You have to understand, you fellows are very fortunate to participate in this thing, or even to be here. Tell you what. I could fill out the report the way you need it for the right price. I'll put down that you slipped on some Martian fungus and I'll neglect to mention the barroom brawl."

"It wasn't a barroom. It was a Biofeed Lounge."

"I don't care where it was. It's going to cost you. You kids spend too much on trashy souvenir trinkets, anyway." The doctor was already completing the falsified report.

"I have very little credit."

"I noticed."

"And if I pay you, and any of my equipment breaks, I might not be able to replace it."

"What about the stipend they pay you to be here?"

"I sent most of it to my mother. I know that's not what it's for, but she needed it more than I did."

"You had better watch your step then, hadn't you?"

"Can you help me or not?"

The Doctor mopped his bald scalp from front to back with a handkerchief. "Sonny, put yourself in my hands. I've been taking care of business since before you were born."

When they completed the illicit transaction, Valdeen ushered Yves out through one door and another man sauntered in from the opposite door.

"Here," said Valdeen to his visitor, when he was sure Loitte had left the outer office. "Do you want his credits, Nils?"

"No, I don't need them. That was funny though. I could hardly keep from laughing when I heard how he spends it all on his mother."

"I wish you could punch out every one of them like you did with Loitte."

"I might just take you up on that. Do you think I've softened Loitte up enough?"

"No. Never underestimate your enemy. Always keep him off balance."

"He's only one skier, and there are better ones I have to worry about."

The older man smiled. He looked directly at his guest but seemed to be looking through him into another time and place. Merris and his predecessors eliminated one way or the other. Then of course, there was Dr. Koutsaflakis, discovered to have been smoking in bed when his house went up in flames. The next target's elimination would have to be more fun if possible.

It all went back to the nine-year-old Havi Valdeen, an avid tinkerer, and very very curious. As an experiment, he had killed another fourth grader by pulverizing the back of his head with a pointed rock. The tinkerer studied the way the boy's head caved in and the things that came out of it. As he had suspected, a hard enough shot brought more than blood.

Valdeen was way too young for prosecution or for having the crime go on his record so it was buried in his past. Getting away with it taught him that not everything you did wrong got you locked up, but he hated getting caught, and going for treatment was bad enough. Valdeen didn't kill again until Sutter Creek in 2012 when he employed more advanced techniques.

He remembered the news conference that followed the death of Edward Merris. They had asked him if the explosion that killed Merris indicated that his partner had made a major discovery. That was laughable. "These things happen," he told them sadly. "Terrible misfortune. Still, I expect it is possible that my careless friend was on to something before he left us with all these unanswered questions."

One reporter prompted, "You were working together for so long. You must know what he was doing."

"No, the explosion that destroyed our laboratory was not in our plans." He pulled out a painful, gentle smile. "Merris must have varied the experiment."

"Can you vary it in the same way under more controlled conditions?"

"Unfortunately his notes and computer were destroyed with him. I can't hope to duplicate them by chance. There are an infinite number of ways to alter an experiment. You may use materials with imperfections, apply a fluctuating current, bring in another element. He may have just been inattentive. Those of us in the scientific community realize that is the way he was, casual to the point of being reckless. My heart goes out to his mother in West Virginia." That last part was a nice touch, he thought.

More than one world is a very different place now, Merris. I was wrong when I said you wouldn't like it. You wouldn't even have noticed. I should have kicked your empty head around like a football or raised it on a spear like the conquerors of old. But, no, you had to be ready for the police investigation. Even in death you spoiled my fun.

Valdeen refocused on the man standing in front of him. "Yes, Loitte is just another skier. Another one to get past. And you've got them running scared, my boy. Just keep an eye on this one."

"You don't think Yves Loitte is any threat to your project, do you?"

"The way he gave up his money, it's hard to believe. But I don't know. Something about that kid makes me think he's going to be trouble. Maybe I should have killed him on the table when I had the chance."

"I didn't ask you to kill him. I just wanted you to mess him up a little. That's what competitive skiing is about, right? Why? He didn't recognize you, did he?"

The doctor warded off the question with a swipe of his hand. "No, nothing like that. He's much too young to know who I am."

The athlete looked sharply at the man in front of him. "What did they really put you away for?" He practically breathed the words.

"In the end, the only charge that stuck was the tax fraud. They said that the lab equipment that I kept but didn't end up using in the government project was supposed to be reported in income." Valdeen shrugged. "Tax fraud. That's what they do to you when they can't find anything else."

"Dear uncle, what more was there to find?"

Valdeen stared back, thinking of Edward Merris' tombstone and the inscription that was culled from his last "words": *Quod erat demonstrandum. Quid nunc?*

What now? indeed.

* * *

Kitty Honera reluctantly welcomed March back into her lower level playpen. He looked out of breath, pumped up from something. She swiveled away from her workstation a bit to watch him.

"Still *nada* from our boy Ingrem," said March with an efficient clap of the hands.

"*Nada*? What's that? And what are you so happy about?" Honera asked, indicating that he could sit in a chair at her level. He ignored the offer, too excited to bend his knees.

"I'm beginning to think we're in the clear. The hacker must have realized he can't touch us. At least not without hurting himself. So he simply slinked back under the rocks." The corner of March's mouth moved a fraction in imitation of a smile. "Your fat's out of the fire, Penny."

Yes, Penny, he called her, instead of her proper name. March never had trouble remembering to use the right pseudonym because he so loved playing games.

"Me? Let's don't start that again. Oh, you're having a grand old time with this Ingrem business, ain't you? I'll tell you something about yourself, Pikey," said Honera, at least using a variation of his code name because he was so touchy about it otherwise. March was a cautious little twit, she could say that much for him.

"What's that, Penny?"

"You always have that smug look on your face, like you've stashed a sense of humor under water, always ready to bubble up to the surface, and it never quite bubbles."

"You're too kind," he answered flatly, without passion, allowing his face to go limp. Honera intuited that he was actually damping his emotion so it wouldn't be recognized as anger. Her boss really didn't like when her comments got personal and struck near the truth. March had once explained that he was raised not to say certain things out loud and he didn't think that others should say them either, even if there wasn't much he could immediately do about it.

"And it's not just the humor," she continued, unrelenting. "It always looks like you're about to have some human being-type expression on your face but that never quite gets there." She enjoyed testing her theories, pushing him.

His demeanor changed just then, just slightly, looking a little dangerous in response to her words. You could only recognize it if you lived with his moods. His eyes, looking

236

straight into her, became hooded in that barely perceptible way of his. His nostrils rounded and the flesh under his chin tightened like a lion willing its prey to stand still. The cat got very still himself in the process. But look there, he squashed it already, let his eyes go unfocused. He's going to sound especially friendly in a moment, she told herself.

"You're under a lot of pressure," he offered with a boyish smile that was almost charming.

"I would have said the same anyway."

"I don't know what you're talking about," he said plainly.

"You can't say you don't suppress your feelings."

"I suppose you're right, in a way. But look in the mirror, Penny. That's what being English does for you."

"Sure, turn it about. Hypocrisy may be peachy where you come from. In my family, we told each other what was what. And you're terribly English for someone who's not too keen on it."

"I suppose there are aspects of being English that I cherish. Being properly brought up English, I mean. I only say it when I'm pressed, but certain classes always have their feelings hanging out all over their faces, you know."

"If that means me, I'm proud of it. The thing that gets me though, is how you're so secretive."

"Secretive, is it?"

"You heard me." She was going to make him a fraction less phony even if it killed her. The right word could hit a nerve with him.

"I'm not secretive at all."

"Of course you are. Here we are in the middle of this whatever-we're-doing and you never say what you're in it for. Even I have my doubts about our fanatic little game.

Taking all these risks and for what? What could someone like you get out of it?"

"Same as you. I'm in for a few quid."

"Oh stuff it. I never once heard you mention money, needing or wanting. Nothing you do says you're in it for the money."

"I like to knock about the established order," he said. "Shake things up a bit."

As repressed as Devon March was, she knew he was also given to sudden bouts of honesty when it suited him. It probably helped to confuse people so they could never be sure of what was real.

"I'll bet you do. This is all some kind of sport for you, isn't it? But why?"

"Why not? See who comes out on top, eh?"

* * *

The Calgary was flying fairly low to the ground when the explosion gripped it, almost enough to get them snuffed out by a rocky outcropping, especially when a numb Grove yanked the stick over like a dead man.

Technology was way ahead of him as the concussive force registered in the on-board navigator. Data from accelerometers and timers told the computer the heliplane's motions were erratic, kicking in the emergency routine and clearing out Grove's headings and commands in order to remove existing lateral thrust and countermand any panic reactions. Checking for other air traffic and finding none, the auto navigator replaced original pilot commands with ground thrust to gain altitude until the spinning lost momentum.

Then in theory, it was back to pilot's control. Seeing no response from the pilot for ten seconds, deciding that Grove was either deceased or disabled, the program utilized one more feature, hovering while seeking emergency landing space.

"What are you, a maniac?" Hrelcik looked like he was ninety and ageing every minute. For him the spinning had not ended.

"I'm sorry, sir," replied Grove, just waking up. "That wasn't me. Someone tried to blow us up. I swear it was the terrorists." In the excitement Grove briefly forgot to be disrespectful.

"Who's flying the damned plane?" shouted Hrelcik.

Grove had to log back on to the computer and answer three logic questions before he could squelch the emergency landing sequence which had them nearly on the ground.

Lifting off again, he took himself and the congressman directly back to the heliport and from there to be checked out at the hospital. Hrelcik made sure he was separated from the maniac pilot by at least a floor. He intended to get some rest.

After one of Hrelcik's aides ascertained that his boss was not badly hurt, he entered the room.

"Sir, you wanted to be notified immediately if the name Chul Huk Chang came up anywhere."

Hrelcik snapped wide-awake. "Yes, has some report mentioned him?"

"He mentioned himself, sir. He's requesting permission to land at Mercury International."

* * *

In Coubertin Square, the center of the Olympic Village, was a giant clock where time ran backwards. In days, in hours, in minutes, it counted down the span remaining before the Opening Ceremonies for the Olympic Games would begin. Yves Loitte and Lou Coburn passed that clock every day on their way to the slopes, admiring its golden icon stylized in the shape of a speed skater. Today as they passed the clock on their way to a special pageant, they memorized its digital legend. It read: 000:18:10. No days remaining, just hours and minutes.

Preview demonstrations of skill in the newest events were used to whet the audience's appetite to build popularity for the fledgling arts. The crowd for the current event had gotten so large that Yves and Lou had to shoulder their way in even with VIP passes in hand. Above them they could see the contenders testing their state-of-the-art wings, gaudy and theatrical, tugging at the ailerons and tightening the harnesses even as they were guided to the starting positions. The first contestant, a young man from Berne, thundered into the wind zone and leapt as high as he could from the ramp, trying to get as much air under him as possible.

"Up-skiers," Coburn snarled with mock contempt. "Anyone who thought I was crazy has to take a look at these guys."

"I know I wouldn't do it."

"They're willing to kill themselves to prove the IOC was right in finally making it an Olympic sport. Of course, none of us Americans qualified."

"You're just mad because that guy has a cobra printed on his parasail," said Loitte.

"That punk is ripping me off. I hold the copyright, I tells ya."

Yves laughed. "Look at that. He caught a draft."

"No shit, he caught a tornado."

It all happened too quickly. After the initial tug, the parasail strings suddenly went taut and the man was pulled up the embankment in a breakneck snap, furiously fighting the towlines like a ten-year-old trying to confine a furious Rottweiler to his leash. A woman in the audience crossed herself, and his coach shouted an oath.

The upskiier opened his vent to cut the drag, but not entirely since he was unwilling to let the draft get away. His coach was waving his arms and shouting something unintelligible. The wind was too strong and the man too cocky. Before he knew it, he ran out of places to go, dropping into a pocket of the mountain, letting out a chilling scream as he went. The wind had released him.

Back in Coubertin Square, the clock said: 000:17:59.

CHAPTER 20
Falling Out

"WHEN WE PASS the red marker, no more talk of blowing up the city," Valdeen whispered to the smaller man beside him as they proceeded to the outside access.

"Stop needling me, Havislaw," said Arazine, "I designed the security system and put the gaps in it myself."

"You have the weight of a planet on you. I'm trying to assist in any way I can." Valdeen's governor friend, Peter Arazine, wore two hats: chief administrator of the first pioneer colony on Mars, and agent provocateur, technically an anti-Earth revolutionary. Even at that, he was no match for Valdeen.

"Anyway, you're wrong," the governor continued, "We're not blowing up the city. We'll destroy only what's necessary."

Havislaw Valdeen looked at his companion to divine if he suspected anything. When Valdeen had separated Arazine from his faithful entourage, he let Arazine think that being alone and undefended was his own idea. Alone with his accomplice. Alone with his executioner. The man was too stupid to live.

When they arrived at the dock, Arazine gingerly placed his chin in the supporting cup to allow a scan of his retina.

"Arazine, Doctor Peter William, oh-five-two-two-seven," he intoned.

Gatekeeper collected his voice print and personal code along with the retinal scan results, and confirmed Arazine to be the highest official on Mars, fully authorized for vehicle use.

This moment was his last chance to save himself and he did not. Had the governor blinked a coded sequence during the scan, Gatekeeper would have known that he was not leaving Olympus of his own free will, and it would have engaged security, perhaps preventing the governor's abduction, and the consequences. But he did not blink for the coercion alarm, and the man who kept to the camera's blind spots did not speak.

Gatekeeper checked the barometric integrity of the next room. "SAFE TO PROCEED," said the distinctive voice.

The dock was a small one, and rarely used. They crossed an unswept floor with patterns of paprika-colored dust from the boots of in-bound travelers. The governor— of his own free will—selected his private Spider for the trip, logged in a semi-fictional geological survey mission, and documented the related equipment as he loaded the pieces one by one.

Valdeen did not assist. The two revolutionary conspirators were never meant to be seen together. Inconvenient as it was, each man dragged along his personal Hybrid to avoid creating a log entry for borrowed suits.

On their way out, Valdeen shoehorned his bulk into a gap in the Spider's machinery and covered himself with a tarp to avoid the next security camera at the exit. Valdeen grunted with effort, and hoped that the sound didn't register as a second person. He kept a small slit open to keep an eye on the governor. As they headed for the Tharsis test site, he could see Arazine trying not to glance with guilty knowledge at his collaborator's hiding place.

Having reached a safe distance, Valdeen said, "That's it. Let me take over the driving so you can run some tests."

"Thank you. I usually have Devon along for that and he's always terrified on these trips away from the domes."

Dr. Valdeen turned off the heads-up display to conceal the weather forecast, and still the governor's interest was not aroused. Thoughts of the mayhem that had already occurred at the Olympic Games and his plans for the next few days kept racing around Valdeen's head. When they were far outside the city, rolling on the narrow stretch of road that dead-ended in the Tharsis desert, Valdeen spoke without glancing over from his driving, "Have you been showing my private work around, Mr. Arazine?"

For the first time since they had known each other, Arazine looked alarmed. Ashen. Valdeen had fed him a question that was unexpected and baited, but they both knew it was much more than that. Arazine tried on a forced, genial smile, and tuned it up until tiny crow's feet decorated the corners of his eyes. Valdeen watched the desolate landscape roll by, tones of red and more red relieved only by the curvaceous white-top paving continually slinking beneath their wheels like the retracting tongue of a snake.

"You have to see my new office," said Arazine, "what they've done with it. It's beautiful with all the sun I get from the skylight. I had them wrap the iron railings around my desk like a giant scroll. I just moved in you know. Of course I still have some of my less urgent junk in Devon's office. He doesn't like that too much, let me tell you." He finished off with a lame chuckle.

"Have you been showing my work to other people, Mr. Arazine?" Valdeen repeated patiently and waited for an answer.

"Private work? I don't know what you're referring to."

"The Valdeen Catalytic Factor that I created and that you want to exploit to run your volcanoes to make yourself far richer than you deserve to be."

"That's a very blunt and uncharitable way of describing a venture that we're both heavily involved in. You make it sound like it's just about profits for me. I'm trying to make this planet independent. You're not a colonist. You'll go back to Earth with your money and live it up like Daddy Warbucks."

Valdeen softly drew in his breath and watched Arazine shift around uncomfortably. "We're completely isolated and far from any help out here so I hope you'll be cooperative, and tell me everything. Have you been sharing my secrets, Mr. Arazine? Have you possibly been sharing them with Chul Huk Chang?"

"What makes you think so?" Arazine did not meet his eyes.

"Oh, Peter, I was hoping a man of your resourcefulness could come up with something better than that under the circumstances," said Valdeen.

"This discussion was not on the table. You don't have a problem with what you get paid in our arrangement, do you?" Arazine asked, in what seemed like a lame attempt to assert himself.

His question went unanswered as they drew up to the end of the road, and Valdeen stopped the vehicle.

The Spider would be found much later, sans the governor, wandering aimlessly after the terrible sandstorm apparently trashed its navigation system. When he had taken care of business, Valdeen set the rover up with a malfunction, parting with it only when he was near enough to the city to ensure a short walk back, and yet far enough to be unobserved.

I should have done that sooner, he thought as he trudged through the crescent dunes. It didn't take up much of my time. Now the contract that Arazine had with Chang is going to be my contract with Chang.

Valdeen and Olympus Colony would never see Dr. Peter Arazine again, the pioneer governor apparently a victim of bad weather.

* * *

Peter Arazine opened his eyes to the empty salmon expanse of sky. On either side stretched a blazing orange land. Everything looked unnaturally vivid in the way that it does after a person has spent some time with a strong sun beaming through closed eyelids. Perfectly still, he was unready to move from his comfortable position. So light on his back, he felt like he was floating in water. So light in his head, his thoughts floated too.

Am I at the beach at Longboat Key? he wondered. *No, I wouldn't be dressed in an airtight suit if this were the beach. And the sun is too small. This must be Mars. I remember that I came to Mars.*

Someone had laid him out in the supine position, hands crossed, with a cloven rock for a pillow. His faceplate had not been polarized against the light so he hoped the radiation filters were working overtime. Peering past the tips of his boots, he thought he recognized Volcano Fourteen, Jovis Tholis, looming no more than a mile away. Except that it sat odd, so maybe it wasn't Jovis but one of the other Tholis formations. Wait, of course it was Jovis, showing its Southern face, which was not his usual approach. The presence of that volcano told him he was in—or at least near—the Tharsis region, and not far from his usual exploration limits.

When the pioneer governor stood up, the blood declined to reach his head, giving him thoughts as fuzzy as his vision, and making him want to lay down again to dream. He couldn't recall what day it was, or even what had happened to him in the last few hours. He faintly remembered that something went wrong, but something else had stolen his sense of urgency. Was Volcano Fourteen actually smoldering, actually come alive? That would be impossible.

No, a gust of wind was driving sand up in front of its crater. False alarm. At least he wasn't hallucinating. A pain began in his head and became a constant throb.

Easing down, he first took notice of what was wrong in his immediate surroundings. The cloven rock had been moved to the position under his head, and pebbles had been cleared to accommodate the length of his body on the ground, forming a crude resting place. Without knowing the events that led up to it, he supposed that he must have made himself a kind of bed when he needed to rest. Who else would have laid him out like that?

Settling further on his back, he formed concerns that were more to the point. It came to him that he had driven out there with the revolutionary, Havislaw Valdeen, to talk business and then said something that Valdeen didn't like.

Or didn't say something that he should have said. At any rate, Valdeen seemed to take offense.

The current ruler of Mars forced himself up again on wobbly legs to check his life support suit. The bio-monitors lit green, no breaches noted. The governor still had the finest protective gear on the planet. And the air tanks, oddly enough, were at full pressure as if he hadn't used any all day, which he must have. Even as he slept, he must have burned something. Someone had the presence of mind to give him a refill not only of the main tank, but the supplemental exploration tanks, and the food and water pouches as well. That was where the good news ended.

The Spider, his only transportation, had gone, and no one and nothing was around to explain things to him. He couldn't recall if he were prone to migraine headaches, but he was sure his ability to think would be clearer if his temples didn't shriek with pain. He discovered he had no operating radio link either to the Spider or to the settlement, and no transceiver to mark his location. The sun rode low in the sky. Valdeen had vanished, yet Valdeen had left him very much alive. Why?

Although Arazine was no angel, he was not as much anti-Earth as he was pro-Mars. He simply did not want fragile Mars tied to an Earth in crisis. Maybe Valdeen looked for more than that.

In any event, there were ways to survive. As soon as night began it would get damn cold, test his limits, but he would be on the move and could manage. In his protective suit on Mars, he was safer than an unprotected man in an Earth desert, where he would soon be a gibbering, dehydrated wreck, if not the victim of an errant rattlesnake. Nothing slithered yet on Mars. He had kept himself in shape and still found the one-third gravity negligible. Since he had no problem with directions, he might be able to walk back eventually, or Valdeen could pick him up again any time, and that had to be the key. Stranding the planet's governor in his favorite haunt was the old convict's way of showing his extreme displeasure. Before it was too late, Valdeen would send help. Arazine could see that Valdeen lived on the edge, but he never expected an outcast to bite the hand that fed him. When he got back he would pay Valdeen off and send him packing. Meanwhile, he had a bit of a challenge and a lot of land to cover.

As he started his long hike, eating up the miles, trying unsuccessfully to remember a song, he turned the mishap into something optimistic, thinking about how interesting it would be to do the whole journey by foot. Given this opportunity, he could notice things that he never would have noticed at forty miles per hour with his head ducked in a mini lab and a whiner like Devon March interrupting him. Ironically, Arazine had no camera and couldn't do a detailed study if he wanted to reach Olympia before his rations ran out. To make up time, he adopted a healthy stride, the Mars Hop as they called it, and made mental notes of geological conditions. His ego convinced him that he could do both things at once.

Arazine covered a mile in the first fifteen minutes. In the first five, one of his hops landed him partly on a small rock and he twisted in the air and fell trying to push off of it. He laughed at himself and went on more carefully. If his Hybrid was damaged in the fall, he didn't notice it.

He found the wilderness much larger and more impressive on foot than within the high-speed shell of the Spider. And he traveled at a time of day he didn't ordinarily get to see. The field of rock expanded toward the horizon, each with a lengthening shadow that pointed back at him. But he couldn't find the trail the Spider had taken on the way out. He recognized his location now as The Devil's Golfcourse, named for its Death Valley counterpart on Earth. Not good.

Trying to find a minor road, he noticed another shadow, this one crawling both above and below the horizon, just a sliver, just an ink spot, in the South—no—South by Southwest to be exact. Where there is a shadow crawling the ground, there should be an aircraft above: surely a rescue ship. He traced a line above the ink spot, waiting for a white dot of metal to come into view, hoping to see the Akagi Shuttle in a flight path that came over his position, and he began to devise a distress signal that could be seen from its cruising altitude. Perhaps if he formed a large "A" for "Arazine," a rescue team would get the message. He gathered rocks and laughed at his good fortune.

Then he froze in his tracks. There was nothing flying to cast that shadow, and the smudge was mounting the sky in a tall column like a cyclonic sand storm. No aircraft above. It was a sand storm.

A Martian sand storm versus a man on the open desert. The odds of survival were...zero? Arazine's heart was pounding like it wanted to rip through his suit. The sweat that burst from his pores taxed his Hybrid's recycling system to the limit. Just a moment ago he was following a game plan for salvation. If he wasn't entirely safe, he hadn't suffered immediate danger either. Now, if he fell within the path of a major storm, a man alone weighing no more than forty pounds in his outdoor suit, what could he do? Even if the ground turned out soft enough to dig a foxhole, it would shelter him but he would never emerge. He would soon be under a mountain of sand even without digging himself under. Forced to figure his options, and instantly finding he had few to speak of, he stood paralyzed trying to perceive, and then inescapably perceiving that the darkness was growing, possibly shifting toward him, though he was unable to tell for certain if it would go to his area directly or grow more one way than the other, moving past, and keeping him safe. *Because it might do that. It really might.*

Though his mindless pursuer expanded like so much multiplying bacteria, Arazine remained as effectively rooted as a young willow in the path of a bursting dam. He knew he should be running for his life on the small chance that he could survive by doing so, yet he stayed anchored to the spot, morbidly awaiting confirmation. This time he was not in the Spider several feet from the gate pushing the buttons that would snatch him from the jaws of death. Instead he was out on the open plain—the Devil's Golfcourse—in a suit designed to protect him from a calm winter day. The smell of his own fear sweat told him all he needed to know. No matter how rational he was by nature, the scientist fleetingly imagined he could be fantastically transported elsewhere if he wished hard enough, the kind of thought you have when you fully realize there is nothing else for you.

That was when something in his pocket began to beep and he wondered whether the item that made that sound was something he could use.

* * *

Peter Arazine blinked the uncommonly vivid landscape into focus through his sun-washed eyes, trying to wish away the disaster that was bearing down on him when he heard the tiny beep coming from his pocket.

Latching onto that faithful tone, any manmade sound the beacon of bright shining hope, he dug feverishly into his pockets after it, expecting to find he had been left something useful after all, perhaps something that would signal a rescuer reaching him before the sand storm arrived.

The instrument he brought out was a long tube with sophisticated attachments, and the tone it emitted was the warning beep that told him in its own feeble way that he was in the very center of a pressure sinkhole. With sickening certainty he realized that his device confirmed the destination of the storm as his own location, the pressure variance measured greater than that in any previously recorded storm.

Dr. Valdeen had left him a highly accurate barometer.

Galvanized, Arazine turned to race for the volcano, still so large behind him, the only possibility of high ground and places to hide above the danger zone. Having hiked so far in the opposite direction, he had a great number of frantic strides ahead. Though he'd stayed fit and could run fast, his goal was much more distant than it seemed, and each giant step appeared only to push it further from him.

One thought kept him going: Whatever I do, decision is better than indecision.

Adrenaline made it easy to loosen up and sprint. As smart as he was, he couldn't help but waste precious seconds twisting back every so often. The front of the storm was a narrow wedge that broadened until it ate up acres of horizon, and cut off the view of anything behind or inside of it. It sheathed the land as it moved, leaving not an inch of air below, instead pressing down, and peeling sand and rock from their rest, slavishly driven ahead, adding to the swollen bulk, and contributing to the destructive force.

Governor Arazine was correct about the height of the volcano being able to save him if he could only get there. The heaviest and most dangerous matter, relentless as it was, stayed low to the ground. The majority of the cloud, its upper reaches, though capable of blotting out the sun in the daytime, was no more than malevolent dust, which he could survive in his protective suit if the bulk of the disturbance moved on.

Leaping through the air on Mars was something that you normally didn't do if you wanted your covering to stay intact, and Arazine was lucky so far that it had. So he bounded through the air, sometimes landing on both hands and feet, pushing back up even harder, and praying that the suit designers were as diligent as they said they were. Even though the helmet's air was isolated from the rest of the suit, an opening in another part could lead to fatal frostbite. Without any other choices, he located one big rock after another from which to launch himself forward. Surprising himself, he covered the distance.

Once past the edge of the lava terminus, he had technically reached the volcano itself, but the part that was nearly flat, before the mountain proper would give him anything near a high perch. Running five hundred meters bought him only ten meters worth of altitude. The front of the sand wall would make it over the lip of the terminus, and drive upward until it petered out. Not knowing exactly how much height he needed to escape, he made for a point where the steepness began early, where the lava had once flooded up the banks of an old river. Another glance backward from his improved vantage point told him the menace was growing faster as it pressed local soil into service. Even for Mars, this was an unusually bad storm. The entire sky faded too rapidly in the premature night.

In a few more giant strides, Arazine reached the round pebble wash of the old riverbank, leapt onto the mountain itself and began to climb, hands and feet on the smooth, loose surface, hapless as an agitated monkey. He would scramble and progress, loosen a cache of grit, and slide back only to redouble his efforts and attack it again.

Stopping for a deep breath, he finally realized that he'd made it to Volcano Fourteen before the storm did, began to think that he could reach high ground, and let himself relax just the least bit, if only to gain better control. Fourteen had gone unnamed for way too long, and he believed he was entitled to call it what he wanted. He christened it Icharus Tholis, the closer to the sun, the further from the storm.

Now he could feel the bare wind fleeing in advance of the monster's path, the rocks beneath him rumbling with the strain. The gale pressed him against the mountain and cheered him on with better traction. He had actually made it to the mountain, feeling that Valdeen had never expected that. He would beat the mangy bastard yet.

Skillfully and rapidly, he made for the distant caldera and safety. A light mist closed around him.

When he was fairly high on the slope, the trembling of the ground shook loose the soil he knelt on and sent him sprawling toward the lower reaches. Bouncing off one rock and another, taking several shocks to the head, his hands fixed into claws caught nothing and he rode the sandy rapids until he came to rest naturally near the bottom of the dry river bank again. Peering feebly back up the path he came from, he was likely to be injured now in ways he could not fully ascertain. Oblivion itself couldn't be much different. Weak, exhausted, determined, the scientist rose to climb again.

"Discipline," he said. "I'm coming to join you, Icharus." He pounced and lifted himself one laborious step at a time, making delicious progress through the thickening air. In the short stretch, he managed to restore four meters to his altitude bank.

"Slow and steady," he croaked softly. "Vibration breaks bonds in this soil, so watch your step, Arazine, because if this governor doesn't make it, who's going to ever know the new name of this thing?"

As he concentrated his efforts, he didn't notice the beauty of the stars that brightly speckled the gloom overhead and got eaten, dozens at a time, by the unfurling mass. He didn't appreciate the golden lining that traced around the edges of the storm and met the stars first.

What he did notice was the pealing of bells, deepening into the sound of gongs. Voices with a pattern, playing out an ancient melody with another set of voices imitating the theme of the beginning before the first set was finished. The following layer was a vibrant booming equally as beautiful, the envy of any church choir. And there were the high bells coming in again to join the tones in progress. He recognized the paradigm as that of a perfect canon. Live music. So strange. To his knowledge, Olympia had no instruments that could produce these sounds.

Arazine dimly recalled that even on Earth there were rare occasions reported where massive sandstorms with their rocks colliding in wind-driven fury and sand pouring over the slip face of high, rolling dunes produced the repeated sound of resonant bells, sweet music for the doomed.

"Now I remember what it was," said the governor in a suddenly clear voice. "Valdeen asked me if I showed his work to anyone. That's what got me into this." And a small but very sharp rock smashed through his faceplate.

The last thing his brain recorded was his futile attempt to breathe dust.

CHAPTER 21
Chang

OLD AS HE was, Chang Chul-huk could remember being in love once, long ago in his homeland. The sight of Mars turning beneath him, a barren and rocky unexplored vastness, made him dream back to the year of the first moon landing and what shape his life took.

Nineteen Hundred and Sixty Nine, when China was facing an uncertain transition and a thought-revolution spilled onto every quiet street. People under constant surveillance took their leisure whenever and wherever they could find it as overt and covert coexisted in balanced tension. One hardly noticed the fighting in Viet Nam for all that transpired on the broad continent. The American achievement in space was the only event that had filled Chang with envy.

It was summer in the small town of Hunchun in his native country, and the heat was considerable as Chang tracked through the soft gravel on his way to the small arms drill for his company. He was the only soldier who had gotten off the last stop of the railway, a pack slung heavily over his shoulder. Sweat traveled down his body in routes he could never have dreamt of.

Many of the townspeople were busy at card games and chess games, hopscotch and table tennis, enjoying a break from their work in the iron foundry. Chang saw an old peasant in from the wheat fields selling crickets in bamboo cages, three boys up on a wooden frame turning the dragon-spine water wheel with their bare feet, ice lollies being peddled in the shade, shoddily clad girls surreptitiously glancing at his uniform and giggling in embarrassment. He ignored the questionable frivolity when he found he could make a purchase of green tea and a pouch of melon seeds to chew while he strolled.

If any of the fools in Hunchun would have attracted his attention, it was the peasant with the crickets. Not long ago, as a member of the Red Guard, Chang might have bashed the old man in the head and crushed his bamboo cages for perpetuating the old traditions and impeding the transition to true communism. The old one reminded Chang of his elder that he had hated and feared, the one who could not adjust to the Cultural Revolution, who beat Chul-huk for espousing the ideas of Mao Ze-dong, his grandfather who had to be denounced and corrected.

But now things were so much quieter. Since Mao had prevailed once again, productivity ran high and some of the old ways were slowly being allowed a longer leash—The Cultural Revolution victorious. For a young successful soldier in the People's Liberation Army, it was time to root out more serious transgressions.

Chang liked what he saw in his assigned province of Kirin, where China, North Korea, and the U.S.S.R. met in one place, less than one hundred miles from Vladivostok. The communes here were properly organized like the one he left in Shensi where his father was a member of the revolutionary committee. He could no longer tell the difference between one commune and another, which was a tribute to how well all of China was conforming to the

Soviet model. Unlike his father, however, the ambitious Chang wished for more than full-time agricultural work and the chance to earn one *yuan* a day. In the army, he did farming for only part of the day, received excellent political and technical training, and drew a regular salary of ten *yuan* per week. As a company commander he could stay permanently with the armed forces to make three or four times that amount. Then he could invest it in the furtherance of the transition whether it be to the Party's benefit or his own.

One of the boys on the dragon-spine looked at the stranger suspiciously when he passed near, but Chang did not censure him. It was healthy to be suspicious of your elders so the boys were entitled. Yes, the old order was upside down, a man's worth was measured by how well he learned the teachings of Mao. Chang chewed his melon seeds as he walked and he patted the pocket that held the green tea close to the picture post card of Mao. If the PLA soldier chanced to discover that anyone passing by did not carry a picture of Mao he would have shot the offender on sight.

Chang would bet that there were very few who did not carry the picture. He called to mind an appropriate quote from the fine works he had memorized, the one that began, "I will never forget the tragic days before the Liberation..." It was wonderful to be so young and so well schooled.

And before he knew it, the graveled path led him to the drill site, the place where he first saw the woman, the one who would make him question everything he had so recently been taught.

CHAPTER 22
Fourth Planet Night

THE LAND MELTED into pools of burgundy with much of the sky directly above a deep gray-blue. Somewhere between the two realms, the sun seeped into the horizon, sending out bright messengers of gold and red to tinge the silver latticework towers as their giant propellers fluttered in the distance. Directly overhead, the white pinpoints of early stars mimicked a slow descent as their murky backdrop retreated to the void, a kind of three-dimensional retrograde motion that some called queasy and others delightful.

Yves and Terri made their way up to the 50-foot platform known as The Asaph Hall Star Terrace, named after an Earth astronomer who specialized in early mapping of the Martian landscape, the man who discovered Mars' moons, Phobos and Deimos.

Broad steps were carved into the side of the truncated pyramid reminiscent of Aztec altars. These they bounded up two at a time, laughing like children in a low-gravity ballet.

They followed the rumor of a surprise dust storm forming at sunset, a spectacular sight, unmatched anywhere. Before coming up, they donned extra heavy thermal suits to protect them from the desert-like shift in temperature that came on in the evening. It would get colder than ninety degrees below zero before morning. For now they didn't need the extra layer of head coverings they brought along so Terri had no trouble seeing her boyfriend's cheek when she examined him closely behind his nitrox feeder.

"What's that cut on your face?" asked Terri.

"It's nothing. Just a little gift from one of the Martian skiers, Nils Barkly. It's a compliment really. I think he wants me to look just like him."

"If I see Barkly, I'll give him a gift that will make his scar look like a paper cut." Yves smiled, touched to hear her say that. He had girlfriends that stuck up for him before, but this was the first one who was so blunt and so capable of actually doing some mischief. If she wanted to, she could crack Barkly's skull with her martial arts skills and he wouldn't even see it coming. All the same, he wouldn't mention Barkly to Terri anymore. It wasn't right to get her involved in something he could handle himself. Some sexist remnant of his reptilian brain told him her intervention would be embarrassing, and Yves' logic brain layer agreed.

They reached the crown of the platform panting lightly, casting around for landmarks. A balustrade hugged the edges, telescoping into the distance, and theater foot lights arranged in rows illuminated the ground below, enough reflected light for them to see just how popular the event was. Scores of stargazers already occupied half of the reclining chairs available. Many who preferred to stand staked their claims at the railing.

Terri scanned the multitude for a three hundred pound man with a tangled gray beard. It took only seconds to find him as the crowd shifted. He reposed on his back with knees bent, feet flat on the walk, hair spilling in every direction. He wore a plain white suit stretched over him, his underside aglow in muted yellow. His chair hadn't been properly extended, yet he was well balanced and comfortable, chin tilted toward the heavens.

"There he is," she said. "That's Andrey Mirovich. Hurry, there's still two chairs open next to him." They ran over and claimed the prized location, practically running off two people who were about to sit down. Yves and Terri joined Mirovich with Terri in the middle between them.

"Okay I hurried," said Yves, "now who is he?"

"Who am I is not important," said Mirovich, whose eyes probed the horizon. The red and gold streaks had become bars of light against dark. The sun was a bloodshot glob on the rim of the world. The stargazer didn't look at the new arrivals. Notwithstanding his usual mirth and bluster he was practically all business when it came to his work.

"Andrey Mirovich is an astronomer. He's the one who figured out there would be a dust storm. Andrey, I'd like you to meet Yves Loitte of the American ski team." Mirovich's gaze flicked over to Yves and back to the dazzling sky, forcing the brief interruption out of reluctant courtesy. Anyone who was blinking would have missed it.

Terri and Yves decided to sit back before dizziness overtook them. "Pardon me professor," said Yves, "but what are we all doing out here if there's a storm coming?"

Terri swatted him on the leg.

"Please, Terri, I meant that as a legitimate question."

"It won't reach us," Mirovich answered. "Now pay attention. It could happen any second."

They waited in silence, breathing evenly. The foot lights fizzled out, all motion stopped.

They heard a sound as soft as imagination itself. The sun's last glow became a fuzzy mass that rose and swept together, captured by beads of quartz in hungry currents of unstable air, feeding upon itself until it gathered into a spinning torrent of light and mass. A susurrus churning reached them. Terri gathered Yves' arm in hers.

An army of tiny crystals, older than the rocks themselves, built the glow into a great, swirling yellow column streaked with muddy orange, exponentially gaining speed and solidity. It carried the sun's fading light high into the darkness, the unseen core black as a cave.

The column moved. Its twisting caused it to catch light in a strobe so that it seemed to vanish at points and reappear at others as it crossed their view rapidly from North to South, assailing the gathering with an inhuman moan as it jumped. The spectators flinched and covered their heads. Some squeezed their eyes shut behind their faceplates. They heard the whoosh of the sand and felt the thunderous wave front of clear air that the twister pushed ahead of it, causing their chairs to shift slightly out of place. Then they noticed a secondary disturbance, the droning sound of wind turbines capturing the fleeting blast for Olympia's energy reserves.

When they looked up again, the glowing column was gone and the 60-foot turbine blades were cranking madly through the last of their momentum, squeezing out a mournful howl. All was ebony except for the twinkling of the blades until eyes adjusted to the gentle light of stars.

Out in the wilderness, at the base of Jovis Tholis, one ruler was deposed, another took his place in Olympia, and Yves felt Terri shudder beside him.

"That was close," someone whispered in the hush that followed.

"Not as close as it seemed," said Mirovich who saw no need to hold his voice down, almost shouting, whose eyes were open the whole time. "Otherwise, you would be smothered in sand," he exalted.

"It was impossible. Hallucination," someone else whispered.

"It was possible," yelled Mirovich. "'I am a thing that thinks, that is to say, a thing that doubts, affirms, denies, knows a few things, is ignorant of many things, wills, rejects, and also imagines and senses.' René Descartes, First Philosophy, Meditation Three: Concerning God, That He Exists." His index finger punctuated his words. The cloud they saw, raised three kilometers high, would linger in the Southern hemisphere for weeks. Mirovich was no doubt planning how he would follow it for further observation.

"How did you know about that event?" asked Yves.

"At such short notice, you mean? That's what I do."

"His astronomy," said Terri.

"The air we've added to the planet has created new weather patterns that we've been charting. When certain conditions coincide, a twister is born inside the Demon's Playpen."

"The Demon's Playpen?" Terri asked. "That's not on any map I've seen."

The chair groaned as Mirovich shifted. "That style of nomenclature is a recent development. When the astronomers stopped naming things and the residents of Mars took over, everything went to hell," Mirovich laughed.

"It sounds like the sort of names they use for ski runs," said Yves.

"Believe me, it fits."

"I thought the International Astronomical Union was in charge of naming the features of planets."

Mirovich laughed. "Oh they used to be. They wanted to continue. Fought for it like their lives depended on it. But in the end the IAU had to admit that Mars was no longer an object in the sky to those who lived there, no longer any of the IAU's business, in fact, and Commission Seventeen was restricted to the six other non-terran planets. The native Martians were right. Would you let an astronomer name the pool your backyard? Name your barbeque and your shed?"

"I see what you mean."

"On top of that, the town of Olympia is suing the Planetary Research Center to stop pointing their Earth-based telescopes in this direction. They say it's an invasion of privacy. Everything to do with Mars and Earth is in litigation, nothing I care to understand. All in all, I'm happier to be over here instead of there. I'm the ultimate escapist."

"What's your job here?" asked Yves.

"I'm overseeing construction of a new observatory on the planet surface."

"Aren't space-based observatories the best ones?

"In some ways yes, but we'll never give up terrestrial or land-based observatories. With the so-called smart optics techniques we can compensate almost perfectly for atmospheric disturbance. Of course there's very little you can do about a wall of sand. On the other hand, there are certain problems with the ones in space. You have to either live there or run it remotely. You can't repair an eye in the sky as easily when they break down. My one big puzzle for my surface project is worrying about what the temperature changes can do to my land-based viewing. I have to compensate for inversion layers. The math changes constantly. That's why I keep such a close eye on the weather systems."

The last blush of light sank quickly and the stars took full charge, filling in the blackness that was left behind. Yves clutched the edges of the chair as the canopy erupted like fireworks with nearly twice as many stars visible as could be seen on a night in the country on Earth. It was shocking and dizzying and heart rending at the same time. Terri must have sensed his discomfort because she sought his hand.

"Enjoy the view while you can," said Mirovich. "You understand why? It will diminish every night as the atmosphere fills in."

Yves couldn't settle down. The night seemed to be continuously changing. He groped for reference points. "I thought I'd see two moons on Mars. But I can't even find one."

Terri spotted the elusive object. "Take a look there, almost overhead. That has to be one of them. It looks like a squashed egg, and you can see it moving against the other lights."

"Oh yeah, I see it. That's not much bigger than a star and it's not even as bright as some of them."

Mirovich laughed. "Come back in forty million years and you'll see it better. It's orbit will send it crashing into Mars."

"Where's the other moon, Professor Mirovich?" Terri asked.

"The satellite you see now is Phobos. You're not going to spot the other one tonight."

"Why does Phobos look like that?" said Yves.

"It's merely a matter of albedo and distance relative to size."

Yves laughed. "You'd better start from the top. I don't know what albedo is."

Mirovich said, "Albedo is the percentage of light that reflects off an object such as a moon. A perfect reflection of one hundred percent is better than the most perfect mirror. A black hole has an albedo of zero. Earth's moon rates an eleven, highly visible for its size and distance. Phobos and Deimos, however, are two of the dimmest objects in the solar system. With an albedo of five, less light reaching them, and a greater distance for their size, they're like coal. Not to mention that Mar's gravity makes the oval moon point to us like an arrow. We never see it in its larger profile. So most of the viewing advantages of a thin atmosphere are wiped out by the lack of surface area over the distance. Deimos is even smaller and further away from this planet's surface."

"Is that why we can't see Deimos at all?" asked Terri.

"No. You can't see Deimos because it is not there. Its synodic revolution—that is, its movement relative to an observer at a fixed point on Mars, like Asaph Hall for instance, takes five and a half days. Right now, Deimos is suspended over the lit side of the planet while we are naturally on the dark side. For us, this is the so called 'new moon' period." He sighed. "Having two moons is not as satisfying as some people thought it would be. We'll see Deimos on another night."

"Do the two of them ever get to spend the night together?" she asked. Mirovich didn't notice that Terri was looking at Yves rather than the sky.

Yves looked at her with a trace of guilt and regret. The pair pushed their chairs together and put on their extra headgear against the closing cold. If the Earth vanished at this moment they would probably ignore it. Mirovich was right. Bearing witness to the forces of nature made you reevaluate the existence of God if you ever had any doubts. As the pop philosophy question put it: "Could a billion monkeys with a billion typewriters accidentally turn out a copy of Hamlet?" Given infinite time, maybe they could. But when he saw Terri's face, at once bewildered and inquisitive, any doubts about God were spontaneously driven from his mind.

They embraced awkwardly and shivered as Yves thought about the days ahead. The uncertainty of here and now, their wasted home world, the whims of nature. Here there were no crickets, no owls, no baying dog sounds to populate the night. There was only the sound of air endlessly rushing to an unknown purpose. The next day, at noon, the Olympic Games would begin. Yves was thinking of the hapless up-skiier he saw that day. "I think I'll skip the Opening Ceremonies and get in some more practice," he said.

Then they held very still and watched Heaven expand its dominion.

* * *

That night, Terri dreamed that she tried to practice her skating and ended up whirring like a top with the ripcord pulled by a maniac.

Something was wrong, she couldn't stop. As she looped around the rink a second and third time, she grew buoyant from the air gathering under her. As gravity seemed to ebb, it was all she could do to keep from flying into the upper seats of the stadium. Her score marks on the ice grew more delicate with each loop, leaving little trace of her passing, scant evidence of her existence. Finally there was so little to hold her down that she lifted off and drifted away against her will, twice her own height from the ground and fleeing the bounds of reason fast.

She fought with mind and body to claw toward the ground. Heavy thoughts, heavy prayers to get back to the ice. She gained against the tide, reaching lower by progress measured in inches to safe haven, at last scratching tiny slivers from the ice surface with her fingertips in a desperate effort to grab hold. Closer still, she laid her fingers flat on the ground, pressing gently as a hand on a pregnant stomach, while hanging upside down in place, and an explosion burst forth from inside the planet, turning her around, shooting her away from the surface and beyond, into space.

Conscious inside the nether regions, she witnessed stars wheel by, so deep in the Solar System that she could see the gossamer rings of Jupiter flying towards her, then turning into crude rocks, bursting against her unprotected body with eyes opened, scattering her debris in every direction.

CHAPTER 23
Investigations

THE NEXT MORNING, against the funeral background, black ribbons darkening every lapel, Lieutenant Governor Marty Richfield took the oath of office as successor to Governor Arazine. A modest, quiet gathering under heavy security in the large hall with the low ceiling. Outside, in Coubertin Square, the Olympic Clock held at zero hour.

Richfield could see Shelly Kastin herself standing ready with her aide, Zack Younger, the way a crocodile waits by a tall reed in the marsh. This pair and their blue-jacketed force searched the eyes of the crowd for signs of unrest. The commander kept glancing at Richfield like he was one of her eggs.

Richfield gave a shaky nod to Kastin and her soldiers. He realized that Arazine's demise was no accidental death. Kastin expected trouble here today, a threat to him this time. It was a good thing she allowed the Opening Ceremonies to continue. That would keep the live cameras pointed at Abdul Harouk and away from the change of power. That was something to be thankful for. Richfield couldn't take it if he had to stare at a bank of lenses. He'd be constantly thinking that every assassin who wasn't actually present would be dreamily watching and planning his end in the comfort of their homes.

Barely able to pay attention to his own ceremony, the lieutenant governor repeated back the words like an automaton. Something about agreeing to faithfully execute... duties and responsibilities... uphold the law...another part where he just mimicked the sounds, and ending off with "So help me God. So help me God. So help me God." The administering judge had to ask him to stop repeating that part.

He had nothing to worry about, he assured himself with his right hand raised and stiff. Arazine was conducting dangerous experiments, wasn't he? Richmond kept away from his activities, never spoke to him, hardly knew him. He had a family to protect.

The judge had to push Richfield's arm back down when the oath was finished. Scowling, he wrestled the bible from under the new governor's leaden hand. Richfield thought of bolting before the music played out but decided it would be safer to remain among the soldiers.

Why did he bring children to Mars? They couldn't defend themselves against his poor judgment. Was any of this worth it?

* * *

In the back of the ceremony hall, the ill at ease formed a muttering section, most of them Arazine's staff wondering if they would stay on with Marty Richfield even if given the choice. A rumor was going around that suggested it wouldn't be safe to do so. At the far corner, away from the regular clutch of hens were Devon March and Havislaw Valdeen, separately arrived, looking properly solemn.

March avoided Zack Younger's gaze by checking the gloss on his shoes.

"Well, Mr. Pike," said Valdeen. "I can't say I'm surprised at what happened to Peter Arazine after all the chances he took." Valdeen was quiet when he spoke, hardly moved his lips at all.

March looked at Valdeen with a touch of amazement. Although the ex-con had never been specific, the governor's counsel had no doubts about what happened to Arazine. Besides which, in public, his name was still Devon March, not Pike. Dr. "Ziljian" shouldn't have been standing there like a boor, shouldn't have been speaking to him with incriminating proximity.

"Yes, quite," was all March could manage. He reflected that it was a good thing Valdeen wasn't running the governor's office given his audacity. He was a fine assassin but he'd make a worthless politician.

March fixed his eyes ahead at the ceremony, the reality that he had helped to create in his own insinuating way. You make a wish, a few consenting noises, and watch a life pass like a formality. Opportunity. With one thrilling and terrifying gesture he made himself the most powerful man in the city. There was no going back now.

"In the wake of this tragedy, it's up to me to hold this organization together," said Valdeen out of nowhere.

March was aghast. "Don't forget I have seniority over here. You're just a bloody consultant. You can go back to Earth when this is through, retire rich and fat." March betrayed an unusual degree of alarm with the noise he was making. His eyes darted around to see if anyone heard him, but no one appeared interested in the content of his conversation. People nearby just urged the two of them to shut up.

"Yes, I agree," said Valdeen in more restrained tones. "That's if you want the responsibility of being in charge."

"Why wouldn't I? You and I can maintain the relationship that you and Arazine had." His voice was a whisper, being strangled like his plans and visions. Wasn't it reasonable to assume he had moved up a notch in the leadership of Red Freedom? That the entirety of his work and the time he put in had led up to his moment of reward? March was the co-founder after all. Marty Richfield would be a puppet governor. Valdeen-Ziljian didn't fit into the equation at all. He felt an urge to flee, to not have this conversation now or ever, and he started to walk away before a strong hand stopped him.

Valdeen loomed over him. "I sincerely hope you make sure Arazine's accident doesn't happen to you."

Polite applause erupted for the new governor.

* * *

Kastin was scarcely back in the office when Younger said, "Chief, Governor Arazine was murdered."

"Do we know that for sure, Zack? Although his radio link might have been tampered with, it might just as well have been defective. And the autopsy showed no evidence of foul play."

"Granted, a medical examination makes it appear that it was the storm that killed him, but I say he was set up."

"You found something in his rover then?"

"Not direct evidence, we're not finished checking, but something that convinces me anyway. I figure that whoever did this, didn't know that we just launched the MGPS."

Kastin nodded. The MGPS, or Martian Global Positioning System was a satellite group similar to the set that orbited Earth. It was a basic necessity of modern navigation. The user's precise latitude and longitude could be correlated to show a traveler where they were on even the most detailed of maps without the need for any visual confirmation. Every outbound vehicle came equipped with a link up.

Kastin said, "It could be that the killer either didn't know about MGPS or didn't realize that our system also keeps a permanent record of where the vehicle has been."

"Right. That's where he messed up. The record indicates that the Spider came—"

"—What spider?" Kastin interjected.

"That's the classification of the rover Arazine traveled in. It's got these amazing articulated—"

"Skip that and go on."

"Well, the Spider went directly toward Jovis Tholis, stopped short for approximately nine minutes, and came nearly all the way back to Olympia for one more stop before it lost control and started off on a random course that took it in all directions. So it appeared that mechanical difficulties left Arazine hanging."

"That was before the storm began, right?"

"That's correct. Now, if Arazine first ran into mechanical trouble that close to home—"

"The second stop."

"Yes. Then he would never have hiked away from the city and ended up where the heliplane found him. That's a helluva wrong turn with a storm coming, and there was no way for a geologist to get lost with the landmarks out there."

"But his work ordinarily took him deep into Tharsis. All we know is the Spider's record of movements. We don't know whether or not he was aboard at any given time. He could easily have gotten off during the nine minute stopover, and seen the Spider leave without him."

"That's where it gets interesting. The point where the Spider stopped the second time was near to the city but hidden from view by a hillock. It waited there awhile before taking off again, and it didn't start going haywire until after the second stop."

"Wait a second. Can this Spider make independent decisions?"

"Yes, that's what the killer wants us to focus on. But the vehicle makes independent decisions for safety reasons only. At stop number one the Spider wasn't in any danger."

"That could have been part of the malfunction."

"True, but if you look at it another way, the pattern of movement indicates that someone was with the governor aboard the Spider. Someone who left Arazine where they wanted to keep him, which would have been far from home, and then got off where they wanted to get off, at stop number two. Whoever it was, brought himself almost all the way back and then fouled up the controls to make it look like a malfunction caused the Spider to strand Arazine in the path of a storm."

"And it would serve the dual purpose of making us think that the Spider is an unreliable tool for us. I'll buy your conjecture so far. But I need to know who killed

Arazine and why. Especially who, so keep digging. Do we have any more of those Spiders?"

"They're not exactly the same models, but there are six more in storage."

"Break them out. We'll soon put them to good use."

* * *

Zack Younger scanned Governor Arazine's office, mentally cataloging a thousand facts to sort out later, his features tight and sharp. Serious, probing and thoughtful, his FBI background was with him still. The picture of a paramilitary superman, even his scalp obeyed, keeping every hair in place. Not that most people could see it up there. Kastin liked to ask him if 6'6" was enough height for him. She also asked why, with all the music in two worlds to choose from, "Sweet Home Alabama" was still his favorite song. He told her "the South will rise again."

The layered security systems he found suggested to Zack Younger that the late Peter Arazine spent his time as something more than a governor and a scientist. He got Kastin down to the scene to see for herself, filling her in about his suspicions.

"He has an encrypted message for someone named Chang," Younger explained.

"Who?"

"Just Chang, no first name. And the message is in Mandarin. According to our translator, Arazine's note says to contact Chang and tell him 'his path is strewn with roses.'"

"Is it someone on Mars?"

"Chang is a common name, but I checked. No one currently on Mars goes by it."

"How often did he speak to this Chang?"

"We have no way of knowing. Everything from before has been erased."

"Why wasn't this one deleted?"

"I'd say he was preparing to send it and never got the chance. It's not as if he knew his computer was about to be tossed for information. If someone gets killed unexpectedly, you find all their unfinished business," he reminded her.

"There's only one Chang that comes to mind."

"If I had to guess, I'd say one head of state contacts another or he contacts the next best thing. Chul Huk Chang from the Chinese government."

"If his overtures were official business, I should have heard about it."

"But you didn't. And it's no secret that the Chinese refused to sign the space treaty that we're operating under."

"I never trusted Peter Arazine, but you're putting together a case of treason."

"I think he put it together himself."

"Now the big question we've been avoiding. What could be so urgent that somebody would walk away, even temporarily, and leave an incriminating message, if you turn out to be right."

"As back channel communications go, it sounds innocuous. If it weren't encrypted, we wouldn't even be talking about it. I don't know what it is."

"It's fairly simple," said a voice behind them. "That line was not his mistake." Their translator, Steve Trebbia had spoken. He worked for Zack Younger and was trained by him, a smaller version of the original. He was sometimes called Little Zack.

"You think he would trust someone else to translate and send it?" Kastin asked Trebbia.

"It wasn't a message *per se*. It was made to look like part of a poem dedicated to someone named Chang."

"How can you tell?"

"The way it was written on the page with a capital coming up in the middle of a sentence when it hit the next line, and the fact that he had a book of verses in his briefcase. Inspiration for his own writing, I guess." Younger hadn't seen the briefcase Trebbia was referring to yet, but Arazine had dozens of different interests. One more didn't surprise him.

"Another layer of subterfuge," Kastin commented. "Our man was complicated. Brilliant, eclectic and not immune to fault."

"Like most crackpots," said Younger.

"We can't prove his duplicity," she said to Younger.

"Which would mean no search warrants for his associates," said Trebbia.

Kastin said, "At least not from that. What does it mean and how does it relate to his killer?"

Younger said, "I have a feeling something else is going to tie him to Chul Huk Chang and that same thing is what got him killed."

"How did the Chinese get involved?" she wondered aloud.

Trebbia cleared his throat. "Every so often in history, great China sets its foot upon the stage of all human affairs." They both looked at Little Zack incredulously.

"Where do you get that load of crap from?" asked Kastin.

Trebbia pointed. "It's right here in one of Arazine's books."

CHAPTER 24
People's Liberation Army

HER NAME WAS Sun Yan and the first time Chang saw her she was firing a pistol for the People's Liberation Army in 1969.

Her skin was pure as the headwaters of the Yangtze, her lips full, her cap worn tilted back to gather her long hair, with bangs escaping like delicate blades of grass to her forehead. In a row with four male soldiers, her sighting eye fully open and left eye closed with barely an effort. A gentle wind blew the corners of her mouth upward, a face of serenity and pleasure.

While the men fumbled uncertainly with their weapons, squinting, fiddling, blaming the gun, looking at each other, never properly sighting the target, there she stood, left hand reposing on her hip with fingers pointed toward the earth, right arm fully extended, body in perfect alignment with the shot.

The simple fatigues demanded by the Chinese Communist Party and Chinese ethics were almost fancy by comparison to what the peasants wore. On Sun Yan they looked like they were tailored to a Parisian model. While alterations to the uniform were strictly forbidden, and Western decadence was clearly undesirable, the effect was strangely attractive.

Chang studied her to see if there was any true difference between the outfit she wore and one the men wore. Was she guilty of tailoring it against the regulations? The uniform came in dark olive, and woven like a sack of rice. The jacket fell slightly short for her arms so the white lining flared like a frill when her shooting arm stretched. A slight twist of her body made the plain tunic appear tapered at the waist. The supply strap that crossed her torso emphasized her breasts as it slipped between them, and the ammunition pouches extended her ample hips. Bang went the discharge.

Then she wore the tilted cap puffed like a small baker's hat, with her brim flipped toward the sky, an acceptable modification. So the standard had been enhanced only by her ample figure, more than most Chinese women were gifted with. No doubt an unusually confident female communist thrived beneath the sack of rice. Everything was in order on that front.

Sun Yan was special automatically since so few women met the minimum standards of the PLA. Even at that, China was far more advanced than America. There was opportunity to fight in the army for anyone who wanted to escape the fields and factories, but they had to be highly fit and able. Chances were that a woman in the army would have to be better than most men even to get there, and this was certainly the case with Sun Yan. Chang was struck by her. The question was, did she learn Mao's lessons, would she also measure up politically?

Chang got his best political indoctrination in the army, as did the other eighteen-year-old conscripts. "The Party is my mother," as the saying went.

If any of the backward thinking bourgeois liberals became dissatisfied with the CCP, a politically conditioned army made military coup by the malcontents unlikely. Survival of the Cultural Revolution confirmed that theory. Thus the fulfillment of Mao's Principle, "The Party commands the gun, and the gun must never be allowed to command the Party."

Some reports claimed that the bold and proud Sun Yan sided with independent factions in the Hunchun Commune, that she held very dangerous views that were contrary to the Party. Were the informants accurate or jealous?

Soon Chang would take his place as commander of the company on the triple border, in the sight of Vladivostok, the country of their inspiration to which he owed so much. Soon he had to decide if Sun Yan was to be arrested.

CHAPTER 25
Competition

PARTICIPATING IN THE opening ceremonies with Terri beside him filled Yves Loitte with trembling wonder. He viewed Mars as the embodiment of the new Olympic frontier with challenges to push humans beyond their imagination. *Citius, Altius, Fortius.* Faster, Higher, Stronger.

The Olympic Torch had taken its longest journey ever. Televised to the entire known universe, the two-planet audience had watched it make a stop at the tomb of Baron Pierre de Coubertin, who had resurrected The Games in 1896 for modern man. Only this time the torch traveled from Greece's Olympia to Olympia Mars via spacecraft for the first time. When it reached the stadium it lit the Olympic Flame, which would burn throughout the Games.

The audience hushed for an announcement. Following tradition, an athlete from the host city, in this case a five-year Martian, would recite the time-honored Olympic Oath. Without preamble, he said, "In the name of all competitors, I promise that we will take part in these Olympic Games, respecting and abiding by the rules which govern them in the true spirit of sportsmanship, for the glory of the sport and the honor of our teams." Brief and to the point. Not a word of the 1896 oath had to be changed for the circumstances.

Behind the athlete, the Martian flag painted the curve of the red planet large in the foreground with the rising sun washing a fiery halo to the periphery. The Earth loomed in the background in a black field amongst the stars. It looked magnificent. Yves could never be pissed off at the Martians. He was in awe of them.

Even against the backdrop of the under-populated future capacity stands, the host city put on a spectacular show. Best of all, Yves and Terri would join in the Parade of Nations, a procession where the athletes of each participating country were announced and circled the stadium in costume, bearing their flags. In alphabetical order, they would not enter at A for America, but U for the United States, promising a long wait.

Yves had no reason to be impatient considering the company he kept. Terri's beauty captivated him equally when she was twirling around on the ice, climbing a rock wall, breaking boards, or sitting peacefully. Even standing still, she was woman he had to work to keep up with. Had he realized his relationship with her was quickly reaching a precipice, he might not have been so complacent.

She said, "I'm worried about you tomorrow. It's so isolated on the mountain, I don't know how you can stand being out of touch."

"I'm used to it."

"Still, I wish you would stay tuned on the wristband for information. By the way, the man you so admire made it to Mars."

"Who's that?"

"After all that raving? Professor Brisini. He must have come in on the last flight."

"You recognized him, huh? Where have they got him housed?"

"I don't know. He was too busy to talk to me. Some big shot."

Yves laughed.

She said, "Hey, I've been wanting a private moment to ask you something."

Yves was grateful she couldn't see his face flush under his armor. "There's probably a billion people watching us. I wouldn't call that private. But go on."

"The cameras are pointed the other way. Are you with or against the location of The Games?"

"We're here aren't we?"

"Yes, of course. We're not going anywhere. But none of the athletes, including you and I, had a say in it. We want to hold a symbolic protest."

"Sure, whatever."

Terri sighed. "For someone with such pride in your Franco-American heritage, you are a hopelessly non-political creature. You're not off the hook yet."

The audience cheered. Below them, the Parade of Nations ticked up to the letter B.

* * *

The morning light grew quickly at the Martian equator, just as it would on Earth. Here however, slanting rays fortified the nearly transparent clouds with whiteness as they raced by. Yves on the day of his first event lived at the very moment when they would give him the signal to make history, for better or worse.

Five of Yves's competitors had plunged downhill already, four of them setting a withering pace as the standard. Karl Hinter, the sixth, neared the bottom of the course, and Lou Coburn had just left the starting gate. Yves had drawn bib number eight, making him the next to follow.

Even from where he stood, near the base of the great Olympus Mons, waiting to ski down a lower fringe that could have been a mountain itself, the tilted land seemed to stretch off in all directions. Rising 78,000 feet from floor to summit, ten *miles* beyond Mt. Everest on Earth by his familiar measurements, Olympus was the highest mountain in the solar system. Not even two Mt. Everests stacked one atop the other would have matched it.

A glance back showed him clouds of ice crystals obscuring the 64-k crater at Olympus' peak along with the top five kilometers of the mountain. Resembling snow, the cloud cover had been dubbed *Nix Olympia* or Snow of Olympus long before man set foot on Mars. As Yves gazed toward the horizon, the clouds became sparse and thin, dark pink smears on the sky. The sun, 49 million miles further away than he was used to, appeared small but bright against the thin atmosphere.

Yves was slightly alarmed when he heard the shouting. He decided it must be the excitement. He had to keep his mind on skiing.

Yves looked at the viewer in the start house and was immediately sorry he did. A skier ahead of him, Karl Hinter, went flying off the path in what had to be a monumental disaster. Yves groaned. First the Games had suffered the upskiier's accident, then Governor Arazine killed in a storm, and now this.

Yves watched Lou Coburn waved off the course three quarters down to ensure that he did not crash into the rescuers. The rest of the chain was put on hold.

The on-the-spot investigation findings had it that a leak in the Austrian's nitrox tank had made him light headed before he hit the ground.

Subcutaneous air bubbles under his arm told them that the broken rib he sustained had punctured and collapsed his lung. If those injuries didn't end his career, the broken hip he suffered surely would.

Yves was now facing the very same slope.

Coburn was down in the finish house sending Yves advice via wristband based on the run that got interrupted by the accident, a low gravity jump off a 90-meter ramp followed by a standard slalom. Slalom meant "a race between flags." Here Yves would test both his jumping ability and his speed on a zigzag course.

On the days to follow, things would get much more complicated. An Olympic athlete today was expected to live up to the ideal of the "four-way" title, a return to the days before World War II, back when specialists were frowned upon. The full title required both Nordic and Alpine skills to complete a program of slalom, jumping, downhill and cross-country. Only now, it also had to be accomplished in combined tasks within a single event. The equipment makers, who thought everything had already been invented in the twentieth century, had a whole new list of requirements to fulfill.

Yves wondered why there was so much controversy arising from the changes in this Olympics. Skiing itself was not an event at the 1896 Olympics in Athens when The Games returned to the modern world or before that. In fact, dozens of events had been added and modified in the last hundred and forty-two years. So what if it took place for the first time on another planet with different gravity? Everyone played under the same conditions. They even used standard Earth clocks so that the statistical comparisons would not be thrown off. And if the Martian colonists had a bit of an advantage this year, it might not be so next time.

To preserve the order, Lou was sent back to the top to do his run over. It was the longest wait Yves had ever experienced. He checked his helmet latches for the fifth time. Did the Nitrox tank lock in properly? Was it at full pressure? It seemed like he was waiting for the starter's horn forever. He could see the cameras and the small knots of people, but he focused on the starter holding the green flag aloft as he checked his watch. To give ample warning, the starter would call "ready," drop the flag, and someone else would initiate a sequence of beeps. At that point, the skier's first forward movement would trip an electronic beam that would mark precision time until the corresponding beam tripped at the finish.

When the ready call came, Yves dropped his outer visor, surveyed at the slope and adjusted visor brightness. All business now. Nothing else existed. A light wind sprayed whiteness across the only landmarks on a snowy course that spread on and on beyond vision.

He turned up the oxygen regulator and dropped into a crouch, his fingers flexing to test his gloves against the grip on his poles. The last thing he did was something he remembered just in time. He dampened the hearing input in his helmet so the sound of the roaring wind wouldn't deafen him. *Too many gadgets.*

He felt the skin creep on his scalp, and relax as he counted off the three distinct tones that followed. At the third, higher in pitch and louder than the previous two, Yves uncoiled, threw his weight forward, and drew his feet up. He poled down in four quick strokes and tucked his knees up to his chest in the classic egg position to pick up speed. Accelerating in seconds to a blurry 108 m.p.h., he made several rapid changes in position to end up in a sail formation, a kind of full body airfoil that formed a tight acute angle with his skis.

The cable bindings unlocked so that his heels could rise off the skis when he leaned forward with his legs straightened. His arms hugged his sides. No matter how many times he did it, he remembered the rules. *Lean over your skis so that your head is nearly even with the tips. Hold the poles so that they are out of the way, pressed against the backs of your arms, pointed toward your head.* Ideally, as in the old days, there would be no poles used for a jump, but he needed them for the combined event.

Had he left his communication band on, he would have heard the broadcasters commenting that his skis were rising as he cleared the curved lip, a sure sign that he would land well. He positioned himself in the air so that the back of the skis almost touched while the front was spread wide to form a "V." The loose boards evenly met the wind to allow a rocking movement like the gentle ebb and flow of a deep-water tide. Yves was airborne for several glorious moments, weightless and invincible, a feeling of euphoria that skiers called *effect.* For some, it was reason enough to endure any type of punishment to get back up there, to heighten the effect. A small dose of it could be had on a rollercoaster ride, even more from a parachute jump, and the most where it was entirely dependent on your own inscrutable combination of skills to put you in the situation and to bring you back safely. On Mars, effect was multiplied by lift, an earnest flirtation with death, settling the question of survival each time.

The ground came rushing back. He balanced and bent his knees again to take the shock before he touched fresh snow over 220 meters distant from his starting point. His heel mechanisms locked back into place one at a time and the stability fins jettisoned on impact to convert his awkward double width skis into something he could carve turns with. In this event, the judges did not look for elegance when you hit the ground. Not everyone could hold onto the landing under the circumstances. A skier was lucky if he didn't go spinning off to the padded retaining walls, or worse.

Land bound again, he tucked down to approached the slalom. In this part of the course, he had to pivot around flagged poles known as gates, passing right of red ones, left of blue. The flexible gates gave way when bumped. There were sixty of them and missing a single one meant disqualification. With his skis offering precious little resistance to the snow, he had to be very careful about his center of gravity in those turns. In this abnormal weight environment the momentum he was used to would now push him off center if he didn't adjust properly. And that would send him sprawling into disaster.

His concentration held keen. The course ran fast in the packed down straight-aways from eighth position, and on a clear, high visibility day like this he could still choose his own line because the snow hadn't yet been carved into unchangeable ruts by the previous skiers. He hardly noticed the markers flop out of the way as he nudged each of them in turn with his passage. He would clip more than forty-five of the gates before he was finished. Only passing on the wrong side of one, "missing it," would invoke disqualification.

Time slowed from his perspective. A thousand vertical feet could be burned up in no time if he didn't concentrate on corrections. His body responded well, but not perfectly. As he bore down on his left ski in the stretch they called the Pressure Cooker, he sent a high mist of snow to rise and scatter in the wind. The added friction would slow him by critical hundredths, maybe even tenths of a second.

Then he saw the unusual tracks in the snow where the Pressure Cooker did its worst, ones made by helmet, elbows and skis crashing end over end. The name *Karl Hinter* flashed through his mind, breaking his concentration for an instant. He had successfully blocked out the Austrian's accident until that point. Yves lost his alignment and regained it, throwing off his time again. But he held on.

When he rounded the final gate, the last flag dipped and rose again hesitantly. He flew out onto the straightaway, past the finish, easing up until his legs were only slightly bent. He pivoted sharply to the right, throwing up a tall spray in order to stop, and raised his visor to see what happened. He gave no victory salute.

The first event results posted on the spot. Yves noted the time transmitted to his wristband. In the previous six finishers, there were three better than him and three worse. As a running tally, fourth was the order he would occupy at best. Nils Barkly had already taken a commanding lead and there were still other fast Martians left to follow. Yves felt sweat trickle down his wrist.

"Congratulations," shouted Lou.

"What did I do?"

"You dog! You've already toppled the three best guys on our team in this event. Even Gingold. Even me. I knew your tryout troubles didn't mean a thing."

"You were a fraction behind me in fifth, Lou. But save the celebrations for the end."

Though no medal came with it, top five meant you were usually a medal contender for the next race, but Yves refused to let that into his head.

Lou was already poling away. "The way you zapped those gates, I think we'll call you The Clipper from now on."

After a time, when Terri made it to the finish house, she ran into Lou and he pointed her towards Yves.

Terri tapped him on the shoulder. He turned to see her smiling face, her eyes glistening. Was it the cold or something else? "Good performance. Your place held up. I need to talk with you. It's important."

Before they could move on, reporters hungry for an American win pressed around and between them to ask Loitte if he was ready to pull an upset.

* * *

The young man joined the lady on the bench, and both kept their attention on their digital assistants while they talked. The young man longed for the days he'd seen in old movies when secret agents used a newspaper to cover their lip movements. He could still obtain a newspaper, but it wasn't worth looking that eccentric.

"You said a little too much to Loitte the other day, Mr. Coburn."

"In Little Green New York? You mean, I'm worth listening to?"

Kastin looked straight at him. "You're lucky it was me listening instead of the Agency. You didn't sound like you were enjoying your job very much."

"I'm doing it aren't I?"

"You're on loan to me and I'm worried about you."

"Responsible for me."

"I want you to drop out of sight for awhile."

"You mean out of Loitte's sight. I'm going to be way too busy to talk to him anyway."

"You're to have absolutely no contact with him. And stop asking questions in the Village for a while. Don't take any chances."

"I finally got hold of something with my idle questions."

"You have something on the Course One fatality?"

"My report will say that Karl Hinter was sabotaged. Even the news anchor noticed that something was odd about his run."

"How would a sports commentator recognize sabotage?"

"Just from watching. Most control problems that end in a spill start early. You make a wrong move, lose your alignment, become unbalanced, fight the wind, fight yourself, compensate, over-compensate and finally fall. Any trained eye can see the struggle from the beginning. With Karl Hinter it happened as suddenly as if an invisible hand slapped him down. And he didn't make a physical mistake, he probably just fainted. I think his problem was in the nitrox. He must have thought his tank was at full pressure before he took off, otherwise he wouldn't have gone anywhere. But the Austrian doctor diagnosed hypoxia when he saw the burst blood vessels in the back of Hinter's eyes. That means that at some point there wasn't any oxygen reaching his blood. I'd say someone gave that skier a heavy dose of nitrogen gas to replace most of his oxygen and fixed it so that the gauge didn't read that way. That's the reason he had nothing to breathe while missing any caution light for low pressure in the tank."

"Does analysis confirm that?"

"We have someone who says he was paid to get rid of that nitrox tank before it could be examined. Hinter's team doctor wanted to get a look at it, too."

"Did the doctor comment? I want to know exactly what he said."

"When he couldn't find the tank, he demanded to know who took it, and he yelled something that sounded like, '*Es ist gegen die Hausordnung.*'"

"It is against regulations?"

"You're very good with your German."

"That still leaves us with a lot of questions. Was it a rival team, or was the killing tied in with the terrorists?"

"We'll soon find out if Red Freedom wants to take credit for it."

"There are fifteen days of competition left, Mr. Coburn, and we have one skier and one governor killed by the end of the first day."

"We should stay a step ahead of everyone else, but I get the awful feeling that we're running more than one step behind them."

"It had better not stay that way. Did Hinter manage to say anything himself when they carried him off the slope?"

"*Beten Sie für mich.*"

Kastin translated, "Pray for me."

* * *

"Let us speak of objectives," Valdeen said to the leadership council of Red Freedom who sat around him in a circle. Devon March stood next to him. "Everything around here is a potential target," Valdeen continued. "Anything we do will hurt them. Be it a building or an outpost or the draining of an enemy's Nitrox tank. Even livestock can be a prime target."

"Livestock?" someone repeated.

"It's their primary meat supply. What are they going to do, go out and hunt up some more? Our first choice, naturally, is to control the most critical elements. Our goal in this conflict is to force Kastin to evacuate her security forces to the orbiting space station. We have to take over as many buildings as possible and take as many hostages as possible to convince her to leave. People and facilities will be our leverage. We will disarm them by destroying as many of their shuttles as we can when her security is aboard them. If they are still on the ground when we strike, we can damage the airfield at the same time. That will essentially put us in control. That's all you need to know. Team leaders each have their job to do. Wait for the signal to act. You're dismissed."

March stayed behind after the room cleared out. "What happens after their military leaves for home?" he wanted to know.

"After? That's the really fun part. We wipe out the traitors and divide the spoils. Plenty of people will be interested in joining us when it comes to that."

March wondered if he or Richfield or even someone else would be left to lead them. He was going into it with his eyes wide open. "And long term?" March asked.

"Then it's propaganda all the way. Eventually, Earth will give in. They won't be able to bring an army forty nine million miles and supply a long distance war effort. Especially after they wasted their treasury on this Olympic nonsense."

CHAPTER 26
Admirer

As ONE WITH her company, Sun Yan used the hoe blade to help peasants turn the soil of their local fields for the 1969 growing season. Thoughts of Chang Chul-Huk, the confident young man who would soon take charge, lightened her swing, his undaunted outlook sparking her hope and feminine desire. Intellectuals among the peasants scornfully claimed Chul-Huk looked like Chiang Kai-shek, and while Sun Yan could not completely deny that assessment, she privately found him far more attractive than the earlier, and no longer popular, revolutionary leader.

From the pictures, Chiang Kai-shek had something of the Spaniard in his face the way his moustache hair grew, and certainly the Spanish were among the colonists who took advantage of China, so it was obvious where the Hispanic influence came from. But worse yet, the man who defied Chairman Mao looked like his mother had been raped by the Japanese. It was unfair to compare Chang to someone disgraced in so many ways.

In Kirin Province, spring wheat gave way to summer soybeans and corn. Since the Hunchun Commune did not encompass what the CCP identified as "a high and stable yield area," the work was accomplished with the occasional help of the PLA and without the benefit of valuable and scarce machines. Ironic that the areas that needed help most, got the least. Perhaps she drove the blade a bit too hard when she thought of the unfairness both to the newly responsible Chang and to the Hunchun Commune. "The Party is my mother," she muttered.

"Learn from Dazhai," said the smirking intellectual beside her, correctly reading the cross look on her face. He was being sarcastic. Dazhai Village in the Northwest was famous for overcoming exceptional poverty and poor production conditions to become relatively wealthy by Chinese standards. In a counter-intuitive experiment, the CCP reserved the best farm equipment and machinery for areas where the soil was rich and historically prosperous. The "Learn From Dazhai" campaign exhorted agriculturally disadvantaged areas to look at the model of the rigged Dazhai Commune and somehow accomplish what they had accomplished. Commune headquarters at Hunchun proudly displayed an enlarged photograph of the beautifully terraced and remarkably productive fields of Dazhai.

No matter what platitudes spilled from his mouth, the intellectual beside Sun Yan, who had been forcibly imported from Peking University to learn the virtues of manual labor, was unconvinced. He was also one of the people who did not like the looks of Chang. If he only knew everything that Sun Yan was thinking.

Sun ignored him, listening to the pleasant chopping sound of blades tilling the land on every side. What the corrupt intellectual did not realize was that Chang Chul-huk was startlingly different from the incompetent men around him. And more genuinely Chinese if you looked for it, she thought insistently. The more rounded line of his jaw was like the hard-working Han of the interior from which the old dynastic rulers were risen. Or better still, from the fantasy world of the Sons of Heaven, like Shun, who was master of the elephants or like Chu Chüan-chung who lived in the Great Luminous Palace beyond the Gate of the Cinnabar Phoenix. Since Chang's arrival, stories of her ancestors swirled in her mind on wings of fiery vermillion.

The curious mixture in Chang's heritage, she decided, was Tibetan in origin. Can such an exotic man admire someone like me? she wondered. The extolled virtues of late marriage would turn out true if it saved her for someone like Chang Chul-Huk. But never having traveled, she couldn't be sure of any of these things, what he resembled or what would meet with his approval.

Regardless of the learning opportunity, it was futile to save your resources for traveling, she reminded herself. Only the army could provide such luxury. Sun lived an average life and knew the value of a *yuan*. Back in the city, her mother shared a kitchen with another family where there were always ample pots and clean towels, baskets strung across the window. They had a wood burning stove and plenty of workspace. The cupboards that still had doors looked better than the ones without but some of the household wood had to be burned in hard times. Going out, her mother wore her best clothes, the ones that had been re-sewn at the seams but not obviously patched. She owned a bicycle that was in perfect repair, still saving up for a radio, and even provided her daughter with paper for a diary. It was never said that Sun's mother did not "hold up half the sky."

When Sun's father lived, he was a good earner. His pay exceeded that of a farmer or soldier but fell short of a PLA commander's envelope. His wages grew as the work and the worker became more specialized. A long-time laborer in the Nanking Fertilizer Factory, he caught on to the new process immediately. Recycling secondary chemical products with patriotic fervor the equal of any. Before her father could pass on his skills, he was accidentally killed by the Red Guard, while foolishly trying to defend a Buddhist temple. "Stay away from the Red Guard," he had often told her. Today her mother held up the whole sky by herself. Sun dug vigorously into the earth.

Were things different outside of Nanking and Hunchun? Who could tell? It was too arduous to get a travel permit, and impossible to find the money. But with the People's Liberation Army, and Chang's blessing, she would travel now.

CHAPTER 27
Taking Chances

KASTIN'S COMMUNIQUÉ TO Earth read:

Date: February 1, 2038
To: The Office of the President of the United States
From: Shelly Kastin, Security Chief, XXVIII Winter Olympic Games.

Re: Crisis in Olympia/ Danger to personnel and equipment.

> Preliminary investigations indicate 1) that the death of Governor Arazine was an assassination; 2) that the death of Karl Hinter of the Austrian Ski Team resulted from sabotage. Be assured that no such information has been made public. Although all counter-terrorist actions have been initiated, I consider it unlikely that Games can proceed without further loss of life and other costly damages. Disruption may be imminent and critical. Recommend immediate suspension and postponement of

Games until threat is identified and
curbed.

Scarcely an hour passed before the response came
back. Kastin read the contents with dismay:

"Kastin: Proceed with original
directive. Under no circumstances
must the Olympic Games deviate
from schedule."

She read the message twice and then inquired with a
copy of same as to whether any portion was missing. In
forty minutes came the answer:

"No."

* * *

Lou Coburn trotted swiftly down the deserted corridor
on his way to Shelly Kastin's office. In possession of a
complete list of conspirators, he couldn't trust sending a
message for fear of interception. Shelly would understand
and would call for immediate action. To get to her it would
take five minutes, tops.

At an intersection in the hall, two men grabbed him by
the arms, another two seized on his kicking legs. The four
of them lifted him uneasily and battered his head into the
wall. While he was dazed, they flipped him over and tied
his hands behind him with two of their knees pressed to the
small of his back. Someone else fixed the gag firmly in
place over his mouth.

As they tried to haul him up, The Cobra gathered his legs under him and kicked and twisted so that he broke free, running with hands tied, still gagged. The leanest of his attackers tackled him and took a boot in the face while the others caught up and started kicking Coburn on the ground. They tried to tear his clothes off, gave up when it didn't work, and the lean man hit him again to cut his squirming. Then they carried the agent, less than half awake, to the nearest airlock, which was back where they first got hold of him.

"He's got a head like a bowling ball," the man at his right elbow commented.

"Hurry and get him out," was the reply.

"WARNING," said Gatekeeper when they pressed for the exit. "IT IS NOW EIGHTEEN DEGREES BELOW ZERO FAHRENHEIT AND FALLING. THE AIR JETS WILL BE TURNED OFF IN THIRTY-SIX SECONDS FOR ROUTINE MAINTENANCE. DO NOT LEAVE THE BUILDING WITHOUT THE NECESSARY PROTECTIVE CLOTHING AND NITROX SUPPLY."

"Thank you for the warning," said one of the men before they opened the second door, flung Lou Coburn into the night, and sealed him out.

Coburn, fully awakened by the cold through his open shirt front, launched himself back at the closing door a moment too late. He whirled around so that his bound hands could try the door controls, closing his eyes to imagine the keypad upside down. The normal sequence gave no response. Gatekeeper patiently explained, "AIRLOCK IN USE. OUTER DOORS WILL NOT OPEN UNTIL INNER DOORS CLOSE." Holding his last breath in his lungs, he punched in his emergency override codes and waited.

"CURRENT AIRLOCK USER HAS DECLARED PRIOR EMERGENCY TO KEEP INNER DOORS OPEN. HAVE ADVISED CURRENT USER TO EXPEDITE. FIVE SECONDS TO AIR JET DISABLING. REMEMBER TO USE YOUR NITROX."

Coburn repeated his request for access.

Gatekeeper told him, "INTERIOR EMERGENCIES HAVE PRIORITY OVER EXTERIOR EMERGENCIES. WE SUGGEST A TEN CREDIT PURCHASE OF GINSENG SCENT FOR INCREASED PATIENCE."

Already The Cobra was freezing and gasping for the remaining air. Any warmth he had generated from the fight quickly evaporated. He didn't know if it would be minutes or seconds before he was completely disabled. There wasn't time to reach another door, and the next nearest one was probably rigged in a similar condition, just in case he tried for it. One thought kept him going: *Barbara will never forgive me if I don't come back.*

He kicked the wall hard, feeling the solid response reverberate through him. Dropping back six paces, he ran towards the wall, swinging his leg and rotating his hips so that his heel slammed into the surface with everything he had. His cries of pain emptied his lungs of precious air. The crack of his bone echoed louder than the sound of the impact that breached the wall, but he had managed to punch through the thin layer of concrete in one tiny spot. His body ended up twisted face down on the ground.

Sensors buried in the wall recorded the problem, activated a spray to re-coat the affected area, and made the proper notation in the maintenance logs.

Before the spray sealed over the spot, and just before he passed out, Coburn turned over, lifted his good leg and pushed it into the hole so that the new concrete sprayed only his foot. He held on until the spray ran out. As he fell senseless, his foot slipped out of place and the hole was exposed again.

Sensors noted the unsatisfactory conditions and summoned a human maintenance operator.

* * *

Rolly Ingrem began his shift on another happy day. Back in Sub-Level Three in the empty and very private room he cherished. Ingrem kissed his terminal right in the middle of the screen leaving a spot of moisture behind.

"You lucky terminal," the Life Giver told it. "You get to keep me." Happily, he wiped the smudge clean with a soft rag, heard the surface squeak like a contented seal. He'd suffered a close call yesterday, but he got to stay in his lovely job. Fellow game jocks would rejoice. Smart thinking that was, using a piece from here and a piece from there to solve his missing passport problem. He'd recommend himself for a promotion if he could figure out how to explain it in governmentese.

Master Detective, which contained the imaging sequence that saved him, was a great game, too, one that snagged his highest rating. If nothing else, old Rolly reigned as king of evaluating programs. That's what his coworkers counted on him for. Why not celebrate his mental prowess? Pull out the long neglected game, call up a few friends, and have a blow out.

He would get some girls down here. He deserved it. That Katy Juno from Sub-Level One had been lonely too long. He would beat some sense into her and she would meet Master Dick.

He already had the game loaded into the hard drive this time so its recall would be quick. Those fast driving cars from the Thunder Track were long forgotten.

Let the babes be red headed and acrobatic. Why not?

Interrupting the program, Ingrem punched in his message and let his database blast out the party proclamation. Just a minute or two now to secure their R.S.V.P.'s. Meanwhile he wanted to take another look at the program and brush up on the rules before the others arrived.

He popped on a second unit so he could work at the same time without sacrificing processing power. It also had the game loaded in. It wasn't until Ingrem kicked it into gear and saw the Master Detective logo flash on with its smoking Sherlock Holmes pipe puffing away, that he thought more deeply about what he had done with the passport program and the way he did it, and realized he had made a terrible mistake.

"Oh shit," he said to himself. "I'm dead, aren't I?"

* * *

Kastin read Zack Younger's report with disbelief. The terrorist activity had come to an apparent standstill. Reports coming in showed zero incidents taking place, not even a subversive leaflet littering the street. No attempts of property destruction and no threats made. This is wrong, wrong as can be, she thought. Shelly Kastin had tightened security to its highest level for the start of the Games themselves, but she fully expected some kind of onslaught after Arazine and Hinter were reported killed. There should have been an increase in activity. The television cameras gave them all the publicity they wanted. Nothing happening meant that they were husbanding their resources for a serious attack. She had to stop it.

The Chief was painfully alert to the possibility that Red Freedom would take every opportunity to import more operatives. Any additional subversives coming would have arrived on the last shuttle. But if someone had slipped in, the fact had eluded her staff so far.

She unsprung the passport and entry visa file that Rolly Ingrem had transmitted to her earlier. Her last coverage of the material revealed no clues. Like before, she went page by page, just looking. This is what her department at Treasury used to call "an investigator's fishing trip." None of the entries were going to be labeled "enemy infiltrator," but the more she learned, the greater the possibility that she would find something amiss. Theoretically, there was one passport and one entry visa for every person that landed at Mercury Airport, the answer in this file somewhere. Unlike amateur anglers, Kastin had never gone on a fishing trip without catching fish.

She scanned them down to the last one, just like before, then asked to start at the beginning again, and ran it more slowly. Only this time, she had it change parameters from name to point of origin. She wondered if she brushed against another key at the same time because something different came up on the screen this time.

"CHANGE NOSE Y/N?" the program inquired.

CHAPTER 28
Correction

THE NIGHT BEFORE the harvest, October 12th, 1969, Chang Chul-huk inspected the moonlit Sea of Japan, smoothing down his four-pocketed jacket and fingering his new ball point pen, the modest items that distinguished commanders in the People's Liberation Army from non-commanders. Although forty percent of Chang's day was given over to political study, on top of it he sometimes stayed up late to ponder the changing situation in China. Clearly he could pinpoint when the Cultural Revolution began but not when it ended, if it had truly ended at all. Who could say it was at an end when the capitalist trend was not fully corrected? Back at the camp, outside of Hunchun, he still saved the armband imprinted "*Hong Wei Bing*" that identified him as a member of the Red Guard. He still carried the "little red book," Quotations From Chairman Mao, and relished his role in the sanctioned destruction of rival gangs. The complacent Red Guards from the city universities had been no match for the teenage Red Guards from the countryside, politically or physically.

As the new commander of his company, Chang had many decisions to make, including ones about the fate of people he guided. His choices had to be based on nothing less than perfect doctrine. Only by being "expert" could he reach the staff level of the parent battalion and the higher ranks of the CCP.

Several of his men were destined for correction. Minor correction could be accomplished through hard labor, and self-denunciation. If an intern learned properly, or if circumstances changed, they could later be rehabilitated, reinstated with rank and privileges intact. If some needed major correction, that would also have to be done. Although there was talk of things soon returning to normal, a good Party member would always err on the side of redness, and disrupt the social order to keep it from becoming stratified. The image of Mao was always at hand to remind you. "Uninterrupted revolution" was Mao's Dictum, and uninterrupted revolution it would be.

The next day, on roads of well-packed dirt, the PLA moved the fruits of their harvest into the reserve granaries. The farm maintained the PLA mobilization to counter the growing Soviet threat. Working beside the lovely Sun Yan in the fields, preparing the soil for corn, Chang elicited the full scope of her political views . By now they knew each other well and Sun Yan did not believe he was capable of tricking her, or that he was inclined to do so in these marginally more relaxed times.

The ascension of Lin Biao to the Vice-Chairmanship signaled to most people that the oppressiveness of the Cultural Revolution was no longer necessary, and like many recruits of her scarce years, Sun was confident of a new era of openness. Unaware of Chang's background, she defended religion and the rights of commune workers to earn money from outside jobs. She believed with inspirational passion that the teachings of Confucius could co-exist with the great wisdom of Mao. She half-believed that the fantastic stories of the dynasties were true. Encouraged by Chang's scholarly knowledge of ancient China and the warmth of mid-day, she even confided her theory that Chang was descended from the Han of the interior, surely an heir to the dynasties himself. Her genuine admiration for him and the inherent correctness of the revolution slowed his hand long after he had ample cause to correct her political errors.

Most interestingly, he in turn admired her great skills with a pistol and her influence among the men. If it was not love, it was as close as he could come. Too bad. If she had not been in a military career, her views would have been somewhat more tolerable.

Without further agonizing over the decision, Chang had Sun Yan arrested. *The gun must not be allowed to control the Party, not if I am ever to reach the staff level of the parent battalion*, he swore.

But Chang was not without sentimental feelings for her. If it would not have tarnished his reputation, he would surely have recommended against her execution.

CHAPTER 29
Forced Hand

YVES RUSHED OVER to the fireplace to see its small blaze, a rare delight he hadn't expected on Mars. He noticed that Terri crossed the parquet floor to the majestic windows. Old World stuff in this room Terri had reserved. No big game heads mounted on the walls, though. He wondered what would constitute big game on Mars. A garden slug?

"Are you listening to me?" said Terri. He hadn't noticed her cross to the couch. "I need to feel like I have your support."

Yves knew fires and this one was going out. He parted the fanfold screen and fed wood through the fire gate where it would best catch.

"Terri, I don't know what to say. I have to be honest." He used the poker to reposition the fuel, eliciting a crackle and a spray of embers. "I feel that we all agreed to the terms simply by coming here. Protesting the location of The Games would be hypocritical at this point."

"We were forced to Mars if we wanted to compete at all."

"But I agree with the IOC. It was a practical decision to have the games here. Mars needs the support and the Olympics needs a new spectacle."

"That's debatable," she said with a finality that belied the concept of debate.

Yves stared at his stylized helmet with its image of a pelican on one side and a hermit thrush on the other, honoring both of his native states. "I don't have time for this, Terri. Neither do you. Why can't we protest when we get back?"

"That's not the way to make a point. Yves, let's try to save the Earth instead of running away from it. I'm not saying that we should prevent The Games from going on. I'm saying that there is nothing wrong with a quiet protest to make our views known. And the venue gives us no better forum for inter-world attention. We're not going to get another chance."

Yves joined her on the couch to adjust his boot bindings. The difference in gravity necessitated several changes and experience told him not to trust the default settings. He also wanted to play around with the tilt and flex options. "You've been talking to Lou. I guess that I have to say I'm not with you guys on this. I see the planet shift as part of necessary changes we have to get used to."

"Fine," she said bitterly. "I was hoping that your stature would lend support to our efforts, but I guess I was wrong." She looked at the fire. It gave her a spit and a hiss.

"Terri, I understand what you're going through with your father. I know he'd be with you if the games were on Earth. I had to leave my whole family behind, so I share a little bit of what you're going through."

"That has nothing to do it."

"Maybe."

Yves knew more than she thought he did about her father's condition. Terri had taken the option of going to the Olympics instead of providing the comfort she felt she owed her dad. She probably imagined it as a kind of betrayal.

Terri spilled it out fast. "You don't understand. My parents spent twenty-five thousand dollars a year on me, a quarter million dollars before I could do a triple-toe loop. I was up every day to skate at five thirty with school at eight thirty. My coach programmed it into me that all I could think about was me. Skate for me, concentrate on me, and think about me. Then if you do a good job, the jealousy comes, and your skates disappear in the locker room, and your dresses, and then your music for the program. So they spend more money. But the rest of my family can't have a life because their hopes and dreams rest on me." Her face was contorted, her voice high and shrill at the end.

Yves didn't plan to say anything for a while. She was feeling the pressure. She wasn't unraveling, but it was a rare venting for her. He just looked at the rough skin on the back of his hands and held still. Before he expected it, she swallowed and got back under control. "I'm leaving now. If you change your mind, I'll be with Doc Ziljian in the stadium."

"Wait. What has Ziljian got to do with all this?"

"He's the organizer of the protest. We'll be holding a candlelight vigil tonight in the stadium, and we have to make plans."

"I don't like Ziljian."

"Why?"

The fire gate popped open. Random sparks leapt and vanished. "I—I just don't. I can't say." He couldn't tell Terri what had transpired between him and Ziljian without lowering her opinion of him still further.

"I don't expect you to like him. He's principled."

He wondered if she realized how much that hurt.

"He believes that the Games should be on Earth," she continued, "so that the Earth is not abandoned. And he believes in Martian autonomy through peaceful means. If the terrorists attack, he's willing to fight them. The only thing you came here for is personal glory." She let the breeze slam the door on her way out.

Yves felt a small pain crimp his chest, but he could tell she didn't mean what she said. She looked as wounded as he felt. Still, he knew she believed in him, and there was a lot of truth in what she had said.

Yves began to go after her, and stopped himself. The pressure was getting to Terri more than Yves ever guessed. He decided he had better let her cool down.

* * *

Kastin froze with a poised finger over the keyboard. The record name on the screen was Travis Ziljian, listed as the American Team Doctor. Why the hell would it say, "change nose?" thought Kastin. And does it have something to do with Ziljian himself? She had that dry mouth feeling that bode well for the investigation but made her fear for the safety of her team.

She entered "Y" for yes, and a full selection of different shaped noses were laid out for selection. *Am I seeing what I think I'm seeing?* She picked a long, thin type, skipped the fine-tuning that was offered, and instantly, Travis Ziljian had a different nose. The image rotated in three dimensions to show her how it looked from various views after the change. Someone had designed the pictures to be altered.

If she knew what she was doing, she would probably find a whole range of variation controls. Probably the original, unaltered image beneath would turn out to be the portrait of an in-bound terrorist.

She patched through to Zack Younger. "Zack, send a unit out to pick up Rolly Ingrem. Bring him to me."

"As an arrest?"

"Yes. Don't do anything that would make him bolt. If he shows the slightest resistance, use force. But I need him alive."

Kastin didn't know for sure how she had summoned the change feature so she couldn't test out the other passports to see if they could also be changed. It might be that only Ingrem had that answer. He took too long to get her the file, so there was a good chance he was doing something funny with it. Meanwhile, she called up the patient record for Dr. Ziljian. Even though there was a waiting list, the only ones he had treated were skiers Yves Loitte and Allen Sanchez, in that order. She placed an emergency call to Loitte. He was able to pick it up on his wristband even though it was turned off.

"You're Chief Shelly Kastin?" he said as though he were expecting a joke. "Are you sure?"

"I need answers, Loitte. Did you get a good look at Dr. Travis Ziljian when he treated you?"

"Yes, he's the team doctor."

"Have you ever seen this guy before?"

"No, he said he was a replacement at the last minute for Koutsaflakis. That was the previous—"

She cut off the call and got Zack on the line again.

"Zack, arrest Dr. Travis Ziljian."

"Him too?"

"Consider him dangerous."

Younger passed along the order to his crew and then stayed on the line. "By the way, you may find this important. One of my men discovered a chair missing in SL3-25. I had him check the room for fingerprints."

"That was a waste of time."

"We found unauthorized access by one Devon March."

"Arazine's corp counsel. Yes, it could be something. Track him down after Ziljian is secured. Where's Ingrem?"

The door popped open and her police pushed Rolly Ingrem into the room and shut the door behind. He looked miserable.

"I can explain," he said lamely.

"You will explain."

Her secretary rang at the same time. "Ms. Kastin, there's a man outside your office who says he's *Congressman* Jim Hrelcik and he demands to see you now."

Kastin turned off the screen, but left the program running.

* * *

Twelve thousand feet up the mountain's flank, two men approached each other behind an ample ridge. Devon March was still officially known to Valdeen only by his Red Freedom name, Pike. It was almost time for action. Unlike Valdeen, March was the usual type of intellectual. Though he didn't have much stomach for achieving his goals in a violent way, he appreciated people who could get things done. Peter Arazine, with all of his faults, had been the perfect example. He had guile, flair and the common touch.

But his old boss was dead. Trapped in a sandstorm and never found. March saw Valdeen as a similar individual, only more worthy of admiration. He was certainly more patient than Arazine when it came to capitalizing on his labors. He could have taken his Valdeen Factor to market any time he wanted, but he didn't. That was an ideological plus. Yes, he had taken up the banner of Mar's autonomy, but without Arazine, the plans had to change drastically, and in his opinion, for the better.

He also was aware that the convict had a whole other reputation. It wasn't exactly a problem that Valdeen had killed the governor, but it wouldn't be polite to bring it up. March enjoyed a duality in his thinking. He could understand someone being knocked off for the greater good. And he was beginning to understand the American concept that no matter how good you think you are, someone can always come along with a bigger set of balls.

They looked around them, making sure no one was in sight, however unlikely that might be. March drew his coat more tightly around him. As the wind was picked up, the temperature dropped, keeping most people indoors. The cold could penetrate even the best protection at these high altitudes. The officials were considering postponing the next day's events if the weather didn't clear. The two men found it difficult to stand still. Valdeen spoke quickly. "For what emergency did you drag me all the way up here?"

"We can't consider the rooms to be safe," said March. "We don't want to lose everything at this point."

"We didn't have to meet at all, you loose-brained boot licker. We have prearranged signals."

Valdeen's tone took him aback. There was nothing more embittering than being slapped in the face by someone you admired.

"I have reason to believe they've cracked the signals." March neglected to mention the disaster they almost had with the passport file. This remote rendezvous was his attempt at being more cautious.

"Go ahead. Make it brief," said Valdeen.

" I want to confirm your strategy. The threat of using your invention to set off the volcano will make the takeover go smoothly and keep the bloodshed to a minimum. We plan to populate this world, not decimate it." While March stayed cool, he wondered if he might have to eliminate Valdeen if things went sour. Provided that circumstances didn't get to him first. He did not admire many people since most of them were like so much cattle. March always sought the courage that he didn't see in himself. Then Arazine came along and gave him something to fight for. He wasn't so bad. He was the one who created Red Freedom as a cover for his operations, and he was the one who brought Valdeen to the planet. Since he was dead and harmless, March was thinking of him more kindly. He would erect a statue to that man when all this was over. *Well, maybe not a statue*, he thought. *Let's not get too excited just yet.*

Valdeen tried unsuccessfully to rub the end of his nose by force of habit, forgetting that the nitrox mask covered it.

March continued, "Triggering the volcano is just a threat, right?"

* * *

The moment of truth. Valdeen thought about his three years in a white-collar prison, a maddening derailment for someone of his genius. Valdeen had learned early on that the way to find out if you were better than someone was to try to take advantage of him. If it worked, then you were superior and they must get out of your way as Edward Merris had discovered. But then the IRS came and locked Valdeen away for the wrong reasons.

So he didn't let the world have the Holy Grail of Chemistry when he found it. It became clear that he needed new goals.

That miserable Shelly Kastin, now *de facto* governor of Mars, was the same woman who had put him in jail. She was the reason he let Arazine convince him to come here. It would be worth it to blow up Mars just to get to her.

He grabbed March roughly by the shoulders and looked straight at him. "This is the last time we will meet without a country of our own. Phase Two begins as we speak. I'm organizing a peaceful protest against the location of the Olympic Games. That will deliver a number of athletes into our hands, the first set of hostages. But remember, we have to keep Nils busy. He's on a need-to-know basis. And he's to be spared if possible. "

"Agreed."

Valdeen thought about his scar-faced nephew for a moment. He was a good kid. *A shame how he lost his parents considering his mother was nearly as smart as me. Maybe...* Then he reminded himself: Only fools live on sentiment. Everyone on this planet is expendable.

* * *

The congressman demanded everyone but himself and Kastin clear the room as a matter of national security. Ingrem was carted off to a holding pen amid his protests that he had cooperated, and they were alone.

"This had better be a first class emergency, mister," said Kastin.

Hrelcik's eyebrows rose in disbelief before his eyes narrowed. "People's Deputy, Chul Huk Chang is requesting clearance to land at Mercury Airport. Your soldiers are refusing clearance and ignoring my orders."

Several things registered on her mind at once, all shocking, with one particular question that demanded an immediate answer. "How long have you known about him coming?"

"We can shoot the bull later. Right now you've got a foreign dignitary—"

"The sooner you answer, the sooner he can land."

"I got radio communication half an hour ago. At that point I requested that the control tower notify me when they were in range to land. The ATC's agreed to do that but now they're making him orbit until they hear from you."

"I'll need clearance from Earth. That will take at least forty minutes."

"You've got clearance from me, sister. I speak for Earth."

"Fuck your clearance. I don't answer to you."

Hrelcik's eyes went round. "What the hell are you going for? Chang's ship doesn't have the fuel to circle around. He will either land or crash. Do you know what an international incident is?"

"Here's what will happen. Chang will be cleared to land at the alternate airstrip at Outpost Nine and he will stay put while we wait for Earth's answer. If you're too antsy to wait the forty minutes you can go hold his hand." She keyed in the commands regarding the disposition of the incoming shuttle instead of saying them out loud so that he wouldn't hear that she was posting heavy guards at the landing site.

"You're exceeding your authority."

"I take my orders directly from the President."

"As the Head of Oversight, I can shut this project down and take over right now. You're right on the edge of having that happen. And you're wrong if you don't think I'll do it."

"Go to Hell." She pressed a button so that one of her guards appeared, and held the door open for the congressman to leave.

* * *

Valdeen's beeper went off with insistent tones and red light flashing. For other doctors, it meant that they had a patient to attend to. For him, the alarm meant that someone had gotten into either his office or his private room. It didn't matter which; they had entered forcibly. That beep was the signal for him not to show up there again. It was time to spring his traps.

CHAPTER 30
Takeover

ALTHOUGH HE HAD slipped in and out of the persona at his convenience, Havislaw Valdeen now left medical doctor Travis Ziljian behind. As Mars' rightful leader-in-waiting, Valdeen tread quietly down to Sub-Level Three. The full body suit he wore stretched tight, made for someone else's dimensions, making the technician's orange look more like a Florida orange.

With the corridors even emptier than usual, he hurried along just the same. He was lucky to meet people one at a time, so no one lived to tell about it. Wiping his hands from his last victim, he chose one of the safe rooms at random, slipped inside and found a workstation. With deft strokes, he opened a channel to Chief Kastin via the terminal. Kitty Honera's password got him in.

Dear Shelly, this is your old friend, Havislaw. Don't try to respond to me now. This is a pre-recorded one-way message. You have a well-trained security force. They will be of no help to you. We've got people on the volcano, in the village, and inside major installations. Only one third of the freedom fighters have revealed themselves. The rest will come out of hiding when you least expect it. We have your athletes held hostage at eight separate locations. Valdeen Catalytic Factor is on the mountain and ready for use. You will read all about it in my press release. It only takes one drop to end life on this planet.

323

I declare this Olympics over. Don't wait for me to hand out any prizes or medals. Evacuate your forces to orbit immediately. Oh, and by the way, I've killed one of your athletes to show that we're serious. I'll be dropping off to you one Lou Coburn.

Valdeen put his message on a half hour delay before sending it. That would give him time to get out of the area and carry out some of the promises he had just made.

* * *

"He's a jerk," Terri said to her roommate, Tara Bantera. "I stand thoroughly corrected in any statements to the contrary. Yves doesn't care about anything." Terri shoved the door shut as hard as she could. It was one that couldn't slam. Throwing herself on the bed, she began to cry.

She pictured her father laughing with steam coming out of his mouth on a cold winter morning as she practiced on the ice. The local hockey team had carved ruts in the ice from their scrambling around. When the game broke up early, the skaters had been allowed to squeeze in some practice time. Terri was attempting a Salchow, a move where the skater takes off from the back of the inside edge of one skate, makes a complete turn in the air, and lands on the back outside edge of the opposite skate.

She remembered how she seemed to complete the move perfectly, caught the rut, and went down hard in a spin, her leg collapsing under her. Her face contorted with pain when her right blade cut through the boot at her left ankle. How the whole group crowded around her to see if she was all right, and her father pushed through them looking so sad and regretful, as though he wished he had mapped every rut in the rink. How she suddenly decided the whole gaggle of gawkers looked funny around her, and laughed to show them she was fine. The consternation on their faces switched to relief.

Then she couldn't help herself. She cried flat out like she was doing now, afraid of the turn her life might take. Only it was never so poignant before today. I should have told Yves, she thought. Why didn't I just tell him?

"Why does Yves have to remind me of my father?" she said.

Tara said, "That's a good thing, isn't it? I thought you love your father."

Terri couldn't help a brief, snorting chuckle. Tara came over and wiped Terri's eyes gently with a tissue. "That's not what I meant," Terri protested quietly.

"I don't know what you meant, but it sounds like you care about this guy."

"I do. I don't know what I'm going to do."

"Hold yourself together, that's what."

"It's not just him, it's the Olympics, it's Mars, it's everything."

"I know. You're suffering from sun deprivation, and home sickness and love sickness all at once."

"Tara, did anybody else ever have it this hard?"

"This hard and worse. I can come back later if you want to cry some more."

"No, that's okay. I think you fixed it for now."

"Fixed it, did I? Maybe it's me that you love."

"Tara, I do love you," said Terri.

Tara smiled and shook her head and they hugged.

"I knew it," said Tara. "Try to get some sleep now."

"No, I can't. I'm going to the rally. Come with me."

"Uh uh, not now. I gotta get some biofeed into me. I'll catch up with you later."

"Okay."

"Oh, listen, I heard they moved your rally thing to room four-oh-two in that building with the Grissom Cafeteria."

"Thanks. Who knows where I would have ended up without you?"

* * *

Shelly Kastin spun past the Security Center stations at her usual high speed, keeping an eye on the instruments and terminals. Senior Congressman Jim Hrelcik was sticking to her and she didn't want him to know about the terrorist round up. That would be the least she could accomplish.

The Olympics and the entire planet were in jeopardy with Chul Huk Chang waiting on the landing pad. So far, all she had managed to capture was Rolly Ingrem. And he wasn't one of the terrorists, just a moron. Now if she could have a congressman arrested, that would be progress.

She was still looking for a way to shake Hrelcik loose short of chaining him up when Valdeen's message lit up the main screen like an explosion.

The congressman near her shoulder read parts of it out loud. "Dear Shelly? Freedom fighters? What is that, some sort of joke? Do you actually know this man?" Hrelcik's loose skin gathered around his frown.

Like Hrelcik, Kastin was seeing it for the first time. "No, Congressman, it's not a joke." She wasn't ready to admit having heard of Valdeen or Ziljian in any respect.

Hrelcik swiveled his face toward her on a thin neck. "You mean we've been taken over? Are you telling me that we can be taken over just like that?"

Kastin was already in motion, copying the message and routing it to her forces with one of her own. Part of her instructions were for security to go to the terminal from which Valdeen's message was sent and to hold him there if he was found in the vicinity. "I'm not telling you anything. It sounds serious, but I don't know that any of what he's saying is true."

Hrelcik scratched his silver crew cut. "How are you going to find out? How are you going to resolve this? How do you plan to keep me safe? My office will want some very good answers."

Kastin pursed her lips in a moment's thought. *It only takes one drop to end life on this planet,* the message said. "Congressman, I'm going to start by keeping you out of my way."

* * *

Landing as directed, Chul Huk Chang came in on the Russian-built Razdolye, named for a Russian concept that roughly meant "spaciousness." Until the Chinese completed a shuttle of their own, the least objectionable foreign model would have to do. Being that Chang saw the Japanese as the greatest long-term threat on Mars or anywhere, one of the things he wished he could do on Mars was to destroy every Japanese-built shuttle he could find.

Although his hated of the land of the rising sun came from feelings of Chinese nationalism and ancient conflicts,

Chang didn't see himself as a government employee representing the Chinese government in his actions. Nor did he see himself as a public servant. His aspirations were those of an overarching entity, a matter of record in the Book of Fate.

Now he occupied the red soil of Mars—*Huo Hsing*, as his people called the planet. It was no surprise to him that Kastin ordered his shuttle detained in a remote area under a special contingent. If she were really as smart as her bloated reputation, she would have had his ship destroyed.

Chang placed his palm on a bulkhead to get a sense of its strength. Being held near Outpost Nine while drawing off Kastin's resources was more than satisfactory to him. It would split her force with guard duty while Olympia came under attack. He could wait out most of the battle in a relatively safe position before taking over at the end.

CHAPTER 31
Blindside

VALDEEN HAD JUST found his way to the restricted area so carefully prepared for him, when Barkly burst in "You said you were going to let The Games finish!" Barkly screamed.

Valdeen looked almost impassive, if not slightly amused. His nephew's orange belt, part of his technician disguise, was undone. "I see you have the same tailor as I do. You found out about this place. That's pretty good. I'm going to have to kill someone for letting that happen." He packed a large black bag with supplies, careful to put the delicate items into separate cases. The room had been well stocked for him by his Red Freedom subordinates.

"You're not supposed to have this thing in motion now," Barkly complained. "That's not part of the plan."

"You never heard the whole plan so you don't know that for sure. Why does it matter?"

"The timing is way off. You can't take over now. We've only gone through one course. You know I wanted to compete."

"Our objectives can't depend on your needs."

"You lied to me then?"

"I have no need to lie to you. I had no choice. Kastin is dim but she stumbled on to something so we had to move right away."

"I didn't say anything to her," he said with a trace of fear.

"I know that, grandnephew. It was some issue with the passport. I know who's to blame, and I hope Devon March is still alive after this so that I can finish him personally. Going off schedule is a problem to say the least." His bag was almost full.

"I wish I could have finished the competition."

"What is the difference? You were obviously winning. I say you won. I'll award you the medals myself. You don't want Earthers to rule Mars, do you?"

"I don't know for sure if I would have beaten the other Martians, and then there's Loitte. Loitte looked surprisingly good out there."

"I'm very busy now. If you want to help, why don't you go see if you can catch Loitte before he knows what's going on. Go up on the mountain and keep him occupied. If you're with him at the right time, you can avoid suspicion if by some small chance our plans fall through."

"That's a good idea."

Valdeen watched as Barkly hurried out the door and cut across the center of the Village where the clock was perpetually frozen at zero hour.

Young Nils, the son of Valdeen's sister, was not obviously from the same genetic branch as his uncle Havislaw. Certainly the alphabet soup of DNA had granted them a few things in common. Big things, such as a burning need to remain unrivaled at any endeavor, and small things such as a propensity for rolls of stuffed cabbage. Yet Valdeen had killed early in life while Nils had not. More than a matter of opportunity, it was a transition to manhood that the ski bum had failed.

* * *

"What are the odds of that?"

The two maintenance workers, known as sweepers, leaned forward at once. "REPEATED WALL BREACH," their monitor said. "MANUAL REPAIRS REQUIRED." According to the log, something had struck a wall in one spot, and right after it was fixed, the wall suffered damage a second time at that exact same point. And there was no major storm in progress. The micro compressor registered an empty refill cell and called the sweepers for assistance.

"That's gotta be a good one."

"It's right near by, too."

"Well, check your suit and let's go."

When they arrived on the scene, they found a man sprawled under the spot in a twisted heap. As they ran up to him, they noticed that he wasn't wearing any weather protection or breathing gear. Curious bruises made black spots on his blue face.

* * *

Yves wore his wristband so he reached to open a channel for an update. Barkly came running into the lodge, hands extended in supplication. "I'm glad I caught you," he said breathlessly.

"This is just what I need right now." Yves' voice was rough. He had been hoping for Terri's return. "Get out of my way."

"No, Yves. I came to tell you that I'm sorry for the way I behaved. Your performance on Course One was much better than I expected. You deserve my respect." He offered his hand.

Unsure how to respond, Yves didn't shake hands but he sat down.

Sitting with him, Barkly said, "I've been a great deal of trouble to you. *Je suis dèsolè, Yves.*"

"I don't speak any French. We moved from Baton Rouge to Burlington when I was two years old."

"Ah, Vermont. Home of Mt. Snow, Killington, and Stowe."

"Don't get too cocky. I've also made trips to Zermatt, the Matterhorn and several other places." He didn't mention that he had also been to Vinson Massif in special preparation for Mars. Vinson was the highest point on the Antarctic continent. It was there that Børge Ousland, scaling the mountain again at seventy years of age, shared his diary with Yves. Ousland had the distinction of being the first person to complete a solo expedition to the North Pole without re-supplying, and the first to cross the Antarctic continent alone in 1997.

"I didn't mean anything by it, I'm impressed. Look, Yves," he continued. "I think it was just nerves that made me act the way I did."

"You knocked me out. I had to go to that lunatic doctor. That goes beyond bad sportsmanship."

"I know. That was crazy. Your remark about my parents got to me. Now that I have a comfortable lead, I feel much more relaxed, and I realize what an ass I've been. I hope you can forgive me, but I will understand it if you don't."

Yves kept silent. He was still weighing the option of pushing Barkly aside and rushing after Terri.

Barkly had a sturdy metal box with him. "Ah, I almost forgot. I want you to have this to make up for the damage I've done." He held the box out expectantly. When Yves just stared at him he said, "I'll leave it here and go."

"No, wait." Yves took the box and tugged it open slowly, directing it toward Barkly in case it was a mail bomb. When he turned it around and it did not go off, he saw that it contained a single yellowed paper, puckered with age. A musty odor rose from the box as Yves unfolded the paper gingerly. He slowly realized that it was an antique document. It seemed to be the paperwork authorizing a medal for Alfred Andersen of Norway. Yes, there was the description. 230.5 points on the 90-meter hill. He made the jump in 1928 in St. Moritz, Switzerland, one of the first Olympic jumps ever. The event must have held a special meaning for Nils Barkly who was from Switzerland, and partly of Scandinavian descent like Andersen.

Yves shook his head. "This is amazing. Where did you get it?"

"I'm a collector."

Yves continued to stare at it with wonder. A priceless piece of the past. Something tangible from the very early days of the Winter Olympic Games.

Barkly cleared his throat. "It's yours now."

"Thank you." He let out a deep breath, then hesitated. He hoped he hadn't shown how much the gift affected him. He was always fascinated by artifacts in skiing history. "Nils, like I said before, I can't afford to keep fighting with you. This is a great present. But you can't expect me to start feeling totally different right away. Not after the start we got off to. I won't try to get even, if that's what you're worried about."

"When you get to know me, maybe some of that cynicism will melt away. But we're late for the next event now. You better grab you're stuff and come with me."

"No, I'll be a few minutes. I'm not scheduled to go first."

"Come. If it's important to you, you'll hurry. We can put everything on when we get to the top." They shook hands stiffly and Yves gathered up his skis, poles and helmet with its attachments but he didn't put them on. The fairings that made his ankles aerodynamic were already built into the suit. But there would be no room for skis in the enclosed cable car and the helmet could go on *en route*.

Just before they left, Yves sent a quick, private text to Lou Coburn, but got no immediate response.

Course Two stretched five times the length of Course One. As long as it took to get there, the two men alone in the lift compartment found nothing to say to each other. When Barkly smiled slightly, the scar down his face grew disjointed. Yves shivered at the sight. Then he had another idea. He texted Al Brisini for a favor.

* * *

The terrorists prodded their captives into a single file for the move down the corridor, an incredulous Terri Finney among them. She shivered under Dr. Ziljian's treacherous gaze. He turned from her to survey the line of athletes under his control disapprovingly. Yves had been right not to trust him.

"Why haven't you got that athlete, Coburn?" Ziljian asked one of the kidnappers.

"The sweepers got him first."

"Sweepers?" Ziljian raised a gun to the man's head.

"Don't worry, we killed him. The only thing they collected was his dead body. What did you need him for? You have all of these other hostages."

"You're right, I suppose," said Ziljian lowering the gun. "We'll make do with these candlelight vigil morons."

One by one, as they reached Room 402, they were shoved inside where other thugs were busy tying them to chairs. Each captive got smashed in the head with a rifle butt to dull their senses and weaken any possible resistance before they were trussed. Most of them flinched or whimpered but they had the choice of the rifle butt or the barrel end with the bullets. No one had resisted so far.

Terri was scared. Not so much by her possible fate or Coburn's reported fate, neither of which she cared to acknowledge, but by what she intended to do. She had practiced the precision moves thousands of times in karate class, alone and with luckless sparring partners. She could bash wooden boards to splinters. She could kick a man bracing up a tackle horse and knock him senseless across the room. It was serious business. This was the time to put her training to use, see if it worked in reality. She just needed to get a crack at someone. As long as either her hands or feet were free, there was still a chance.

* * *

Half an inch of yellow and red sand covered the seats in the Olympic Stadium. The shelter dome was still under construction and the air jets only functioned during an event. Al Brisini had found the large doors yawning open and walked in. This was where they were supposed to be holding the protest that Terri was involved in. Brisini had promised to keep an eye on Terri for Yves. He had a strong feeling that she could take care of herself but it wouldn't hurt to discretely keep watch.

Those two were a pair of hellcats, the sort of relationship where anybody but the couple themselves could see how strongly they were attracted to each other. Brisini saw them ending up together in the long run no matter what went on between. Separation would bring them to their senses.

Brisini walked along the open racetrack with its spongy surface that added urgency to tired feet. Terri wasn't there. No one was. A cold wind whistled through the stands bearing still more sand. It looked very different than the pageantry of the Opening Ceremonies. The only thing recognizable was the Olympic Cauldron continually gushing a plume of orange fire. Dedicated air jets kept the howling currents from whipping the blaze to a sputter.

Brisini walked up the empty stairs and searched the corridors behind the stands. They were vacant as well, so different without the vendors and the screaming kids. He speculated the protest got called off.

Then Brisini saw the hand written sign that told him where everyone went: Room 402. Of course, they would have moved the meeting inside because of the weather. Out here, a room in the four hundreds meant that it was the fourth floor below ground. The only thing that rode above the first story were the air traffic control towers. He admired the planning. As early man discovered untold years ago on Earth, some underground hollows could maintain a temperature as high as 59 degrees Fahrenheit all year round without any additional heating. Underneath the surface of Mars, you could count on having about 29 degrees as your head start, and that was a boon since it took only a few extra degrees of heat to get above freezing.

The teacher shook his head. Olympics on Mars. Terrorist threats. Candlelight vigils. *And Boom Boom Brisini was there.* He wasn't really called Boom Boom Brisini, but he would have so much to tell his wife Madelyn when he got back. And ample material for his lectures! At the top of the list, he would have to admit he was wrong about Mars having no magnetic properties. Mars was the biggest people magnet he had ever seen.

Brisini threaded his way through curving corridors, still getting the feel of the place, halfway between familiarity and confusion. He resolved to study the map very carefully tonight.

Meanwhile he found the stairwell that only led down from his level. And there was the picture window with the breathtaking mountain view. Now he knew where he was. He headed down the stairs and emerged again into another corridor. Remarkably, there was the picture window again with the same image projected down from above. Only the big red number beside it reminded you that you were underground and told you how far. What a beautiful scene. It was like going on a very peaceful vacation. Not a hint of the winds outside. Losing his bearings again, he began to look for a posted directory on the fourth sub-floor when he saw a sign for the meeting room itself and entered.

Someone pulled him by the collar and pressed cold, hard reality against his face. The smell of metal and lubricant filled his nose from a gun recently cleaned and oiled. He saw dozens of men and women moaning against their bonds. Some sat with ugly purple bruises or cuts on their foreheads. A handful of men with nitrox masks hiding their faces hefted rifles at varying degrees of readiness. A couple of other new victims were just being led into the room from a door on the opposite side. Their belongings piled in a corner.

His tense stomach clenched harder. One of the captives was Terri Finney, who he had promised to look out for. So far he was doing a terrible job of it.

"I thought this was supposed to be a peaceful demonstration," Brisini said, playing for time. Think Al! Think and then act. You can do *something*.

Only the man known to them as Dr. Ziljian chose to show his face. "We'll kill this one first to show that Red Freedom means business." Ignoring Brisini, he indicated Terri.

A squat man who styled himself of a black-clad ninja, gave Terri a gratuitous jab between her shoulder blades with his rifle. "The bitch?" he asked. She took it stiffly.

Al Brisini didn't wait for things to get worse. He shouted to the skater, "Terri, get out!" Then he lunged forward to gouge at Ziljian 's eyes. He missed his target organs but held a savage grip on Ziljian 's head while the others rounded on him. Terri twirled sideways, immediately making herself a narrower target, one arm pushing the rifle in another direction. At the same time she stepped in closer so that the end of the barrel pointed past her. Her other arm swung the ice skates in her hand so hard that the edge of the blade went clear through the mask and buried itself in the Ninja's head. She got hold of the rifle when it slipped off his sagging shoulder and she sprayed its fire toward a cluster of the terrorists as she backed out of the room. Other captives tried to run, duck, or throw their chairs over. Pandemonium reigned.

One of Terri's bullets slammed into Ziljian 's arm and he fell back out of Brisini's grasp. Then the butt of another gunman's rifle swung down onto the back of Brisini's neck. One vertebra popped loudly and he went stiff. As he crumpled to the floor, his head twisted sideways and he laid choking in his own blood, his eyebrows high in surprise. Terri froze, hesitating in the doorway, staring at the gruesome sight until Ziljian yelled to his men, "Don't get near her. Get behind that door, shut it, and secure this room."

Brisini mouthed, "Go," and she backed out, firing a few sloppy rounds high to cover her escape.

With Terri out of sight, guards were posted outside, the door sealed and bolted. Valdeen restored order inside the room with random executions. Some Red Freedom members lay on the floor beside their victims. The other captives stared in silent horror, and listened helplessly as the man who started the brief captive's rebellion struggled noisily for his last breath.

Al Brisini gasped until he seized up. Unable to display any outward sign of life, it surprised him that he had these last few moments of observation and clarity. Then Ziljian spoke to him, "It was your own fault, you know. That's right." He stopped as though listening to an answer from the almost-corpse. "Don't look at me like that. What's the matter with you?"

Someone moaned in hysterical fright and it made Ziljian turn to them with a cross look. Then he stared back at the other faces. "You can all stop worrying so much about him," Ziljian said quietly to the group while pointing to Brisini. "None of you will get out of here alive." As if to prove Ziljian's point, Brisini's last sight left him.

* * *

Yves and Barkly arrived at the Course Two summit to find the observation post and the start house unmanned. Their boots rang on the empty floor. The two of them glanced at each other, then walked around outside a bit and met back at the cable car they came up in. There wasn't far to go, or much to investigate.

"There's no one here," said Yves.

"We're early."

"I thought you said we were late." Yves turned on his wristband to find out what happened. "*Now the Martian Separatists say they are planning to dump a substance called Valdeen Catalytic Factor into Olympus Mons itself if officials do not accede to their demands. They have already taken hostages.*"

"What's that all about?" said Barkly.

Yves turned it up so they both could hear. "*Sources revealed that one Havislaw Valdeen, with a criminal record that included only a tax fraud conviction before this, may have developed an extremely volatile substance made up of natural elements. Highly placed sources say the explosive was under development for government use at the turn of the century, and now Valdeen may have sold it to the Martian Separatists. Dr. Valdeen, posing as the American team's physician under the name Travis Ziljian, is claiming that his Valdeen*

Factor is the most powerful explosive compound in the universe, and he's proved it to be the easiest weapon of terror to smuggle across international or planetary boundaries. They demand—"

A ski pole slammed into Yves' wrist, cutting off the sound.

"What's the matter with you, Barkly?"

"Sorry. I was pointing. I thought I saw someone, but it was a shadow. The situation is making me nervous."

Yves paled. Terri's Ziljian was Valdeen. "We have to get down there." He headed for the emergency transport, running. Barkly followed close behind, shouting in his ear.

"Hold on. Let the experts handle it. You'll get everyone killed."

"Listen to me, Nils. Our team doctor is mysteriously missing. This Ziljian or Valdeen is a ruthless bastard. Terri said that Ziljian was leading a protest she's involved in. I think she's down there as a hostage."

Barkly seemed to react to the tug of the wind kicking up. He said, "I think you're jumping to an awful lot of conclusions."

"We can't afford to take the chance that I'm wrong. But if I'm right, then Terri needs our help right now."

Yves stopped himself at the transport. "Hold it," he yelled. "That thing's not fast enough. We had better ski down."

"I can ski down faster," said Barkly.

"We'll both go."

"Sorry, Yves, it has to be me, I'm faster. On the length of this course, my speed will make a difference. My helmet is out of nitrox, and I snapped my bindings on that last run so I'll need to borrow your equipment. You can take the trans car and meet me. C'mon, we're wasting precious time."

Yves relinquished his equipment reluctantly, but swiftly. He made sure Barkly took off down the slope, and watched him melt into the snow. It seemed odd to him that he didn't see where Barkly put his own stuff. He headed for the emergency route, the trans car.

Heliplanes lifted injured skiers, but the ten passenger trans cars were the only permanent facility that moved quickly down the slope for an emergency. The only other ways out were the leisure-speed guest cabs and V.I.P. cars, and the line for the remote camera, which moved as fast as any skier but might not support his weight and couldn't be switched on from his location.

Yves remembered the launch lacked an operator. He had no alternative but to learn how it worked. He popped open the cabin and went back inside the building to find the automatic controls.

"DOOR OPEN," the trans car warned him loudly as he walked away.

He surveyed the board and found a lever marked "EVAC," which he guessed was for evacuation. He lifted the safety guard and gave the lever a tentative pull. Green lights appeared across the board except for the last two, which were red. Again he heard audio, "SECONDARY MALFUNCTION. DO YOU WISH TO PROCEED?" He couldn't identify the problem. Since it was secondary and he had an option, he said, "Yes."

"ARE ALL OTHER PASSENGERS ABOARD?" the automated controller inquired.

"Yes!" he yelled into the air.

"THEN YOU MAY PROCEED."

He saw the car begin to ease slowly out of its bay. Yves realized he was still holding the metal box Barkly had given him. He tossed it in, hopped in after, and slammed shut the door as his transport moved out along the rail. The trans car picked up some speed before maxing out to safe limits.

He wasn't used to being reduced to a spectator. Within the first five meters, he grew impatient, pounding rhythmically against the safety bar, rocking back and forth. Couldn't the damn thing go any faster?

Ten meters out, he tried to turn on the wristband Barkly had damaged to get more information. Several hard raps later, the unit came back to life in a burst of static. The current report that came across was nothing but a recap. Shaking with humiliation and impotence, Yves railed at the son of a bitch Valdeen, and at himself for not warning Terri about him more specifically. Twenty meters out, and high above ground.

Then he got the new information. "*Valdeen's grandnephew, Nils Barkly of the Martian Team, has been identified as a key figure among the Martian Separatists.*"

"Damn it!" he shouted. He looked in every corner for the controls to turn the launch around. There weren't any. Trans cars were not designed to reverse before they got to the bottom. Yves could see the distance to the ground increasing.

Under the seat there would be an emergency switch to stop it at least. He forced the heavy bottom to swing back ponderously on its hinges. Frayed wires blossomed where the switch should have been.

Yves turned and strained at the door handle of the moving vehicle. The lock held. Below that was a red push bar. Yves strained at it until he noticed it had been welded in place, making it impossible to unjam. Grabbing hold of the safety rail, he braced his back against the seat and kicked feverishly at the giant window above. He didn't know how many times he kicked it before began to separate at its seams, first at the bottom and then up along the sides. Giving it one more kick so that the plastic sheet tore off the top and sailed out, he jumped.

CHAPTER 32
Executive Order

SHELLY KASTIN STOOD in front of a forty-nine square foot grid that represented the Olympic Village, the host city, the volcano, and the surrounding area. Security Control formed the center. If any object were fitted with a homing device as their own resources were, the grid tracked it. She observed several moving lights on the board corresponding to each vehicle, eying one nervously as it crawled past the air factory. Friendly or no, it reminded her that both air and ozone would be a prime targets. She punched the intercom. "Zack, it's Kastin. Triple the guard on Oh-Two and Oh-Three. And I need intel fast. Out."

Of course almost everything here was a prime target. As helpful as the grid could be, it offered no advice on terrorism in an ongoing hostage situation. Fortunately, Shelly Kastin needed no advice. The intelligence reports would inform her decisions. She kept one eye on the tableau as she began to pace. "What are we waiting for, Mr. Culpepper?" she demanded.

Harris Culpepper, an older gentleman in charge of personnel, was not used to locating people at a moment's notice or completing any transaction that was not on electronic paper. She had reminded him that with the new system in place, she could see he was hiding in his office. Embarrassment moved him fast.

Culpepper looked as though he was about to say something impolitic and then changed his mind with an almost imperceptible shake of his head. "Chief Kastin, we are waiting for the arrival of Dr. Logan Avery, one of the experts you requested. He's the volcano specialist."

Shelly Kastin wasted no time being annoyed with people in the middle of a crisis even if they told her things she already knew. She plowed ahead. "I know that, Mr. Culpepper. What's keeping him?"

"There's a bit of a dust storm kicking up. To get to us he has to travel through enclosed corridors only." For an afterthought, he added, "As you know, that takes longer."

Shelly Kastin just grunted in response. She was well chosen for her position as Security Chief, a woman who always saw past roadblocks and found solutions. She would move Heaven and Earth, and Mars as well if she had to. The terrorists would not succeed. It was unthinkable. The last time Kastin was on Earth the President of the United States instructed her to use "whatever means necessary" to insure the safety of the Olympic Games on Mars. "Insure the future of the planet itself." He might have added that it was more for the sake of Earth than Mars or the Martian settlers since that was the truth.

It wouldn't have mattered if he had said that. Even though she was appointed by the President, Chief Kastin had no partisan agenda; she took her responsibilities very seriously. The need for security on Mars or anywhere else was explanation enough and no one had to convince her of a mission. She had always been that way. When she worked for the Department of Treasury, she saw to it that Havislaw Valdeen got jail time. He was responsible for a murder the Justice Department couldn't prove when the evidence was ruled inadmissible because of the way it was obtained. They approached her with that information and asked if she could press an income tax evasion case against him. She was more than willing considering he was guilty of that too. Eighteen years later, she didn't recognize the bastard in time. He passed right through screening. But now he was in her jurisdiction again. Now she would have to stop him for good.

She hit the intercom switch that put her through to maintenance. "Borgo, do you have the modifications on the X-1?"

"Almost ready."

"Do it. Meanwhile, I want every land rover, sightseeing or otherwise, in motion around the perimeter. Fully armed."

"We can't do that Chief."

"Did you understand me?"

"Chief, rover numbers 4 and 5 are down with dust damage. We don't have enough people to clear it out and still do the other things you asked for."

"Then you get the athletes to help you clear it or some lard butt spectator, but you do it on the double."

"What do I tell them if they don't want to do it?"

"The truth. It's an emergency. I don't care if you inform them they're under Marital Law or give them a big wet kiss. Whatever works quickest."

"Oh."

Kastin didn't wait for Borgo to break the connection. She concentrated on setting the grid to search for the location of anyone above fifteen degrees latitude, the staging area for all skiing events. There shouldn't be anyone on the slopes now. She had already issued an advisory that the Games would be delayed and everyone should stay indoors. It went out over the wristbands. Any strays out there now couldn't be helped. She rang Zack again.

"Ready," he answered.

"What's the word on who they've got hostage?"

"Near as we can tell, they have a score of tourists, two missing reporters, a film crew that was on the mountain shooting a commercial, and maybe a dozen of our athletes."

"Did you say shooting a commercial?"

"Yes. The athletes won't be home for at least seven months so they shoot commercials right after each event."

"Thank you," she said calmly.

From the corner of her eye she noticed that Culpepper was taking the opportunity to try to become invisible, edging slowly towards the door. She wondered if she was really that frightening. Years ago, she learned that her life after the divorce was most rewarding when she did something meaningful. She didn't know why people were always shocked at her decisions when something had to be done. It was unquestionable that she had to get things under control without worrying about the etiquette involved in telling people their priorities. She was helping them. Those people would live. In fact, this might be the only way they would.

She became marginally aware that Hal Grove, the only one of two chopper pilots available, sat in another corner of the control room. Grove had one hand on top of his thin red hair and his lower lip bulged slightly. He may have sensed he was about to be sent on a suicide mission because he shook his head and mouthed, "No way. No way."

* * *

Dr. Logan Avery traveled indoors in an enclosed cart with a driver and an armed guard, precautions imposed at the behest by Chief Kastin. A ten-minute drive gave as many minutes to think, and Avery needed it. Kastin was probably going to ask him if Mars was volcanically viable, if one last volcano could still flip a switch after a hundred millions years of silence as Valdeen implied. Here he was on Mars, finally able to study the damned volcanoes up close and he still wouldn't know whether there could be an eruption unless it actually happened.

One of his geology students back on Earth once asked him if Mars has hidden subduction zones where crust and plate and mantle meet and struggle for eminence like in a living planet. In the gentle rocking of the runabout, Avery mused that the volcano question was the same black box of mystery whether it was framed simply or cloaked in sophisticated terminology.

Did you ever try to close a faucet that was just the least bit leaky? he had asked the student. Did you do it on a quiet night when you couldn't sleep? Afraid to bust it, you twist the handle shut a fraction at a time, and it drips ever more slowly until you can count off whole seconds between drops. You tighten it more firmly than ever, surprised that it's got more left to turn. Then a whole minute goes by and it seems to be done. Maybe you see one last, leftover drop bulging there, holding firm, not quite strong enough to form a coherent sphere, not quite massive enough to break its bond with the faucet and plummet to the stopper. Quickly, you wipe it off with a towel and wait though you can't see the next drop forming. Maybe you wait two more minutes just to be sure. Then you lay down for what feels like five minutes holding your breath, wondering where would it get more water after all this time? It has to be done at some point. And just as you've forgotten about it, and find yourself drifting off to contented sleep, out of nowhere comes the next one. Put that on a scale of a billion years, and there you have the behavior of a volcano.

* * *

Kastin watched Dr. Logan Avery, the Great Red Hope of Martian geography, enter the room. He was a pleasant looking man in his late forties with a ruddy complexion, well-groomed prematurely white hair, and black-rimmed half glasses. Only his suit jacket seemed out of place, too small for his broad shoulders and bulging arms, like no formal jacket could contain the otherwise mild man. The equipment cases in tow bespoke great preparation. When he got closer, it looked like he had lost some sleep.

"Here's your Dr. Avery," Culpepper muttered unnecessarily.

"Thank you, and don't think you're going anywhere, Culpepper. Now Dr. Avery," Chief Kastin began. "Let's get right to the point. How much damage can Valdeen Catalytic Factor cause here on Mars?"

Avery looked at her with unabashed appreciation, making her wish she didn't need to be so painfully direct. Another place, another time...

With a deep breath he said, "It depends on how much material they use, where it was placed, a multitude of factors. There's no way I can judge. I've never even seen the tests. In simple terms, I don't know how reactive it is."

"Could the quantity of material concealable in a carry-on travel bag be enough to set it off?"

"Again, I don't have the facts, but intuitively speaking the answer is no. On the other hand, we have to assume he secured the quantity he needs. He could easily have smuggled the ingredients to Mars one chemical at a time."

"Bottom line: What can an explosive, any explosive, do to this volcano that we're sitting on?"

"I do specialize in volcanology, but the Martian volcanoes are not yet fully understood, and that's an understatement. On Earth, even landslides have been known to bring on eruptions."

"Speak to me, Logan. We're running out of time. What's the worst that can happen?"

"If it gets down there and lowers the boiling point of the magma—assuming there is any magma—it can potentially set off the volcanic process." He closed his eyes as he said the words. His face looked a bit redder than usual.

For a moment, she thought about questioning Avery's conclusion, but she knew better. He was a cautious man, a proper scientist who would not speak outside the realm of possibility. It looked like it cost him something to say what he did.

Zack interrupted, "Chief, we've got an unauthorized vehicle in Orange Four." Orange Four was a sector of the volcano's flank.

"How could that be? What type?"

"It's not a Spider. It's an earlier model, the Beetle, but it's fitted with an MGPS."

"They meant for us to find it. What's it doing?"

"Its course looks randomized."

"Decoy," she shouted. "Get some eyes on the ground and find the one they don't want us to see."

* * *

Devon March's war-footing assistant, young Moss Guidry, had a small contingent in Beetle 2 bearing a dose of Valdeen Catalytic Factor up the mountain. Although the Beetle he yanked out of storage was an earlier model than the Spider, it comfortably carried six people and a payload. Beetle 1 had been sacrificed. Considering that decoys were needed to make this trip and they were up against Earth security forces, Guidry did not feel safe at all.

They made good progress by the standards of the vehicle's time until he heard the demand to stop. Amplified though it was, Guidry could just barely hear the message because it wasn't directed at them. Someone on the ground had spotted a vehicle that wasn't equipped with MGPS. Then the shooting started. No one was there to fire back.

Beetle 3 boiled up as a cloud of smoke on the horizon, and Beetle 2 continued.

* * *

Avery waited patiently until Kastin got back to him. After trying to find out why she had never heard of the Beetle transports in storage, or the fact that they had been raided, she said to him, "I have no illusions that we're out of the woods, but what if we can prevent the terrorists from reaching the crater?"

"It's a plus. If they don't reach the central crater, you can reduce their chances of success."

"Why only reduce?"

When Dr. Logan Avery got a question that required a complex answer he usually communicated more by making eye contact over the top of his glasses instead of answering verbally. It made people understand they were wading out of their depth. Today he wouldn't do that. The Chief wasn't asking because she was stubborn. She had to examine the issue from every side. Even the obvious conclusions had to be questioned at a time like this.

"Chief Kastin," he began, thinking about how to phrase it. "Shelly. Olympus Mons is a shield type volcano over five hundred sixty kilometers in diameter. Yes, most of the lava erupts from the central vent located at the summit, but it also erupts from vents on fractures anywhere on the flanks of the cone. These vents trace back to the central shaft. A small fraction of the total area is covered by our artificial snow. That hides some of the vents, but the rest of the cone is exposed. All the terrorists have to do is get to one of those vents. The magma can punch through at any point that becomes weakened."

"So what are you saying in terms of defense?"

The muscles around Avery's eyes tightened and drew down his heavy white brows. He was visualizing what would happen when uncounted tons of volcanic runoff came rolling into the town of Olympia. With the visitors they'd added to the thousands of residents, it would make Pompeii look like a backyard barbecue. Had the settlement been sleeping under an active volcano? Olympus Mons had not erupted in over two hundred million years. But if there was still activity in the mantle, and a potent catalytic factor was added, that activity could find its way out somehow.

It wasn't easy to talk to Kastin when she was in her command mode. She could make you feel like a natural disaster was your own fault. Avery could see Culpepper and Grove squirming in the background. He could imagine what they had gone through before it was his turn. Avery took a deep breath. "I'm saying that against this kind of attack, Olympus Mons is indefensible."

"Indefensible my ass," said Kastin. "Avery, I want you working on something to neutralize Valdeen's formula. Right now we're gonna take out their leaders. Grove, I want you airborne with a sharpshooter. Don't stand there. That means now!"

To Avery's surprise, he felt some strange mixture of surprise and relief. Kastin was as direct as he remembered her, and today he was thankful that she had that quality. He had walked in there low on both information and optimism, yet with this Heaven-sent woman they would go down fighting.

Avery and Grove started moving out but had to stop short. A wild-eyed girl with a rifle blocked the doorway. Their jaws went slack when they noticed she wielded a pair of ice skates dripping something that looked like blood. "Ziljian controls the ozone factory," she said. "Some of his men are down though."

Kastin walked right up to her. "Terri, I need your EPA experience. I have a job for you."

CHAPTER 33
Power Struggle

YVES HIT THE snow feet first, allowing himself to crumple and roll. Then he spread himself like a starfish against the momentum of his slide until he stopped. Pulling himself to his feet, he struggled back up the mountain to the trans car station, fighting the wind and the disheartening idea that he might be too late. Though the gap he had to cover was the better part of a football field, he wouldn't be able to recall one centimeter of it later.

When he finally got inside the trans car station, he realized that there was only one place Barkly could have hidden his equipment. Tracing the cables back to their housing, he found Barkly's helmet, skis, and poles stashed under the enormous gear mechanism, undamaged. The helmet had plenty of nitrox left. So that was a lie too. He would give anything to have his hands around Barkly's throat.

When he got it together, Yves poled anxiously toward the descent. What could he really do if he caught up to Barkly? Hand to hand combat as they roared down the slope? Centuries ago, Vikings actually fought some of their wars on skis, proving it was possible. He had plenty to fight for.

Yves focused and crouched. On this course, at least with the beginning of the stretch, he could accelerate to high speeds. It started off with a straight bowling alley corridor. Conscious of the wavering wind, he snapped up and threw his weight forward. With every push of his poles he remembered to do a full stroke follow through before he finally tucked down to accelerate.

Barkly had an almost impossible lead by now. To beat the Martian skier, he would soon have to risk leaving the course and travel off-trail on snow that was not specially packed and groomed. It would be treacherous. He meant to avoid some of the short jumps later in the course, and the sweeping turns. The air resistance between the edge of a jump and the ground below could slow you down unless you chose to drop like a rock, and curves had to be avoided because they simply increased the distance. Because all of the snow was artificial, and it was well maintained and specially patrolled for the Olympics, he was counting on the fact that he wouldn't have to deal with typical backcountry ground cover. It wasn't the thick, soft powder that would sink him and it wasn't crud. He would deal with the pitches, rolls and terrain changes as they came.

Yves pushed over to the right and took off. He could envision the fall line that would take him on the shortest path but he had more to consider than the ideal angles. His greatest danger with the wind picking up on untested snow was the possibility of a powder avalanche. Vigilance meant avoiding the areas that appeared to be classic collapse paths. Barkly would know every one of them, but wasn't about to share that information with his rival.

As he went, Yves continuously calculated a line alongside the course to minimize natural jumps and twists, and generally avoid the rock formations that might be fatal at this speed. He could never pause his forward motion as he planned his next move. Experimenting as he went, he sometimes hugged the downhill side of moguls, sometimes hopped over them to see what gained him more speed.

Though he made good time, tortuous lengthening slices of the clock slipped by before he sighted Barkly on the course, a distant figure appearing out of the blankness. Barkly never looked over his shoulder. He had no idea Yves was anywhere near. It must never have occurred to him that Yves would risk leaving the confines of the course, even temporarily. So the Earther at least had the advantage of surprise.

At this juncture Yves didn't like the loose terrain he saw ahead. He wanted to rejoin the course, follow Barkly directly. While he was looking for a way in, the sequence of a nightmare scenario began. His skis passed over a stress point and triggered a snow slide. He heard a whoosh and then a steady, building hiss like a steam pipe about to burst. The loose particles traveled down with him. As he tried to outrace them, he prayed the snow would find its equilibrium. He didn't want to do anything to disturb it further, yet he couldn't help but turn his head to see the wall. It formed a cloud and then a conglomeration of small chunks approximating a nebulous ball that grew larger and more solid. It wasn't a skid cloud for sure.

Yves held his breath without realizing it, and prayed for Terri. He squeezed his eyes almost shut, going by what he had seen ahead and his visualization skills. Unexpectedly, an image of Terri's father came to him, they way he looked before his daughter left for Mars. Then he seemed to grow younger, more robust. He said, "I'm counting on you, kid."

The air grew quiet and Yves felt tight, solid snow beneath his feet, just ahead of the slide. Slowly, gradually, the ball that chased him began to break up. Without additional loose snow to build it, the slide distributed itself and dissipated like the last leaves of autumn.

At the same time, Yves found an opening to rejoin the course. Moving into the transverse with the sacrifice of some forward motion, he was able to line up directly behind Barkly.

It looked like Yves would catch up at that rate. He was almost within striking distance before the snow began to burst outward in every direction. The rotors of a heliplane pressed down on them. The machine ranged close enough for Yves to hear the damned reporter broadcasting from inside, his voice amplified over the noise of the engines. *"The first hostage, a man identified as Lou Coburn, has been killed and no one is taking any chances. Nils Barkly has been located on the slope and will be surgically removed by a marksman. I am here with the sharpshooter on the scene."*

The report of Lou Coburn's death delivered a shock wave to Yves' psyche. His mind froze on the news so that he didn't hear the rest. He could easily have lost control at that moment, but he held on. Swallowing back the lump in his throat, he remembered that many other lives were at stake, including Terri's. He tuned the visor to a fog penetration setting to compensate for the sand darkening the air.

In the heliplane overhead, the marksman focused his crosshairs on the distinctive ram in a crimson circle painted on the top of Barkly's helmet with Yves' head in it, and fired.

* * *

Terri made her way through the tunnels at a lope with two of Kastin's security crew keeping up with her. The city blueprints were in and out of her pocket frequently as they ran.

Evaluating the enormous caverns with the pipes, cables, and catwalks crammed into every space, the place reminded her of the dockside paper mills of Thunder Bay where she used to hide as a kid. The manufacturing process was a frenzy of activity where she loved to spy on things being made. The strangest part for her came when she would watch them hauling out the black sludge by-product and transferring it to container cars. She finally asked someone what it was and where it was going. They told her that it contained lignin, which the paper mill would recycle to make plastic resins.

Later she found out that those same plastic resins replaced ones made from toxic chemicals. She also learned that the valuable lignin that came out of wood was destroyed throughout most of the twentieth century, sixteen million tons of it incinerated annually. Every bit went to waste because no one thought of what it might be used for. That was the first time she realized she wanted to study environmental planning.

Terri endeavored to manage as few detours as possible, referencing the posted markers they passed. One of the two security men with her lagged behind to guard the rear. They used no advance guard since hadn't decided exactly where they were going. The other of Kastin's men, with his heavily muscled upper body and long blonde hair, stayed close to Terri. They had a long way to go and the markers didn't come up often so she didn't mind the interruption when her escort started asking questions. "What is this place?" he said.

Terri noted the name Ostermark stenciled on his coverall and unconsciously said it out loud. "Right now we're under the nitrite warehouse."

"I never heard of nitrite. What do they do with the stuff?"

"It's used for the colony's fertilizer, gunpowder, and electroplating. It's also needed to dilute oxygen for the air we breathe. Not to mention that nitrogen bucky balls launch our rockets into space." She said it admiringly. Buckminster Fuller, for whom the chemical marvels known as bucky balls were named, happened to be one of Terri's heroes. It was he who said, "Pollution is nothing but resources we're not harvesting." Carbon-60 molecules, originally called Buckminster fullerenes because of their resemblance to Fuller's geodesic domes, were the inspiration for the volatile nitrogen-60 molecules. They were frozen and compressed clusters, rearranged by a high-powered laser. When exposed to enough heat, these nitro buckies, released enormous bursts of energy. She spared Ostermark the full details.

"Whatever bucky balls are," he said, "they sound extremely valuable."

"They are. On Earth, the only reliable nitrite deposits are in the deserts of Northern Chile. Not only does Mars have its own source, but the accumulation near Olympus Mons is bigger than anything we've ever seen."

They stampeded past the opening they needed and had to look around in confusion for a few moments. After re-tracing their steps with the map, they ducked into a narrow green corridor that sloped further underground. "Where are we going?" asked Ostermark when they continued.

"I'm still figuring out how to get there, but we're headed for the ozone factory."

"What for?"

"Red Freedom intends to shut down the electric generator and dismantle it."

"How'd you find that out?"

"When I was captured they were planning how they would attack the Oh-Three power frame to get to the armature, and what to do with the commutator rings. Oh-Three is ozone and the other references have to do with the generator fittings. They didn't think I would understand."

"I don't get it."

She glanced at him. "The ozone factory, like everything else around here, has its own power plant. You zap ordinary oxygen with a current and you get ozone. Those tall stacks outside give a canopy of protection against the ultraviolet rays of the sun. The terrorists want to cut that off."

Keeping pace with her, he said, "Isn't ozone something we normally have? I thought Mars is an Earth type planet."

"One day the planet will generate its own ozone as sunlight falls on the new atmosphere and the lightning storms begin. Those two events are the main sources of ozone if nothing interferes."

"I thought ozone on the ground could kill you. How come we can release it here?"

"You're right." Ostermark was better informed than she expected. Kastin picked right. "I didn't want to get into the particulars, but that's why the stratospheric ozone is released from one of the orbiting space stations. Some of the electricity produced here is beamed into space with microwave transmissions so that the ozone can be made and distributed up there. But some of the ozone is still created and contained on the surface because Olympia needs it for water purification."

"Why doesn't the air need to be purified also?"

"The water comes from an aquifer, an underground permafrost they discovered here. The ozone cleanses harmful bacteria from existing water. But the oxygen and nitrogen we combine for air are pure since we extract them in elemental form."

"Why doesn't our distance from the sun protect us from the ultraviolet rays?"

"Quiet," she whispered over the constant hum. "We're under the generator. Look at the diagram. If we go up right here, we'll be directly in the middle of them."

"Surrounded."

"I hope not. It's the only way in for us."

They moved up the vertical ladder and came to a secure hatch with a circular screw handle. Ostermark turned it with painstaking slowness so he wouldn't attract attention in the room above.

Terri went back down the ladder for a few moments. She worked behind an access panel, out of his sight.

Ostermark noticed the humming sound grow lower in pitch as he rotated the handle. "Am I doing that?" he asked.

"That's the generator shutting down!" she called frantically. "Get through. Get through."

Ostermark twirled the last quarter inch in one snap, and threw the heavy hatch open. The sound got drowned out by the last dying moan of the power supply. He lunged up the hole, scrambling out at the next level. The room was enormous, filled with a bewildering array of complex machinery. He brought up his rifle as he searched, and swung it around until he acquired a target. Terri clambered out of the hatch after him. She saw him pointing the weapon at the right people. They were a man and a woman perched on the enormous commutator rings, preparing to disengage the brushes.

Terri brought up her own handgun and spoke to them. "You can stop now."

They continued working, but the woman looked up for a moment. "If you know anything about where we are, you won't fire those things in here."

"Maybe we will. And maybe we won't," Terri told her slowly. "But if we delay you long enough—"

The hum came on with rising fury. The two engineers still had their hands in the machinery. They were jolted and rocked back and forth as the current flowed through them. They screamed until their cheeks puckered and foam came out of their mouths. This went on until their own weight dragged them down.

Ostermark had the calm his training instilled in him, but he looked at Terri questioningly.

"I re-activated the auxiliary power from the lower level. The way I fixed it, Red Freedom won't find it easy to turn it off again."

The doors around the room opened simultaneously. Red Freedom fighters came pouring through the entrances. There were ten or more, with the man they knew as Ziljian among them.

Kastin's other Martian security man came through the hatch to join them so Terri's team stood back to back with three guns in their hands, as much firepower as they were going to get. Dumb as it was to fire before, it seemed an even worse idea to start a shootout now.

* * *

Since Kastin kept track of all her resources, she maintained contact with her agent at the hospital. "Give me an update," she prompted. "I understand Lou Coburn is not dead."

"Yes, but I'm afraid he's as good as dead if you want him for your war. He's crippled and in a coma."

Kastin stayed quiet.

"Did you hear me?" he said.

Worried about Terri, Kastin had wanted to hear some good news and she didn't get it. In the background she heard frantic footfalls, the clatter of metal and glass, the public address system blaring. The hospital was preparing for heavy casualties.

Two thousand years ago, all wars were suspended during the scheduled Olympics, thought Kastin as she cut off the connection. Today we are not as civilized.

CHAPTER 34
Downslope

THE FIRST BULLET tunneled into the snow just in front of Yves, and the second came even closer, between the skis. He would have flinched if he realized immediately what was happening. When he replayed the broadcast in his head, knowing that he was being shot at and that someone intended to kill him, he felt a weight in the pit of his stomach. He had no way of signaling that he was one of the good guys.

Yves tried to calculate his chance of survival over the next few minutes. He was, after all, a moving target being shot at from a moving vehicle. The professional shooter would take a few moments to adjust. Anything could happen in that time.

When the third bullet came, it slit open the back of Yves' suit, and the cold air rushed against burned flesh. His teeth ground together beneath the mask. He slipped behind and Barkly faded out of sight. Yves' muscles were weakening. By necessity, that couldn't happen.

He thought of Lou and of Terri, one lost and one in jeopardy. He had to come out ahead for both of them. At the same time, he had to stop bracing himself against what had already happened and what else he would find when he got there. It was a beginner's mistake to let trepidation slow you down. He reminded himself to let go of the mountain and the tension left him. He forgot his pain. Tuning out the next shot, he formed the perfect egg and relaxed until his legs were flawless shock absorbers. He saw the ground move toward him at an increasingly high velocity as the heliplane downdraft lent him more familiar weight and drove him forward.

When Barkly came into sight as a gray spot on the snow ahead a bullet penetrated Yves' boot and he stiffened with surprise and renewed pain. His legs cramped. The spot vanished again as he slowed. He knew he had to release the pain no matter what level it reached, just as he had released the mountain.

Yves recalled the image of Killington, Vermont that he had conjured up earlier. Biofeed allowed you to continue the benefits outside the machine. He could see the white snow superimposed over the pink. Yves moved faster, drawing on whatever residual was left. The gray spot reappeared. He wouldn't let it go again. It became the center of his existence. This was the day he won his first race; there was no way to lose. He closed the gap between himself and Barkly until they were less than half a meter apart. All this speed and no one to record it. It was then that he noticed the shooting had stopped. He heard the words of the reporter again.

"Our marksman, Thomas Canfield from Bristol, England, now refuses to fire, as the terrorist may be too close to an innocent bystander who is apparently trying to flee... And now they are skiing into the Olympic Village itself. That is sure to cause further difficulties for our security team."

As momentum carried them along the flat ground, Yves looked for an opening, listening to the reporter on his wristband when he couldn't hear directly.

"The leader or chief negotiator has emerged from Building Five, possibly to allow access to their--" The last comment drowned in a burst of static, and the damaged wristband gave out altogether. Yves hit the release and tossed it away. Concentrating on the spectacle ahead, he watched a small group of people, just visible out in the open.

* * *

March's Threat Team, as he called them, perched in the same line of sight on the mountain at a fracture in the volcano. They stood ready at a trigger to bend the forces of nature to their will. Only the lawyer knew that the mechanism was hobbled.

Now however, March raised his telescope and saw four figures near the building, Havislaw Valdeen looming larger than the rest. March quaked. The troubled scientist may not have disabled his own apparatus.

* * *

Valdeen had warned Chief Kastin that he would not wait for her to make a move. He wanted the security forces evacuated off the planet for a start. She hadn't done that. None of his demands had been met. Now Valdeen was forced to arrange a small-scale demonstration of what his Valdeen Catalytic Factor would mean to human life. He moved slightly away from the building with Hrelcik, Medcamp, and Terri, all of his favorites tied together like mountain climbers on a towrope. He wanted the television cameras to get a good view. The three captives shivered without their thermal jackets. They wouldn't be needing them, thought Valdeen. He held a small quantity of his discovery in a double-chambered black box.

Though Hrelcik was roped up front for recognition's sake, the woman who escaped earlier and ruined his plans at the ozone factory would be the first to die, followed by the nosey politician, and lastly the puppet man. It would be interesting to see Medcamp burst into splinters. He had Kastin waiting on Line One to hear all about it.

He looked up, startled by the sound of the heliplane. A skier came into view and another behind him. Who would dare? His eyes went from one skiing figure to the other. The one with the red Martian helmet was slightly behind. The one in front was signaling with crossed arms. Valdeen had excellent vision but something was odd about them. One of them looked like his nephew but he wasn't sure which.

"Stop," ordered Valdeen.

Neither man stopped. Two suicidal fools.

"Stop!" Valdeen shrieked.

* * *

They were still a great distance, and Yves could not see what Valdeen was holding through the blowing sand, but he saw the hostages and slowed down. Barkly kept sailing along, quickly fading out of reach. The shooting started again.

Yves was forced to pole forward in Barkly's direction as the bullets pressed behind him. Without a solid plan, Yves removed the ram's head helmet and launched it at Barkly. It hit him in the elbow, making him veer off slightly, but he recovered fast.

With Yves' headgear off, he looked up and was immediately recognized as an innocent by the heliplane crew, now almost on top of them. He saw Tom Bristol readjust his sights to try shooting at the other man. If Yves didn't want a stray bullet to hit Terri he would have to take Barkly out himself. Calling upon the Viking spirit that seemed to emanate throughout the Nordic-influenced winter Games, he threw his ski pole like a javelin, going for the broadest target, center chest though the back.

He realized immediately how badly it flew from his untrained hands. The pole landed closer to Valdeen, but posed no threat to him either. Yves followed the pole's trajectory with the bullets now raining in front of him. Before Yves' new line took him far, Barkly slowed and pivoted. The Martian went down low and used Yves' own momentum to scoop him into the air. The 58-pound skier arced over Barkley's head. He covered three meters before he hit the snow and then slid along for another meter.

One ski had come off. As he searched for it in a daze, a rope ladder appeared in front of Yves, and it took him a moment before he realized it had come from the heliplane. He dropped his poles and clambered up hand over hand, concentrating on keeping his feet from being tangled in the spiraling rungs. Yves released his remaining ski to enter the craft, and watched the shape twist harmlessly to ground. Then he saw the reporter, the sniper, and the man who controlled the heliplane. Coburn had mentioned this pilot who had "GROVE" stenciled on his uniform, someone with a lot of skill but limited patience.

Yves looked down. Barkly had almost reached Valdeen when Bristol's gun jammed.

Valdeen raised his bullhorn. "Land that helicopter. I have enough explosive power to knock you out of the sky."

Grove said, "That makes him the new boss. Say goodbye to this scene."

Yves warned the pilot not to do it.

"We're fish in a barrel up here," Grove blurted as he pulled back on the control stick. "I'm getting out."

Yves said, "I'm sorry." He grabbed the reporter's microphone, raised the pilot's faceplate, and jammed the microphone into his teeth. Then he pushed the stick forward directly toward Valdeen. The heliplane's nose lurched toward the ground, spreading a lateral wave of snow.

The wind from the rotors knocked the box Valdeen carried out of his hands and against the chest of the man following him, Representative Hrelcik. When the box turned over, it mixed the contents of the chambers, as the scientist had designed it to do. Valdeen watched in fascination as the explosion laid the man's rib cage bare. What was left of him collapsed in a heap. Valdeen ran. Barkly hurried toward his granduncle's side as the recovering pilot steadied his craft. The shooter finished Barkly with a lucky shot, but missed the scientist who then managed to drop out of sight.

* * *

The Red Freedom remnants watching from upper slopes were supposed to trigger the volcano if they saw their leaders fall. Devon March's assistant, Moss Guidry, was up there shaking. The movement had lost Arazine and couldn't locate Valdeen. Guidry was out of contact with March, and in no position to take over. No one was. He ignored the plunger and headed north. The rest took off after him. They would take their chances in the wilderness, preferring to suffocate in the thin air rather than wait for retribution.

Guidry would happily leave the failed revolution up to Chang.

CHAPTER 35
The Earth Of Mars

CHUL HUK CHANG cursed the day he set out in a craft that was not of Chinese manufacture. His men were glued to the windows watching Kastin's forces spread out and surround them, not only planning to keep them from coming out of the shuttle, but also laying down wheel bursting barriers to keep the Razdolye from taking off. The situation was desperate and Chang's men were anxious to take some action. Kastin's forces had not been nearly as split and spread thin as Chang had promised.

Commander Tang Lin looked to his master for orders with many sets of eyes behind him. His men appeared just as curious about what Chang would say to Tang Lin. They would follow their commander to any outcome.

The glance was as good as a question but Chang did not answer. In his hand he held a jade Pi from four thousand years past, from the oldest known dynasty, Hsia. The center hole symbolized Heaven. Stresses of the journey may have been too much for the artifact as now it was shattered. Chang had meant to carry the symbol with him like the Chinese Kings of old until the day it was to be placed in his grave. Now Heaven was broken.

"Supreme commander?" said Tang Lin, with a nervous glance behind him.

Again, Chang did not answer. Instead, he rose lithely, went to the bulkhead where the character *tao* was mounted exactly like the one in his painting gallery, and there assumed his meditative stance. Through drooping eyelids he blanked out the world, allowing his thoughts, disagreeable and otherwise, to float by unmolested, and so to release them.

He thought of Peter Arazine and his last electronic mail communication congratulating The People's Representative; he thought of Havislaw Valdeen in his art gallery with his stubbly face and horrid breath; he contemplated the suffering people he tortured in prison, including Abdul Harouk's children, and wondered whether they could ever come back to reach him; he saw the eight symbols of divination circling the back of a white turtle.

And finally he thought of Sun Yan, whom he had personally sent to the Great Luminous Palace in her youth, and wondered if he himself would ever see the Gate of the Cinnabar Phoenix. Having betrayed her, how would he get past the first gate, Luminous Virtue? In Sun's memory, he tried to think of something Confucius had said, and could not.

* * *

Tang Lin awaited his orders. After a long pause, Chang's arms seemed to drift up of their own accord the way a magician levitates his assistant in a stage act, keeping the limbs in tandem with each other until they reached shoulder height. Then they startlingly reversed direction, still together, leading with the wrists, giving a subtle push

373

forward, invisible force exposing the palms, the way seaweed moves in a changing current, rhythmic and dynamic, complicated nuances wrapped within simplicity.

Now like two staffs, Chang's arms arced in collapsing parallel to one side, and before the next change, Lin recognized that Chang was performing *tai chi ch'uan*, the Chinese system of exercise sometimes known as soft karate, believed by the Chinese to be far more powerful than the Japanese martial arts. It baffled Lin to see Chang engaged in frivolous exercise when a crucial decision was needed immediately.

Chang swept his arms in round loops at his sides as a wader luxuriates in the water, snapped the limbs up and together quick as an imploding vacuum, almost but never quite coming to a complete stop, with the fingers of one hand pointed to the opposite elbow, and the fingers of that arm pointed up in a perpendicular fighting stance, continuing the entire exercise in a single endless movement. Knees slightly bent, rolling gently on his heels and the balls of his feet, light came through his parted fingers to cast barred shadows on his face, echoes of *yin* and *yang*, the forces of darkness and light. The motion was seamless as a circle so that the *tai chi ch'uan* practitioner could attack or defend from any point and remain unpredictable.

On the long journey to Mars, Chang had told Lin he believed he had found his *chi*, the life force, after eighty years of searching. More fundamental than *Yi*, the mind force, his continuing task was to focus his *chi*, learn to use it so it could turn the strength of others against themselves, make them fly away like marionettes at the end of a puppet show.

Chang continued his dance, forever it seemed to Lin, with the versatility of a flute laid across the supplest of lips. When Lin was nodding off, nearly asleep, the display ended, delicately as it began. Softly, Chang uttered the words of Yi Jing, "Be not sad, be like the sun at midday." Then the supreme commander was barking out orders.

Tang Lin radioed for his agents to replace Valdeen's men on the mountain. They were to set off explosive charges, followed by Valdeen Catalytic Factor pumped into the depths in long tubes. Six out of eight charges heard in the distance successfully detonated as planned, biting into the crust of Olympus and making an opening to help funnel the catalyst to its destination.

Under the distraction of the explosions, Chang's men burst out of the Razdolye on a suicide mission to destroy the critical fuel factory. They scattered so that each was of minimal value to artillery shells.

From nowhere they were overrun by bobbing and dodging metal arachnids with mounted guns. The machines, which ignored the chaos on the mountain behind them, seemed to be remote controlled or programmed to deal with random evasion. One Spider went down with men tangled in its legs but the rest went on with guns fixed on targets. In heavy fighting, the entirety of Chang's soldiers, including Tang Lin who was last out the door, were killed without reaching their goal.

* * *

One of the remaining Spiders, facing no opposition, found an opening in the Razdolye. Upon discovering the

Chinese leader in the main chamber, it paused as though taking his measure. The machine was out of ammunition.

Chang focused his newfound *chi* on the metal beast in an attempt to make it fly away. *Yield to my strength.* It didn't budge. With no life force, there was nothing in it he could reach.

His triumph came when the Spider engaged him and he used its own thrust to easily toss it aside, rattling and sparking on the walls with only minor injuries to his wrist and shoulder from the throw. Nonetheless, the Spider self-destructed inside the Razdolye with an explosion that indeed looked very much like the sun at midday.

* * *

Some of Tang Lin's agents on Olympus Mons had done their work in poisoning the rifts. He heard four explosions, each coming within a second of the last. The Valdeen Factor leeched into the earth of Mars, seeking to find and exploit weakness as its creator intended. While the lower rocks under pressure were like plastic, the Valdeen Factor worked like plastic solvent. One of the four rifts gave way. Then another crashed.

For the first time in centuries, if not millennia, the volcano exhaled wisps of steamy gray air, shaping a cloud of rippling billows, gathering and regrouping until it looked like stalks of gray cauliflower. For the first time in millennia, Olympus dislodged a spray of superheated matter that spewed yellow streaks transformed to black ash and fell like rain, coating everything, burning everything it touched, spreading fear and casualties where it went.

The scarred walls of Olympia shook with seismic waves. Rock surfaces ripped and rippled. Scores fell dead. Just when it seemed that Avery's greatest fears, Valdeen's revenge, would smother them in ash and lava, the ground rumbled with one last convulsion and stilled. Or was it the last? Survivors held on and wondered. Communications to Earth were jammed with goodbye messages.

Yet somehow the venting ceased and the plastic rock within Olympus hardened, unable to attain the critical mass and pressure needed to escape. Not enough from that dose. A bit more Valdeen factor applied and they might have had a different outcome.

Tang Lin's men fled back to where the Razdolye had been for further orders, but found nothing left. Without a credible threat to wield, the Martian Separatist's cause and their fight for independence would eventually have different leaders, and would wait a little longer.

CHAPTER 36
Man On Earth

AT THE CLOSING ceremonies, officials quenched the Flame for two more years when the Summer Games would rekindle it back on the home planet. Yves and Terri stood on the field with the other athletes grouped by nation, one thousand strong under a volcano-polluted sky. They watched the IOC personnel wrap things up in the Olympic Stadium as the athletes waved dutifully for the cameras, which were mostly aimed at Terri. The clean linen of the great flag, with its five linked rings representing the colors of all nations, slowly lowered, while a special honor guard fired off a salute with three rounds from each of seven guns, or twenty-one shots in all.

Yves noticed that it took fourteen people to haul down and carry away the giant Olympic Flag to insure that no part of it touched the ground. When the flag was secured, the efficient men and women in uniform fired off three more rounds to commemorate those who had died during the Games. Everyone in the stadium stood with their hands over their hearts and flinched each time the powder exploded in remembrance. The national flags from each of the countries that suffered a loss were displayed separately at half-mast. Most people were in tears. Yves and Terri hugged each other until their arms ached.

IOC Chairman Abdul Harouk appeared on the podium looking somber. "In the first Olympic Games held in 776 B.C.," he said, "a foot race was the only contest and an olive wreath the only prize. But what some saw as poverty, and others saw as humble elegance, did not last. The Games' popularity grew, the number of contests and participating nations grew, and it became an ancient luxury. Eventually the prestige of the games was such that the winners were made rich and distinguished citizens, celebrated throughout the known world. In the rush to gain these coveted positions, bribery and sabotage became commonplace. After nearly seven centuries, the Olympic Games were so corrupt and dangerous that Emperor Theodosius banned them in 393 A.D. and they remained banned for fifteen hundred years. We've come full circle to today's dangerous times. Rather than explain my resignation from this institution, I will let that sad illustration of repeated history speak for itself."

Then the Governor of Mars, Marty Richfield, came out to make an announcement that he too was stepping down for an early retirement. He explained, "I tried to name Security Chief Shelly Kastin as my replacement, but failed to convince her to stay. Devon March will take over as governor."

March looked smug standing there. In Terri's informed opinion, March had managed to pin his treason on his assistant, Moss Guidry.

After the ceremonies, the crowd spilled out of the stadium planning what to do until the next ship left for Earth. Ash had been scrubbed from the walls but pockmarks remained. Yves and Terri rejoined each other after a pass through their respective locker rooms. They took a long walk together, Yves limping a bit on his bullet-creased heel, and found themselves at the Olympic Gardens that Terri had discovered on The Big Orange Tour. The floral shock troops were hamstrung with frostbite and shriveled aspirations. Only the illustrations above them were perfect. They captured the period of a day or two when the flowers had stubbornly burst into bloom dominated by the waxy plants like notch-leaved kalanchoe in a profusion of lavender, looking like hundreds of slices of wax fruit, and blue kleinia with its delicate water color fingers.

Strong as they were, the kings of the Earth desert were already starting to wither. Larkspur, penstemon and verbena never took hold at all, which was just as well since the bees needed to pollinate them had also died. The saffron and lime colors in the "Antarctic shrubbery" remained in ascendance close to the rocks in their safe microclimate. Crawling among them in wondrous abundance were golden pharaoh ants.

"You know something Terri? I think the Cobra would have beaten me if he stayed in the race."

Terri didn't believe that for a moment but she wouldn't contradict him. She wondered how she would feel in Barbara's place if Yves were shipped back to her in the state Cobra was in. She didn't even want to see Yves get started on Brisini again.

So much senseless loss. She couldn't believe she had killed three people herself. At least three. There was the Ninja, and the two in the ozone factory, and others she shot at during her escape who might have been mortally wounded. Aunt Shelly certainly didn't treat her like a kid anymore.

On the other side of the moral abacus, she was now free of the notion that she had somehow killed her great grandfather by inflicting disappointment. Nothing could seem more absurd in the context of what she had just been through. Here was real, deliberate death, killing for survival. It added to the list of indelible relationships between her and those who were gone, making her realize it was a good time to think about something else.

"You were right about Ziljian or Valdeen or whoever he was that got away," she said. "I'm sorry I doubted you."

"No, I had a lot to learn, too," said Yves. "Lou told me to listen to you. I sat up last night thinking, and somehow I seemed to hear everything he ever said. Things we did together came flooding back to me for hours."

Terri said, "How did this Valdeen get his bomb to Mars? How did he get those chemicals through customs?"

"They were ordinary items, some sent in advance. Nothing too strange for the medical doctor he was posing as."

"He was a sick man," she said, examining the bag with her skates.

"Yes, but it wasn't just him that screwed things up. The way I heard it, the things that happened at Olympia's Games were an embarrassment to several countries. Lou found out a lot of the details because of his work. He'll be there to fill us in someday."

"Colonizing Mars is not going to save us in the immediate future."

"The good thing that's come out of it is they're going to put a lot more effort into repairing the Earth's ecology. And I hear they'll be testing Valdeen's volcano theories on the far side of Mars. Disgusting that he may get the credit after the damage he did."

"Whatever happened to him?"

* * *

Yves, Terri, and most others returned to Earth where they could find dirty air, foul water, and excellent pecan pie. In the months that followed, Yves put Barkly's helmet, skis, and poles inside a glass case in the home he and Terri shared. That idea came from Terri's father who had held on long enough to see his daughter claim the top of the platform.

Yves and Terri became minor celebrities for the next few years, endorsing products and giving interviews. They pooled these earnings to help create the Doctor Edward Merris Foundation, a fund to promote development of clean energy. Its main building, located on Mars, was named in honor of Al Brisini.

Yves gave his bronze medal to Lou Coburn's family.

EPILOGUE
The Rest of Valdeen's Story

2012: SUTTER CREEK, MARYLAND

Deputy Marsden saw the sheriff's lip curl in distaste as he took in the human destruction mingled with institutional debris. Even in unsophisticated Sutter Creek, an investigation of any unnatural death was mandatory. This one also counted as spectacular.

Marsden said, "Are we treating this as a homicide, sir?"

Sheriff Meyhew, a forty-five year old African American of raw umber complexion, chipmunk cheeks and serious eyes was accustomed to thoughtful consideration and keeping his options open. He said, "Preserve the scene."

"No classification then?"

"We're not in the business of classifying just yet. Doing your job properly means never having to say you're sorry. Grab me the best forensic team you can get, and don't schedule the clean up yet. Do we know next of kin?"

"Carol Draper."

Mayhew widened his eyes. "Oh this is going to be interesting."

* * *

The sheriff brought Valdeen right up to the chest-high yellow police tape where he could see the remains of Dr. Merris congealing in the slanted rays of afternoon sun. A team bagged most of the head in one area, an arm in another.

"Don't tell me you want me to identify the body parts?" Valdeen laughed.

Mayhew studied him. "Now that you mention it, yes. Marsden, show Dr. Valdeen his friend's head up close and personal."

Marsden brought the transparent plastic bag over and made Valdeen look at the ruined face.

Valdeen recoiled in suspicion, but not horror. "What is this, sheriff?"

"I'd like you to take a good look and tell me why seeing your friend like that doesn't bother you."

"I'm a scientist. If anything, I find it interesting. If I had something to hide, I'd make a big show of grief for you, wouldn't I?"

"Lots of ways to play it."

Before Mayhew was through with him, Valdeen's inconsistencies in relating the story made him suspicious enough so that no additional impetus was needed to take a good hard look at him. Nevertheless, Dr. Merris' family was wealthy and capable of injecting themselves into the investigation. As a beleaguered Sheriff Mayhew described it, "Poor people *interfere* with police work. Rich people *get involved*."

No one currently working in the police departments from Sutter Creek to Baltimore had ever come across such a gruesome crime scene. With the splatter and separation of limbs so much greater than what guns could do, they wondered if more than one man had been killed.

When all the body parts had been accounted for, however, and cause of death was not in doubt, only one forensic fact excited the investigators. During the autopsy, a piece of paper with writing on it was found concealed in the dead man's right hand. If foul play were involved, they and the family hoped that slip of paper was a clue that might identify his killer.

The letters appeared to have been written at an odd angle and loosely scribbled. Since Merris often jotted things down without looking at the surface on which he wrote, the examiners had a basis for comparison with this note. It looked like the capital letters OEDQN.

Merris' Aunt, Carol Draper, who was chairperson of the English department at the private school she financed, said that O.E.D. was a common way of referring to the Oxford English Dictionary.

"He had little time to write," she said. "And he needed to provide us with a clue. The dictionary is the most potent tool for packing information in a small space by way of reference, and you would want to show which dictionary a particular definition came from, hence the first part of the abbreviation."

The letters that followed, "QN," provided a second abbreviation, commonly used for the word "queen." Therefore, she suggested the authorities look to the Oxford English Dictionary for their definitions of "queen," as a clue to the killer. The possible homosexual angle sounded promising to Mayhew only because he knew that spectacular murders often involved intimate relationships. He checked out both Valdeen and Norrick extensively, the only people Merris saw on a regular basis, and neither one of them seemed to have had that kind of relationship with the victim.

Aunt Carol also pointed out that her nephew played chess. "The queen is the most powerful piece in a chess game," she said, "capable of moving any number of open spaces horizontally or diagonally. In this case, he might be referring to something highly potent, pointing again to Valdeen or the project they were both working on. If the chess definition of QN were number six in the O.E.D., then the number six itself might be significant."

It wasn't. After a good waste of time puzzling out Aunt Carol's additional theories, Mayhew traveled up to MIT. That was Merris' alma mater. The sheriff began by showing the scrap of paper with Merris' writing on it to three faculty members gathered in a chemistry lab, professors Halsey, Tamarind, and Wichefsky. They recognized the reference immediately, and starting laughing.

Tamarind said, "No sheriff, it's nothing to do with the dictionary."

The first fuzzy letters were "Q.E.D.," not "O.E.D." It stood for *quod erat demonstrandum*, meaning, more or less, "that which was to be demonstrated has been demonstrated." Typically, "QED" was something written at the end of a mathematical proof to indicate completion. Since Merris was apparently conducting one of a multiple-year series of chemistry experiments, he was not likely to have been engaged in a purely mathematical exercise at the time of his death. So, the MIT boys reasoned, the cryptic letters probably meant that Merris had not just a single demonstrated proof, but his comprehensive proof, a breakthrough discovery.

"Could grabbing full credit for a discovery like that be enough motive for murder?" Mayhew asked them.

Professor Wichefsky said, "Have you ever worked with scientists, sheriff? For some of them the answer is yes, any day of the week."

When the sheriff confronted Dr. Valdeen on the Q.E.D. explanation, he vehemently contradicted any suppositions of a scientific breakthrough. Slyly, he added, "My records don't reflect anything like that, do they?"

Valdeen wasn't too pleased with other aspects of the investigation either, especially the Aunt Carol part. The sheriff breached protocol by allowing her to be present when he did some of the questioning, and even participate.

If Valdeen had ever bothered to ask while his partner was alive, he would have found out that Merris could have funded the research out of his own inherited millions, with more yet to come.

"Edward was my favorite," Carol told Valdeen with a pointing finger. "He was a naive soul, and I had to make sure no one cheated him. That's why I will never rest until his degenerate killer pays for the crime."

The revelation of a hidden fortune must have made Valdeen wonder what else he had missed, a worry that prompted him to be more careful. Although Mayhew watched him closely for several years, Valdeen published no scientific papers related to cold fusion in any journal. He and his work disappeared into a government lab to sort out the stubborn instability problem, and no usable evidence of murder ever turned up.

The MIT faculty members that Mayhew had visited spent those same years recounting Merris' cleverness at the breakthrough moment. The last two letters in the deceased scientist's note, Q.N., written just before he exploded, meant *quid nunc*, "what now?"

* * *

2039: RENO, NEVADA

Edward Merris' Aunt Carol had a mantelpiece plaque with the letters Q.N. emblazoned on it. "What now" reminded Aunt Carol to never rest while Havislaw Valdeen was a free man. She remained convinced that her nephew had been murdered by his overweening partner.

Setting up residence in the rumored vicinity of his government lab in Reno, Nevada, she knew that Valdeen had to surface one day. Either he was going to be carried out in a casket or she was.

For the next twenty-seven years, she used her family fortune to pay local tipsters to watch for him while she read his work on other subjects, trying to get a handle on him, and compared it to that of his partner. Her conclusion from those studies was that her nephew was far more methodical and inwardly focused than Valdeen. It would have taken the proverbial bat to the head of a mule for Edward to make a monumental mistake. Valdeen had the motive, he was untouched by the explosion, and to her those grains added up to murder.

She had circumstantial evidence and an avalanche of intuition, which was no good in court, but that didn't stop her.

Though she missed the Ziljian years when he took time out to visit Mars, she eventually got the call that someone resembling an age-altered photo of Valdeen stood at the counter of the Silver Screen Coffee Shop in Reno, ordering a Triple Mocha-Pacino. Driving recklessly and breathing hard with excitement, she arrived in time to confront the scoundrel with his hands full in the parking lot, fishing for the key fob to unlock his classic Audi S6. With the passage of time and the more important things he had to do, Valdeen no longer recognized his minor adversary.

"Who are you," said Valdeen, "and why are you blocking my way?"

Carol stood fast without any noticeable flinching, and addressed him as if it were the day immediately after the reported accident.

"I know that my nephew was goofy," she said between gasps, "but he would never have mixed dangerous chemicals without some deception and encouragement on your part...Havislaw."

"Nephew? And chemical mixing? Oh you must be Aunt Carol," said Dr. Valdeen with a hand to his forehead. "You're just as dopey as Edward with his heavy-handed potassium nitrate. Rather ancient to be chasing people down, aren't you?"

"I'm fine," she said.

"Don't you wonder why I've emerged, the reason that someone as inept as you could find me?"

"I assume all snakes have snake business to tend to."

"I've worked out the instability problem on the cold fusion process. As soon my patent comes through, your fortune will be insignificant compared to mine, and Merris will remain forgotten. So what have you got in that purse you're holding so tightly? A recording device maybe?"

"Maybe."

"Well, it doesn't matter what actually happened, and I don't give a damn what you think. I'm never going to admit to anything, so you won't be able to prove your charges."

"Oh hell, don't I know it, you lousy s.o.b."

Aunt Carol pulled a .22 from her purse and emptied it into Valdeen's chest. With the small caliber and the way her hand was shaking, it took the whole magazine to drop him. But her greatest weapon was that she didn't care who was watching. The only way to get him with his guard down was to do it in public, and she believed in taking responsibility.

Over his dead body and spilled coffee she said, "See, if you've got a pinch of sulfur and charcoal to mix in, gunpowder is another thing you can do with potassium nitrate."

#

ACKNOWLEDGEMENTS

I originally drafted this novel in the late eighties and early nineties just before the revival of Mars in science fiction. Like some of the big name authors, I thought the wealth of newly available scientific information made the subject ripe for hard SF. When I circulated the manuscript, another author's wife, who may have considered me a rival, convinced me that the subject of Mars was publishing poison, and would never be resurrected. She need not have worried. Whatever flair of mine scared her, I wasn't ready for such an ambitious project. When I picked up the manuscript for revision a decade later, it still had a long journey ahead.

Many thanks are in order for Blueberry Lane Books' outstanding editorial assistant Kim Weinberg, as well as Miranda Suri for the overview; remarkably supportive WDCers: Susan David, Metina, Meyoline, and Chy; then Sam Rappold, Amy Lau, Kat Hankinson, and Ken Altabef for their comments on Valdeen and Merris; and Elias Fixler for his suggestion of nitrox and other input way back when.